Choice of Evil

ANDREW VACHSS

Alfred A. Knopf New York 1999

THIS IS A BORZOI BOOK
PUBLISHED BY ALFRED A. KNOPF, INC.

www.randomhouse.com

LC 99-61596
ISBN 0-375-40647-6

Manufactured in the United States of America

First Edition

ALSO BY ANDREW VACHSS

Flood

Strega

Blue Belle

Hard Candy

Blossom

Sacrifice

Shella

Born Bad

Down in the Zero

Footsteps of the Hawk

False Allegations

Safe House

Choice of Evil

for *Richard Soney Allen*
uncaged, finally

and for

Leslie Haines
who hauled the weight until she saw the sun, finally

Choice of Evil

I nosed the Plymouth carefully around the corner, checking the street the way I always do when I'm heading home. The garage I use is cut into the closed-off base of an old twine factory, converted into upscale lofts years ago. Above the designer-massaged floor-through apartments is what the yuppie occupants think is crawl space. That's where I live.

A pal had tapped into their electricity lines and installed a stainless-steel sink-and-toilet combo. A fiberglass stall shower, a two-burner hot plate, a duct to the heating pipes below . . . and it turned into my home.

I've lived there for years, thanks to a deal I made with the landlord. His son got himself into a jackpot—an easy enough feat for a punk who thought ratting out his rich dope-dealing friends was a fun hobby—and ended up in the Witness Protection Program. I stumbled across him while I was looking for someone else, and I traded my silence for a special brand of rent control. Didn't cost the landlord a penny, but it bought his punk kid an anonymous life. And safe harbor for me.

Some of my life is in that building. And when I saw the pack of blue-and-white NYPD squad cars surrounding the back entrance, I knew that part of it was over.

I just sat there and took it. The way I always do—fear and rage dancing inside me, nothing showing on my face. I've had a lot of practice, from the hospital where my whore of a mother dropped me—dropped me out of her, I mean—to the orphanage to the foster homes to the juvenile joints to prison to that war in Africa to prison again and . . . all of it.

It didn't matter anymore. Nothing did. Somebody had dimed me out. And the cops would find enough felony evidence up there to put me back Inside forever once they connected it up.

I watched the cops carry Pansy out on a litter, straining under the huge beast's weight. Pansy's my dog. My partner, not my pet. A Neapolitan mastiff, direct descendant of the original war dogs who crossed the Alps with Hannibal. I had dreamed of having my own dog every night in prison. They'd taken my beloved little terrier from me when I was a kid, that lying swine of a juvenile-court judge promising me there'd be another puppy in the foster home they were sentencing me to. I remember the court officer laughing then, but I didn't get the joke until they dropped me off. There was no pup there, and I had to do the time alone, without anyone who loved me.

I never saw my dog again, but I did see that court officer. It was more than twenty years later, and he didn't recognize me. When I was done, nobody would recognize him either. That's the way I was then. I'm not the same now. But I've only changed my ways, not my heart.

I'd raised Pansy from a pup. Weaned her myself. She would die for me. And it looked like she had. Standing up all the way. She'd never let another human being into my place when I wasn't there.

I said goodbye the way we do down here—promising her vengeance. I was using the little monocular I always carry to get a close-up when the screen shifted focus: I saw Pansy stir on the litter. She was still alive. The cops must have waited for the EMS Unit—they carry tranquilizer guns. So I didn't need the badge numbers of the cops anymore—I needed my dog back. I U-turned the Plymouth slow and smooth and aimed it toward a place where I could make plans.

"Honey, I called around for hours. We know where she is," Michelle said, her lustrous eyes shining, reflecting the pain in me. She's my sister—my pain is hers.

"Where?"

"The new shelter. The one in Hunter's Point, just across the river? In Long Island City."

"Yeah, I heard about it. It's private, right? Part of the fucking Mayor's giveaway plan."

5

"Baby, relax, okay? Crystal Beth ran over there the second I called her. It could get a little stupid . . . Pansy's got no license, no papers . . . but Crystal knows how to act. Just sit tight, and—"

"When did she leave?"

"Honey, stop. You're *scaring* me. She's been gone almost . . . three hours now. You don't expect her to haul that monster on the back of her motorcycle, do you?"

"I don't care how she—"

Michelle put her hand on my forearm, willing me to centered calmness, reminding me of all the years I'd invested in learning the path to that place.

"Can you get Max for me?" I asked Mama. She'd been hovering nearby since the minute I'd come in.

"Sure. Get Max. Come soon, okay?"

I just nodded.

"Burke, you don't need *Max* for this," Michelle told me. "Jesus! It's not like they're gonna care, right? So she doesn't have a license. So Crystal Beth has to pay a fine . . . or what*ever.* It won't take long. . . ."

I stayed inside myself, waiting. Felt Crystal Beth's small hand on my shoulder before I heard her approach. Smelled her orchid-and-dark-tobacco scent. Didn't move. She came around the table and sat down across from me.

"Burke—"

"What happened?" I cut into whatever she was going to say, already knowing it was bad.

"The . . . license thing wasn't a problem. Just like Michelle said. They were willing to let me take her. But they wouldn't bring her out—they said I had to go back and get her myself."

"And . . . ?"

"And she was in a cage. A big steel cage. Like a tiger or something. There was a sign on it, in red; it said: DANGEROUS! DO NOT APPROACH! The . . . attendant, he told me she wouldn't take food. Even when they shoved it into the cage, she wouldn't eat. He warned me not to come near her, but I did anyway, and she . . ."

"What?"

"She tried to kill me. She lunged at the bars, snarling and snapping her teeth, and . . ."

"They don't know the word," I said, half to myself. I had poison-proofed Pansy when she was still small. Unless you said the right word, she wouldn't touch food, no matter how hungry she was.

I had a friend who ran a little auto-parts joint. He had a shepherd, a real nice one. He used the dog to guard the place at night, so nobody could help themselves. Some degenerate tossed a strychnine-laced steak over the fence. When the dog helped himself, he died. In pain.

I'd trained Pansy so that would never happen to her. And I should have known she wouldn't walk out with anyone but me.

They try and get dogs adopted at the shelter. If they can't, they gas them. Who was going to adopt a sixteen-year-old, hundred-and-fifty-pound monster who could bite the top off a fire hydrant? But Pansy wasn't going to wait to be gassed—she'd loyal herself to death first.

Not a chance. I owed her at least what I'd always promised myself. That I wouldn't die caged.

"Michelle, go find the Prof for me," I told her.

A few hours later, I was with a piece of my family, waiting on the rest.

"I can't scam her out," I told the women. "I mean, I could go there myself, and she'd come with me. But if I show up . . . the cops know where they got her from, and they might be expecting that. I'm surprised they didn't try and follow Crystal Beth. . . ."

"I was on my bike, honey," Crystal Beth said, her face calm with assurance.

I knew what she was telling me. There wasn't a cop car made that could keep up with Crystal Beth on that motorcycle of hers, especially with the steady rain that had been falling for days. For the first time, I noticed what she was wearing—a full set of racing leathers.

"But how were you gonna get Pansy on—?"

"We had a car standing by. If I got her out, I was just going to load her in there and—"

"Whose car?"

"I don't know, Burke. The Mole lent it to us. Some big dark thing. He made me a new license plate for my scooter too. Even if the cops saw it, they won't make anything out of it."

"The Mole was gonna drive? Jesus, I—"

"Not the Mole," Michelle interrupted. "Terry."

"He's not—"

"Yes, he is," she said, a trace of sadness in her voice. "My little boy's almost a man now. He doesn't have a license, but he can drive."

Terry. Had it really been that long since I'd pulled him away from a kiddie pimp in Times Square? Since Michelle took him for her own? Since the Mole had raised him in his junkyard? Since . . . ?

Then the door swung open and the Prof walked in, Clarence at his heels.

"What's the plan, man? I got the word, came soon as I heard."

"We have to get her out before they—"

"I said the *plan,* fool. You know I'm down with the hound. So gimme the four-one-one, son. They gonna be laying in the cut, waiting on you to make your move. We gotta be quick, but we also gotta be slick. Otherwise . . ."

"Let me think," I told the only father I'd ever had—the one I met behind the Walls.

"Everybody got it?" I asked. It was almost nine o'clock at night by then, more than sixteen hours since my life had been torn apart.

Everybody nodded. Nobody spoke. I looked over at the big circular table in the corner, now piled high with what we needed.

"You sure they're open twenty-four hours?" I asked Michelle.

"That's what they *said,* honey. But I don't know if they'll actually open the doors, even if you say it's an emergency. It's not a medical place. All they do there is keep the dogs and . . ."

"Kill them," I finished for her. "It doesn't matter anyway." I turned to look at Crystal Beth. "You got the floor plan?"

"Right here," she said, unrolling it on the table in front of me.

"Mole," I called, summoning him over. Then I started to explain what I needed.

"There *have* to be women there," Crystal Beth said, standing to one side of the table, little hands on her big hips, face tightened against any argument.

"Look, this is—"

"You say 'man's work' and I'm going to—"

"No, girl," I said soothingly. "I wasn't saying that. It's just you don't have any experience with—"

"With what, hijacking?" Michelle interrupted. "That isn't the way to do it. You and the Prof, sure. I know you even got Max to go along sometimes on that crazy stuff you used to do, but if you think—"

"I am going too, Little Sister," Clarence said in his dignified island voice, blue-black West Indian face set and resolute. "You are not to blame Burke for this. Yes, I would follow my father, wherever he walked. But I love that great animal too. She is not going to die," he said softly, his hand caressing the 9mm semi-auto that was as much a part of his wardrobe as the peacock clothing he draped over his lean body every day.

"That's not the *point.* I don't want—"

"Michelle, I am going," the Mole said. Soft and gentle, like always. But not, like always, deferring to her. "Not Terry. You are right. He is my boy too, not only yours. And he is too young to risk . . . whatever there is."

"Will you morons fucking *listen* to me?" Michelle yelled, standing up so suddenly she knocked a couple of glasses to the floor. She walked over and stood next to Crystal Beth.

"This isn't about what you imbeciles *think* I'm trying to tell you." Her creamy complexion flushed red with anger. "It is *not* a hijacking, even with all those . . . guns and things you have. It's still a scam, right? And they are *not* going to buy it unless you have a woman doing the talking, understand?"

"Girl's telling it true," the Prof said. "We don't work it right, they ain't gonna bite."

The Mole nodded, slowly and reluctantly.

"Yeah," I said, surrendering.

9

It was near 3 a.m. by the time we were ready to ride. Michelle and Crystal Beth were both dressed in military camo-fatigues, complete with combat boots. Max and I went for the generic look. Crystal Beth sat in the front seat right next to me, her left hand on my thigh, transmitting. Max and Michelle were in the back, Michelle yammering a nerve-edged blue streak, the mute Mongol warrior probably grateful he couldn't hear. I had decided the Plymouth wasn't much of a risk—I always keep the registration on me, and the car got a fresh coat of dull-cream primer last night.

I waved across to where Clarence sat behind the wheel of what would pass for a Con Ed truck if you didn't look too close. If you did, you'd be looking at the wrong end of the Prof's double-barreled sawed-off. Somewhere in the back of the truck, the Mole was preparing his potions.

We caravaned along until we got to the pull-off spot on the FDR. I pointed to a white semi-stretch limo with blacked-out glass. "That's yours," I told Crystal Beth. "The rollers won't look twice at a car like that this time of morning. It'll look like someone's coming home from clubbing. Besides, it'll hold everyone."

"I'm staying with you," she said.

"No, you are *not,* girl," I told her. "Max can't drive worth a damn, and the Mole would crash it for sure. Clarence is the best wheelman we got, but we need him in the truck. We're *leaving* the truck when we're done, and everyone can't fit in the Plymouth. You just park it where I told you to, and we'll all meet up before we hit the place."

"Burke, I—"

"Crystal Beth, I swear I will throw your fat ass out of this car right now, no more playing. Drive the limo, or we'll do this without you."

She punched me hard on the right arm and got out. She walked over to the limo, opened it with the key I'd given her. I waited until I heard it start up, then I took off.

The Animal Shelter was freestanding—a long, low concrete building, T-shaped at the back end. I pointed out my window for Crystal Beth to pull over. She parked the big limo perfectly, left it with the nose aimed straight out. When she got into the front seat of the Plymouth, I said: "They're going to take the truck around the back. Mole'll stay with it. The Prof and Clarence will meet us out front. Then we do it. Ready?"

Everybody nodded. Nobody spoke.

I stashed the Plymouth just around the corner, out of sight from the front door. We all got out. The Prof and Clarence slipped around the corner and linked up with us.

"How we getting in, Schoolboy?" the Prof asked. "Scam or slam?"

"Slam," I told him, showing the handful of Semtex I was holding. "Me first. Stand back."

I walked up to the door. Put my ear to it. Nothing but a few random, doleful barks—the Captured Dog Blues—no sound of human activity. I patted the Semtex all around the knob and the lock, then made a long seam-tracer for the door's edge. I jerked the string loose and ran back around the corner.

The second the door blew off the hinges, we all charged, faces covered with dark stocking masks, hands gloved. I was first in the door. The attendant was at his desk, face slack with shock. I showed him the pistol.

"Touch the phone and you're dead," I promised him.

Max slid past me, unslinging the huge set of bolt-cutters from over one massive shoulder. The Prof stepped into a corner, his scattergun weaving, a snake looking for a passing mouse. The lights flickered, then went out—the Mole saying he was on the job.

Crystal Beth stepped up, shoving me aside, shining a halogen flashlight in the attendant's face.

"This is a message from the Wolfpack Cadre of the Canine Liberation Front," she proclaimed in a perfect liberal-twit revolutionary's voice. "You may no longer imprison our brothers and sisters without fear of consequences!"

"Look, I—"

"Silence, lackey!" Crystal Beth snarled at him. "This is a jailbreak, not a debate."

A soft explosion rocked the back of the building. Then another.

The attendant moved his lips like he was praying, but no sound came out.

I walked past him. Saw Max's broad back bent over as he severed the heavy lock on the door to the cage area. Then we both popped the cages open, one by one. The dogs milled about uncertainly, until one spotted the gaping hole in the side of the building. He ran for it, and the others followed.

Pansy was there, her cage standing open. On her feet, daring Max to come closer.

"Pansy!" I called to her. "Come here, sweetheart!"

The big beast's head shot up. She bounded over to me. "Good girl!" I told her, patting her huge head. Then I gave her the hand signal to heel and we merged with the river of dogs flowing to freedom.

As soon as she saw the car, Pansy knew what to do. I popped the trunk and she jumped inside, curled up on the mat next to the padded fuel cell, and looked up expectantly. I handed her a giant marrow bone, whispering "Speak!" at the same time. I closed the trunk lid, knowing the air holes I'd punched in it years ago would let her breathe just fine. And if anyone heard her pulverizing the bone, they'd just think the old Plymouth had a bad differential.

Even with us working the wrong side of the river, some citizen could have called the cops by then. We had to move fast. I stepped back inside the front door just as Michelle was taping up a cardboard stencil warning the world against the unlawful imprisonment of dogs. Clarence sprayed the blood-red paint with one hand, the other holding his pistol steady.

"Don't think about the phones after we're gone," I told the attendant, just to get his attention. As he looked up, Max materialized behind him and did something to his neck. He wouldn't be making any calls for hours.

"They all out?" I asked Clarence.

"All gone, mahn. Every one."

"Scoop the Mole—he's back there somewhere. Then get in the limo and fly. I'll be right behind you."

I tossed a smoke grenade into the back of the joint and dashed for the Plymouth.

I read all about it in the afternoon paper, Pansy stretched out next to me in Crystal Beth's apartment. On the top floor of her safehouse.

The papers were full of it—in all respects—for the next couple of days. The Mayor said it was terrorism. Pansy yawned when she saw his face. Even the camera was bored.

Most of the dogs made it to freedom. The waterfront's not fully developed over on the Queens side. Yet. Maybe some of them will form a pack like their counterparts had in the South Bronx—go feral, evolve their own breed.

Like we have, the Children of the Secret.

Some of them will bond. Some of them will prey on anything that crosses their path.

Some of us do that too.

I started rebuilding my life.

"You know who this is?" I asked.

"Yeah," was all the answer I got.

"You want to meet me? In the alley?"

"Yeah."

"Say when."

"First thing tomorrow."

I hit the off button. Even if they traced the call, all they'd get would be the bogus number of the stolen cell phone—the Mole had installed a cloned chip to make it work.

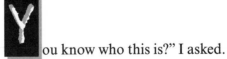

13

If anyone else had been listening to that few seconds of talk between me and a pit bull of a cop named Morales, they still wouldn't know that "first thing tomorrow" meant midnight and the alley was Mama's restaurant. And even if they did know it, they wouldn't come there without a SWAT team—it's not a safe place for strangers.

He strolled in five minutes past midnight, a cheap brown suit and wash-and-wear white shirt with clip-on tie covering the surgery scars from the bullet he'd taken a few years back. A bullet from another cop: that homicidally insane Belinda. I'd left her dead on the rooftop of the building where they'd had their last meeting, making my getaway while Morales was being carted off by the EMTs. Later, the brass made it a tidy package by declaring Morales a hero. In their version, he'd killed Belinda in a shootout.

Morales was an old-time harness bull, a dinosaur who couldn't evolve but refused to die. He'd flake a drug dealer, phony-up probable cause, whatever it took. And he carried a throw-down piece in case he had to smoke a suspect. A brutal man who saw it all in black-and-white. Mostly black—my color in his eyes forever. He wouldn't pay for information—thought that was what God made blackjacks for—but he'd trade for it. And the weight of the debt he owed me was heavy on him, so we didn't waste time with prelims.

"What do they have?" I asked him, flat-out.

"They know you lived there. *Didn't* fucking know it till they tossed the place, though."

"I figured no landlord had enough juice to get NYPD to do evictions, so . . . ?"

"So the cocksucker called in a nine-one-one. Said he just discovered some Arabs was secretly living in his building. And that the place was a bomb factory."

"He didn't warn them about my dog?"

"Not a word, pal. But as soon as they started with the battering ram, they could fucking *hear* about it, so they waited for the Animal Control guys to get there before they finished breaking in."

"There weren't any fucking bombs—"

"Uh, I *know* that, all right?" he cut me short. "What they found was . . . well, bottom line, that you lived there. I mean you, Burke, okay? Not from the papers, from the prints."

"The papers . . . ?"

"Yeah. You better forget about Juan Rodriguez, pal. That ain't you no more. Not this Arnold Haines guy either. Or any of the others. Man, you sure had yourself some serious ID."

"'Had' is right."

"Yeah, well . . ." He dismissed my problems with a short chop of his stubby hand. "Look, the guys who tossed your joint said it was clean as a prison cell. It wasn't till your prints came up that they made you."

"And . . . ?"

He shrugged. "And you ain't been on parole for years. No wants, no warrants. They found a bunch of letters—somebody's been stinging freaks, promising them kiddie porn, stuff like that—but it was all run out of some PO box in Jersey . . ."

That one's gone too, I thought to myself.

"Only thing they found that looked like a crime they could connect to you was the tapped lines," he continued, "from Con Ed and all."

"I never did that. Probably the landlord himself."

"Yeah. That's the way they figure it. Probably an off-the-books rental. You paid him in cash, right?"

"Right. Speaking of cash . . ."

"They didn't find any," Morales said, flesh-pouched eyes steady on mine. "Didn't find no guns either. You got a problem with that?"

"Not me," I assured him.

"That motherfucking landlord," Morales muttered. "Coulda gotten a couple a good cops killed, they'd a broken in there with that dog of yours. . . ."

"And they didn't find any bombs."

"That too. That piece of shit's lucky they didn't charge him. But the punk-ass ADA said the cocksucker had a 'good-faith belief' or some other such crap. Still, little weasel deserves to be fucked up."

I raised an eyebrow.

"Don't even think about it," he warned me. "Right now, you walk away. Start over, I guess. Something happens to that one, Ray Charles could see through any alibi you come up with."

15

“I wouldn’t even know where to find him,” I said truthfully. “He sure doesn’t live in that building.”

Morales nodded, not speaking.

“Funny how people look at things,” I said softly. “This landlord, he never said a word about my dog. You guys, you’re mad because a couple of cops could have gotten chewed up. Me, I know what would have happened if it went down like that—they would have shot her.”

“Whatever,” Morales said, standing up to leave. He stuck out his hand for me to shake. That isn’t his usual thing, but I went with it.

As soon as he was out the door, I read the little piece of paper I’d palmed when we shook hands. Just a phone number, Westchester area code.

“He would have killed my dog,” I said to Crystal Beth later that night.

“Burke . . . stop it! You’re so . . .”

“Why did he have to do that? Pansy never did anything to him. We had a deal. A square deal. I always kept my piece of it.”

“Maybe he didn’t—”

“Didn’t *what*? He *had* to know I wasn’t around when he made the nine-one-one call. If the cops had knocked on the door with me inside, I would have let them in, let them look around, whatever they wanted. Or told them to come back with a search warrant, if I thought I could have gotten away with it. Or called Davidson, anyway. A lawyer comes over, the cops have to watch what they’re doing. He knows I would have told them *something,* and he didn’t want to take the chance. So he must have been watching, made sure I wasn’t there. But Pansy was. And he knew what she’d do. He was trying to get her killed.”

“Honey, you can’t *know* that.”

“I do know,” I told her. “What I don’t know is why. Not yet.”

"¡*Buenos días!*" the cheery voice at the other end of the line greeted me.

"You a Latina today, Pepper?" I asked her. "Pretty good."

"Thanks, chief," she answered. "It's a lot easier than being an alien, like I was in the last show." Pepper works with Wolfe's crew. She's an actress, among other things. When she's not teaching kids gymnastics. Or singing in a choir. Or working the lifeline between Wolfe's outlaw-info outfit and the players who pay for her services.

"I don't need a meet for this," I said. "Just some answers." Then I gave her the landlord's son's name. "He's in the Program," I told her. "Can she get me—?"

"Okeydokey," Pepper said, as if I'd said something else entirely. Then I was listening to the fiber-optic hum of a dead phone line.

"Call for you," Mama said, nodding her head toward the bank of pay phones between the kitchen and my booth in the back.

"Who?"

"Girl. Say you know her."

I walked back, picked up the phone. "What?" is all I said.

"He's gone," the woman said. Wolfe—I'd know her voice in a subway tunnel, even with the train coming.

"Disappeared?"

"Dead."

"From?"

"The feds didn't need an autopsy. He was Swiss cheese."

"Ah. Any suspects?"

"*Too* many. He must have been big-time stupid to go into business for himself in Vegas."

"Thanks. How much I owe you?"

"Two large will do it."

"I'll have Max drop it by."

"No rush."

17

"You think I ratted him out?" I asked softly.

"How did you get this number?" the landlord wanted to know, his voice trembling.

"Oh, I always had *your* number, pal. Just answer my question."

"It *had* to be you. You were the only one who knew—"

"He went into business for himself. Out there, I mean. Your kid, he had a disease. He *liked* being an informant, even when his own case was over. I had nothing to do with it. You wanted me out of there, all you had to do was ask."

"I . . ."

"You knew my dog was there," I said quietly.

"Look, if I was wrong, I'm sorry. I mean, we can still work something—"

"You'll never see it coming," I promised him, cutting the connection on my last word.

That was it, then. Humans are the only pack that tolerates predators of its own species. Most think "family" is a biological term. Not my family. My family is my choice, and I belong to them like a wolf cub does to a pack. Only I'm grown now. All of us, grown. Only babies—some lucky babies—get that "unconditional love" the talk show psycho-flashers are always bleating about. We know better. For adults, there's *always* conditions. And one of them is that the pack survive, that the house stay safe.

We had killed to do that, all of us, together. And when it was over, Crystal Beth asked me if I was going to stay. Not here, not in this cesspool of a city where I was born—stay with her.

I told her the truth then: I didn't know.

But I was there now. Me and Pansy. Trying. Living in Crystal Beth's safehouse, seeing if it could maybe be my house too. That's when it started.

People don't kill for no reason. What the cops don't get is that sometimes no reason *is* the reason.

They thought it was random, that first one. A target of opportunity. Like the victim of a bomb dropped from above the clouds, the pilot certain everything down below was the enemy. Killing things, not people. Following orders.

But not all bombers are military. And some take orders only from inside their twisted-circuit heads.

When people from the other side started to fall, the cops got it all distorted. And once they worked it backward to me, they were sure they knew the motive.

It fit me like a good pair of handcuffs.

It's hard to say it even now. Hard to say her name. When Crystal Beth died, so did my chances.

It didn't happen the way she thought it might. It wasn't one of the risks she knew she was taking. She wasn't even supposed to be there. It didn't have anything to do with that "purpose" she was always talking about; the one her mother had tribal-tattooed on Crystal Beth's teenage face before she went out to meet her own destiny. Crystal Beth's purpose was the safehouse. The network. Fighting stalkers and protecting their victims. Why even *go* to a gay-rights rally? I remember asking her, deep in the quiet darkness of her room on the top floor.

"It's not you, girl," I said.

"Why not?" she answered, her soft voice as rich and round as her thighs. "You know I have . . . I mean, you know I did . . . with Vyra and all. It wasn't her who started that, it was me."

Vyra was gone now. My old . . . what? Not girlfriend. Not even friend. Sex partner, I guess. I never saw any *real* piece of her until the wheels came off last year. When my own house was threatened by a pack of race-haters and my brother Hercules went into the fire to save us. Homicides happened. And when it was over, Vyra left with Hercules. To new lives, out of mine.

But before she went, I saw her and Crystal Beth make love to each other. Right in this room, on this bed. I wasn't a spy or a voyeur. They wanted me to stay, wanted to show me something. Much later, when Crystal Beth was sure I'd seen what was really there, she asked me if I was going to love her.

I told her I didn't know. Lying is encoded in my genes. I learned lying so I could keep them from hurting me. It didn't always work, but it was all a little kid had. Later, I learned better ways.

Couples who want to make a baby tell everyone they're "trying." It always makes me sick to hear that . . . like they're making me *watch* them try. But I understand what they mean. I was trying to love Crystal Beth then. I'll never know if I was going to get it right.

"That doesn't mean you're gay," is what I told her.

"Because I'm a woman? That's the way *men* think. If *you* have sex with another man, even once, then you're gay for life. That's the fear, isn't it? When a little boy is raped, he's afraid he's going to be just like the rapist . . . only he doesn't think 'rapist,' he thinks 'queer.' But if you're a woman, it's like . . . okay, right? Just an experiment. Just playing. You know what, baby? Gay people don't like my way either. I'm not *out* enough for them. Not for the lesbians, anyway. If I still have sex with men, I'm not *really,* see?"

"Really what?"

"Not really real. Not . . . myself, whatever that's supposed to mean. You know, 'yourself' . . . the person someone *else* wants you to be. For them, not for you. Funny. Gay people are discriminated against, hated, feared . . . and they do the same thing to themselves. I'm bisexual. And they have no tolerance for me just as straights have no tolerance for them."

"So fuck them. Why go?"

"Because they're *wrong.* I belong there too. And I'm going."

"No, you're not, bitch."

"Don't sweet-talk me," she whispered, flashing her smile in the darkness. "I took your orders when we were in the middle of . . . that thing. But it's over. *That's* over, I mean. This is me, now. Me, no matter what a pack of fools think."

"It's not about being gay," I said. "Who cares? But why go where you're not wanted? It's just another bullshit demonstration anyway—it's not like it's gonna change anything."

"Tell that to the Freedom Riders."

"Hard to talk to dead people," I said, warningly.

"This isn't Mississippi, Burke. It's not even close. The climate has changed. And it didn't change by itself. We helped *make* it change. I'm going."

"Crystal Beth—"

"Shush up, now," she mumbled against my chest. "I've got something better for you to do."

It was just cracking light when I left the next morning. I looked down at Crystal Beth, sleeping on her belly, soft cheek against the pillow. Heavy-haunched and glistening in her own dew, her face open even with her eyes closed. I thought about giving her a kiss but I didn't want to chance waking her up.

I never saw her again.

The papers had it pretty close to accurate. I know because I went down there. Not to the scene—to where I could find the people who saw it. People who wouldn't talk to the law.

Crystal Beth wasn't even one of the speakers. She was just in the crowd, toward the back. Not a big crowd, maybe a couple of hundred or so. Right on the rim of Central Park, west of the Ramble. Protesting another fag-bashing episode, demanding the Police Commissioner send some undercover cops in there to stop it. The speaker was saying something about how they used undercovers to bust straights looking for hooker sex, but they wouldn't spare any to protect gays. Talking about voting as a bloc . . . knowing as he spoke that you might tip an election for a local City Council seat with a threat like that, but it wouldn't make the Mayor blink.

A car swept by. Nobody saw it good enough to say much except that it was a dark color, moving fast. Gunfire poured from the windows. At least two guns—they found that from the ballistics lab later. Five people went down. Two dead. One of them was my Crystal Beth. The car flew north, disappeared somewhere in Harlem.

That didn't prove anything—didn't mean it was their home base. There's a hundred ways out of Harlem: bridges, tunnels, alleys. Underground garages where you could stash a car and switch to the subway.

The first thought was that the drive-by had to be about the dope business—a typical triggerboy spray-and-pray hose-down job. One of the guns had been a Tec-9, so that sounded right. For about a minute. Then it went on the books the same way the streets already had it—as a hate crime.

Fag-bashers all over the city were high-fiving.

Then they started dropping.

The first three weren't hard to connect. They'd been convicted of beating a gay man to death after luring him into a playground at night. Aluminum baseball bats and bicycle chains were all they needed, although one of them stabbed him a few times after he was dead. Didn't take a psychologist to figure out that last part.

One rolled over immediately, took a short manslaughter hit in exchange for his testimony. The other two went to trial. The lawyers got a lot of camera time. And their clients got a lot of time Upstate—a pair of life sentences.

But then the appellate courts reversed all the convictions—said the cases should have been severed for trial. So everything was voided, even the guilty plea. All three got bail pending a retrial. The gay community protested. Got a lot of TV coverage. Changed nothing.

Then two of them got done. They'd been living together. Sleeping together too, I guess—they were found in the same bed, what was left of them.

The third one, the informer, he must have figured it out—or thought he did. He called the cops, asking them to take him back Inside while he waited for the trial. The cops said they were sending someone right over. I guess the guy opened the door himself. Whoever he opened it to stuck an ice pick into his spine. Then hacked his head off with a butcher knife while the fag-basher watched himself die, paralyzed.

The reason the cops knew that, they found the victim's phone had been tapped into. And rerouted. When the third one had dialed 911, he'd been talking to his doom.

And while the cops were wasting time grilling the family and friends of the gay man who'd been murdered, some "Christian" organization took out a full-page ad saying homosexuals needed to "convert" or burn in hell.

That night, every TV news show ran clips of the organization's spokesman saying, "AIDS is God's cure for homos," and other, similar sound bites.

The next day, the spokesman was napping in a hammock in the backyard of his estate when a long-distance rifle shot opened his left eye. Opened a bigger hole in the back of his head.

One of the picketers at the funeral of the murdered gay man—the one holding the sign saying his death was God's Good Riddance—got a UPS package. And got a real bang out of it.

But it was the poisoned black-market steroids that killed the bodybuilder—the one who kept in shape with fag-bashing—that finally persuaded the cops.

They managed to keep the connection between the victims out of the papers. But the killer trumped them by going public.

> Be warned! These attacks have not been indiscriminate. All the targets were predators, and homosexuals were their prey. Queer-bashing is no longer a risk-free sport. For too long, the gay community has tolerated assaults in the vain hope that protection would come from outsiders. Be warned: now *we* hunt.

The first radio station to receive the tape with the machine-altered voice had played good citizen and turned it over to the cops. But it wasn't long before another station decided it couldn't pass up the chance for a ratings score. Once it went out over the airwaves, the dam was breached. The flood followed.

A short time after I met Crystal Beth, we got into a war. A war to keep our house safe. It took all of us. And all we had. Just before I left for the showdown, Crystal Beth said she wanted to have my baby. That last time, as we parted before I went out to do my work, she asked me. Of all the women in my life, she was the only one who'd ever asked. Flood had told me she'd thought about it, had been thinking about it, but she went back to Japan and I never saw her again. Belle loved me. Died for me. But she knew her blood was bad—she was her sister's daughter, and she'd never pass that along. I've had sex with so many women. I liked some of them; some of them had liked me. But it was only Crystal Beth who'd wanted my child.

I'd told her the truth then. I can't make babies. Had myself fixed a long time ago. Not because my blood was bad, like Belle's. I don't know my blood. "Baby Boy Burke" is all it says on my birth certificate. It's not my blood that stopped me—it's that I know blood doesn't mean anything.

But the cops had this much right: when Crystal Beth was taken from me, I needed to spill some.

Only I couldn't find the shooters.

And while I was looking, this other guy kept killing the tribe they came from.

Trolling for freaks in this city is no different from poling a skiff through a swamp, hunting for gators. They don't have to be smart to be dangerous. And you better not fall in the water.

The gay community already had one of the usual arrest-and-conviction bounties out on the drive-by killers. There was government money too. The lame Mayor caught so much heat the last time he opened the public coffers for reward money—for that "gay serial killer" who'd never even crossed our borders—that he was an easy mark. But even a total of more than a hundred grand didn't turn up a trace. Oh yeah, the pay phones were clogged with quarters from informants, but not a single tip proved out.

Then a skinhead clubhouse in Queens blew up. The whole thing. Maybe a half-dozen of them inside. Impossible to tell—too many body parts to match into complete sets. The radio stations played his tape right away this time. Short and sweet:

> Skinheads all hate fags. This was always stupid. Always a mistake. Now it's a mistake to *be* a skinhead. A *fatal* mistake. See you soon, boys.

They should have known what would happen at the gay-pride parade. The cops, I mean. It takes them longer because they act as a herd.

Or maybe they thought he'd only react to actual violence. When the first two drunks jeering at the queers dropped like they'd suffered heart attacks, the cops started running toward them. But by the time they figured it was him—*had* to be him, firing from a rooftop, scoped and suppressed—he was gone.

So were the two drunks—heavy-caliber hollowpoints tend to do that to you.

A pervert who ran something called *Homo-Haters Gazette*—a website featuring news of "successful actions" against gays around the world—must have thought the letter he got was fan mail. The cops couldn't determine from the few fragments that they found. And they couldn't interview a guy with a severed brainstem.

"They want you for it." Morales, on the phone, voice like a bulldozer in a garden.

"Get real," I told him.

"Just did," he said. "Straight up. They don't know where you are, but they're looking."

"So . . . ?"

"You should come in. I know this one ain't yours."

"Thanks."

"For what? You not slick enough to be sending no letter bombs, pal."

"I can find out," Davidson said, puffing on his cigar. "But if I make the inquiry, that alone will . . ."

"I know," I told him. "Do it."

"Give me a call, uh, tomorrow. Before ten."

"Done."

"Burke . . . ?"

"What?"

"Anything you want to tell me?"

"I got nothing to do with this one. *Any* of them."

Davidson nodded, not doubting. If I'd killed anyone, I would have told him. He was sure of that—I'd done it before. He was a good lawyer, knew all the tricks. He wanted to get paid, but he did the work. Better than most, that last part.

"You can't stay here," Lorraine said, the second she crossed the threshold to Crystal Beth's place.

"I know," I replied.

She didn't know what to say to that; a look of surprise froze on her face. "I . . . didn't mean you had to get out this minute," she said stiffly. "I just meant . . . I mean, you know why we set this place up. You know what we do. Having a man here . . ."

"I understand. I'll be out in twenty-four hours. It's not like I got a lot of stuff to pack."

Pansy's enormous head swiveled back and forth, following the conversation but dismissing the woman as a threat.

"Burke . . ."

"What?"

"I never liked you," Lorraine said. "But I know what you did for . . . us. Before, I mean. And I know you loved . . . her."

"Crystal Beth. You can say her name."

"Maybe *you* can. It . . . hurts me just to . . ."

"All right. Never mind. I told you, I'll be out in—"

"Do you think they'll ever catch him?"

"The guy who killed her?"

"No. The guy who's killing all of . . . *them*."

I shrugged.

"You don't care?" she asked, an extra-aggressive tone sliding into her already hard voice.

"What are you asking me, Lorraine?"

"If he were to . . . kill them all, he'd get the one who killed . . . her, right?"

"Kill every fucking fag-basher in the city? Right. That'd do it."

"I wish he would. I wish *I* could."

"So why don't you give him a hand?"

"You wouldn't understand."

"Why? Because it's a gay thing?"

"It's a woman thing."

"Yeah? Then how come you keep saying the killer's a man? It's easy enough to alter a voice on tape."

"He *is* a man. Everyone knows that. I meant . . . Crystal Beth. Her. And me. Between us. You could never get that."

"And *that's* what you hate me for?"

"I didn't say I hated you. I said I never liked you."

"You know what, Lorraine? I never liked you either."

"That matter we discussed the other day?" Davidson's voice, treading carefully over the line at Mama's.

"Yeah."

"Your . . . surmise was, in fact, reasonably accurate. The individuals to whom you referred have expressed a desire for an interview, but they cannot seem to locate the . . . object of their interest."

Meaning: yes, the cops want to talk to you, and no, they don't know where you are.

"You think this 'interview' should take place?" I asked him.

"Assuming the factual content of the material you imparted during our prior conversation is unchanged, I do. If only to . . . reorient their interest."

Meaning: yes, if I really had nothing to do with the murders, I should go in and talk to the cops, answer their questions, show them they were wasting their time so they'd leave me alone.

"Set it up," I told him.

"What do you need a lawyer for, you coming in here to assist us with our investigation and all?" the sandy-haired plainclothes cop asked me, nodding his head in Davidson's direction.

"Oh, I'd be scared to come here by myself," I told him. "I heard you guys do terrible things to people when nobody's watching."

"A comedian, too?" his partner asked, a short guy with a round face and a boozer's nose.

"Me? Nah. I even heard you guys sometimes put a telephone book on top of a guy's head and whack it with a nightstick. Doesn't leave marks, but it kind of scrambles your brains."

"Where'd you hear that?" the sandy-haired one asked.

"My brains are still scrambled from the last one, and that was a long time ago," I told him, nice and quiet, but letting him know I was done dancing. "You've been looking for me. Okay, here I am. You want to ask me some questions, do it. You don't, see you around."

"My client is here at the request of the DA's Office," Davidson put in. "Since he's not a suspect, I assume you won't be Miranda-izing him?"

"Sure, counselor," the one with the boozer's nose said. He opened a notebook, looked over at me. "Name?"

"See you around," I said, getting to my feet.

"Hold it!" the sandy-haired one said. "What's your problem?"

"I don't have a problem. You guys do. I came here, in good faith, because I thought *you* thought I could help you. You know who I am. You got my rap sheet and my mug shots right there in front of you. What else you want to know?"

"A current address would be nice."

"Sure as hell would," I told him. "Problem is, I don't have one."

"You're homeless, right?"

"Yep."

"So you're sleeping in the shelters?"

"I look that fucking stupid to you?"

"Hey, Johnny, relax," the boozer-nosed one said to his partner. "Burke here, he got a lot of friends he could stay with. Besides, they don't let no dogs in the shelters, right?"

"What dog?" I asked him.

"Ah, it's gonna be like that."

"Last chance," I said, meaning it.

"Okay, okay. Relax. Come on. Let's just deal like men, all right?" the sandy-haired one lied. "We know your girlfriend was one of the ones killed in that drive-by, at that queer rally."

I looked at him like I was watching a TV test pattern.

"And we figured, maybe, you'd like to find the guys who did that."

I kept looking at him.

"And we know you've been asking around. . . ."

"Do you?" I said, uninterested.

"Yeah, we do. We got a witness to it, all ready to walk in and talk to a grand jury."

"And the crime is . . . what? Asking questions? That was true, all reporters would be doing life."

"And we got a *bunch* of fucking murders," he went on. "All fag-bashers. So, the way we figure, somebody don't like fag-bashers. Brilliant so far, huh?"

"About up to par," I acknowledged.

"And we figure, there's at least one, maybe two, or even three fag-bashers that *you* don't like."

"Oh. You mean, you solved that case? You got the shooters."

"You're one sarcastic motherfucker, aren't you? How about this one, *Mister* Burke. How about you tell us where you were on the thirteenth? Say, between four in the afternoon and eleven at night?"

"I can't remember," I said flatly. "You know how it is, drifting around, looking for a place to stay."

"So you got no alibi for that time?"

"I got no alibi for *any* time," I promised him.

"You fit," boozer-nose said.

"Fit what?"

"The profile. Everyone knows you're a revenge freak. They killed your girlfriend, so you . . ."

"I what? I don't know who did it. You know, why don't you tell me, find out if your theory's correct?"

"We don't know," the sandy-haired one said. "And we figure, you don't, either. So maybe you're just working your way through the whole list."

"You know why I came in here?" I asked him. "You know the real reason?"

"No. Why don't you tell us."

"I came in because I thought you guys were actually trying to get whoever killed Crystal Beth. I thought maybe you knew who it was, but you didn't have enough to arrest them. And that maybe you were going to let that . . . slip, understand? Then you'd close the case. Call it 'exceptional clearance' and keep your stats up. But now I see what's going on. All this bullshit game-playing crap. You think it's *me*? That I'm a fucking serial killer? Jesus H.—"

"Hey, pal, it's not like you never—"

"Never what? Went around whacking people for the freakish fun of it?"

"Nothing freakish about it," boozer-nose assured me. "Somebody did *my* girlfriend, I'd wanna take 'em out too."

"And if you knew it was a Spanish guy, you'd kill every Latino in New York?" I asked him.

"Gentlemen," Davidson interjected. "It is quite obvious that my client is unable to meaningfully assist in your investigation. *And* that you are not going to arrest him. I am quite certain of the former. Unless I am mistaken about the latter, we are, in fact, leaving."

I followed Davidson out the door. Neither of the cops said anything.

"That's really why you wanted to come in?" Davidson asked me in the car on the way over to his office.

"Yeah. It happens. Some cases, they close 'em that way: 'Exceptional clearance.' Means they know who did it, but they can't prove it. Every once in a while, it eats at a cop, and he lets a name slip out . . . to somebody who just might do something about it."

"You figure they wanted you to kill the guys who—?"

"How could they lose? Not only do they close one case, they get a beautiful new felony handed them on a platter, complete with perpetrator. One step closer to that gold shield."

"I thought *I* was cynical," Davidson said.

"You are," I assured him.

But nothing happened. Nothing changed. There's a million places to live in this city, but it's hard to find one off the radar screen. The Mole had done it. Even if you suspected he lived in an underground bunker in a Hunts Point junkyard, you wouldn't go poking around there to make sure. The Prof used to live in the subways until he hooked up with Clarence. Then they found a crib over in East New York, right off one of the prairies. Bought the whole building, a gray brick eight-flat, for a song and started the rehab. Only they're never going to have tenants. They offered to let me stay, but they blended into that neighborhood and I didn't. It wouldn't take long for somebody to notice.

Plenty of places I could hole up, but not for long. I even called a girl I knew from a few years ago on the off-chance . . . And I scored. She was by herself again, and wanted to have a try. Asked me if I was ready for a commitment. Not hard to lie to her—comes naturally to me, and I hate extortionists anyway—but once she saw the size of my commitment, all hundred and fifty pounds of Pansy, she decided the whole idea was overrated.

31

I know a lot about junkyards. Fact is, I own one. And Juan Rodriguez, he used to work there. Simple enough scheme: The guy who runs it for me, he writes me a check every two weeks. I cash it, kick back most of it, and I got that Visible Means of Support thing knocked. Being Juan Rodriguez is the same as being John Smith, only it doesn't trip the IRS alarms, at least not coming out of New York. I protected that identity for years, never risked it doing anything wrong under that name. Always kept up the Social Security, Workman's Comp . . . everything. Juan Rodriguez wasn't just a citizen, he was a *good* citizen.

Such a good citizen, matter of fact, that the guy who runs the junkyard for me made a mistake about him. I dropped by, told him he'd be hiring someone else pretty soon. No big deal. But he got stupid. Told me, after all, it was *his* name on the title, right? So I gave him a history test. Asked him if maybe he remembered how his name got there. And who I got the place from. And how I got it.

He passed the test.

Now all I needed was a new set of papers, starting from scrap.

I know plenty of people who can make paper. Any kind you want: Passports. Birth certificates. Bearer bonds. Social Security cards. Only problem with them is that they're merchants. I don't trust merchants. Today you pitch, tomorrow you catch. Anyone who sells you outlaw stuff is always a risk to sell *you* if the Man makes the right offer. I never worried about that with the Juan Rodriguez stuff. I'd built it up myself over the years, slow and careful, starting with a dead baby's birth certificate—a baby who'd be around my age if he'd lived. But I didn't have time for that now.

Until last year, I didn't know Wolfe could get paper made. But she'd shown me different, manufacturing a Jew in the background of a dead guy to buy my brother Hercules a ticket into the White Night underground. And she had one credential none of the other paper-makers did—I knew I could trust her.

I could never say why. Not out loud. And never to anyone who wasn't part of me. But I know I'm not wrong. I've known Wolfe since she was a prosecutor. We worked opposite sides of the law then, but sometimes we got close enough to the line to hold hands over it. Never more than that. And never for long.

I guess I . . . I don't know why I can't say it different, say the truth: I always wanted her to be with me. But alligators don't mate with egrets, even if they live right next to each other in the same swamp.

When Wolfe had been chief of City-Wide Special Victims, she was working in a counter-evolutionary world where you could travel faster on your knees than standing up. And if you stood up too long, they took you down. She'd sneered at the firing squad. Everyone on both sides of the line respected her for it.

I never could tell Flood I loved her. She went away from me knowing it, but never hearing me say the words. Women know it, somehow. Before you do. I did tell Belle—it was the last thing she asked for before she left, full of bullets she took for me.

I never told another woman since.

I couldn't tell Wolfe. But I could call her.

"What?" A man's voice, not Pepper's. Not sweet either.

"How you doing, Mick?" I asked.

"What?" he said again, like he hadn't heard me. I don't know what Mick does, except it's something with Wolfe's crew. I know he's Pepper's man, know he's some kind of fighter. Big guy, good-looking, like an actor. But his eyes are flat and he's got that *ki*-alert radiating all the time.

"You know who this is?" I asked.

"No."

Fine. All right: "It's Burke. I want to see Wolfe. Can you tell her?"

"Yeah," he said. And hung up.

33

I lost almost all my tapes too. Hundreds and hundreds of them, put together over more than a dozen years. Oh, I still had a whole bunch in the Plymouth—I circulated them between my major stash and the car so I always had a fresh batch to listen to—but most were gone forever. I didn't know how I was going to replace some of them. Judy Henske, that probably hurt the worst. Magic Judy is hard to find on vinyl. And her voice . . . impossible to find anywhere else on earth, period. I had some bootleg stuff of a couple of her live club dates that were just plain unreal.

Ah, fuck it. I know where to get more. But it just . . . hurt, somehow. I mean, I knew the thieving cops would appreciate the cash and the guns they "found" there, but the tapes . . . They were probably already in some Dumpster. Or maybe some techno-geek was patiently listening to every one, hoping for something incriminating. Well, good luck, sucker. You'll never find anything, but you'll be in love with Magic Judy by the time you're through.

Replacing the guns was nothing. I'm not one of those loons who has a favorite piece. When it comes to firearms, I'm strictly a use-it-and-lose-it man. This city's got some of the toughest gun-control laws in the country. Some of the harshest penalties for dealing drugs, too. And every drug-boy in town packs heat.

Michelle was more upset about the clothes than anything else. "Oh, baby, not your alligator boots? And your beautiful suits, the ones I bought you? And the lovely—"

"It's all gone, Michelle," I told her, not insane enough to mention that she'd bought it all with *my* money. "They got it all. Everything I didn't have on my back."

"Well, you know what, baby? That's really a good omen."

"Huh?"

"Honey, even with my careful, meticulous shopping, your wardrobe was hopelessly out of date. Now we can start over."

If there was a God, I would have cursed him.

I tried the area around the Greenpoint riverfront, but even with the HAZARD buoys floating everywhere in the slime that passed for a piece of the East River, the area was lousy with artists and entrepreneurs. Next thing would be a Starbucks on the corner. I kept looking.

The reclaimed swampland out around JFK had too many other operations going, besides the quick-trick motels and the topless joints. Too many warehouses without signs on them, too many rotting big rigs parked together like an elephants' graveyard.

South Ozone Park was good once, but it's chop-shop heaven all along Atlantic Avenue, and too many neighborly citizens in the little houses just beyond.

Most of Queens is lousy, in fact. The DA out there is so lame he can't even make an organized-crime case at the airports. Pitiful. The feds have to do all of that stuff.

And you're always reading about rapists and murderers who capture their victims in another county and truck them into Queens because it's a softer spot if you get caught.

Everybody knows. And, sooner or later, dead meat brings flies.

I finally found a place. Not far from the Eastern District High School in Bushwick, right in the middle of the badlands. Just over the Brooklyn line, past a foul little river that ran under a rusting drawbridge beside a concrete plant. It was an old factory that the sweatshops hadn't taken over because it needed way too much work—the life-support systems were all gone; even the copper tubing had been stripped for cash. No danger of pedestrian traffic in daylight. The area was deserted except for the buses that ran along Metropolitan Avenue, like spot-labor vans that cruised the corners picking up whoever wanted a day's work. Only the bus cargo was all regulars—born-unlucky refugees who couldn't even say "green card" in English.

And after dark, the only signs of life were the strip bars and the fast-food joints. Once you left the main drag, you could see more action in a graveyard.

I got Pansy used to our new home by camping there with her for a few nights. The Mole welded some steel stairs to the roof, and Pansy was accustomed to depositing her loads up there at the last place, so there wasn't really any learning curve. One thing was different—a two-pump gas station on the Avenue had a little fenced-off area with dogs walking patrol, so the night was never quiet. But Pansy didn't seem to care.

I put the place together slow. Real careful. Worked at night, coming and going. When I was finished, it still looked abandoned, but if you checked the city property records, you'd find out it was owned by a corporation. If you traced that corporation, you'd eventually dead-end. But it was mine, and I wasn't worried about a surprise condemnation proceeding from the city, because Davidson was listed as the corporation's agent, and he'd get notice in plenty of time.

The first floor was empty, and I left it that way. For a while, the occasional wino would try and catch some sleep there, but it was too full of rats big enough to hunt cats . . . and dogs hungry enough to go after *them.* A swirling river of predators. Didn't smell great either, especially with the pigeons who visited through the broken windows, looking for leavings and leaving more than they took every time.

The rust-covered steel door on the side of the building got brand-new locks, multiple spikes driven deeply into the four-inch frame. The best pick man in the world might have beaten it without a key, but even if you could convince thieves of that class there was anything worth stealing in this neighborhood, even if they put together a watch-your-back team while one worked on the door, even if they got inside, they'd just see a blinking red light and a keypad. And a digital counter, working its way down from 30. At that point, they could start punching numbers or start running.

Past all that was another staircase, with a motion-sensor-and-trip-wire combo that would stop a counter-terrorist sweep team.

On the top floor was Pansy, roaming loose. That's where I lived. Different from the last place. Lots more room, lots less light—a trade-off for the one-way glass. I used a generator for electricity, so nothing registered with Con Ed. No phone, but I had a steady supply of cloned cellulars from the Mole. And a bunch of fresh extra-sweet pineapples for deodorizers that I replaced every couple of days.

I parked indoors, using a million-candlepower hand-held spot to clear the area every time I pulled in. It always drove whatever was there back far enough for me to make it to the stairs. Nobody could get into the Plymouth, even with a crowbar, so I didn't worry about that much either.

None of the rats made it upstairs, but occasionally a mouse would flit past in the corner of my vision. Mice and rats don't coexist, so I guess the rats preferred the lower bunk.

Mice aren't the real problem in city apartments anyway. I remember one day in the joint, we were all out in the yard, swapping stories. Throwdown was telling us about a place he once had. I never knew his citizen name. We all called him Throwdown because he was the sweetest guy in the world, big black dude with a lot of miles on him. But if you challenged him, he'd just go off. He was one of those anesthetics, didn't feel pain. The hacks discovered that when they tried to club him out once. And mace only made him mad. After that, one of the Goon Squad always carried a hypo full of Thorazine when they came for him.

"Rather have mice than roaches any day," Throwdown said. "Mice at least got the good taste to stay away when you got company over, you understand what I'm saying? Motherfucking roaches, they see people, they think it's a business meeting, and they all invited. Now, I had 'em *both,* okay? So I figure, I'll do somethin' about them mice first. They was in the closet. I could hear 'em moving around. So I get me this trap. Now, I know you supposed to use peanut butter, 'cause the little motherfuckers'll just pick the cheese right out, but I didn't have none, so I used a piece a salami, okay? Anyway, I'm kicking, doing a dube, waiting for my woman to show, and I hear the trap *snap!,* right? So I figure, I gotta get that dead mouse outa there before I get company. I opens the door, and there's this big-ass roach hauling the fucking salami away!"

"Damn! What'd you do?" one of the guys asked.

"Booked," he said, grinning.

The Mole could have hooked me up with air conditioning too, but window units would have given away the game. And I wasn't looking forward to winter, even with the space heaters we had lining the walls. But, right then, the asphalt was boiling and getting out was the best way to deal with the weather, so I saddled up the Plymouth and took Pansy to the park.

We got settled in and watched. One guy was going through a complex ritual with himself—stretching, flexing, getting ready for . . . whatever. One of those boys who thinks his body is a temple, I guessed. I lit another cigarette, scratched Pansy behind the ears, both of us grateful for the shade.

A gorgeous redhead with legs longer than a bust-out gambler's last hope swiveled by. She took a glance at the temple and decided she was an atheist. Watching her walk away was almost enough to make me do some jogging of my own.

The day went on. Close to that special twilight where everything is outlined in black against the sky. Wolfe said she might meet me there, but not to count on it. I'd give her another hour and roll down to Mama's, hang out there until the commuter traffic vanished.

I wanted a woman. Not the hard-eyed ones I'd been playing with ever since Crystal Beth was taken. Yeah, those were the ones I thought I wanted—as far away from love as I could get, now that mine was gone. But . . . I can't explain it. Women can fake orgasms, but they can't fake that wonderful big-eyed look they give you when you'd done something fine.

I wanted to do something fine. See that look.

I don't buy what citizens mean by "faithful." Sex isn't love. But I had to be faithful to Crystal Beth my way. So, before I could search for that look in a woman's eyes again, I needed to see some dead bodies.

Pansy spotted a squirrel hauling a hunk of discarded pizza back to its nest. An hors d'oeuvre in motion, but even Pansy's brick brain knew she'd never score, so she contented herself with just watching.

Like I was.

Wolfe never showed.

The heat got worse, visible waves hovering just above the ground. TV cranked it up more. CNN especially. Not the weather reports—the footage of Hutu and Tutsi slaughtering each other on both sides of the Rwanda border again. The mass-homicide images flashed me back. Headaches. Fevers. Night sweats. And that terrifying visitor they call ague: cold, bone-marrow-deep, so bad you can't close your jaw or your teeth will crack like dry twigs from the chattering, an electric shaking that has to work its way through your body before there's any peace. It never announces its coming—it's just *there,* and all you can do is ride it out. Biafra, that genocidal nightmare, intruding now like it never had before. Pansy recoiled at the smell coming off me.

I took some of the quinine they'd given me years ago, but it just made my ears ring. I went to a doctor who specialized in tropical diseases. She said the ringing was tinnitus. Common thing for malaria victims—the tiny cilia in the ear become brittle and snap. Nothing can be done about it. The ringing would just come and go for the rest of my life. *Like* the rest of my life.

I asked Mama. The herbalist she sent me to was so ancient he would have been New Age in the Roaring Twenties. He made about a dozen piles of stuff, then dealt a heavy pinch of each into six little brown paper bags. It looked like: thick white Popsicle sticks, basil leaves like they use for topping veal marsala in Tuscan restaurants, tiny clumps of twigs like from a finch's nest, sections of tree bark—dark outside, pure clean white inside—gnarled lumps of dark reddish roots, big rubbery slabs of mushroom cap.

"You have malaria, yes?"

"Once."

"Africa or Asia?"

"Africa."

"Never go away," he promised. "You soldier?"

"What difference?" I asked him.

He shrugged at that truth. Said, "Parasites, back now. Go away soon, you do medicine. You put this in big pot, okay? Boil into tea, drink three times every day. Two, three weeks, all gone."

So I did it. Washed each glass down with a hit of dark chocolate between sips.

And he was right.

39

I'd met with Wolfe by then, too. She backed her hammered maroon Audi sedan into a spot between my Plymouth and a Dumpster, managing to scrape a little off each.

"Nice work," I told her.

"Parking a car is like docking a ship," she said. "It's a controlled collision. You do it slow enough, you can't hurt anything, not really."

"Terrific," I said, indifferent to another welt in the Plymouth's flanks. Then I told her what I needed.

"You're talking a *big* number," Wolfe said, eyebrows going up for emphasis, the white wings in her long dark hair flaring along for the ride.

"I have no choice. The cops got everything when they took my place away."

"You're really going to start over?"

"Not . . ."

Her gray eyes watched me, waiting.

"Not my life," I answered her question.

"Too bad," she said, so softly I almost didn't hear it.

"Why?" I asked her.

"Because you . . . it would be . . . I mean, it would be cheaper. There *is* a real you, right? A real Burke, I mean. There's a legit birth certificate somewhere. You could apply for a Social Security number, start over. . . ."

"I'm not changing my ways," I told her, making it clear. Meaning: I was going to thieve. Maybe not at gunpoint anymore, but I was going to take stuff from other people and I needed a shield-screen of fake ID to do that. And still more to keep the IRS off me if I ever stepped on the wrong land mine.

"You hear about that Canine Liberation Front thing?" Wolfe asked, a sorceress smile on her lips.

"No. What the hell is that?"

"Ah. I figured you don't read the papers much. Never mind. I can understand. If somebody ever took my Bruiser from me, I'd do . . . whatever to get him back."

The stallion Rottweiler stuck his head out the side window of Wolfe's Audi and snarled agreement.

"You can do it?" I asked her. Not really a question.

"You have the cash, sure."

"You need it all up front?"

"It's not like, say, a shipment of guns," Wolfe said, her smile thinner now that she knew I was going back to my old ways, making it clear she knew what some of those were. "You know, ID; it's not something you can just turn around and sell to somebody else if the buyer defaults."

"I wouldn't—"

"And a lot of it has to be fronted at my end. Besides, you never know if your client's going to be around. . . ."

"Yeah." Nothing much else to say. Wolfe was telling me that, no matter what I called myself, she'd always know who I was. Truth is, she'd always known. Only now she'd know the names I'd be using, too.

"Want to set up a—?"

"No need. I got it right here," I told her, nodding at the trunk of the Plymouth. "You okay carrying that much? I don't see any of your crew around. . . ."

Bruiser growled at me again. I got the picture.

Her price was actually a few grand short of what I'd guessed. I popped the trunk, opened the false bottom next to the NASCAR fuel cell, and handed her enough cash to buy a new car. A *nice* new car. She opened her sling purse and I dropped it in. She never glanced at it. Even trust is a different thing down here. I'd never stiff Wolfe a penny on the fee, never slip her funny money or a Chicago bankroll. And she knew that. But . . . who'd stiff anyone holding the key to your whole new ID anyway?

"Could take a while," she said.

I shrugged. It was out of my hands.

"I'll get word to you," Wolfe promised.

The Audi belched oily black smoke as she fired it up. She waved a quick goodbye and pulled out. The Rottweiler's head swiveled to watch me until they were out of sight.

41

The new place felt safe, but it wasn't . . . the same. Anyway, I didn't spend much time there, so Pansy started riding with me a lot.

She was with me for that first meeting on West Street. And she wasn't the only one in the joint wearing a collar and leash.

It had taken them a long time to get in touch. Mail was stacking up in PO boxes of mine all over the city, but they were never going to be emptied. I hadn't left the keys or the addresses in my old place, but a lifetime of playing it to the far side of safe kept me away.

So a few wannabe mercenaries wouldn't get stung, a few kiddie-porn collectors wouldn't get a ticket to the slammer instead of more trophies, some assorted chumps wouldn't get taken. No loss.

All the names I used for stings were gone. But anyone who wanted Burke bad enough could find a phone number if they asked in the right places. The number for a Chinese laundry in Brooklyn, set on permanent bounce to the pay phone at Mama's.

The ones who wanted the meet, they didn't know me. The only ticket they had was a name. A dead man's name. It was me they wanted, but they didn't know where to look. So it took a while before the word came in. I returned the guy's call, told him I'd meet him, and he told me where. I figured it was a job. And a job was one of a lot of things I didn't have, then.

"You can't bring . . . that in here," the bouncer said, crossing his arms over his chest.

Pansy took my hand signal and stood rock-steady. She watched the bouncer with disdain, her ears slightly perked in case I told her to sit. If I did, she'd nail the muscleman before he could scream—high-thigh chomps are her specialty. And then all he'd *do* is scream until he passed out from pain or blood loss—Pansy's a one-bite beast.

"I'm supposed to meet someone here," I said mildly. "He'll okay it."

"Who would that be?" the bouncer asked, arms still crossed, flexing hard, unable to keep his gaze away from Pansy's ice-water eyes, and wishing he could.

"Lincoln's all he told me."

"You mind waiting outside?"

"Me? No. I don't mind *where* I wait, pal. I just mind how *long* I wait, understand?"

I made another hand signal. Pansy wheeled and followed me outside. I lit a cigarette and leaned against the outside of the one-story black-walled building. The traffic was all gay, mostly leather, a few tourists in business clothes. Some looked at me; none spoke. I wasn't sporting a handkerchief in a back pocket, wasn't pierced, not even a lousy earring, and I was dressed in what people went to work in when they got paid by the hour. Pansy lay down at my feet. She doesn't like concrete much at her age, but the sidewalk was still warm from the day's heat and it probably felt good against her arthritis.

I wasn't halfway done with the smoke when the bouncer came outside. "You mind going around the back way?" he asked. Polite now, not like before.

"Nah."

"Okay. You just walk toward the corner. You'll see an alley. You turn left and—"

"Ah, that sounds complicated," I told him. "Maybe you'd better show me the way, huh?"

"I can't leave my—"

"Sure. I understand. Tell this Lincoln guy that I came by to see him, okay?"

I gave an imperceptible tug on Pansy's leash. She lumbered to her feet. "Wait a minute," the bouncer said.

I stopped.

His face looked like he was making up his mind. "I'll show you," he finally said.

"Lead on," I told him.

He started walking in the direction he'd told me to go. Suddenly he stopped, turned, looked at me: "You gonna walk behind me all the way?"

"Sure," I said; meaning, "What else?"

He nodded, as if confirming a deeply held suspicion, but he started up again. When he turned into the alley, I unsnapped Pansy's lead and she trotted ahead of him. He practically slammed himself into the alley wall to get out of the way as her dark-gray shadow flitted past. He whirled around and said: "Wha—?"

And then he saw the pistol I was holding. "Just a simple precaution, pal," I reassured him. "You're taking me someplace nice, I'm gonna thank you for it. Otherwise, you're not gonna need to look up 'crossfire' in the dictionary, understand?"

He put his hands up.

"Put 'em down," I told him. "Relax. Just do whatever you were gonna do."

He walked down the length of the alley, fast now, Pansy trotting alongside him like she was heeling. I could barely make out her shape, but I knew the hair was up on the back of her neck, ears flattened, tail whipped between her legs to protect her genitals. Ready to deal out a more certain death than anything I was holding. Guns jam. Shooters miss. Pansy never did either one.

The bouncer rapped a couple of times on a bright-yellow door. It opened immediately. There was light coming from inside. I could see maybe half a dozen people. Except for the guy answering the door, they were all sitting down.

"All right?" the bouncer asked me over his shoulder.

"Sure, pal. Thanks for your help."

I stepped inside, Pansy's bulk against my leg. I could feel her vibrating, still ready.

"My name is Lincoln," the man said as he closed the door behind us. "I'm the one who called."

He was medium height, early thirties; his body looked trim in a pastel T-shirt and white pleated pants, but his face was older. Prominent cheekbones, thin lips, a full set of capped teeth, brownish hair frosted a lighter shade at the forelock. He wore a diamond stud in his right ear, and his grip was strong, self-assured.

He walked over to a sofa where some other people were sitting, nodded his head at an armchair off to one side. "Okay with you?"

I sat down without saying anything, Pansy dropping down on my left. Farther in that same direction, a pair of women at a café table. One, a busty brunette in a pink tank top, showing off her muscular arms among other things; the other, a slender blonde with long, lank hair falling on either side of her head, bangs covering her eyes, wearing some kind of middy blouse.

"We didn't expect you'd bring . . . company," the guy who called himself Lincoln said.

"You worried she's gonna talk?" I asked.

The brunette laughed. Nobody else made a sound.

"No. I was just . . . Forget it. Vincent didn't say anything about you having a . . . partner." Making sure I heard the name, keeping the connection alive. Vincent was an old friend. A gay man, emphasis on the second word. *Heavy* emphasis.

A lot of gay guys I'd met over the years said they started with being molested. I was ignorant enough to think that was the root until I met Vincent. His family was the real thing—loving and warm and supportive. He explained to me how being gay was hardwired, present at birth. Genetic. "It's not a 'choice,'" he said, explaining it to me. "It's not a 'preference' either. It's what we are. It's what I am."

Vincent was in what he called the "literary world." I never understood what he did. Or maybe I never paid attention. What I remember most was how he hated . . . them. Baby-rapers. I was hunting one when we crossed paths, that's when I found out. But he didn't hate them because he was one of us. The Children of the Secret, we're a big tribe, but we're not united. We don't fight under the same flag. Vincent wasn't a draftee in that war; he was a volunteer. He hated them for what they did to children . . . not what was done to him. That was the kind of man he was.

Vincent was a man in a lot of ways, it turned out. He had to do some jail time. Not much, a few months. He wouldn't talk about something the grand jury wanted to know, and some pontificating pervert of a judge locked him up for contempt of court. The black-robed ass-kisser told Vincent he'd stay there until he talked. Once the appellate court figured out that was a life sentence, they cut Vincent loose.

I couldn't help it. I was young then. So I asked him if he had sex in there.

"No," is all he said.

I remembered what it was like Inside. How guys who weren't close to gay on the bricks got turned in there. "Turned out" is what the cons called it. Turned *over* is what it was. I didn't know how to ask him about that . . . rape thing, so I just said, "How come?"

"I didn't meet anyone I fancied," he said, his deep-blue eyes telling me that someone in there had mistaken gay for weak. And learned the difference.

That was a long time ago. Vincent's gone now. But his name would still key my lock . . . at least enough to make me listen.

"What *did* Vincent tell you?" I asked the guy who called himself Lincoln.

"He said you could . . . that you were some kind of private investigator. But . . . off the books."

"Meaning I don't have a license, or I get paid in cash?"

"Both, I guess. But that's not what I meant. I mean, what *Vincent* meant. He said you could . . . find someone. Even if they didn't want to be found."

"Okay. That's what *you* want?"

"Vincent said you'd never go to the police," Lincoln said, meaning it as a question.

"You're tap-dancing," I told him. "I don't know what you asked Vincent. I wasn't there when you talked to him . . . if you did. And nobody can ask him now, right? My résumé is in the street—that's where you have to ask whatever you want to know. You gonna ask a liar if he lies? How would you know anything comes from my mouth is righteous? Either go with what Vincent told you, or get somebody else, friend."

The guy who called himself Lincoln glanced around the room like he was taking a vote. I couldn't see anyone respond, but he went on like it had been unanimous.

"We want . . . the man who's killing all the . . . gay-bashers. The 'Avenger' or whatever name the tabloids are calling him this week."

"You *want* him . . . ?"

"We want to find him," Lincoln said. "We want to . . ." He glanced around the room again, waited until he was satisfied. ". . . to help him get away."

The whole place went quiet, like a bomb had just dropped and they were waiting for the smoke to clear to determine the body count. But I'd had a lifetime of knowing how to answer the question he never asked, so I aborted their pregnant pause and said: "Why tell me?"

Then they *really* went quiet.

Another mistake. I just sat there—a frog on a lily pad, waiting to see if they were flies. I reached down, scratched behind Pansy's ears, my face just this side of bored.

Waiting.

"Vincent told us—" Lincoln started.

I held up my hand in a "stop" gesture. "Vincent's not here," I reminded him.

"Not about . . . you. Vincent was the first one who . . . Look, gay-bashing is . . . lynching, okay? Like that poor kid in Wyoming. I mean, what happened to him, it's always happened. But it doesn't get reported much. Not for what it is. And—"

"And you're all over the map," I cut in. "Lynching is when they string a guy up for stealing horses without waiting for a trial. When they total a gay guy for *being* gay, that's a hate kill. And those're never about individuals."

"I—"

"He's right, Lincoln," the brunette in the tank top said, her voice harder than her face. "Save the politics, okay? If I listen to one more dumb-fuck discussion about whether we're 'queers' or 'gays' or 'homosexuals,' I'll hurl. Just tell him what Vincent told us . . . told *some* of us, anyway—I wasn't there." Reminding him. A smart, tough girl, that one. I couldn't tell where she was from. There's no such thing as a "New York" accent. Brooklyn, Queens, the Bronx . . . they all carry speech-markers. Her voice didn't have any of them.

Lincoln made a gesture like he was wiping sweat off his brow, but he wasn't sweating, so I took it for some kind of prelude-habit. Then he said: "Vincent said it was never going to stop by itself. He said we had to . . . hit back."

I waited, but he'd obviously said his piece. Or thought he had, anyway.

"Is this supposed to be some kind of test, pal?" I asked him. "Am I supposed to guess the rest? Or maybe you want some . . . what, credentials? Look, far as I'm concerned, you can all—"

"Vincent said that," he cut in. "That's what he said about you. He said you were the most unprejudiced straight man he ever met in his life."

"So you went through all this to give me some kind of award?"

"What Vincent said," he continued, like he hadn't heard me, "was that you just plain didn't give a fuck. One way or the other."

"That hasn't changed," I told him. "So what? You got something to say, let me hear it. And it better end in cash."

"To maintain your wardrobe?" some little twerp in a Godfather-movie gangster suit threw in.

I looked over at him, still patting Pansy. "No, pal. To feed my dog. She eats a lot. And she's not the only bitch in this room, I see. Look, I don't do dish, okay? Show me some cash or show me the door."

"That's enough, Sean," Lincoln told the twerp in the gangster suit. "Mr. Burke, what Vincent told us was that we needed to . . . practice violence. Deliberate violence, not self-defense. That we needed to patrol our own streets and . . . interdict the enemy."

"Sounds smart to me," I told him.

"Maybe it was," Lincoln said. "But none of us would go for it. It sounded too . . . ugly. We didn't want to turn the other cheek or"—some fool cackled far in the back, but I couldn't make out what he said—"anything, but we're just not . . . like that."

I guess Vincent hadn't told them everything about our past dealings. One of his friends had ended up with a steel plate in his head after a night in the Ramble. Vincent convinced the guy to go to the cops. They caught the perps easy enough—the little freaks were trophy-takers, and one of them still had the gold chain he'd pulled off the guy whose skull they'd bashed in. And the DA even prosecuted. But only one of them got time, and he didn't get much of it. That's when Vincent first came to me. Later, I was working a job and I needed a place to meet a guy. A place I could haul him out of against his will, if it came to that. Vincent set that one up for me. He was glad to do it. He hated baby-rapers worse than fag-bashers, and that was a lot of hate.

"Who's 'we'?" The brunette challenged the silence Lincoln's little speech had produced. "If I had been there, I would have—"

"Sure, Nadine, we know. We heard it all from you, a thousand times," Lincoln told her without taking his eyes from me. "Anyway, we took a vote. And Vincent lost. That was the end of it."

"So?" I asked him.

"I mean, it was the end of . . . 'us,' I guess. Vincent said he didn't want anything to do with us. He . . . mocked us. He said, when we traded in our leather drag for lavender bullets he'd be back."

"So?" I asked again.

"So he . . . died. From a heart attack. But now it's like he's . . . back."

"You think it's *Vincent* taking out all these freaks?" I asked him. "You should've gone to Ghostbusters, chump."

The brunette laughed again, more harshly this time. Her body went along for the ride—quite a sight, and she knew it. When she caught my eye, she shrugged her shoulders to write that in italics.

"Look," Lincoln said, "you're not making this any easier. But I . . . we didn't expect you would. We don't want you to do anything illegal, all right? There's nothing against the law in looking for somebody. Or solving crimes either."

"You said a lot more than that," I reminded him.

"Lincoln *always* says more than he has to," the brunette he'd called Nadine said, snorting. She got to her feet, walked over to stand next to him. She was shorter than I'd thought she'd be, legs as heavily developed as her arms. "What we want you to do is find him," she went on. "That's all. Just find him, and tell us where we can find him too."

"Vincent said—" Lincoln started, but Nadine chopped him down quick with: "Nobody fucking *cares,* okay, Lincoln?" She turned to face me, hip-shot, her eyes asking me if I liked her as much from the waist down. "*Vincent* told them you had contacts outside the country. That you'd been a mercenary, and that there was a . . . 'pipeline' or something you could send somebody down if they wanted to disappear."

I let my eyes tell her she was, in fact, just as fine from the waist down. "Now you *are* talking about committing a crime," I said. "Whole bunch of crimes if I remember my legal training."

"You're a lawyer?" she asked.

"No," I told her truthfully, "but I've been in plenty of courtrooms."

"So you're not interested?" she asked, a quick lick of her lips telling me she knew how double-edged her words were.

"In what? Solving some crimes? Or committing some?"

"Right now, I'll settle for either."

"I might be . . . in the first. If the money was right."

"What makes you think you *could* solve . . . I mean, find him?" Lincoln asked.

"I don't know, pal. What makes *you* think I can? Vincent?"

"Vincent said you . . . do things for money. He said he . . . helped you with one, once."

"That's nice," I replied. "Only thing is, I don't have any old stories for you, friend. You want to check me out, do what you have to do. Or maybe you already did that. But I don't have a crystal ball. Or promises either."

"But you could *try,* couldn't you?"

"Sure. I could try. But I don't do bounty hunting."

"What does that mean?" Nadine asked.

"It means I don't do COD, understand?" I said, holding her eyes. "I get paid for work, not for results. You want to pay me to look, I might do that. You want to pay me only if I turn him up—if it's a 'him' at all—forget it."

They all went silent again. Nadine turned and walked back to her little table, showing off what every man on the planet was missing. I could tell she'd had a lot of practice.

I went back to scratching behind Pansy's ears. If they didn't learn anything else from all this, they'd at least discover I could outwait a tree.

Lincoln went over to a far corner. A number of them clustered around. The skinny blonde at Nadine's table started to get up, but Nadine grabbed her wrist and wrenched her back down.

I couldn't hear what they were saying. Nadine and I played with each other across the distance. It was as good a way to pass the time as any.

Lincoln finally came back. "We . . . can't decide," he said. "But we will. Soon. If we agree to your . . . terms, we'll reach out for you."

"You don't even know my terms," I told him. "The money has to—"

"The money, the money," he said dismissively. "Don't worry about money. Your terms are that you'll . . . work. Like you said. Yes?"

"Sure."

"You can find your own way out?"

"Sure," I said again, getting up. Pansy slowly got to her feet, then we walked toward the door. As we passed her table, Nadine shot out one hand, grabbed at my jacket.

"Ahhh," she said, mock-sorrowfully, "you didn't even ask for my number."

"I already know it," I told her. "And it's a wrong one."

I went through the door into the alley. It was empty. Pansy was the only one disappointed.

"I do not like them, mahn," Clarence said, back inside Mama's an hour later.

"Them?" Michelle's voice, scorpion-under-glass if you knew how to read it.

Clarence did. And he wasn't going anywhere *near* there. "No, my little sister, I do not mean their . . . sex. That is their business. I mean, I do not trust these people who come to Burke. Something is wrong with all . . . this."

For Clarence, that was a long speech. And for him to *start* a conversation was rarer still. I exchanged a long look with the Prof. Max just waited, as always.

"You make the call, you got to tell it all," the Prof finally said.

"Yes, Father, that is what I am saying," Clarence agreed, not understanding that the Prof was talking about him, not about the crew I'd just visited. "Why don't they . . . fight the ones who attack them?"

"Remember the Haitian guy over at the Seven-Oh in Brooklyn?" I asked Clarence.

I didn't have to say anything more. A couple of cops supposedly took him in the back room and sodomized him with a nightstick. An ugly-filthy Tontons Macoutes–style power display. Ruptured his bladder. Told him if he screamed they'd kill his whole family, muttering about "teaching niggers a lesson." There's a big Haitian community here, and they sure aren't all nonviolent. But they stayed with peaceful demonstrations, expressing confidence that the authorities would get the job done.

The young man nodded, his face unreadable.

"Maybe it's the same thing," I said. "Maybe they're waiting for the public to fucking *get* it, I don't know."

"Mahn, they do *not* get it. The Haitian guy, it happened when the Mayor was running for re-election, yes? And it was on the front page of the papers. Every day. Big coverage. TV, radio. No place to hide. Most of the time, when the . . . homosexuals get attacked, it never even gets out, you know? They don't even go to the cops. Those little demonstrations, they are nothing."

I nodded, against my will, agreeing with him. Thinking of Crystal Beth. Dead and gone. Just because some freak who couldn't face what was in himself had to go and . . .

"This 'Avenger' guy, he is speaking sense to me, mahn," Clarence finished my thought. "They kill your people, you kill them."

"Like the Israelis and the Arabs?" Michelle challenged, pink beginning to creep into her peaches-and-cream.

"Israel is still standing, Little Sister," Clarence said. "Would it be so if she waited for the United Nations to protect her from her enemies?"

"That clue is true," the Prof said. "Ain't a motherfucker on the planet don't know the Israeli bible."

Michelle looked a question at the little man.

"*Two* eyes for an eye," he answered her. Then he turned to the rest of us. "Been pretty quiet since this 'Avenger' guy started playing his number. . . ."

"And *that* is who they want you to find, mahn?" Clarence asked me.

"That's what they say," I told him.

"But . . . what?" Michelle asked.

"Clarence has got a point," I said. "Why me? Sure, I was tight with Vincent, and he might have told them a few things. But they got beaucoup cash. Made that clear. Why not just . . . ?"

"They told you that part, Schoolboy," the Prof said. "I think they're for real on it. The Man wants to stop him before he hits again. But these boys, they want you to stop him before he gets *caught.* Better than wasting their cash on a lawyer."

"Well, it doesn't matter for now," I told everyone. "They'll get back to me if they want to play."

I didn't want to play. I wanted to watch the slime who killed my woman die. I thought about that. A lot. Would Crystal Beth have wanted revenge? She was raised a hippie. Peace and love. But her father died protecting a runaway from a biker pack who said they owned her. And her mother followed him later, taking his killers along for the ride. Much later, Crystal Beth got into the business too. Running that safehouse for stalking victims. Until she became one herself. That's when I came in. And by the time we were all done, the walls were splattered.

Would she have wanted it? I couldn't puzzle it out. So I faced the truth. *I* did. Me.

But I didn't have a clue. And if the cops did, they weren't saying. So I thought I'd get myself an alibi and see if the Avenger would do some of his work while I was covered.

I hadn't been in the basement poolroom for years, but the old man nodded like he'd seen me yesterday. My cue was still in the rack, held in place by a tiny little lock. I took it down, unscrewed it, checked the hollowed-out compartment in the heavily taped butt. Empty. Nobody'd left me a message there for a long time.

Been a long time since I'd played too, and it showed—only took ten minutes to attract one of the slowly circling sharks. I waved him off. I wanted witnesses, sure, but I wasn't going to pay for them.

Hours slipped by. Toward the end, the cue ball was finally starting to obey orders. I spent the whole night working on my stroke, not paying any attention to pocketing the balls. It was after three in the morning when I settled my tab with the old man.

Nothing on the news next day. Maybe he'd really gone quiet. Or, like one of the tabloids speculated, taken his own life. Dying of AIDS, that was another rumor.

I didn't buy any of it.

I went to the track that night. Been years since I'd been to Yonkers. The whole place had changed. NO SMOKING signs everywhere. Quiet. Damn near empty. The horses were a sorry collection of low-rent claimers and nonwinners, with a few burnt-out old campaigners thrown in. Purses were real low too. Handicapping wasn't the same either. They'd added a flexible rail, so the short stretch wasn't the big factor it used to be—horses could pass on the inside coming home. And they ran at a mile and a sixteenth for some stupid reason. I had no experience with any of that, but I invested a few bucks, making sure I went to the same window every time.

I didn't hit one all night.

Neither did he.

The way to establish an alibi is to be visible. But I'd spent my whole life being the opposite—even in prison, where profile maintenance can get you dead real quick—and when I made my list, I didn't come up with much. I'm not known as a gambler, so making the rounds of the various games in town would get me *too* noticed.

If I wanted to play the slots, I could always go to one of the strip clubs, but those siliconed androids wouldn't remember one john from another if the cops ever asked, and they sure don't give receipts. Baseball interests me about as much as antique-collecting. And the movies are a good place to hide, not be seen. My crew would always stand up in court, but there wasn't one of them that didn't have a sheet or wasn't known to be my partner. Not good.

I asked around. Got offered a sure-fire deal from a sleazoid lawyer I know. His client wanted some video of his wife in the sack . . . with anyone but him, he wasn't particular. All I had to do was romance the woman—"She's an ugly old pig," the lawyer told me, "probably even go for a guy like you"—and they'd get me an alibi that'd pass anywhere. It was good money. I hated to let it slide. But I recouped a bit by going to see the woman and telling her what her husband had planned. She was real grateful. And she wasn't anything like what the lawyer had described. I might have gone back to see her again if she hadn't offered me major money to kill her husband.

I thought about getting locked up for something petty, but that bullshit only works in movies. Nobody who'd ever been Inside for a minute would go back just to prove his whereabouts. Besides, the killer was off the job. Or quiet, anyway. And I couldn't alibi myself twenty-four-seven if I was sleeping alone.

I was still thinking it over when he went back to work.

This one was harder to connect. Fact is, the cops probably wouldn't have put it together on their own. It was at a college residence, uptown. The usual stuff:

ALL FAGS MUST DIE!

spray-painted on a dorm door. The same door someone had been slipping nasty little notes under. Somebody threw a rock through the kid's window too. All reported to the campus cops, but not to NYPD. They had some suspects, but not enough proof to go to the Student Court or whatever other impotent nonsense they used there. The gay kids had a demonstration in the Quad. Got some local coverage. But nothing happened—no ID on the perps.

But the hunter must have figured it out. The target was alone in his room. On the third floor. It was a hot night—I guess he left the window open while he slept. Maybe he felt the first burning slice of the razor, maybe not. In the morning, they found him in strips.

Turned out the kid who died was one of the suspects. But that wasn't enough for a connect until the hunter launched another communiqué at the papers.

> Night will not protect you. The darkness holds no safety. Your shield is now my sword. Another of you has joined his cow-

ardly comrades. Do not deceive yourselves. The design is not deterrence—it is extinction. Either we will be allowed to live in peace or you will not be allowed to live. The next one will be close to home. Welcome to a new food chain, prey.

There was one big difference to this note. Apparently he didn't care for the "Avenger" title the media came up with. So this time it was signed: "Homo Erectus."

The tabs went crazy. "Profilers" filled the talk show stages. Gay groups got center stage . . . and used it to go on and on: They understood how this killer *felt,* blah-blah, but they were *very* careful to denounce violence, playing their role. All the editorials read the same: Fag-bashing is bad, so is killing. Two wrongs don't make a right. The kind of trenchant, cutting-edge stuff that makes them so relevant. The "re-enactment" shows ran fake violence-video of the murders, but they didn't have an image of the killer, so the "Most Wanted" stuff went unanswered. Rewards increased.

The father of the kid who got razor-ripped called a press conference, saying his son was the innocent victim of a maniac. That can of spray paint the cops found in his room—the one with his fingerprints all over it—so what if it was the exact same brand that had been used on the gay kid's dorm door? Was that *proof*? Even Jeffrey Dahmer got a trial, for God's sake! What kind of country was this, anyway?

And, of course, he sued the school.

I kept adding to my new refuge. Never anything bigger than I could lug in the Plymouth. The Mole looked like one of those TV aliens with his huge goggles as he arc-welded away. Max wasn't any good with techno-stuff, but he understood mechanics and leverage as perfectly as he did his own kinetics, and the loading-bay door he designed pulled up into the roof, silent as cancer, when I touched the dashboard switch the Mole installed. Now I could turn the corner, cut my lights, and, if I timed it right, slip inside the building as if I'd just vanished. Much easier than in my old . . . place. I didn't have to carry the spotlight anymore either. A pair of them blasted on automatically as soon as the Plymouth's front end broke the motion-detector beams. If you weren't ready for it, you'd go instantly blind. Nice for uninvited visitors.

I spent some of the money I'd stashed, fixing the place up. Gave a little chunk of it to Michelle for clothes, and she went through it like a dope fiend the night before detox.

And I kept the lines out too, but I didn't hook anything. When you're in the freak-scamming business, you meet a lot of humans who hate gays, but you also meet a lot who hide behind them . . . like those "man-boy love" groups who masquerade as homosexual and try and march in the gay-pride parades—as if fucking a boy is the same as making love with a grown man.

I was at the table, ready to play, but all I drew was blanks.

If I got a hint, I was ready to do some ugly things. If I thought anyone in particular knew the answer, they *were* going to tell me. But I didn't have . . . anything.

I knew better than to go back to working my scams until I got the new ID. And I didn't really need the alibi anymore. Morales had nailed it—mail bombs weren't my style, and whoever took out that last one was either a ninja or in a lot better shape than I was. The *federales* knew I had the horses in my stable—the Mole could fit enough bang-stuff into a suitcase to take down a big building. And Max could climb walls like I could climb stairs. But they weren't showing any interest, and I didn't expect any. Whoever—or whatever—this Homo Erectus was, it was all local.

Still, I made the rounds. Shot a lot more pool than I had in years. Took Max with me down to Freehold to watch some *real* trotters—the Meadowlands is closer, but only the half-mile tracks really show you any action—and even hung out in some after-hours joints.

After a while, I didn't know what I was waiting for, so I told myself it was the ID.

I was in the restaurant, playing another round of our life-sentence card game with Max. It was gin for a long time, but we'd switched to casino ever since Max had a once-in-forever winning streak and refused to play anymore for fear of insulting the gods.

For once, Mama wasn't lambasting him with her incompetent advice—he'd brought his daughter Flower with him and the little girl was watching, patient and quiet. Like her mother, except the child was actually interested in the game, missing nothing. Max was convinced she'd bring him luck. But casino's not like gin, and there was no wave of fortune for him to catch. Oh, he could win a hand once in a while, but he'd never get close to breaking even. The trick was making my deliberate blunders slick enough so he wouldn't snap that I was tanking the game. I don't do that often, but, with Flower sitting there watching me with those grave and glistening eyes . . . no choice. He got back a couple of thousand off his deficit before Immaculata came in there to collect the little girl.

"Are you ready for the museum, child?" she asked, her face blazing with love.

"Could we wait a bit, Mother?" Flower asked politely. "I am helping Daddy."

"And how are you doing that?" Immaculata asked.

Max signed "good luck" to her. She bowed, and took a seat next to me. Mama brought her some tea, serving it personally, a sign of deep respect. Their elaborate thank-you ritual took long enough for us to play another couple of hands.

"Are you . . . all right now? In your new place?" Immaculata asked me.

"Yeah, it's fine, Mac," I told her. "Better, even. It was time to go anyway."

"Ah," she said, as if she understood. That I was lying.

Needless to say, with Immaculata added to Max's arsenal, I started losing *every* damn hand. Max would have sat there for hours—when he hit a winning streak, he went absolutely immobile, convinced that any alteration would change his luck. But Immaculata wasn't having any. "It is time to go now, Flower," she said.

"Yes, Mother," the child said. She stood up and kissed Max on the cheek. Max signed that he loved her, that he would always protect her, that she was the most precious thing in his life. The child's face reddened slightly, just a trace of embarrassment showing.

Watching them took me away.

When I was little, I was in custody. They called it an orphanage, but we all knew what it was. All except those chumps who thought they were going to get adopted one day by the privileged people who came around and looked us over like it was a petting zoo. They didn't want any of us—they just wanted babies—but we got displayed anyway. I hated them all. By that time, hate came easy.

Once they took us to watch some Little League game. Out in the suburbs, all us State kids on a bus. Same kind of bus they used to take me to prison years later, only this one didn't have that steel mesh over the windows. Anyway, it wasn't like we were going to play or anything; we just got to watch.

This one kid, he was a fat clumsy little goof. Every time they hit the ball to him, he flubbed it. And when he got up to bat, his swing was spastic. But his father was running around the stands cheering like the kid was the second coming of DiMaggio, shouting encouragement, applauding everything. I could see it embarrassed the fat kid, his father making such a fuss over him and all.

I hated that kid.

I wanted to kill him.

And take his place.

I wanted to . . .

"Burke. Call for you."

Mama, tapping me on the shoulder, that look on her face telling me it wasn't the first time she'd tried, but I hadn't been there.

I shook my head to clear it. Immaculata and Flower were gone. Max was sitting across from me. Cards still on the table. Score sheet to my right. But it was—damn!—half an hour since I'd been in the room.

"Thanks, Mama," I said, like nothing was going on. I saw her exchange looks with Max.

"What?" I said into the phone.

"Aw, you never *did* call, huh?" A woman's voice. But not one I . . .

"Nadine," I said.

"Sure. Who else? You have *other* girlfriends?"

"What do you want?" I asked, flat-voiced, just this side of harsh.

"Ah, what a list *that* is. But, for now, I'll settle for this: We want to meet with you again."

"Lincoln—"

"Yes, Lincoln. All of us."

"What's the—?"

"The point," she interrupted again, "is that we've come to an agreement. And we want to propose it to you."

"I told you—"

"Yes, and we *listened,* okay? You can have what you want. How many times a day do you hear *that*?" she mock-purred.

"I *hear* it all the time," I told her.

"Well, you play your cards right, you'll get to *see* it too," she said, a play-sexy catch in her low voice.

"You want entertainment, watch TV, bitch."

"You scared?" she challenged.

"Sure," I said indifferently.

"Hmm . . . that works on most men," she said, whispering now, breathy. "What works on you, Burke?"

"Money," I said, neutral-voiced.

"Well, then, you got your wish, mister. Interested now?"

I didn't bother with the bouncer this time. Or backup either. If there was going to be trouble, it would have been last time. Anyway, my crew knew who everyone was, and where to find the place. If those people knew enough about me to offer me a job, they knew enough to figure out that double-crossing me was a sure ticket to Payback City. And that it wouldn't be a round trip.

The yellow door opened a split-second after I rapped. Nadine. In baggy pink jersey sweats, her thick dark hair tied behind her head.

"You ever go anyplace without her?" she asked, nodding at Pansy.

"Sometimes," I replied, looking over her shoulder. The place was empty. "Where's everyone else?"

"Oh, they'll be along. Don't worry. I just wanted to talk to you first. Alone."

"Talk," I told her, walking past her and sitting down at the same table she'd been at the first time.

She strolled slowly over, hauling the sweatshirt over her head with both hands as she moved. Underneath was a white jersey bra with heavy shoulder straps. She needed them. Pansy watched her, not moving. She doesn't rely on smell like most dogs, never makes guesses. If I told her to, she'd let the strange woman pat her head and not make a sound. Or lock on to her like a crocodile with an antelope that ventured too near the water's edge. All the same to Pansy—she's a pro.

Nadine sat down, rummaged in a small black nylon bag sitting on the table. The only light was somewhere in the back room. No noise. She came out with a hypo, hit herself on a fleshy part of her upper arm, and pushed the plunger. If she felt the spike go in, I couldn't see it in her eyes.

And if she expected a reaction from me, she didn't see it either. "What is it you want?" I asked her.

"To find out . . . something. They're going to hire you, but I have a . . . proposition. Maybe. I need to find out. . . . Did you ever know a lesbian? I mean, really know one, not watch a couple do it in some movie?"

"I live with one," I told her.

"Huh? *You?* Who is she?"

"She's right there," I said, pointing at Pansy.

"I guess I don't like your sense of humor much," she said, her voice sharp around the edges.

"Pansy's gay," I said, telling her the truth. "Or whatever it is that means she wants nothing to do with male dogs. She's a Neapolitan mastiff, from one of the finest lines. I could get an easy fifteen hundred bucks for one pup, and they usually have real big litters. So I paid a ridiculous stud fee for this famous brute Neo, over in Brooklyn. And even though Pansy was in heat, she wouldn't get busy with him. No matter what he did, she wasn't having any."

"Maybe she just didn't like him?"

"*Like* him? A bitch in heat? Sure. Anyway, I tried it again. Couple of times, in fact. No Sale."

"Didn't they want you to tie her down so he could—?"

"Yeah, they did. You think I'd let anyone rape my dog?"

"Well . . . you were going to breed her, right?"

"I was going to *let* her have sex, then *let* her have puppies. That's it. I thought she wanted to. And I was wrong. Truth is, I thought she would—she loves puppies."

"You really think she's gay?" she asked, leaning forward, moving her elbows in to display the cleavage.

"Sure."

"I didn't think dogs could be—"

"Why not? Some monkeys are. It's just brain chemistry, right? Hormones trigger differently. I heard it from other guys too, about their dogs."

"How about male dogs?"

"I . . . don't know. I don't see why not. Be harder to tell with them, though."

"Why?"

"They're pack animals. When the bitches go into season, the males fight. The winners get to mate. At least, mate first. Maybe their blood gets up even if they don't want to have sex, and they fight anyway. I don't know. Never paid much attention."

"But you seem to know a lot about them."

"Dogs? Sure. Pansy's my . . . partner."

"Is she . . . trained, like?"

"You mean, can she do tricks?"

"Yes. I mean, I guess so. What else could—?"

"They got food in that joint? The one around the side?"

"Sure. What would—?"

"Go get a nice piece of raw steak, no bone, I'll show you a trick."

She gave me a quizzical look for a long second. Then got up and walked out the door. If running around in her bra bothered her, you couldn't see any evidence of it.

I lit a cigarette. "Ready to show off, girl?" I asked Pansy.

She didn't say anything.

I was almost done with the smoke when Nadine came back in, a big slab of bloody steak in one hand. "Now what?" she asked.

"Just give it to her," I said.

"She won't . . . bite me?"

"She won't do anything unless I tell her to. Go ahead."

She handed the steak to Pansy. The big Neo sniffed it appreciatively and immediately started to slobber. With Pansy, that means quarts, not drops. But she didn't move a muscle.

"How come she won't—?"

"Drape it right over her snout," I told her. "Go ahead—it's perfectly safe."

She did what I told her. I got up, walked behind Nadine. Pansy's eyes were only on me. "Tell her she's beautiful," I whispered into Nadine's ear.

"You're *beautiful,*" she said, just as I made the hand signal for "Speak!" to Pansy. The beast expertly spun her huge head, dewlaps sending a spray of drool all across the room as the steak disappeared into her maw. It was gone in a few chomps. She sat up alertly, waiting for more.

"That's enough, you pig," I told her, walking back to the table.

"She only takes food when you tell her she's beautiful?" Nadine asked, a tone of wonderment in her voice. Really curious now, not playing.

"You know how some women are about their weight," I said.

"That's . . . amazing. Does she do other stuff?"

"Lots of stuff. But I couldn't show you most of it."

"Why not?"

"There's nobody here to show it *on.*"

"Oh. She's a . . . what do you call them . . . attack dog?"

"She's a *protection* dog," I said. "Just about all her tricks have something to do with that."

"She doesn't, like . . . I don't know . . . roll over or play dead or anything?"

"What good would any of that be?"

"I don't know. I see people with their dogs . . . in the park. . . . Does she play fetch? Or Frisbee?"

"Pansy doesn't *play* anything. She works. Just like me."

"Oh, you never play?" she asked, a wicked grin making her face look softer.

"Not word games."

"Me either. No matter what you think of me."

"How do you know what I think of you?"

"Oh, *that's* not hard. I'm a cock-teasing queer cunt, right?"

"'Queer,' that's your word. I don't know anything about the rest."

"So what *do* you think?"

"I think you want something. And that you're going to tell me what it is."

"Because . . . ?"

"Because, unless you're lying, the others are going to show up, and you don't want to ask me whatever it is in front of them."

"A lot of strippers are gay," she said, as if that was an answer to a question.

"Why tell me?"

"To explain what I said before. I have girlfriends who strip. They have to . . . sit with the guys, it's part of the job."

"You mean sit *on* them, right?"

"Yes. But it's not a whorehouse."

"You take off your pants for money, then you're a . . . what? Actress?"

"Men *hate* that," she said, as if I hadn't said a word. "They find out you're gay, it's like they've been . . . tricked or something."

"'Tricked' is exactly what they've been. You pay some broad to wiggle on your lap, what are you *except* a trick?"

"You don't understand. They wouldn't care. . . . I mean, they wouldn't get *mad,* if the girl was straight. I can't explain it. They just—"

"Yeah, whatever. You got a point to all this?"

"Yes," she said quietly. "I do have a point. You already have one gay partner. You want another?"

I watched her face, staying on her eyes, little chunks of cobalt, looking for . . . I don't know what. But I came up empty.

"What's that mean?" I finally asked her.

"If you're really going to look for him, there'd be places you'd have to go. It would be a lot easier . . . easier for you . . . if you had someone with you, understand?"

"You think I'm going to look for a serial killer in gay bars?"

"No," she said. Eyes alive, mouth tense. "That's what *they* think. I mean the . . . others. Lincoln and all. Or maybe not. I don't have any idea. But . . . neither do they. That's the point. All they know about you is . . . what they heard. They don't know what to do, but they want to do *something,* okay? It's more . . . symbolic to them, I think. I mean, they can't expect you to really find this guy. How could you? Every cop in the city is looking for him, and . . . Anyway, they just want to be able to tell themselves they *tried* . . . like they were being 'supportive' or whatever the hot word is this week. I mean, with that deal you wanted, how would they even know if you ever looked at all?"

"Ah. So the idea is, you tag along, you make sure I'm earning the money?"

"No. I think . . . I know about you too. And not from where they do."

"Which means . . . ?"

"You think the only gay cops on the force are in GOAL?"

I knew what she meant—Gay Officers Action League. Like the Guardians, the organization for black cops. Every group inside the department has got some kind of organization of its own. It took major *cojones* to come out in the open like the cops at GOAL had, but it wasn't news, not anymore. I just shrugged an answer at her.

"They're not," she said, firmly. "I mean, they're not all . . . out. Not because they're afraid, but because they have . . . work to do. And it wouldn't get done if the brass knew the truth, no matter what NYPD's PR people say."

"So?"

"So I have a friend. And I got to learn a little about you from . . . my friend."

"I'm giddy with anticipation," I told her.

Pansy grunted, convinced, finally, that she'd seen the last of the steak.

"You've been arrested dozens of times," she said. "And you've been in prison too."

"That's your idea of a secret?"

"No," she said, leaning closer, dropping her voice. "This is: A cop was killed a couple of years ago. A woman cop. Belinda Rogers. She was bent. Bent bad. Killed some women to make it look like a rapist did it. Her boyfriend was in prison. In New Jersey. He was just finishing up there, for some other crimes, and then he was coming here for trial. It was copycat killing she was doing—like that crazy woman in California who tried to copy one of the Hillside Strangler's crimes because she was in love with one of the guys who actually did it."

"What's this got to do with—?"

"The cop who killed her? It was a shootout. His name is Morales. He's still on the job."

"If you say so."

"You had something to do with it," she said flatly.

"With killing a cop?" I asked, raising my eyebrows with the ridiculousness of the idea.

"No. But the word is that you were the one who found her. Found her *out,* I mean. That you were the one who tracked her down."

"That's some weird 'word' you got," I said gently, just shy of mocking her.

"No, it isn't. I'm not going to argue with you. I'm not trying to get you to admit anything. I'm not wired," she said, sticking her chest out as if that would prove she was telling the truth, "and this isn't a game. What I'm telling you is . . . I know you *could* find this man. And you might get into places where you'd have to . . . convince people that you weren't a bounty hunter, understand?"

"No."

"Look. A *lot* of people are trying to find him. There's some major reward money out there. And word is that there's a mercenary team looking. That's another thing I know about you too. You *could* hook him up . . . get him out of here if you wanted to."

"If your source for that is as good as—"

"Never mind. You know whatever your truth is. All I can do is tell you mine. Bottom line: If you get in . . . contact with him, why should he trust you? But if I'm there, if I'm in it, then he'd know it was legit."

"So I'm gonna call him on the phone, tell him I'm really a nice guy, and prove it by bringing you to our next meeting?"

"I know it won't be like that," she said, biting at her lip, trying for patience. "I don't know *how* it would happen. But if it comes down to . . . credentials . . . if I was there, I could answer any questions. You see what I'm saying?"

"I *hear* it. But I can't *see* it," I told her. "You got some ragtime story from some loony pal of yours on the force; you got some *pssst-pssst* bullshit about mercenaries; you think it adds up to you partnering up with me? Not this year."

"You don't trust me."

It wasn't a question, but I still answered it for her. "No."

"I don't blame you for that. You don't know me. But I'm telling you the truth. Not about"—she waved her hands as if dismissing those stories about me she'd heard—"that stuff. About this: I want to find him. And I want to help him get away before they bring him down. The others, they're just role-playing. Even Lincoln. All that macho rap, it's just for style points. That's what it'll come down to if he's ever caught: courthouse vigils, talk shows, letters to the editor . . . not what they *say* they want."

"Why you?"

"You know how gay people always wonder if some part of them isn't straight? No, I guess you wouldn't. Well, we do. I don't mean we want it . . . although some *pray* for it . . . but we always . . . wonder. I don't even know how it works. If you have sex with . . . you know what I mean, does that make you bi?"

"You're asking the wrong man."

"Meaning you never did. Or you just don't know."

"Both."

"I didn't come out right away. It was . . . years. Before I figured out . . . before I . . . Never mind. If I had sex with men once, and I have sex with women now, what am I?"

"I'm the wrong man to ask."

"You're the wrong man to ask a lot of things, seems like."

"True."

"I love him," she said suddenly.

"Huh?"

"The . . . executioner. I love him. I never met him. Or maybe I did. None of us could know that. Maybe he was right in one of the . . . places we go. But it doesn't matter. I know I love him. And I want to be with him. Even if he's . . . even if we could never have . . . I mean . . . It doesn't matter. I love him and I want to be with him. So I'll . . . do things. Whatever things, it doesn't matter. Things that could help you find him. Understand what I'm saying?"

"Yeah. I always seem to have the same problem with you, Nadine. I understand what you're saying. I just have problems with believing any of it."

"What kind of proof could I show you?"

"I don't know. I don't know if there *is* any. It's not the kind of thing where you—"

"Just think about it, okay?" she whispered, her hand on my forearm, nodding her head sharply to tell me what Pansy's pricked-up ears had told me a few seconds ago—the rest of them were coming.

I never turned my back, letting Nadine's eyes mirror their approach for me. She was the first to speak too.

"About time!"

"We *are* on time." Lincoln's voice. "How long have you been here?"

"About five minutes," she lied smoothly.

Lincoln walked around behind me and took a seat next to Nadine. "We want to do business," he said, no preamble.

"Everybody wants to do business," I told him. "It's the terms and conditions that hold things up."

"What do you want?" Lincoln asked, as shadowy figures filled in behind him. Some of them stopped behind me . . . no way of telling how many. Pansy was alert, but relaxed, still within herself, not feeling any heat.

"I want you to understand what we're all doing here," I told him. "Me, I'm a public-spirited citizen. Or maybe I'm a treasure hunter. For the reward. Yeah . . . I like that better. You all, you're . . . investors. You finance my investigation, and you get a piece of the pie when and if I turn him up. How's that?"

"Wait!" A voice behind me, male. "I thought you said we were going to—"

Lincoln held up his hand for silence. "But since we're the . . . investors . . . you'd naturally report your findings to us before you . . ."

"Naturally," I told him, straight-faced.

"How do we know he wouldn't just go to the—?" Another male voice, this one from somewhere in the shadows to Lincoln's left.

"I'm sure Mr. Burke has professional standards," Lincoln said, cutting him off, trying to put an aura of threat around his voice.

"Oh, I do," I assured him. "But I don't have a private investigator's license. I don't need one if I'm working for a lawyer, though."

"We have—"

"Me too," I told him. "And I want to use mine. What you have to do, see, is hire my guy. Then *he* hires *me.*"

"That seems like a good deal of trouble for—"

"For who? Not for me. And I'm the only one I got to look out for here."

"Fine," Lincoln said. "If that's the way you want it, that's the way we'll do it."

I slid Davidson's card across the table to him, not saying another word.

"And the money . . . ?" he asked.

"What money? Me, I'm not taking any money. Not from you. If this lawyer you're going to hire decides he wants to compensate me for my trouble, that's his business. Not yours."

"That's all there is to it?"

"Yeah. And forget progress reports. This happens or it doesn't. Understand?"

I could feel the electric current crackle around the room, call-and-response, question-and-answer, voting in silence. I went back to patience, watching only Nadine's hard bright eyes.

"All right," Lincoln finally said.

"How am I supposed to set a fee for something like this?" Davidson asked me later.

"You charge by the hour, right?"

"Not for tort litigation. That's all contingency. And I front the investigation costs. The client doesn't pay anything until it's all done."

"But in a matrimonial . . . ?"

"Sure. That's an hourly rate. But if I'm representing the non-moneyed spouse, it all has to come from a counsel-fees award. And that's never guaranteed, I assure you. The only time I get paid in a lump up front is for criminal defense," he said, nodding at me to indicate that I should know that part real well.

"And *that's* all cash, right?" I said, reminding him that I'd always paid him that exact way. And that I'd been a lot of things in my life, but IRS-informant was never going to be one of them.

He nodded, waiting.

"Let's say you were approached by someone who fears he might be a . . . target of a police investigation, okay? Let's say he's totally innocent. Got nothing to do with whatever the Man is looking at. But, still, he's worried. Let's say he knows there has to be a bust soon. The media's all over the cops, and that means the politicians can't be far behind. So this guy, he's worried. He could hire you, right? For a flat fee? And he'd need an investigation too. From your end. Just in case."

"That hypothetical has a certain structural validity to it," Davidson acknowledged warily.

"And the new IRS rules, they can make you disclose who paid you any fee in excess of ten grand, right?"

"Yes. That was just ratified by the—"

"Sure. So, maybe, just to protect a client, you wouldn't want to report a fee . . . immediately. You understand what I'm saying?"

"I do not," Davidson said, primly.

"Let's just . . . take a number, okay? Say, a hundred thousand, all right? Now, this client, this *hypothetical* client, he thinks he may be the target of an investigation, okay? But he also has *other* legal issues. Maybe real complex ones . . . like he wants to get married and—"

"—he needs a prenuptial agreement?"

"No. And he's gay. So he needs some kind of highly complex 'partnership' agreement. Something that would protect his interests no matter how it turns out. Let's say he . . . and his partner . . . they want to adopt a child too. After they . . . formalize their relationship. Raises a lot of legal issues, doesn't it?"

"Certainly. Although I must tell you, I would not myself participate in any premarital agreement concerning custody of children. The courts won't uphold them . . . and they shouldn't. Children aren't property, and their best interests cannot be determined prior to—"

"Yeah, sure," I said, stopping the flow before he got really wound up and spewed for hours. "Pay attention, okay? So this guy comes in and he plunks down a hundred large. In cash. You report it—report it all, no problem. What it's for is the partnership stuff. And then *you* need a partner. For the investigation. That costs you, say, fifty. Half."

"And that's for you?"

"Sure. What do you care? You're declaring it all as income, and you can freely disclose the name of your client. What's the problem?"

"The problem is that I would be declaring a hundred—and paying tax on it—but I would only be getting half of that."

"You'd be paying tax on whatever you declare," I told him. "A hundred large is a pretty big fee for what I described."

"So is fifty."

"Sure. But you have to get paid for representing me, right?"

He nodded.

"And there's no way you're declaring *that,*" I told him, not a question.

He didn't move his head an inch, but I took that for what it was.

"So if a guy calls you, name of Lincoln, then you'll know what to do?"

This time he nodded, slightly.

"Can you find him?" I asked the delicate-featured young woman. She had taxicab-yellow hair, short and straight, with a black X dyed into the left side. Her face was symmetrical, with just a trace of baby fat. She wore a silver ring in her puggish nose. And her dark eyes looked as sharp as the razor-blade earrings she sported. I didn't know her, never met her before then.

Lorraine was the only link I had left to Crystal Beth, but it wasn't a real link until I finally went over to the safehouse and told her I was hunting the humans who'd killed my woman. She didn't blink, just asked me if I wanted any help.

"I looked everywhere I could think of," I told her. "And I drew blanks. I need a tracker."

"I don't know any—"

"Crystal Beth said you did," I told her. Then I told her what I meant. And how I knew they'd have what I needed.

"Her name is Xyla," Lorraine finally said. "She'll be in touch."

So now this Xyla was sitting across from me in my booth at Mama's.

"Can you find him?" I asked again.

"If he's in Cyberville, I can," she said. Not bragging, confident. "But I can tell you, people are already looking."

"Looking?"

"Posting open messages for him. On newsgroups, bulletin boards, like that."

"What kind of messages?" I asked her.

"The whole range: journalists who want an interview, gays saying 'Go for it!,' threats, challenges, target suggestions . . . everything."

"And they think he's going to answer them?"

"Netizens are real naïve," she replied. "Most of them are kids. In their minds, anyway. There's over a thousand profiles with the name 'Avenger' in them on AOL alone. That's what the papers called him. Until he wrote that last letter. So now the geeks will just search under this 'Homo Erectus' handle. And there'll be a ton of matches there too."

"And they think he's got an . . . address?"

"Sure. Someplace. And it's already happening—there's messages posted that are *supposed* to be from him. As if the FBI isn't watching all that traffic," she said contemptuously.

"So how could you find him?"

"I think he's on-line. I think he lurks."

"Lurks?"

"Watches. Hops on the Net and visits these different places. As long as he doesn't post, he's pretty safe."

"Pretty . . . ?"

"If he stays on long enough, or hits a website with our software on it, we can finger him."

I looked a question over at her.

"Locate him. His cyber-addy, anyway. That wouldn't find him—he could be using any ISP, and the server could even be out of the country."

"So what good would—?"

"If you found his addy . . . if it was really him, then, if you could hack into the ISP's own files, you could get his billing info. You know, the credit card he uses—you can't buy ISP services for cash, you need a credit card just to sign up."

"But anyone can get a phony credit card. As long as you pay the bills, they won't care what name you use."

"Sure. And some of the ISPs give out e-mail addys for free just to build their lists too. That's where . . . someone else comes in," she said.

"Okay. You'll take a shot?"

"I'm with Lorraine and the others," she answered, like that was all the answer I needed. "But there's something else too. Another way, maybe. I don't know if he's high-cyber or not. But if he is, I could send a message myself. Send it encrypted, so you'd need a program to open it."

"What happens if you don't have this program?"

"You just get a bunch of gibberish—numbers and symbols—it wouldn't mean anything. But if he *is* lurking, he might be intrigued enough to open it up."

"And . . . ?"

"Then I could find him," Xyla said, flashing a quick smile. "And you know what? I don't think he'd mind."

"Huh?"

"Look, he writes to the newspapers, doesn't he? It's not as if he's being quiet about the whole thing. But he hasn't posted to Cyberville yet. How come?"

"I can answer that one for you," I told her. "The newspapers are turning over everything to the cops before they print it. This many murders, even the tabloids wouldn't screw around."

"So what?"

"So he has to be authenticating his communications somehow. Telling them some detail about the crime that wasn't in the papers, enclosing something from the crime scene . . . like that. No way he could get that done over the Internet."

"That's true," she said. "Cyberville is nothing but Impostor City. So I'd need something myself . . . some, what did you call it, authentication, right?"

"Right."

"Can you get that for me?"

"I'll see," I told her.

But she wasn't done. "You're not trying to . . . catch this guy, are you?"

"Why?"

"Because, if you were, I wouldn't help you."

"I thought you said—"

"I said I was with the network. But I don't know if anyone asked you that question."

"If I was trying to . . . You *like* this guy or something?"

"I don't know if I like him," Xyla said calmly, dark eyes steady on mine. "I haven't met him. But I wouldn't be part of trying to stop him."

"You like what he's doing, then?"

"Not even. But I sure don't like the people he's doing it *to,*" she said, standing up to leave.

"Hi." A woman's voice answered the phone, soft and sexy. But the disguise wasn't even a good try.

"You know who this is, Nadine?" I asked her.

"Sure," she replied, shifting texture. "You change your mind about wanting a partner?"

"Maybe. Depends on what you can bring to the table."

"I told you. I—"

"Not now. Not on the phone. Not ever," I told her. "You got a car?"

"No."

"Want a ride in a nice one?"

"Is *she* going to be along?" Like Pansy was the other woman.

"Yep."

"Why? You scared to be alone with me?"

"Yep."

"Ah. Okay. You know where I—?"

"No," I told her. "I'll pick you up in front of the same place we met last time, okay?"

"Sure. What time?"

"Say . . . midnight?"

"Ooh. It's *dark* then."

I hung up on her.

I was there at a little past eleven, parked across the highway, the Plymouth lost in the shadows, watching the front of the joint through the night-vision spotting scope I'd held out of an order I'd middle-manned. A little inventory shrinkage is something you have to expect when you deal with crooks.

The scope worked even better than the seller had promised—kind of a greenish wash over the whole scene, but bright and clear enough to pick out individual faces. Nadine showed way early, around eleven-forty-five, the skinny blonde girl with her, Nadine holding her wrist as if she expected the other girl to bolt. Or maybe just making a status statement. Ten minutes later, she said something to the blonde and let go of her wrist. The blonde went inside the joint. Nadine stood there, arms folded under her breasts, shoulders squared, waiting.

I wheeled around and came from the downtown direction, pulled up just before midnight. Nadine walked over to the passenger side of the car boldly, stuck her face inside as the window slid down.

"You're on time," she said.

"Just get in," I told her.

"Where's the seat belt?" she asked me as I pulled away.

"It doesn't have shoulder straps. There's a lap belt right on the seat next to you."

"Geez. How old is this thing, anyway?"

"About your age," I told her.

"You're sure not," she shot back.

"Damn! You don't miss much, huh?"

"Why are you so nasty to me?" she asked as we passed the Meat Market and forked left for the West Side Highway.

"I play them the way they're dealt," I said.

"So if I was sweet to you . . ."

"I'd take it for sarcasm."

"So, I'm . . . stuck, right?"

"What's your beef?" I asked. "This is what you want, isn't it? You made your point, first time I met you. You want to keep making it over and over, get your kicks that way, it's all right with me."

"You don't know anything about the way I get my kicks."

"And I don't have to, right?" We were into the Thirties by then, in the sleaze zone that surrounds the Port Authority Terminal. You don't see much hooker traffic there anymore, although it's still around, but it's a good place to buy whatever they don't sell in stores. "You got a friend on the force," I said, setting her up for what I was going to pitch later. "You got some info, heard some rumors . . . and you made all your decisions. One of those decisions was that I was judging you . . . and you started out with an attitude just for that. Now you want to do . . . what? Flirt with me? Do your little Mae West thing? You don't like men. Straight men, anyway. That's your privilege. Me, I don't give a good goddamn what you are. All I care about is what you do. You're not pro enough to play it the same, sit there and pout. Or snarl if that makes you feel more top. You said you could do something. Now I want to find out if you can. That's all this is about . . . all it's ever gonna be about."

"Wow! That's the most I ever heard you talk."

"Don't get used to it." We were on the upper roadway by then, Riverside Drive on the right, the Hudson on the left.

"Where are we going?"

"Someplace where we can talk. Privately."

"I know better places. And why can't we just talk now?"

"We can, if you want. I can just cruise around while we talk. Or I can go where I was headed and park. Pick one. But we're not going anyplace I haven't been before, case closed."

"Oh, go ahead," she said.

We drove in silence until the Cloisters loomed ahead. I pulled over. It's a kind of Lovers Lane up there. Cops wouldn't pay much attention to a couple talking outside a car. A sex-sniper would. Or any of the wolfpacks that roam occasionally. But I docked the Plymouth back end in first, and I had something else to even the odds.

"Come on, girl," I told Pansy, opening the back door. She took off at her usual slow amble, circling, mildly interested in the new turf, but not about to go running off into the woods. Pansy's a tight-perimeter beast, more comfortable in small circles.

Nadine let herself out, stood next to me as I leaned against the Plymouth's flank and lit a smoke.

"Those make me sick," she said. "I don't see how you could poison your body like that."

"The doctor prescribed them," I told her. "There's a chemical—lecithin—in cigarettes. Improves concentration. My mind kind of wanders sometimes. These help."

She gave me a wondering look, trying to read my face. Good luck.

"If that's true, how come the cigarette companies don't advertise it?" she finally asked.

"You can get it other places besides cigarettes," I told her. "In stronger doses too. Over-the-counter, any health-food store."

"So why would you—?"

"These taste better," I said.

"Oh. So what you really are is a junkie, huh?"

"Nah," I told her, "I could stop anytime I wanted."

She folded her arms again and stared hard at me. I wondered if she'd go for it. For me, quitting cigarettes is a sucker bet. I can do it. Done it a bunch of times. It's just a shuck. There was a girl once. In another town. Another world. Her name was Blossom, and she was a doctor. She bet me I couldn't stop smoking for a week. I still remember the payoff. And her promise—the one she made when she left. The one I'd never hold her to.

But Nadine wasn't having any. Or maybe she wasn't a gambler. "Sure," is all she said, not leaving the door open enough.

Pansy strolled around, sniffing occasionally just for the fun of it. She knew she couldn't snarf something off the ground—I'd trained her never to do that—but she liked the smell of discarded fast-food containers anyway.

"So what's this about?" Nadine asked, once she realized I was just going to relax and have my smoke without saying anything to her until I was done.

"There might be a way you could help," I told her. "It all depends on whether you're telling me the truth. And if your pal was telling *you* the truth."

"What does that mean?"

"And how good a pal he really is," I continued, like I hadn't heard her.

"*She's* a *really* good pal," Nadine said.

"We'll see. There's no risk pulling up a guy's rap sheet. Even if they check the computer log-on record, she wouldn't need much of an excuse to explain why she wanted to know more about me . . . especially with this open pattern-killer running. But taking a look at *those* cases themselves . . . "

"What do you mean?"

"Is this pal of yours actually assigned? I mean, is she on the task force they got or whatever?"

"I don't under—"

"There's a case running, right? A bunch of them. The killings in the park, that's one. I already talked to the two slugs who're working it. But the others—the ones this Homo Erectus guy is doing—no way there's only a two-man team assigned to *that.* There's got to be more. A *lot* more. Too much press for it to be otherwise. So, first thing, is your pal involved in *that,* yes or no?"

"I . . . don't know."

"Jesus. Look, like I said, I don't know how you play. And that's none of my business. But I also don't know how you talk, and that *is,* understand?"

"No, I *don't,*" she snapped back, turning toward me, face tilted up, jaw out-thrust, hands on hips.

"Well, then, I'll explain it to you," I said, keeping my voice as measured as my words. "Every crew has its own language. Sometimes it overlaps, sometimes it doesn't. In prison, they call everything outside 'the World.' That's what they call it in the army too. But if someone told you they were 'waiting to get back to the World,' it wouldn't mean squat, right? Okay, you say someone's your friend, what does it mean? Depends on your *own* language, see? I need to know what words mean to you if I'm going to do anything with you. Otherwise, we're walking down a trail, I say 'Duck!,' and you think I'm pointing out a fucking mallard."

"You think gay people—?"

"How about if you actually try listening to me, okay? I'm not talking about subcultural crap, I'm talking . . . just you, all right? Just tell me, Nadine. Tell me this. When you say this woman's your 'pal,' what's that mean? You took a roll with her one time? You're in love? You go back to high school together? You can trust her? How much? With what? You understand what I'm saying now?"

She moved her hands to behind her back, flexing so her biceps popped. Took a step back. Looked up at me. "She's my . . . you know that skinny blonde I was with? The first time you came to the place?"

"I remember her."

"This one's like . . . her. She'll do what I tell her."

"That doesn't overlap," I told her.

"And what does *that* mean?"

"It means just because she'll lick your boots or whatever master-slave games you play doesn't mean she'll do what you tell her out*side* of sex."

"You don't know—"

"Yeah, I do. I know it enough not to trust it. And that's all I ever need to know."

"You think she wouldn't obey me? I could walk her on a leash right up Broadway if I wanted."

"Yeah, how very dom of you. It's not the same."

"Maybe not between men and women. Or even men and men. But with me, they all—"

"Sure. Look, I'm not going to argue with you. I'm not about arguing."

"So what *are* you about?"

"Testing."

"And what's the test?" she said, moonlight glinting in her cobalt eyes, lips slightly apart, excited now, eager to show me how much control she had over her pets.

"I might have a way to get in contact with this guy," I said softly. "A long shot. But I'd need a credential. Something to prove I was in the know. And something to test him with too—make sure I was dealing with the right guy."

"What are you talking about?"

"Ever since they started working these murders as a group, they've been keeping all the evidence in one place. Forensic stuff, I'm talking about. Crime-scene photos too. The papers say a guy was stabbed to death, all right? But they *don't* say anything about how many times he got stuck, or in what places, or even whether it was a Bowie knife or an ice pick. . . . You get the picture?"

"I . . . think so."

"When something like this happens, it brings out the loons. I promise you, guys with loose wing-nuts have been confessing for weeks. On top of that, you get freaks who thrill themselves pretending to be the killer. No way the letters the papers have been printing are the only ones they got. So how would they know which ones were righteous and which ones were scams? *Details.* He sends them a little something each time. Just so they know they're dealing with the real thing. That's what I need too."

"How come? Why would *you* need—?"

"Look, let's say there's a place I could leave a message. Not for him, specifically, but a place where he might look for messages. I tell him I want to talk, okay? He's got to know I'm the real deal. And if he answers, I've got to know *he* is too, see?"

"I *don't* see. How could you . . . ?"

"That's my problem. Your problem is whether you can make this other girl do what you tell her outside the bedroom."

"Just tell me what you want," Nadine said, voice hardening.

"Just a piece," I lied. "A little piece. Something they'd use as a polygraph key—tell your pal that, she'll know what you mean."

"Yes, but *I* don't."

"Then ask *her,* okay? Or order her, however it is that you all communicate. I don't have time to screw around with this. Either you really have something to ante up or you don't."

"I . . . All right, you're saying I get this 'polygraph key' and then I'm in?"

"That's what I'm saying."

"And if I don't, I'm out?"

"That too."

"Even after what I told you?"

"What? That fairy story about how you love this guy? You're a power freak, so what? I already figured that one out."

"Kiss my ass."

"The only thing I want to do with your ass is watch it walk away," I told her.

She stepped close to me, stood on her toes, her chest brushing mine. "You're a liar," she said softly.

"Behavior is the truth," I answered, blocking her game-player's jab. Then I turned away and snapped my fingers for Pansy to come.

She was quiet on the drive back. At least for a few minutes. When I lit another smoke, she pointedly hit the switch for her window. I did the same for mine.

"I'm cold," she said, something different in her voice . . . too ghosty for me to grab.

"You want the heater on? It's got to be seventy degrees out."

"No. I'm just not . . . dressed right," she said, hugging herself. She wasn't wrong about that—the lemon silk T-shirt she was wearing showed her off real good, but it was about the same as going topless when it came to weather protection. And you didn't need X-ray eyes to see she wasn't wearing anything under it.

"I've got a blanket in the trunk," I told her.

"Why can't I just wear your jacket?"

"Because it's full of stuff that's none of your business."

"Like . . . what? A gun?"

"There's that thing about language again," I told her. "What does 'none of your business' mean to you?"

"Fine," she sniffed.

I snapped my cigarette out the window. "Thank you," she said, sending her own closed. I did the same.

"Better now?" I asked her.

"Yes."

She went quiet again. I shoved in a cassette, turned one of the dials to crank the bass heavier toward the rear of the car—Pansy likes the bass lines best.

"Who's that?" she asked after a couple of minutes.

"Judy Henske."

"Oh, wow. She's . . . great. I never even heard of her. Is she, like, old or something?"

"How old does she sound?"

"Like she's about thirty-five . . . and like she's lived a couple of centuries."

"Good call," I told her, letting Judy's fire-and-velvet voice roll over us both. That particular tape was all estrogen—KoKo Taylor, Katie Webster, Etta James, Marcia Ball, Irma Thomas, Little Esther, Janis, La Vern Baker, Big Mama.

"I never heard *any* of that," she said toward the end. "Ever."

"Then you've been cheated, girl."

"Are any of them . . . alive. I mean . . ."

"Marcia Ball was in town last week. Judy's on the coast. KoKo's still working. Sure."

"Would you take me? I mean, take me to hear some of that . . . what is it, anyway?"

"It's what you call it. To me, it's the blues."

"But it doesn't *make* you blue. I mean, the songs are . . . sad. Some of them. But that one, the engineer one, that was . . ."

"Raucous?" I asked her. Magic Judy's "Oh, You Engineer" puts it right in your face—you want her to ride your train, you better have one hell of a motor.

"Yeah. She sounds so tough."

"She's a mean woman, no question."

"Not like . . . nasty, right?"

"No. One who can take care of herself."

"And you like that? In a woman?"

"That's all I *do* like," I said, telling her the truth for once.

"What you said to me before . . . when I told you to kiss my ass."

"Yeah?"

"I shouldn't have said that."

I didn't say anything, thinking of where my line had come from: a stripper I knew a long time ago, standing in front of a mirror, looking back over her shoulder to make sure the black seams on her nylons were straight . . . "My butt is my best feature. The only time a man ever really fell in love with me was when I was walking away from him."

Silence filled the car. I didn't switch tapes—we were only a few blocks from the joint where I was going to drop her off.

"You don't know what to do with an apology, do you?" she finally asked.

"Sure."

"No, you don't. I apologized for what I said. Now it's your turn."

"I got nothing to apologize for," I told her, pulling to the curb.

She opened the door, turned to face me, said, "You know you lied," and slammed the door behind her.

Things were quiet for a few days. I invested a lot of time trying to put a sweet little sting together, but it wouldn't mesh. So I passed. That's the way I do business—safely or not at all. Impatience imprisons.

The city stayed edgy. Then the director of one of the above-ground pedophile organizations turned the key to start his pretty new car and drove straight to hell. The radio report said the car exploded right in the freak's driveway.

First Amendment absolutists wrote frenzied letters to newspaper editors, bemoaning a country where a person could be executed for expressing unpopular opinions. They didn't sign their names. Talk shows were loaded with pious pigs droning about the wages of sin. The cops said they had some suspects, but no prime ones.

For all that, the smart money was that the hit was personal, not political. The major pedophile organizations love to publish their little "Enemies Lists," especially on the Net. But if they knew how long that list really was, they'd spend the money on bulletproof vests instead.

Still, the group the dead man had headed decided they needed it to *be* political, milk it for the mileage. So they announced a candlelight vigil would be held outside Gracie Mansion—the Mayor's house.

They were standing there, mourning their loss for the TV cameras, when somebody who knew how to use a grenade launcher took seven of them out with one blast.

The snuff film was a big hit on the networks. But nobody put it together—in fact, most of them were a hundred and eighty degrees off—until the next letter arrived.

> There are many ways to oppress gays. Fag-bashing is the most obvious, but not the most devastating. Physical attacks on homosexuals are not only tolerated by the general community, but covertly encouraged. These are known facts. What is *not* known is that much of the animosity against gays is fueled by the utterly false belief that a pedophile is a homosexual run amok. Journalism has been complicitous in this fraud. The very newspaper in which this is being printed is a prime example. Remember the headline: "Teacher Arrested in Homosexual Child Abuse"? That story involved a kindergarten teacher and a five-year-old boy. Ask yourselves—and this is addressed to the journalism community as well—if the victim had been a little girl, would the headlines have screamed "Heterosexual Child Abuse!"? You know the answer. Much of this is ignorance, but some of it is by design. Pedophiles have carefully self-styled as "gay," seeking to extend the continuum of tolerance for homosexual relations between consenting adults to the rape of children. How many pedophiles have camouflaged themselves as "gay activists" in order to use the old "First they came for the Jews" canard to terrify gays into some "common cause" nonsense? Gays hate child molesters as much as straights do. Some of us, more so. Some of us *victims* much *more* so. After careful consideration, I have concluded that pedophiles who insist on being labeled "homosexual" are

equally guilty of fag-bashing. Now they will pay the same price.
Watch your language!

It was signed with the "Homo Erectus" tag. Nobody questioned its authenticity—the body count had wiped out any doubts.

The city reeked of fear.

I missed not paying taxes. Juan Rodriguez died in the attack on my office. Sooner or later, IRS would go looking for him. That wasn't a problem, but the No Visible Means of Support was. Or it would be, if I got popped again. And I felt that coming—IRS wasn't in a hurry, but the cops were. They would have paraded one of the outpatients who confessed in front of the cameras by now, doing the whole Perp Walk thing, but they knew what would happen next—the killer would show the world that it was phony. And who knows? Maybe he'd decide that promoting a bogus confession was a kind of gay-bashing too. Nobody wanted to walk into that minefield. But arresting me was no big risk. They wouldn't have to tell the papers I was suspected of the actual murders, just recite any lame routine about "conspiracy" or "aiding and abetting" and it would take the heat off them for a while. With my record, I'd qualify perfectly for remand without bail—history of violence, no roots in the community, significant risk of flight to avoid . . .

The best way to lock in a bogus ID is to have it keep up *its* tax payments while you're someplace where *you* couldn't. I figured I was going down soon as the cops found me, and I wanted the new name in place first. That way, I could start the withholding and Social Security and all the other government crap rolling first, and let it build while I was Inside. Davidson would spring me sooner or later—it's happened before—and I could get *something* out of it.

But I couldn't hunt from Inside, so I couldn't stay there too long. My plan was to have Davidson walk me in again, soon as Wolfe came through with the ID. Pansy can get her own food. I have this six-foot-high metal box with a lip at the bottom that she can shove with her snout to make the dry dog food drop. And a hundred-gallon water bottle inverted in place so she can drink, too. It'd be good for a couple of months, minimum, and there's plenty of space for her to roam around. It's not perfect, and I felt bad the last time it happened, but there's nobody to leave her with. I mean, she wouldn't go after Max, but she wouldn't go *with* him either.

We talked it over once, me and him. If I ever went away for a long stretch again, I told Max to tranq her out and then move her over to Elroy's. He's a crazed counterfeiter who lives in a shack out in the country with a pit bull who gets along with Pansy. I know she'd stay there peacefully—she did it before. Elroy had wanted Pansy and his dog to get together, create a brand-new breed. But they were pals, not lovers, and he finally accepted it.

There was nothing else I had to worry about. Everyone in my family could take care of themselves. And each other. I didn't have bills to pay or a landlord to worry about. My family had too much sense to come on visiting day. *Crystal Beth would have come no matter what they told her,* I thought. I cut that off quick, before it started to hurt.

I was ready, just waiting on the ID.

Then I got a call, and everything changed again.

"Yes, say that," Mama told me, adamant.

"She said she was my *girlfriend*?"

"Yes. Say that. I ask her who this is, right? She say, Tell him his girlfriend called."

"You recognize the voice?"

"No. Maybe . . . not sure. Hard to tell with Europeans. All sound alike."

"She didn't leave a number? A message?"

"Just call, okay? Ask for you, okay? I say you not here, call back, okay? Who you? She say, 'His girlfriend,' then hang up. No more."

I didn't waste time trying to figure it out. "You seen Max around, Mama?"

"Sure. Here before. With baby."

"He coming back?"

"Always come back," Mama said. Something *was* wrong—the whole song was a beat off.

"What is it, Mama?" I asked her, looking her full in the face—something you do with her only when you're dead serious.

"What you do with these . . . people?"

"What people, Mama?"

"Crazy people. What you do with them?"

"Mama, I'm not following this, all right? I'm working."

That should have ended it. Working was sacred to Mama. And she knew what kind of work I did. Same as hers, only I played it different. But we were both thieves in our hearts. All of us in my family were. We might have had different reasons, but nobody ever asked. Sometimes we told—I knew about Max, and I knew about Michelle—and sometimes we didn't—the Prof never explained, he just taught. Nobody ever asked Mama. And if she told Max, he kept it to himself. I've known Mama forever. And the only time she was ever upset with me was when I *wasn't* working. But her face was stone and her eyes were harder.

"It's just a job," I tried again.

"You go after that girl, right?"

"Girl? What girl? You think the killer's a woman?"

"Not killer. The girl. The one you bring in here. The one you marry."

"Marry? Mama, what the hell are you talking about? I never—"

"Crystal Beth," Mama said. No description, an actual name. Very strange for her. "You live with her, yes? Love her, right?"

"Mama, I—"

"You go where she is, Burke? You go to be with her?"

"Me? Mama, *no!* You think this is some kind of kamikaze run, I—"

"Huh!" is all she spat back at me. I realized I'd screwed up halfway through the word. Mama hates anything Japanese, even their expressions.

"Mama," I said, dropping my voice, going into my center for patience, calling on the credit I'd built up, "you know I don't lie to you."

"Uhn," is all I got back from her mouth. But she nodded, unable to deny what I said.

"This isn't about suicide. I know there's nothing . . . there. Crystal Beth's down in the Zero, right? She's gone. I can't find her. And people don't come back from the dead."

"Some people not die."

"What does that mean? She's dead, Mama. No question about it. Dead and gone."

"So you look for . . . who? People who kill her? Or man killing . . . them?"

"What?"

"Your woman killed. Accident, right? I mean, not *her* they killing. Just hate those . . . people."

"Homosexuals?"

"Yes," Mama said, looking as close to embarrassed as I'd ever seen her. "Hate . . . them. Not her. Not . . . personal, right?"

"Right."

"This other one, *big* killer. He kill them too, he find them, right?"

"Sure. Looks like he'd happily waste any fag-basher on the planet."

"But you look for him, right? You find him, then he stop. No more killing, right?"

"Ah. I don't know, Mama. That's not my deal. The people who want me to find him, they want to *help* him. Help him get out of here, get safe. They sure as hell don't want me turning him over to the cops."

"Sure sure. But he still *stop* then, right?"

"Yeah. I guess so."

"So the ones who kill your woman . . . ?"

"Mama, I don't know who they are. I don't have any way to find them. And thanks to this 'Homo Erectus' guy, every fag-basher in the city has gone to ground. People are even afraid to *talk* about it, much less do it."

"All wrong," Mama said.

"What?"

"All . . . timing, yes? All wrong, also. Your woman die. Not the only one, right?"

"Right. They just sprayed . . ."

"Yes. And then killer comes walking."

"Right. That must have blown his fuse. Last-straw kind of thing, I don't know."

"I know," Mama said.

"You know . . . what?"

"How many die?"

"I don't know. A few dozen, at least. He's been—"

"Not him. With your woman?"

"Just one other. The rest were wounded, but . . . Jesus. Mama, you saying it was a hit? And they just made it look like a fag-bashing?"

"Not . . . how you say, credit, right?"

"Right," I said, thinking it through. Sure. What terrorist kills without bragging about it? And nobody had. So when this Homo Erectus started making his move, everybody thought they knew why, but, maybe . . . ?

"So you think . . . maybe it was just a murder? And Crystal Beth died for camouflage? They knew who they wanted, but just covered it up? Like setting fire to a whole building full of people to kill one of them—the cops think it's an arson, but it's really a homicide. Sure, could be. But the only man I ever knew who worked like that was . . . "

Mama looked at me. Into me. I got it then. That was *his* style. Almost his trademark. You paid him for a body, you got a body. If he had to make a whole bunch of bodies to cover his tracks, so what? I remember the first time the Prof had pulled my coat to the truth. Years after we'd all been released. "No man knows Wesley's plan, brother. Nobody knows where he's going. But everyone knows where he's been."

"Wesley's dead," I said to Mama.

She just shrugged.

The pay phone rang about an hour later. I picked it up, said, "What?"

"Didn't the Chinese lady tell you I called?" Nadine's voice, edged with irritation.

"She said someone who said they were my girlfriend called. Somehow, I didn't think to make the connection."

"I told you before," she said softly. "You have to start telling the truth. I always do."

"My platonic girlfriend, then, right? I guess they didn't get the joke here."

"What joke? Your nose is so open I can see your brains."

"That's what happens when you use those fake-color contact lenses, bitch. They really cloud your vision."

"Keep playing, honey. It doesn't change anything. I've got what you want."

"Not a chance."

"In fact," she purred into the phone, "I'm holding it right now."

"There's guys who'd pay you three ninety-five a minute for that kind of crap—why you wasting it on me?"

"Oh, I'm not wasting anything. And I'm not playing with myself either. I was playing with this. . . . Listen!"

What I heard on the phone was the sound a sheaf of paper makes when you riffle it against your thumb.

"Where and when?" I asked her.

I almost didn't recognize her when she first showed, striding along the sidewalk in front of the joint like a yuppie businesswoman going to an important meeting, a fitted dark suit with a white blouse over plain dark pumps and sheer stockings. Her hair was in a tight bun. And the requisite attaché case was in her hand, a tasteful shade of blue.

I swung the Plymouth into place. She opened the door like it was a cab she had hailed, only she got in the front seat.

"Where's your partner?" was the first thing out of her mouth.

"She's working," I told her.

"I thought you took her everywhere."

"Not everywhere," is all I said. Pansy had been sick all day. Some kind of flu, my best guess. Upset stomach, lethargic. I kept her warm, gave her some homeopathic stuff I got from a vet. She was running a little fever, but her appetite wasn't that much off, so I wasn't worried. But she needed her rest.

"I don't know what kind of old heap this is," Nadine said, "but at least it's got plenty of legroom." She demonstrated by crossing her legs. Her perfume smelled coppery—the way blood tastes in your mouth.

"You wouldn't understand," I said.

"Wouldn't understand . . . what?"

"This 'old heap,'" I replied.

"Oh Christ, you're sensitive about *that* too? You love your dog, you love your car. You should be driving a pickup truck with a gun rack behind the cab."

"If I was, in this city, you think people'd remember seeing it?"

"Well . . . sure."

"You think anyone's gonna remember seeing this?"

"I . . . Oh. I get it."

"No, you don't. But the kind of broad you are, you always think you do."

We were just pulling onto the highway when she said: "What does that—?" But she lost her breath as I mashed the throttle and the reworked Mopar 440 fired a giant torque-burst down the driveline to the fat rear tires. The Plymouth rocketed past traffic like it was a multi-colored picket fence. I slid across three lanes and drifted it around the exit ramp, scrubbing off speed with a downshift, and merged smoothly into the Riverside Drive traffic. The Plymouth went back to purring, its stump-puller motor barely past idle. Quiet inside enough for me to hear her whisper "Jesus Christ!" when she got her breath back.

"This thing is purpose-built," I told her. "For work, understand? Not for show."

"I get the point."

"Good. Let's stop playing, all right?"

"I haven't *been* playing. I was just—"

"Playing, gaming, teasing . . . I don't care what you call it. You got this whole 'I-never-lie' routine you want to run, go for it. What you're really good at is making judgments, little girl. Bad judgments."

"Little girl? Take a look, mister," she said, sucking in a deep breath so none of her subtlety would be lost on me.

"I'm not talking about your age. Just your experience. I've seen it all my life. You know stuff, but it doesn't translate, understand?"

"No. No, I don't."

"When you're a tourist, the natives all look slick to you."

"Huh?"

"You know all about the . . . stuff you do. The roles you play, the language you use, the . . . props, whatever. You don't know a damn thing about the *only* thing that's happening where you and me are concerned."

"And that is . . . ?"

"Hunting."

"I'm not trying to tell you your business. I was just—"

"—running your mouth," I finished for her. "That's the part you need to keep in neutral, all right? I don't do word games. This isn't about getting me to admit I want to fuck you, understand?"

"I—"

"That's *all* you've been doing since I first laid eyes on you. What do you want that's so important? You don't need me to tell you you're a fine-looking woman."

"Maybe I want to fuck *you,*" she said, matter-of-factly.

"Maybe you do. But I'm not interested in being one of your trophies."

"Oh, I get it. A real Alan Alda you are. You only want commitment, huh? Won't settle for anything less than true love."

"I had true love," I told her softly. "It died. And the killers are from the same tribe this 'Homo Erectus' guy is hunting."

"How could—?"

"She was bi," I said. "And she was one of the people who got done in that drive-by in Central Park."

"You mean you have your own—?"

"I *had* my own," I cut her off. "I never minded sex with a woman who wanted sex . . . just for that. Truth is, that's mostly what I did . . . do. But people with agendas scare me."

"Agendas?"

"Yeah. I'm a good man to have sex with if you're married. I'm not going to fall in love with you, I promise. So when you decide to break it off, I won't beef. I won't stalk you, and I won't blackmail you either. I'm nice and safe, see what I'm saying?"

"I see—"

"Shut up and listen, okay? Give it a chance, you might like it. I'm a good man for some things. Like I said. But if you're married, I'm not going to kill your husband for you just 'cause I want some more of your pussy either. You get it now?"

"Yes. All right. But I don't—"

"You don't . . . what? You been preaching about what a liar I am all along, haven't you? But you say you're in love with a serial killer you never met, and I'm supposed to buy that, make you partners with me on this deal?"

"I didn't say I was *in* love with him. I told you—"

"No, I told *you.* I don't know why you're all dressed up tonight, but whatever's in that case you're carrying better be a present from your girlfriend on the force. You know, the one you bragged about? So here's one you must have heard when you were just sprouting those things you're so proud of now: Put out or get out."

"I don't put out in cars," she said, giving her lips a quick little lick. "But if you want to take me home and try your luck . . ."

"I don't have a home," I told her.

"You mean you're married."

"I guess your friend on the force *really* knows nothing, huh?"

"Fine. You don't have a home. I do. Want to see it?"

"I want to see what's in that briefcase."

"Then take me home," she said.

She lived right at the edge of Turtle Bay. And even if she'd scored a rent-controlled deal, it was still a pricey neighborhood. I aimed the Plymouth at the Triborough, planning to loop back on the FDR on the off-chance anyone else was interested in where I was going. That's why I'd really pulled that highway stunt—if the cops had been tagging me, it would have smoked them out. The rearview mirror had been empty of anything suspicious. That didn't cover everything—the *federales* are pretty good at box-tags. But I still didn't think they were involved in this. And NYPD wouldn't spare the numbers, not with the whole city screaming for an arrest.

I slapped a new cassette into the player. The car was wrapped in the blues. KoKo's version of Howlin' Wolf's "Evil," backed up by Jimmy Cotton on harp. You know how artists "cover" a record? Michael Bolton imitating Percy Sledge, Pat Boone white-breading Little Richard . . . ultra-lite fluff. Plenty buy it, though. Probably the same people who watch *Hard Copy* and think the emphasis is on the first word.

But KoKo didn't cover the Wolf, she twitched her hips and bumped him right off the stage. Then the tape moved on to Albert Collins and Johnny Copeland teaming on "Something to Remember You By," and I thought of Crystal Beth . . . and what she'd left me with. I was still thinking about that as the tape started to travel through hardcore Chicago, with Son Seals at the wheel, his *Bad Blood Blues* searing the truth out of that branding iron some fools call a slide guitar. Nadine sat silently through it. Didn't say one word until I took the Thirty-fourth Street exit from the Drive. "Who was that?" she finally asked.

"Another mix," I said, thinking she was talking about the stuff at the very end of the tape. "Mostly harp men: Butterfield, Musselwhite, Wilson—"

"Oh, I know him. Kim Wilson, right? From the Fabulous Thunderbirds. But I never heard him play anything like . . ."

"No," I told her, flat-voiced. "That was Blind Owl Wilson. From Canned Heat. It's a different planet."

"Judy Henske's planet?"

"Yeah."

"Surprised I remembered?"

"No," I told her truthfully. "It's not hard to see you're a real smart girl."

"And that's good, right?"

"No. It just . . . is. A good mind's like any piece of technology. Neutral. Like a gun or a knife. It's not what you have, it's what you use it for."

"That's another way of saying you don't trust me?"

"How many more ways would you like?"

"There's a spot," she said, pointing with a transparent-lacquered fingernail at a Mercedes pulling away from the curb. I parallel-parked, thinking of what Wolfe's Audi would have done to the pristine BMW behind me, and we got out. Once I saw her building, I could see rent control wasn't an issue—it was a major-league high-rise, built within the past few years.

Nadine smiled at the doorman's "Good evening," but didn't say anything back. We got on the elevator.

"Go ahead," she said, nodding toward the row of push-buttons. "I'm sure you know which floor's mine."

"Nope."

She snorted. Tapped the 44 button.

When the elevator stopped, she stepped out ahead of me. I followed her down the heavy-carpeted hall. The plain pumps had enough heel to keep her mass in motion, so I couldn't tell if it was inertia or she was putting on another show.

When she got to 44J, she inserted the key she must have palmed when I was watching the mass in motion, and then we were inside.

"Careful," she said, showing me what she meant by moving slowly down a couple of steps into a sunken living room. She hit a wall switch and a soft rosy light suffused the entire room. It was long and narrow, with the far wall almost floor-to-ceiling glass, flanked on each side by a black acoustical tower. On the right, an audiophile extravaganza spread across a single shelf that flowed out of the wall so smoothly it must have been a custom job. Along the left, the major focal point was one of those giant-screen TV units with a trio of leather recliners and matching ottomans—one black, one white, and one red—arranged with their backs to the right-hand wall.

"I'm not out at work," she said, as if that explained the decor. "Have a seat."

The window glass looked fixed in place—they don't have balconies that high up—so I took the chair closest to it, the white one, spun it so it was facing the door.

Nadine walked over to where I was sitting, pulled the ottoman away, and perched on it, crossing her legs again. "Open it yourself," she said, indicating the briefcase on the floor. "It's not locked."

I popped the small brass latches at each end. Inside, nothing but paper. Photocopies. Crime-scene reports. Even down to the photographs. Maybe a couple of hundred pages in all. I started to leaf through them, asking, "Is this—?"

"Just one case," she interrupted. "My . . . friend says she didn't know what the . . . I mean, she *did* know what you meant—the 'polygraph-key' thing—but she didn't know which ones they would use. She said ninety percent of this stuff never made the papers, so they had a lot to choose from. And it isn't her case, so . . ."

"Ssshh," I said, reading.

Even in the soft-rose lighting, it was easy enough to figure out which of the cases it was. The best one for polygraph keys—one of the first ones—the guy who'd gotten the ice pick in the spine. A blown-up car wouldn't give away much. Oh sure, if the lab guys were good enough, they might find the triggering device . . . or a clue to it, anyway. Maybe even tell you the type of explosive. But there's nothing like a face-to-face homicide to produce a crime scene you can vacuum all to hell.

And they had. I finally found exactly what I was looking for. The ice pick the newspapers had reported hadn't been one at all. The weapon had been a ninja spike of some kind, a triangular piece of tempered steel with notches for finger grips at the thick end. On the top, where it was the thickest, there was an engraved icon, inset in red. I knew the color only because someone had written the word "red" with an arrow pointing toward it on the photocopy. I guess either the Department didn't have color copiers or, more likely, Nadine's playmate didn't have access to one.

"Have you got a—?"

I looked up and realized I was talking to an empty space. Nadine had gone somewhere. I glanced at my watch. I'd been in that chair for almost two hours. I guess I'd gone somewhere too.

The apartment was sealed-off quiet, no street noises penetrating the thick glass, the rich gray carpet muffling anything else. Where was she? There had to be at least a bedroom and a kitchen. Bathroom too. But I didn't want to start cruising around. And everything past the circle of rosy light I had been reading by was a pool of blackness.

"Nadine?" I called out, medium-voiced, pitched to carry past the living room, no more.

No answer.

It didn't stink like a trap does. And the decor wasn't a clue either. You walk into a room where everything's covered in plastic, floor to ceiling, you better start shooting before they go to work with the baseball bats. But this . . . ?

Nadine was a girl who loved her games. I could walk out and take the papers with me. Or get up and look through the other rooms.

I didn't like the choices, so I pulled the cellular out of my pocket and dialed her number. I heard it ring, somewhere back through the walls. If there was a phone in the living room, I couldn't see it. Or hear it.

She had it by the second ring, her voice awake and sharp even though it was almost two in the morning. But some people wake up just like that, so I couldn't tell.

"Hello?"

"You mind taking a little walk?" I asked.

"Oh! It's . . . sure. Just give me a minute."

I wanted a smoke, but I didn't even think about going through with it. There wasn't an ashtray in sight. And one of those air-filtering canisters sat in a far corner whispering its work.

Then she seemed to just materialize out of the side of the wall. Nude.

"I was asleep," she said, as calmly as if we were talking inside an office. "You were so . . . absorbed, I didn't want to disturb you."

"I didn't want to disturb *you,*" I told her. "And I didn't want to . . . invade your privacy."

My eyes never left hers. Still cobalt, hers were. So either she was lying about being asleep or they weren't contacts like I'd first thought.

"That was very considerate," she said, calmly. "Are you all finished?"

"Not quite yet. Have you got a magnifying glass of some kind? And a better light I could use for a minute?"

"Sure," she said, spinning on her heel and disappearing again.

She came back with a large rectangular magnifier, the kind that comes with the Oxford English Dictionary inside that little tray at the top of the two volumes. And a clip-on gooseneck halogen light. "How's this?" she asked, bending forward like a stewardess. In a porno movie.

"Perfect, I think. Let me try it."

I attached the light, turned it on. Then I placed the magnifier over the photocopy of the icon. Blown up, it turned out to be a meticulously drawn little dinosaur with *T. rex* jaws and monstrous talons, but much shorter in every department—almost like a miniature.

"I got it," I told her.

"You mean . . . you mean you know who he is?"

"No. But I know something I can use to find him. Maybe. If he wants to be found."

"Wants to be—?"

"It's . . . complicated," I told her.

"And you can't tell me?" she asked, perching herself back on the ottoman the same way she had hours ago.

"Not now."

"But I did what you wanted, right?"

"Yeah, you did," I admitted. "In spades."

"So you believe me now?" she questioned, rubbing her eyes like a sleepy child, but showing me she was all grown up at the same time.

"I believe you have a friend on the force," I told her. "One that'll do what you want."

"She did a *lot,* didn't she?"

"Sure did. This had to take some time. And it'd mean her job if she got caught."

"I know. Do you think they'd . . . suspect her?"

"How would I know? I don't know who's got access to—"

"I don't mean suspect her of making the copies. I mean suspect her of being in with . . . him."

"Not a chance," I assured her. "The sleaze tabs broke the mold when they published autopsy pictures of that little girl who was raped and murdered in her own home. Remember, the baby beauty queen?"

"In Colorado? Oh God, yes! I couldn't believe when they . . . and they *still* haven't caught the people who . . ."

"Yeah. Anyway, these pictures, they'd be worth a fortune to one of the rags. *That's* what they'd think she was up to."

"Oh," she said, sounding more relieved than I would have expected.

"Anyway, she sure as hell can't put these *back,* right? I mean, they aren't originals. And there aren't supposed to *be* any copies. So I'd better keep them."

"You?"

"You want them around here?" I asked her. "It'd be insane to burn them—there might be a real clue in here somewhere, even though there's stuff missing."

"Really? When I saw how much it was, I thought she got *everything.*"

"Is that what you asked her for?"

"No. I just . . . what you said. The 'polygraph-key' thing."

"Well, you can tell her she came through, no question."

"Me too."

"You too, what?"

"I came through too, didn't I?"

"Yes. I already said that. You made . . . you *proved* your point."

"So I can . . . help you with this?"

"Yeah."

"When do we start?"

"We already did," I told her. "I'll get back to you, let you know when the next move is."

"That's it?"

"What did you expect? You want to put some clothes on and go running after him right now?"

"Oh. I didn't think you noticed."

"Noticed?"

"My . . . clothes," she said, trailing the back of her hand across her breasts.

"Hard to miss," I said.

"Look good to you?"

"I'm not *that* old." I laughed.

"I didn't mean you were . . . old. You're older than me, sure. But I can see you're not too old to . . ."

"No, you can't see anything," I told her. And it was the truth. Her eyes were on my crotch, but it was about as active as the Vanilla Ice fan club.

"How come?"

"What?"

"How come I *can't* see anything? *You* can see everything. And I know you like girls."

"You scare me, Nadine," I told her, letting her see the truth if she wanted it. "And nothing turns me off more than fear."

"It doesn't everybody," she said in a throaty whisper. "Some people get very excited by fear. Do you know what it's like to be wearing a mask? A leather mask with only a zipper for your mouth and two little holes to breathe through? To be chained. And waiting. Not knowing what you're going to get?"

"You know what?" I told her, my voice quiet, but harder than any silly leather games she liked to play. "I *do* know. Not about your little masks and whips. But I know exactly what it's like to be chained. And to not know what's coming next. But knowing it's going to hurt. Hurt real bad. And not being able to do a thing about it."

"You mean for real?" she asked, leaning forward, listening now, not on display.

"Oh yes," I promised.

"When you were in . . . prison?"

"Prison? Prison was a fucking joke by the time I got there. For me, it was like going to college after prep school. No. Not in prison. When I was a kid. A little kid."

"You mean your parents—"

"I didn't have parents. I had the State. That was my mother and my father and my jailer. I served time in POW camps before I was old enough to go to school. You like to play around in your little 'dungeons,' wear your costumes. . . . You try it sometime without mercy-words, try it when you can't pick your partners, you stupid little game-playing bitch—see how much fun it is."

She gasped, swallowed some words. Sat back on the ottoman and looked at me like I was whatever had crashed at Roswell that the government wasn't talking about.

I took out a cigarette and lit it, hating myself for losing control. I bit deep into the filter, feeling the pain lance through my jaw, ready to grind the butt out on her pretty carpet when I was done.

She didn't move, a piece of white stone in the rosy light.

I blew a jet of smoke into her face.

"I'm sorry," she said.

"You *are* fucking sorry," I told her. Then I stood up. She started to do it at the same time and we bumped. She fell to the carpet. I didn't look back.

"Can you get word to . . . your friend?" I asked Lorraine over the phone.

"Same place?"

"Yeah. Whenever's convenient for . . . your friend."

"I'll reach out. When I link up, should I . . . ?"

"Just leave word. Whenever the meet's made for at your end is okay—I'll be here."

"All right," she said.

"Crazy, yes?" Mama challenged the minute I sat back down in my booth.

"Yeah, Mama. Crazy. You're right."

"So?"

"So I'm going to see it through," I told her. "And I'm going to get Max to help me," challenging *her* now.

"Good," she said, surprising me. "Balance. Good."

Sure. I got it. At least *Max* wasn't crazy. Thanks.

I went back to my hot-and-sour soup. Mama disappeared. I don't know how she reaches out for Max. There's a lot of ways to get messages to deaf people, but Mama was a techno-phobe. She'd use an abacus to work percentages on six-figure scores without missing a beat, but she didn't trust anything electronic, doling out words on the phone like they were her life savings.

I went out the back door.

Pansy was glad to see me. Always was, no matter what. If she thought I was crazy, she kept it to herself. I dumped the entire quart of beef in oyster sauce I'd taken from Mama's into her steel bowl, waiting the thirty seconds it took her to make it disappear, then let her out onto the roof to do some dumping of her own.

When she came back down, she stood next to me, both of us looking into the night. I wondered what she saw.

I didn't like what *I* did.

When I got to Davidson's office, he had the cash waiting. I asked him if he'd heard anything from the cops. It took him about ten minutes to say "No."

I got on the drums and sent word out to the Prof. I couldn't get him to pack a cellular except when we were working a job, but I had years of experience finding him even when he was homeless-by-choice, so I wasn't worried—he'd connect up sooner or later.

No point calling Wolfe. When she had the stuff, she'd get it to me.

So I drove back over to Mama's to wait for word from Lorraine.

When I came through the back door and saw Mama wasn't at her register, I knew Max was around someplace, probably in the basement. One of the waiters brought me a covered tureen of hot-and-sour soup, not saying a word. I know most of them by face, and that's enough to get me through the door even if Mama isn't there to vouch for me, but they treat me like I'm invisible anyway. I was getting the soup because they knew Mama believed I had to have some every time I entered the joint, but I could fucking well serve myself. . . . At least that's how I translated the Cantonese he mumbled as he put the stuff in front of me.

Fine. I was on my third bowl—the house minimum—when Mama and Max came upstairs. I bowed a greeting to each of them. Mama sat down beside me as Max took the opposite bench.

I signed as much as I knew of what was going on to Max. I spoke the words too—I know Max can read lips, I just never know how much he's getting.

Max looked pointedly at Mama. She snapped her fingers and barked something. Could have been Mandarin, Lao, Vietnamese, Tagalog—she speaks a ton of Asian languages I can't even distinguish, and pretty good French and Spanish as well. A pair of her so-called waiters popped out of the back to clear the table. Then they wiped it down scrupulously, not the way they usually do. One of them brought out a black linen tablecloth and snapped it out over the surface. Then they vanished.

From inside his coat, Max took a small metal bowl with a faint yellowish tinge. He placed it carefully on the table between us. Next, he took a thick wooden stick shaped something like a pestle and struck the edge of the bowl as if it was a gong. Then he whisked the stick around the perimeter. A sound like I'd never heard vibrated in the air. It . . . stayed there, drawing me into it. The only way I can describe it, it was like I got when I looked into the red dot I had painted on my mirror. Outside myself. Away. Dissociating the way I'd learned to when I was a kid. When I couldn't run from the pain.

Where I go is the place where I think. About things I couldn't if I was . . . here.

I pointed at the bowl, made a "What is this?" gesture.

Max held up both his hands, one spread out full, the other with just two fingers showing. Seven. Then he took out a quarter and tapped it, making the sign for "seven" again.

Then he made a hand-washing gesture. The sign for mixing, melding, blending . . .

"It's made up of seven different metals?" I asked aloud.

"Yes," Mama said. "Called 'singing bowl.' Very sacred. From . . ." She hesitated, catching a warning look from Max. "Tibet," she finished.

I understood that part. Mama's Chinese. Mandarin Chinese. She can trace her ancestors back to way before Christ, or so she says. In fact, she can trace *any* goddamned thing to her ancestors, from gunpowder to telescopes. It's not political with her. She fled to Taiwan a long time ago, and she thinks the Chinese government—Mao Chinese, she calls them—are the scum of the planet.

Everyone takes Max for Chinese, but he's not. He's a Mongol, from Tibet. Something happened to him there when he was a kid. He wasn't born deaf. He showed me once how they *made* him deaf, and it makes me sick to even see it in my mind. I don't know if Max can't speak, or he just refuses to—I never asked. He goes along with the game that he's Chinese because Mama took him for her son. Mama wants to claim that it was the Chinese who invented haiku, that's okay with Max. She wants to say Max's daughter Flower is pure Mandarin, hell, *royal* Mandarin, no problem. But he was damn well going to claim this "singing bowl" for his own country . . . and Mama got it.

He handed me the bowl, showed me how to strike it, guided my hand in smooth whisks around the rim until I could make it sing too. Then he bowed and handed it to me. A gift.

I held it in my hand, still feeling it vibrate faintly. I could feel its age and its power. And I knew why my brother had given it to me.

I put it aside and we started to play casino. Max was into me for another ten grand by the time the Prof breezed in the front, Clarence in tow.

"What's up, Schoolboy?" the Prof greeted me. "I know you been looking and cooking—the wire's been on fire."

I brought him up to date, even down to what Mama had been saying . . . or not saying.

"Can't be." The little man dismissed it with a wave of his hand.

I just shrugged.

"Why you doing this anyway, son?" the Prof asked.

"Fifty large. Paid up front. No refunds."

"Cool. But why *try*? The sting's the thing."

"Yeah, I know. But it's all . . . connected, right?"

"How could this be connected, mahn?" Clarence, speaking for the first time.

"Whoever killed Crystal Beth, they were killing queers, far as they knew, right?"

"That's what it say in the papers," the young man replied, tone telling what he thought of that source.

"The *next* thing happens," I said, ignoring his tone, "is that this 'Homo Erectus' guy starts killing *them* . . . fag-bashers, right?"

"That deal is real," the Prof put in. "Man is taking heads, and dead is dead."

"Okay, so the cops, maybe they thought I was involved. Some of them, anyway. But they know better now . . . even though I still think I could get rousted if they need headlines bad enough. But, if he could kill *all* of them, he'd get the ones who killed Crystal Beth in the bargain, right?"

"Bro, you too dense to make sense. He was gonna do all that, your move is: Get out the way, let him play."

"Sure. But the people who hired me to find him, they don't want to turn him in, they want to help him get away."

"Maybe the boss plans a cross," the Prof said.

"You mean . . . play for the reward? Nah. He's already out a hundred G's—Davidson got half."

"Not for money. Who knows, bro? Everybody got game, but it ain't all the same."

Nadine flashed in my mind. I just nodded.

“I’m gonna meet someone,” I told them all. “Meet her right here. I think I got a way now.” Then I showed them the picture of the little dinosaur thing.

“What’s that?” Clarence asked.

“I don’t know. Not exactly, anyway. But I know who will.”

“Want to go for a ride, honey?” I spoke into the cellular.

“You mean . . . work?” Michelle asked, clearly less than excited about the prospect.

“I’m gonna visit an old pal. Thought you might like to tag along.”

“Someone I know?”

“No question about that, girl. I guess what everyone wonders is, how *well* you—”

“That’s enough of your smart mouth, mister. I’ll be ready in forty-five minutes.”

“Forty-five minutes? I’m just down the block. Come on. I’ll meet you out front in—”

“Forty-five minutes, you gorilla. Not one second sooner. I am not going *anywhere* dressed like this. Go amuse yourself or something.”

Then she hung up on me.

Aargh. I slammed in a forty-five-minute cassette, lay back, slitted my eyes against the midday glare, and let the music take me to someplace else. The Brooklyn Blues. East Coast doo-wop. The Aquatones’ classic “You” set the scene . . . and the river was flowing deep into “Darling Lorraine” by the Knockouts when I came to. Checked my watch . . . perfect.

I cranked up the Plymouth and motored over to Michelle’s. She was standing on the sidewalk in a burnt-orange parachute-silk coat, tapping the toe of one black spike heel impatiently.

“It’s *hot* out here,” she bitched as she climbed into the front seat.

“You keep *me* waiting forty-five minutes; I’m ten seconds late and you’re already running your—”

“As much as you know about women, I’m surprised you’re not still a virgin,” she snapped, cutting me off.

I surrendered without firing another useless shot, heading uptown toward the only place I could ever be sure Michelle would always want to go.

But I was thinking about what she said, even as we crossed the bridge.

"Michelle, could I ask you a question?"

"Who better?" she wanted to know, still not mollified over the enormous wait I'd put her through.

"About what you said. About women?" I stalled, thinking Michelle was the only person on the planet I ever asked about women. As if the vicious trick nature had played on her—she'd been born a transsexual, into a nest of maggots—had made her an authority. And how I'd never say that.

"I am waiting," she said, tapping her long, burnt-orange-tipped nails on the dashboard to show me how patient she wasn't going to be with me for a while.

"What is it with bisexuals?"

"That means . . . what?"

"I met this girl. . . ."

"Go figure," she sneered.

"Michelle, come on. You're *this* mad at me for being a few seconds late?"

"How do I look?" she asked, opening her coat to display an ivory blouse over black pencil pants.

"Fabulous," I assured her. "But you always do, for chrissakes."

"And you don't think it might be nice to . . . reassure a girl once in a while?"

"I never thought—"

"Because you are, in your heart, a pig," she reassured *me.*

"All right, already. I'm a pig. A late pig too, okay? I was going up to see the Mole, figured you'd like to ride along, and now I get all this?"

"Sweetie," she said softly, one hand on my right forearm, "I am trying to teach you something, all right? Little Sister's not mad at you. But ever since that . . . ever since Crystal Beth died, you haven't really been yourself. A new woman is *exactly* what you need. And, knowing you, what it's going to bring you is more pain. Maybe if you knew how to act around a *normal* girl, you wouldn't always be—"

"How do you know I'm—?"

"Baby, how long have I known you? A million years? This bisexual you asked me about, that wouldn't be Crystal Beth, now would it?"

"No."

"Huh!" she half-grunted in surprise. "Really?"

"Yeah. Really."

"All right, Burke. What do you want to know?"

"I guess . . . what I asked you."

"This is a bisexual woman, then? The one you met?"

"Yeah. At least I think so."

"And Crystal Beth was—?"

"You know what, Michelle? I never knew *what* she was. I mean, she *said* she was. And I knew she had . . . I knew her and Vyra—"

"Vyra!" Michelle spat the name out. "The one with the shoes, right?"

"Yes. But she's gone now. Remember?"

"No, I do *not* remember. I had no dealings with that one. Don't *you* remember?"

I didn't know how to reel her in. Michelle was all tangents when she wasn't working. But I tried another route anyway.

"Forget Vyra, okay? And Crystal Beth, all I know is that she *said* she was bi, okay? That's why she went to that rally, even though she said the others didn't really want her there."

"The others?"

"Gay people. She said bisexuals were, like, caught between the two worlds."

"I don't think so," Michelle said. "It's not that. They're caught between stereotypes, that's all."

"What?"

"Look, if a woman, a straight woman, if she has lots of lovers, she's a slut, right?"

"I didn't—"

"Oh, never mind what *you* think," she dismissed me. "I'm talking about . . . them," she said, indicating the rest of the world with a sweep of her hand. "But straights, they think *all* gays are promiscuous, right? All they know about are the glory holes and the quick meets in the park—the anonymous stuff. You tell them a couple of gay men are together, really *with* each other, and they, like, can't quite get it, see? Now, a bisexual *man,* what everyone assumes is he's really gay, all right? Maybe he can close his eyes and make it with a woman, but how many times you ever hear of a gay male telling his lover it's all over, he's found out he's straight and he wants to be with a woman?"

"I never—"

"Me either. But the reverse, that's all the time, yes? Man's been married twenty years, getting some on the side in the gay bars, but profiling straight. He tells his wife the truth, she's busted up, sure. But the *rest* of the world, it just nods its head and says, 'Sure,' like it was going to happen sooner or later."

"Yeah, but . . ."

"Bisexual *women,* it's like there's no such thing. Not to . . . *them.* So when a woman says she's bi, the only thing *they* figure is she's fucking everyone on the planet, right?"

"I don't—"

"Oh, who *cares*? That's what *they* think. Any married couple wants to jazz up their sex life, first thing they do is advertise for a bi girl, am I right? But what's this got to do with anything, anyway?"

"This girl? The one I met?"

"Yessss . . . ?"

"Well, she's bi. Or she was once. I don't know. She says she's a lesbian now. Heavy-duty top too, the way she fronts it."

"But she's coming on to you?"

"Yeah. At least . . . I think so."

"Because you're dense? Or because . . . ?"

"Because she's . . . ambiguous. She doesn't say anything about herself. Just about me. How I supposedly want her so bad, and I'm not admitting it."

"Roles are . . . weird. Like it's . . . I don't know . . . safer, maybe, if you have a role. If you know what you're *supposed* to do, you can't make a mistake. But if she's a top, maybe she's just plugged into your testosterone, honey."

"What does that mean?"

"It means every man wants to spank a dom. The ones who don't want to take it themselves, that is. That's what the scene-players believe—that everybody would be doing what they do if they had the guts. And if you play that way, sometimes you *stay* that way. You can get . . . stuck. And you never think there's a middle. So if she does men too . . ."

"I don't know. She only said—"

"Doesn't matter. If she's a top, she knows other tops. And some of *them* do men. Big money in it. Even over the phone. Little Sister knows *that* part by heart, honey."

"So I—?"

"So you . . . what? You like her?"

"No. She's not real . . . likable, I don't think. But . . ."

"You want to fuck her?"

"Not even that. Michelle, look, she wants to work with me. On this . . . thing I'm doing. What I'm going to see the Mole about. Says she's in love with this 'Homo Erectus' guy."

"The one who's killing all those—"

"Yeah."

"In love with . . . what he's doing, maybe. Or the . . . power thing. But she's pushing you too?"

"It . . . feels like all she wants me to do is bite, so she can pull the apple away and laugh."

"There's those," Michelle conceded. "But it wouldn't have anything to do with her being bi."

"You sure?"

"Yes, honey. That's just a label. Even gays don't really want people like her in the club. I mean, they *say* they want *everyone,* right?"

"No. Crystal Beth said they didn't—"

"What they *say,* baby. Even when I was . . . Back then. Before I had the operation. There was room for people like me too. 'Transgenders.' Isn't that special? Like they want us all, but they only mean the roles. And if you don't fit one of *those,* they all think you got a piece missing."

"So there's no—"

"Baby, the only thing for sure is, this girl, whatever she wants, it's not as simple as how she likes to play."

Hunts Point never changes. It continues its celebration of quick violence and slow decay no matter how many times some star-gazer tries to turn the Urban Renewal trick. The development money always vanishes, swag cut up by elected thieves. And the blight stays—a permanent resident, building its strength, awaiting the next impotent assault.

Michelle went quiet as soon as we turned off the boulevard and moved deep into the prairie. She's seen the same route a thousand times, but it never fails to make her sad. All hope has been vampired out of this place, cut down past the bone, into the desolate marrow.

But she perked up as soon as I nosed the Plymouth into the V made up of rusting cyclone-fence gates wrapped in concertina wire. The dog pack moved in even before I shut off the engine. They were more curious than dangerous—so confident they could take down any intruder that they didn't need to put on a show. Besides, none of them would make a move until Simba showed. That beast had a lot of miles on his odometer, but he still was the pack leader, and none of the young studs had so much as tried him yet, far as I knew.

The chopped-down Jeep the Mole uses for a shuttle rolled up on the other side of the gate, its unmuffled growl blending with that of the pack. Terry was at the wheel. He took one look through the Plymouth's windshield and jumped off his seat so fast he almost stomped on a couple of the dogs.

"Mom!" he called out, running toward us.

Simba was there by then, but he didn't challenge, just stepped back and watched mother and son embrace. I couldn't tell anything from his wolfish grin, but he looked safer than he usually does. I stepped out while I waited for Terry to open the gate so I could stash the car inside.

"Go ahead, Burke," the kid called over to me. "Take the Jeep. Mom and I'll walk over, okay?"

The kid wanted to spend some time with her alone, I guessed. I took off quick. Let Terry deal with Michelle trying to walk a quarter-mile of junkyard in four-inch heels.

Simba trotted alongside the Jeep, easily keeping pace—anything over ten miles an hour was a life-risking move on that terrain, and the trail was marked so faintly I had to steer mostly with my eyes anyway. When I got to the clearing near the Mole's bunker, I saw the cut-down oil drum he uses as a lounge chair was empty, so I sat down on it myself and lit a smoke.

"Mole?" I asked Simba.

The beast knew the word. But he gave me another close look, not moving. I got it then. He wasn't a sight hound, couldn't be sure it *was* me. Only thing to do was let him hear my voice some more.

"Simba," I called out softly. "Mighty Simba-witz, Lion of Zion. You remember me, boy? I sure remember *you.* Such a valiant warrior you are. Come on, Simba. Go get the Mole for me, okay?"

The big dog nodded his head, accepting me, aural memory kicking in. Then he took off, a rust-colored shadow in a city the same color. I wasn't even done with my smoke by the time the Mole appeared. Like he always does, without a word.

"Mole!" I greeted him.

And he returned the greeting the same way he answers the phone—silently, waiting to hear whatever you have to say.

"Can you take a look at something for me?" I asked him.

Again, he was silent. But he moved close enough for me to show him what I'd brought: a blow-up of the little icon from the top of the handle of the killer's ninja spike. "You know what this is?" I asked him.

"Terry . . ." he started to say, just as the kid himself walked up, Michelle on his arm.

"Look, it's Mom!" the kid practically shouted. The Mole's only reaction was to blink rapidly behind those Coke-bottle lenses of his, standing rooted to his spot. Michelle closed the ground between them, wavering a bit on the spike heels, but making progress. The Mole didn't move, just watched her, his mouth open in the same amazement he always shows every time he sees her.

Michelle planted a chaste kiss on the Mole's cheek and he turned a dozen shades of red. "Well?" Michelle demanded, doing a spin in front of him to show off her outfit.

"You look . . . beautiful, Michelle," he finally said.

"Yes, I do. And you can tell me all about it later," she said, her head nodding toward the opening to the Mole's underground bunker. That about finished the poor bastard, and I knew I had to move fast if I was going to get mine before he got his, so I said, "Mole, what about this?" and practically shoved the photocopy under his nose.

"Terry knows about that," the Mole said.

Which, of course, got Michelle interested. "What *is* that? Some kind of dinosaur?"

"It's a velociraptor," Terry said confidently, looking over her shoulder.

"A what?" I asked him.

"Wait, I've got a whole book about them," the kid said, taking off like a shot.

"He's a genius," Michelle gushed. "Just like his father."

The Mole looked everywhere but at Michelle, back to total silence.

"Terry's interested in stuff like that, Mole?" I asked. "Dinosaurs and all."

"He is interested in everything," the Mole replied, unable to keep the love-pride from clogging his voice. "His CD-ROM library is . . . extensive. And I . . . help too."

Sure. Terry was probably the only kid in America home-schooled in a junkyard, but his tutor was light-years ahead of anything walking around a university. Terry wouldn't be there much longer. College was coming. And when they weren't fighting about where he'd go—Michelle wanted him *close*—they were caught up in that proud sadness when your child turns a major corner. And moves another step away.

But now the Mole and Michelle weren't moving, they were waiting. Another couple of minutes and the kid came bounding out the opening to the bunker, his arms full of books. "It's better on the computer," he said, "but I thought . . ."

He didn't have to finish—Michelle and the Mole were already on their way downstairs, and spectators weren't what they were going to need for a while. The kid slapped together a desk from wooden milk crates and assorted planks, then he laid out his stuff for me.

"Mongolia's got the best fossil beds," Terry told me. Not a trace of officiousness in his voice, just the facts. Like his old man. "In the Gobi Desert. Near the Flaming Cliffs. That's where they found the first one. About seventy years ago."

"The first . . . ?"

"Velociraptor," the kid said. "It means 'swift plunderer.' It was maybe about the size of a turkey, but it really packed a wallop."

"I thought raptors could fly," I said.

"They can *now,*" the kid said patiently. "There's a system—it's called cladistics—to identify extinct animals and group them according to the characteristics they share. Scientists usually only have skeletons to look at, so they concentrate on stuff like a certain bone in the wrist, a hole in the hip joint . . . even the number of toes on a foot."

"And this . . . velociraptor was like a bird that way?"

"Sure. They both have three primary toes on their hind feet. And necks that curve into an S shape. And, see here," he said, pointing, "velociraptor has long arms, and a wrist bone like a bird's wing. There's other common characteristics too: like how nerves travel from the brain, the air spaces in the skull, and the construction of the hips and thighs. It may even have built nests like birds and tended its eggs and all."

"But not fly?"

"Not in that . . . stage. We don't know if it disappeared, or just evolved into something else. Like the eohippus into the horse, see?"

"Sure," I said. The kid was already talking like his father—what I really needed was a translator.

"Look at the skeleton," he said, pointing again. "From the sizes of the various bones, and the light, delicate structure of the limbs, you can see it was probably a fast, nimble runner. It wasn't huge or anything, but it was well armed. See this?" he asked, pointing to a large, hook-shaped piece coming out of the toe joint. "They call it a 'killing claw,' so it was probably used to hunt other animals, not to dig in the ground or anything. Velociraptors had more than *eighty* teeth, some of them over an inch long, and each with a sharp, jagged edge. Awesome, huh?"

"Were they . . . I don't know . . . smart?"

"Probably," the kid assured me. "The brain was large and complex. That means that they were probably intelligent, with good hearing and eyesight, and even a good sense of smell."

"So they were like predatory birds—hawks and all—but they worked the ground, right?" I asked him. Thinking how human vultures never have to fly to feed.

"We really don't know," the kid said solemnly. "Only one truly great specimen was ever discovered—a fossil. And it shows a velociraptor and a protoceratops locked in deadly combat."

"But nobody knows who started that one?"

"Or who finished it either. Like a movie where you have to leave before it's over. But, from all I read, it seems like velociraptor was a great hunter. And a great fighter too. The evidence . . . I mean, what they found . . . it had characteristics of both birds and crocodiles—that's those rows of teeth and all. And those are both still around—birds and crocodiles, I mean. So I don't think it died out, the way the bigger ones did—it was too well adapted to its environment. It probably just . . . evolved into something else."

Was that his message? I thought to myself. *That he hadn't died, just evolved? That he was a perfect predator for the times, and he'd move along once his work was done?*

"Which do you think?" I asked the kid.

"What do you mean?"

"Well, you said it had characteristics of both birds and crocodiles, right? So it had to go in one of those directions if it was going to survive."

"Birds," the kid said, unhesitatingly.

"Why? Crocs are ancient. I mean, they go all the way back to . . ."

"They both build nests, right? Birds and crocodiles. But only birds take care of their babies when they're born. When the baby crocs are born, they're on their own."

"And you think that's the key to survival?"

"For the higher life-forms? Sure. It makes sense, right?"

"If it does," I asked him, "what the fuck are *we* still doing on this planet?"

The kid—this kid whose bio-parents had sold him like a used car—looked at me for a long moment. Then he said: "We're not all like . . . that." And then he glanced toward the bunker where his real parents were being with each other.

I nodded, agreeing. But not believing. The human race *is* a race. And I'm not sure parents like Michelle and the Mole are winning it.

"Would anyone be likely to recognize this?" I asked the kid, showing him the icon again, working for a smooth transition, moving as far away from the other as I could get.

"Sure, if they knew anything about the subject. Like a paleontologist. But not from the name."

"Huh?"

"'Velociraptor' was the name they used in *Jurassic Park.* You know, the movie? But the ones there were nothing like the *real* ones. If you said 'velociraptor' to the average kid, he'd never think it looked anything like *this.*"

I lit another smoke. "You did great, Terry," I told the kid. Thinking maybe I had something to make that polygraph key really sing, now that I had lyrics to go with the music.

Michelle was quiet on the drive back, and I knew better than to break the silence. She could dissect my sex life for hours without batting an eyelash, and she'd turned every kind of trick there was before she took herself off the streets and went to the phones to make a living, but even mentioning her and the Mole together was total taboo.

Terry was always a safe topic with her—she loved that kid way past her own life—and she would have been proud about how he'd helped me out. But she was so inside herself that I didn't even tap on the door. Just took her absentminded kiss on the cheek before she slipped out in front of her place and then motored over to Mama's.

Red-dragon tapestry in the front window. Maybe Lorraine had found Xyla already. Or maybe not. I pulled around the back, flat-handed the metal slab of a door, and waited. One of Mama's crew opened the door, a guy I hadn't seen before. I could swear his face was Korean, but I knew how Mama was about things like that, so I kept the thought to myself. He said something over his shoulder and one of the guys who knew me answered him. The new man stepped aside to let me pass, his right hand still in the pocket of his apron. Whatever was out front wasn't *that* dangerous, anyway.

It was Xyla. Sitting in my booth, facing toward the back, working her way through a plate of dim sum someone had provided. Good sign. Mama served strangers toxic waste—her real customers never came for the food.

"What's up?" she greeted me. "Lorraine said you were looking for me."

"Yeah," I said, sitting down. "Be with you in a minute."

It was less than that before the tureen of hot-and-sour soup was placed before me. I filled the small bowl myself, drained it quickly. I glanced toward where Mama was working at her register, but I couldn't risk it—had two more bowls before I waved at the waiter to take the rest away. I didn't offer any to Xyla, and she seemed to understand . . . just sat there, chewing delicately on her own food, waiting.

"What kind of name is Xyla?" I said, my tone telling her I really was interested, not putting her down. I wanted to start cutting her out of the herd if I could, form my own relationship, just in case Lorraine's old hostility flared up and she tried to cut *me* out first.

"My mom gave it to me," she said, chuckling. "It comes from 'Xylocaine.' . . . Mom said if it wasn't for Xylocaine my old man never could've lasted long enough to get her pregnant."

"Damn! That's cold."

"It was a joke," she said, watching me carefully. "The kind you tell your daughter when she's old enough to ask where her father is . . . and you don't know the answer."

"Ah."

"Yeah," she said, dismissing it—an old wound, healed. But it still throbbed when the weather was wrong.

I'd made a mistake. My specialty with women. So I switched subjects as smoothly as I could. "I got the word I want you to use," I told her. It's 'velociraptor.' Can you—?"

"Like in *Jurassic Park*? Sure. How do you spell that?" she asked me, pulling a little notebook from the pocket of her coat.

I did it, thinking how on the money Terry had been.

"Okay," she said. "But why would he—?"

"Doesn't matter," I told her. "It's just a word. One he'll recognize. You got a secure address? For yourself, I mean. One he could go to with an answer if he wanted?"

"I can make one," she said confidently. "Take about a minute. No problem. What do you want me to do, exactly?"

"Look, I'm no pro at this stuff. You said a couple of things, remember? One, people are looking for him on the Net, right? And two, he could be out there . . ."

"Lurking."

"Yeah. Lurking. He could *see* the traffic . . . but without him banging in, nobody would know he was there?"

"Sure."

"Okay. So I want to send him a message too. Only I don't want to make it public. And I don't have his address. You could post like a . . .

I don't know . . . *general* message for him, only put it into encryption, so he'd need a program to open it and read it?"

"I could do that. But if the message itself said it was encrypted, and I used one of the regular programs—to *make* it encrypted, see?—anyone could open the message if they had the same program."

"And he'd know that?"

"Yes," she said, in one of those elongated "Isn't it obvious?" tones all young girls can do.

"Doesn't matter," I said, maybe trying to convince myself. "I'll be able to figure out who's who."

"Okay. So exactly what do you want to say? And is it context-sensitive?"

"What's that mean?"

"Oh. Well, it just means, does it have to be exactly in a certain form. Like, if you wrote it like a regular sentence, you know, with capital letters and periods and all, and I just sent it in all lower-case, would that matter?"

"No. I don't care. Here's all I want to say, all right?"

She nodded, pencil poised.

"You just address it to him, right? To 'Homo Erectus,' yes?"

"Sure. And I'll multi-post it. If he's lurking on any of the newsgroups or on BBS stuff, he'll see it."

"Okay, say this: 'I am the real thing, same as you. Here's proof: "velociraptor."' Put that in quotes, okay? 'I am not a cop. I have something you need.'"

"That's it?"

"That's it. If he sends you a message . . ."

"Oh, I'll get *lots* of messages," she assured me. "Problem'll be telling if any of them are him."

"I think I can do that . . . if he bites. Just get word to me. I'm counting on you, all right, Xyla?"

"I'm straight-edge," she said, finger flicking at one of her razor earrings.

I sat there for a long time after Xyla left, thinking it through. Even if the killer got in touch, I wouldn't be any closer to him, not really. Sure, he had to be in the city—or, at least, he had to have *been* in the city—to do his work. But he could have already vanished. All we really had was his footprints. And, like the Prof had said about Wesley, that trail only ran backward.

Still, I couldn't see this guy living some double life. Couldn't see him as a stockbroker or running a bodega. He wasn't making his own porno flicks, the way a lot of serial killers do. And he didn't roam the way most of them do either. He had no definable piece of work he had to finish—the way a mass murderer who comes into the workplace shooting and then eats his own gun does, or a wife-beater under an order of protection who's going to take himself out as soon as he blows her away.

No, this one was a different breed. And he was . . . close. Had to be. As if he wasn't so much compelled to do his work as to see its results.

Maybe he was just nuts. Or I was. I couldn't track him in my mind the way I could other kinds of predators. Those, I knew about. Spent my life with them. They raised me. I did time with them. And I studied them close—because I knew someday I'd be hunting them. That was the prayer I put myself to sleep with every night, from when I was a little child. That I wouldn't be prey. Inside, where I ended up, there was only one alternative to that.

That's why he said he was doing it too—revenge. But I couldn't connect with him. Couldn't see him . . . feel him. Nothing.

"Burke, you take this one, okay? Say important."

"Huh?" I felt Mama's hand on my shoulder. Figured out she must mean the phone. Glanced at my watch. I'd been there . . . Jesus, almost three hours. That kind of thing happened to me every once in a while, but ever since I'd lost my . . . home, I guess . . . it was happening a lot.

I got up, walked to the back, picked up the dangling receiver.

"What?" is all I said.

"It's me." Wolfe's voice. "I have your stuff."

"Great. When can I—?"

"Now, if you want. Remember where we were the last time you saw Bruiser do his stuff?"

"Sure."

"An hour?"

"I'll be there," I promised.

There's places along the Hudson River where you can pull over. Sort of big parking lots. Maybe the city planners thought the rich folks on Riverside Drive would promenade over for picnics, who knows? Today, the spots are used for everything from romance to rape. Daytime, they're pretty full, especially when the weather gets nice. At night, it's a little different, but there's enough room to give everybody space to operate, and the assortment of cars parked there didn't set off any of my alarms.

I backed the Plymouth into an empty space—too near the middle for my taste, but the corners were already occupied. I was twenty minutes ahead of the meet, so I kicked back and watched.

It wasn't long before that rolling oil refinery Wolfe calls a car rumbled in. I shuddered as she reversed, slowly and deliberately, then backed in so she was close to me . . . but this time she missed by a couple of feet. I opened my door and waited, not surprised to see that malevolent Rottweiler of hers jump right out the passenger-side window and pin me balefully, waiting for the word.

"Bruiser, behave yourself," Wolfe told him. Not a command I'd ever heard for a dog before, but the brute seemed to understand, visibly relaxing. At least as far as I was concerned—his heavy head swiveled as he swept the surrounding area, maybe remembering the last time Wolfe had met me here. Some clowns in a four-by didn't see me—just Wolfe standing alone—and thought they'd try their luck. Then they saw Bruiser coming for them—a skell-seeking missile already locked on to his target—just in time and peeled out before he could do his job.

"I got it," Wolfe said by way of greeting.

I hadn't expected a hug and a kiss, but this was a bit cold-edged, even for her.

"You also got a problem?" I asked her, getting right to it, ignoring the cheap white plastic briefcase she held in one hand.

"I might have," she said evenly. "The word's out that your . . . friend may be back."

"You believing rumors now?"

"Not any more than usual. But I know a trademark when I see one."

"Spell it out," I said quietly, understanding now why she wanted the meet outdoors.

"I'm still . . . in touch," Wolfe said. Not news to me. The cops Wolfe had worked with for so many years hadn't broken off contact when she'd gone outlaw. They knew what she trafficked in, and they'd made more than one beautiful bust off info she'd provided. The only way she could walk into a courtroom and *own* it the way she had for so long as a prosecutor would be as a defense attorney, and she just wouldn't go the side-switching route like so many ex-DAs. So, even though her license was gathering dust, she was still law enforcement in the eyes of a lot of working cops.

"What is it you want to say?" I asked her, watching her gray eyes.

She took out a cigarette, waited for the wooden match she knew was coming from my end, hauled in a deep drag, leaning back against her Audi's crumpled hood, and blew a jet of smoke into the darkness.

"You trust me?" she finally asked.

"Yes," I told her. No hesitation. I could maybe never tell her how I really felt about her, but I could tell her that. And even as that one simple word left my mouth, I knew it was a commitment . . . that I'd have to prove it.

"The drive-by—the one that started this all?"

"Yeah?"

"Two shooters. Plus one driver, okay?"

"Far as I know. Although the driver could have been shooting too . . . so maybe one less man."

"Seven victims, two fatal."

"I thought it was less, but . . . okay."

"One of them, your girlfriend. This Crystal Beth?"

"Yes."

"Only her ID didn't say that. It said she was someone else."

I shrugged. The woman asking me the questions was holding a briefcase full of documents as phony as a talk show host's tears for the pathetic parade of damaged creatures she used and abused every day.

"You know one of the guns was a Tec-9, right?"

"That's what I heard."

"You hear a lot. But not enough, I don't think. You know what the other piece was?"

"No," I said, focusing now.

"It was a Magnum Research Lone Eagle."

"Oh Jesus . . ."

"Chambered for .22 Hornet."

"So it had to be a—"

"Hit. That's right. An assassination."

I lit a smoke of my own, more to have something to do with my hands than anything else. She was right—what else *could* it be? Magnum Research is a subsidiary of Israeli Arms. And the piece she was talking about was a Mossad special: single-shot, with a rotary breech like an artillery cannon. You rotate the breech cap to expose the chamber and slide in the cartridge, then you lock it up again. No way to reload it in the time a car would pass by . . . impossible. But a sharpshooter, even using open metal sights, could hit a half-dollar at a hundred feet from a moving car with a piece like that. And nobody could be sure the car even *was* moving before the spray from the Tec-9 started.

"They found the slug?" I asked her.

"A piece of it, anyway. He was hit right in the base of the skull, dead before he dropped."

He? "So it wasn't Crystal Beth who—?"

"No. The way they have it doped, she was hit by cover fire. The target was the guy who got the special delivery."

"If all they have is a piece of the slug, how could they know it was a—?"

"They have the weapon," Wolfe said softly. "It was in the car."

"The . . . what?"

"The car. The drive-by car. It was a Lincoln Town Car. You know, the kind most of the limo services use . . . not a stretch, a regular sedan. Black. Tinted windows. About as noticeable as a taxicab in that part of town . . . real good choice."

"Where'd they find—?"

"In a long-term parking garage on Roosevelt Island. A couple of days later. The way they figure it, the driver must have caught the Triborough and hooked back through Queens, come into the garage from the other side of the river. That's probably where they had the switch car waiting."

"So the murder weapon was in the car. Don't tell me they left a bullet in it?"

"Oh, they found a slug, all right. In the back of the head of the guy in the passenger seat. The driver got the same dose . . . only from a different piece. A regular .22 short. The techs found that one too."

"And when they vacuumed . . . ?"

"Nothing. Both of the dead men in the front seat had sheets, but no trace of whoever was in the back. And the weapons were all purchased legally. One in Florida, the other two in Georgia. About three years apart. Straw-man buys. Local drunks or crackheads. All you need is proof of residence there. Then a quick run up Handgun Highway. No way to figure out how many times they changed hands since."

"The dead guys. Their sheets said . . . what?"

"They were both made men," she said. "Family guys."

"So somebody wanted the guy in the park and . . ."

"Contracted it out, sure. That's the way they're playing it. That's why not a word of this has leaked. It's bad enough that this Homo Erectus maniac is slaughtering people. Now it looks like it all started over . . . something else. It wasn't a fag-bashing after all."

"Christ."

"Yes. But that's not all. What's got everyone spooked isn't the hit. It's the word about the hit man."

"I don't get—"

"Yeah, you do," she said flatly. "Who else does that but Wesley? Who else can shoot like that? Who else kills a bunch of people just to get one? Who else leaves the weapon right there when he's finished? And maybe the boss wanted those other guys gone anyway. It's just like Wesley to get paid for three jobs and hit the trifecta."

"Wesley's dead," I said.

"Is he?"

"You going for that handjob too?" I asked her.

"They never found a body."

"Hey! He was inside a school, all right? Surrounded by half the cops in the world. Locals, mounties, feds. A couple of *hundred* people died in the blast. Remember? Not just the dynamite he had in his own hand; the truck he had parked right outside—the one with the poison gas. It was like a bomb hit the place."

"He could have gotten out. . . ."

"Where? They had helicopters in the air. They checked for tunnels under the place and they had them all blocked. They kept a cordon around the site for *weeks* picking through the corpses. So they didn't find his . . . whatever would have been left of him anyway. . . . So what?"

"I don't know," she said. "I know about the note . . . the one you turned over. But I also know you're holding something back. You have to know something more about it than that note he left."

"Even if I did," I said, hedging, "what difference would it make? It might get me out of a beef sometime, if I could add something to what they already know. But alive? Forget it. There's no way."

"Listen to me," Wolfe said, stepping so close her face went out of focus, voice dropping below a whisper. "The feds have a man inside. They turned him a long time ago. It's a RICO thing. They're looking for the whole Family. Probably got more than five years invested already. And this guy, he heard the boss set it up. On the phone. A pay phone—there was no tap in place. But . . . Burke, he was talking to Wesley. That's who he made the deal with. Wesley's not dead. Or he's back, if you want to believe that. But one thing's for sure—he's *making* people dead. And that's what Wesley does. That's all he does."

"There's got to be some other—"

"That's what they say too," Wolfe told me. "After all, they 'solved' that mass murder up in Riverdale, right? Laid it on Wesley. That's their story, and they're sticking to it. But now . . ."

"And you think I—?"

"I don't know what to think. I know you go back with him. I know he . . . did things with you, I'm not sure what. But I'll tell you what they know down at One Police Plaza, Burke. When you turned in that suicide note of his, it may have gotten you off the hook for some stuff.

They know where *you* got it . . . just not how. Or when. They don't want you for any of these fag-basher killings. They don't believe it was you, not for a minute."

"They think it's . . . Wesley? That's nuts."

"Because he's dead?"

"No," I said. "I'll go you one better. Because how would he get paid? Where's the money? Wesley never killed anyone for fun in his life."

"Yeah, well, maybe you should put your ear a little closer to the ground. If you did, you'd hear something real interesting."

"Like what?"

"Like a body-count fund."

"Are you for real? What kind of—?"

"All I know is they call him the Trustee."

"Like in prison? One of those guys who—?"

"No. Like from an estate. The word is, some crazy rich old queen left a fortune in cash to this 'Trustee,' all right? And his only instructions were he wanted fag-bashers murdered. So the Trustee reached out to Wesley and . . ."

"Offered him so much a head? Change your medication."

"*You* explain it," she challenged. "And you may have to . . . in court. Watch your back, Mr. Askew."

"Huh?"

"Your new ID," she said, handing over the briefcase. "If your . . . partner is back in town, or back from the dead, or whatever . . . it doesn't matter. The way they're thinking, they already know who's doing all this. And you're the only connect. Don't worry. You're about as bust-proof as a diplomat. For now. They're letting you dangle. Understand?"

"Yeah. But I—"

"Don't even tell me," Wolfe said, voice cold. "If it's not what it looks like, I'll have plenty of time to apologize."

I just stood there while she got back in her car, her face grim. As the Audi pulled away, the Rottweiler looked at me like he was just waiting his turn.

"From where I sit, I like the fit," the Prof said. "You want that kind of fun, Wesley's the man to get it done."

"He's dead, Prof," I said. Tired of saying it.

"What do we know, bro? I mean, we wasn't there. All we saw was a bunch of stuff on TV. Explosions. That green cloud of whatever crap he let loose. Wesley, he was never like . . . people, you know? There's an old hoodoo . . . 'Reaching Back,' they call it. But even if you believe in that stuff, someone has to *want* you to come back. And they have to bring one to get one too."

"What's that mean?"

"Just what it sounds like, son. The legend is there's supposed to be a Gatekeeper. Could be a man, could be a woman. Could be anyone, anyplace. And nobody knows how to find 'em either. But, if you look hard enough, they're supposed to appear. Anyway, you want to bring someone back, you got to bring some to get some, understand?"

"No."

"The way it's told, you can't bring no *good* people back, okay? Just the evil ones. And the way you got to do it, you got to bring them one soul for every soul the evil one took, see?"

"No," I said. And not because I couldn't understand what the Prof was saying.

"Burke, mahn, my father is telling you true," Clarence put in. "There is the same legend in the islands. If a man has killed many times, and you want to bring him back across, you too must kill as many times as he has. So the Gatekeeper will allow the passage. A trade, understand?"

"Yeah, I understand. Bujo bullshit is what I understand. I want that, I'll go shopping in a botanica. You ever see it happen?" I asked him.

"See this? No, mahn. It is not to see. Not for me. My loss was my . . . mother, mahn. And if I thought I could return her by taking a life, I would have done that. You know I would. But it cannot work that way. My mother was good. In her heart and in her spirit. Where she is, the Gatekeeper has no power."

"If that was true . . . and it isn't, for chrissakes . . . but if it was, somebody'd have to kill a whole *ton* of motherfuckers to bring Wesley back."

"And this Homo Erectus guy, he ain't doing that?" the Prof challenged.

"Not enough. Anyway, why would he want Wesley back?"

"Sometimes, if the killer dies too easily, the family . . . the family of the people he killed . . . they want him back," Clarence said.

"So they can—?"

"Yes, mahn. So they can send him over again. But with much pain."

"That would make them as bad as . . ."

"Sure," the Prof cut me off. "That's why it so crazy. Don't make no sense. I ain't arguing with you 'bout that. Not saying it true. But I know this. Some people *believe* things. And if they believe things, then they *do* things."

"So you think this maniac is trying to raise Wesley from the dead? Because he wants him to die all over again? Only . . . hard this time?"

"It ain't strong," the Prof conceded. "But it may not be wrong neither. What we gotta do, we gotta find out more about the guy who died."

"You mean the guy in the park? With Crystal Beth?"

"Yeah. That's the one. Not the others, that's not Wesley. Some of those guys this new guy did, they died slow. Wesley did a lot of hits, sure. But they was like . . . surgery, okay? He wouldn't torture nobody—he was a killer, not a freak. Except for that one . . . on Sutton Place, remember?"

I did remember. Impossible to forget an image that I never saw but that was still whispered about. This was back when Wesley had the only kind of dispute he ever cared about—he hadn't gotten paid. So he started killing people. When that wasn't enough, he decided to spook them, start them running wild. Same way a stalking cheetah shows itself to a herd of antelopes—the stampede reveals the cripples. He got into the Sutton Place apartment of a connected guy's daughter. When her husband came home from work, he found what was left of his wife . . . arms and legs spread wide on their bed, wired to the posts. With her severed head propped up between her legs, staring at him. They say he's still in a padded room.

That started the stampede Wesley wanted. He'd left a message—on the bedroom wall, in the woman's own blood—saying the butchery was the work of some lunatic cult, but that was just to dazzle the cops. The wiseguys knew he was promising a whole lot more.

And he kept it up, right to the end. They never found him. Wesley went out by his own hand. Not because they were closing in—they were too busy hiding to look for him. And not because he was afraid—the ice-man didn't have any of that in his once-in-an-eon DNA. He left because he was tired. Sick and tired. He didn't want to be here anymore, it was that simple.

A lot of us felt like that. Some of us all the time. And some of us went out that same way. But only Wesley decided he knew who the "them" was that we—all of us State-raised kids—blamed for what had happened to us.

Wesley was pure hate. The kind that metastasizes, year after year. The kind that never goes away, no matter what treaties are signed, no matter whose hands are shaken, no matter who intervenes. Permanent. As deep as your father's father's father's father's firstborn.

Only difference is, Wesley's father was the one he hated. The one we all hated—the State. That viciously uncaring, humiliating, experimenting, lying, exploiting, torturing, unstoppable juggernaut. Wesley's hate was a match for all that. He was us—distilled, crystallized, hardened beyond comprehension, focused past megalomania.

When Wesley went out, he wanted company: the seeds "they" were cultivating for the next generation.

So even if the poor insane bastard on Sutton Place who'd come home to that horrible greeting wanted to bring Wesley back, to give him a greeting of his own . . . and even if the legend was true, and even if he could find this Gatekeeper . . . he couldn't ever bring enough for the tolls, like the Prof said.

It didn't leave me anywhere.

Wolfe wouldn't help me anymore. Maybe she wasn't sure . . . but I could tell, from the way her gray eyes looked at me just before we parted, that the weight was mine to carry. And I'd have to carry it a long way before we could ever be . . . whatever we were to each other . . . again.

She'd given me all I was going to get. The new ID. And the information.

So I made the phone call.

"Why do you want to come here?" Nadine asked me. "You didn't seem so . . . fascinated the last time."

"You said you wanted to be in on it," I told her. "There's more to do now."

"You mean you—?"

"Not on the phone."

"Can you come tonight?"

"Yes."

"Now?"

"What happened?" is how she greeted me, still wearing her business clothes, even though she'd had plenty of time to change.

"I may have found a way to—"

"Find him and—?"

"No! To get a message to him. And to put enough in it so he'll read it, anyway. Now, what I need is to put something in the next one so he'll want to *see* me."

"And you want me to . . . what?"

"Your friend on the force?"

"Yeah . . . ?" she said, warily.

"I need some other stuff. Not about the murders, okay? She doesn't have to go near any of that. Not anymore. But there's another case. The one that kicked all this off."

"The drive-by?"

"Yes. But I don't want anything about that one either. At least, not anything direct. The cops . . . they know a lot more than they're letting out. Not because they got a sudden dose of class, or because they want to play it professional. This piece, the one they're holding back, the media would have them for lunch if they knew about it."

"And you want her to . . . get it?"

"Not 'it.' Not the whole thing. Just a name. And whatever information they have about the name. That's all."

"How is that going to—?"

"I've got a . . . theory. Probably a long shot, I don't know. But it's the only card I have to play. I've been looking everywhere," I lied, "asking everyone. But there isn't a trace of this guy. He's about as lone a wolf as it gets. No partners. Whatever stuff he's using he got a long time ago. Like he's got a warehouse full of it or something. Like this isn't anything new."

Her eyes flickered when I said that. Flickered, not flashed, the blue going from cobalt to cyanotic and back, switching on and off for just a split-second. If she noticed me staring, she didn't react.

"Anyway, she can do that, right?"

"I . . . don't know."

"I thought you said she'd do anything you—"

"Anything she *can* do," Nadine snapped back. "I'm not insane. If it's there, and if she can get it, I'll get it, sure. But I don't know. . . . She told me they have, what do they call them, 'firewalls' or something, inside the department. 'Access Only' places, when they're working on stuff. Mostly political, I guess, but she doesn't know. And I sure don't."

"It's nothing like that," I told her, with a confidence I didn't feel. "I even know where it probably is. NYPD has the same thing as the feds—some Organized Crime unit, whatever they're calling it this week, I don't know, but it would be the same thing. *That's* where she has to look."

"He would never . . ."

"*He?* I thought you said—"

"Not my . . . friend. Him. He would never have anything to do with organized crime."

"Not even to kill a few of them?"

"Oh! But why would he . . . ?"

"I don't know. I don't even know if it's true. But before I can ask my questions, I need what I told you."

She stood up and started to pace, unbuttoning her jade silk blouse, leaving the off-white blazer on over it. The black bra underneath was frillier than I expected, for some reason I didn't focus on. "Sometimes it's hard to breathe in all this stuff," she said. "When it's hard to breathe, it's hard to think."

There was so much truth in what she said that I focused on that, slitting my eyes as she walked back and forth. She stopped at one point, stood on one leg, and pulled off her shoe, then switched legs to do the other, so she was in her stocking feet. By the third circuit, she was down to sheer pantyhose.

"Men hate these, don't they?" she said suddenly.

"Huh?" I'd been somewhere else. Not far away, but just . . . apart.

"Pantyhose. Men hate them, don't they?"

"Hate? That's a pretty strong word for clothing."

"Okay, fine. Men don't *like* them, all right?"

"I'm not following you."

"You ever see pantyhose in a skin magazine?" she asked me. "It's all garter belts and fishnet stockings and thongs, right? Pantyhose, it's too . . . practical. Like shoes. You think men would wear spike heels? They *hurt* once you have them on for a while. But they make your legs look good, so what the hell, right?"

"What do I—?"

"That's, of course, if they're interested in *big* girls, right?" she snarled, angry beyond anything I could imagine having done to her. I couldn't figure what had ignited all that, so I just rode it—waiting, knowing there's always a reason in the eye of the tornado . . . if you're around long enough to take that look.

"Some of them like little plaid pleated skirts and Mary Jane shoes and white socks . . . and white cotton panties too. A garter belt would spoil all that, wouldn't it? The . . . image, I mean. That's what it's all about for . . . them. Whatever they see. Their *eyes.* You know even blind men are like that? I have a friend. A dancer. She says they get blind customers in there too."

"And this is all about . . . what?" I asked her, as neutral as I could, no sarcasm anywhere near my voice.

"It's all about . . . this!" she snapped at me. "This . . . killer, you call him. What*ever* name you call him. He's a man. But he's not like the rest of you."

"Because he's gay?"

"You think *that's* a difference? You think gay men don't look at us the same way? Oh sure, maybe they don't want to fuck us. Or maybe they do and just . . . I don't know. But who do you think runs the damn fashion industry?"

"Frederick's of Hollywood isn't exactly Versace," I said.

"It's the same thing," she shot back. "It's all about what men want."

"So . . . these women who silicone their chests out to all hell, the ones who rake in a couple of grand a night under the same tables they dance on, they're all fashion victims?"

"I didn't say that. I'm not saying it *isn't* true, but that's not what I'm saying. I'm just saying . . . the way things are. And any of us can feel it. We know. Some of us play along. Some of us just play. But we all know. And I'm telling you something about him. Something important, if you'll listen. He's not like you."

"I already know he's—"

"*Not* because he's gay," she said.

"Fine. Because he hates fag-bashers. Because he kills a lot of them. Because he's a fucking superior specimen of humanity, for all I know."

"He is," she said, calmly. "And before I do anything more, I need to know more about you."

"Me?"

"Yes, you. You're a mercenary, aren't you? Lincoln says you have a 'code.' Some bullshit he picked up from the movies. You're a 'professional,'" she sneered. "You'd *never* double-cross a client. Your word is your bond. So, even if you could trade this . . . man to the cops instead of helping him get away, you'd never do *that,* would you? Even if it would help you get out from under a bunch of trouble of your own, huh?"

"You trust this friend of yours?" I asked her. "Not Lincoln—your playmate?"

"I told you—"

"You told me she'd kiss your ass in Macy's window. So what? I don't mean do you believe she'd play whatever game you ordered her to—I mean do you believe *her* when she says something."

That stopped her in her tracks, as if she'd never considered it. She crossed her arms under her breasts, lifted them deliberately, looked down at herself like she was thinking about how one would taste. Then she looked over at me.

"Why do you ask?" she said.

"Ask *her,*" I said. "All you got so far is what anyone could give you, insider or not. Yeah, I got a record. A nice long one. And, yeah, the cops are always on my case—they got a bunch of Unsolveds with my name on them. I'm a thief. Been one since I was a baby. And I'll be one until I die. Those 'codes' . . . You're right: it *is* all movie bullshit. Any one of those slimy little gangsters'll rat out any other. Happens all the time. But me, I got no gang. No crew. No fucking 'Mafia' or anything like that. I've got a family. Not my blood, but more true than any DNA could be. Truly mine. I wouldn't sell any of them no matter what the price was. My life? Fuck that. I don't care that much about it myself anymore. So ask your little slave friend *that.* You know my name. She knows it. There's cops been around long enough to know it too. I been the same since forever. My name is in the street. It's fucking *engraved* there, you know where to look. It's not all true. None of that stuff ever is. But stick your ear anywhere you want, you come back with anything that says I'd shop one of my own, I'll kiss *your* ass, bitch."

"Look, I wasn't—"

"Save it," I chopped her off. "This guy. This . . . killer. There's people who think I know who he is already. People who think *they* know who he is. They're wrong. The guy they suspect—he's dead. Dead and gone. But if he *was* alive, I wouldn't trade him either, not for anything. I came up with him, and he saved my life. More than once. I don't judge him. . . . I know him. Hell, I wanted to *be* him once. But I . . . couldn't."

"Why couldn't you—?"

"That's not your business. And it never will be. I just told you the truth. You're always telling me what a liar I am, right? You know it all, don't you? Trouble is, your yardstick don't work on everyone. You want to sit in, you have to ante up. You don't have what it takes to back your own hand, get out of the game."

"But if the police are wrong . . . ? If it's not this man they think you know . . . ?"

"Yeah, if they're wrong, if it's someone else, what have they got to offer me anyway? A pass on some cases? If they really *had* me on those cases, I'd be Inside right now. They had me down to the precinct once already. If they had any kind of hammer, they would have showed it to me. Fuck, they would have *used* it on me."

"What's the bottom line?" she asked, standing up suddenly, looming over me, breasts swinging down close to my face.

"You think we're all alike," I told her. "Men, anyway. You're wrong. You think because I like your legs better in spike heels *that* tells you I'd turn rat? *That's* your idea of knowing stuff? You don't know anything. You sure as hell don't know anything about me. Want to know some truth? Go ask this friend of yours. Ask her to ask . . . Ah, I'm not giving you any references—you'd just think it was a setup. Let her ask anyone she wants about me. Tell her to ask two questions: Would I rat out my own? And what would I think of a guy who's going around blowing up baby-rapers? When you're all done with that, you still want to help, let's do it. You're not satisfied, go your own way." I finished, getting to my feet, forcing her to step away from me.

I stopped near the door, turned to face her. "If you make that decision . . . if you go your own way . . . you better stay the fuck out of mine," I told her. "Ask your little friend about *that,* too."

If she said anything, I couldn't hear it through the door.

"Is it true?" I asked Morales. "NYPD really believes Wesley's back in town?"

He rubbed the blue-black stubble on his face, like he was deciding how much to tell me. But I knew the gesture for what it was—a habit, not an indicator. We were standing under the overpass to the LIE, just off Van Dam Street. A good place to meet if you wanted to do a deal and keep the peep for the rollers at the same time. Even better if you wanted anyone watching to think that *was* what you were doing.

"Yeah," he finally said. "Some of them do. The older guys. But nobody's saying it out loud."

"You?" I asked him bluntly.

"Nah. Motherfucker's dead. The feds've pulled some strange shit. . . . I know that whole thing about 26 Federal Plaza last year stunk, okay?" He gave me a hard cop-look when he said that. Another habit—he knew it wouldn't get him anything, just wanted to tell me I was a suspect. Again. In another crime. Nothing changes with a cop like Morales.

I gave him a blank look back. Nothing changes with me, either.

"The way I figure it, somebody's glommed his action," Morales said. Not sure of himself, just throwing it out.

"Wesley's?"

"Sure. He was the best, right? Money in the fucking bank. You paid—you got a body. Never a problem. Fucking Torenelli had to go off, start that war. That was bad enough. Then Julio double-crosses Wesley. Stupid motherfucker *had* to know what that was gonna cost."

"You think Wesley did Julio before he—?"

"No way. I think the Family took him out. They knew whose fault that whole thing was. You don't pay Wesley, you open the gates of hell. If they hadn't offed Julio, fuck, Wesley, he would've wasted every mob guy in the city, the way he was going. They just cut their losses, that's all. Not the first time."

He didn't sound like he was fishing. Good. The truth was buried with the body. I was innocent of a lot of things I was suspected of, but Julio was mine all right. I had met him at the spot where we were going to make a trade: a letter he wrote a long time ago—a letter about a little girl—for a bundle of cash. As we made the exchange, I vise-gripped his hand. He struggled to get free, his eyes insane with what he knew was coming. Max took him out. While Strega witch-watched from the shadows, a little girl no more.

That killing had been part of a trade. And Wesley kept up his end, like he always did. I hadn't lied to that crazy Nadine. Wesley was a pure sociopath; that's what all the psychs said. But they didn't know. There was a piece of him that still connected. Not enough to keep him here, but enough to give me that one last gift.

At least this Homo Erectus loon had his own motives. All Wesley ever had was a list. And all it took to get put on it was money.

Money. Maybe Morales was right after all.

"You think someone's stepping in? Taking over?"

"They'd have to blood-in, right?" he growled back at me. "No way anyone's gonna fork over the kind of bucks Wesley got without knowing they was getting the real thing. This guy, whoever the fuck he is, he knows how to make bodies."

"So what? They're just random hits," I said, fishing now myself. "It's not like anyone ordered them done. Not like these guys had bodyguards or anything. Any freak can do a lot of kills if there's no motive, you know that."

"Yeah," Morales agreed. If he knew anything about some mobster hiring a hit man he thought was Wesley, it didn't show on his face. And I bought it too—Morales isn't that good at keeping his face from talking even with his mouth shut, and he wasn't the kind of cop they'd let in on an organized-crime thing anyway. Maybe the brass had called him a hero in their press conference when he got the credit for killing that psycho Belinda, but he was marked forever as a dinosaur street-roller. They couldn't let him work narcotics, because they knew him for a flake-and-bake guy from way back. Put him in the gang unit and you'd have corpses by the end of the week. Vice was out of the question—he was too full of puritanical rage to work anything that took delicacy. Undercover was impossible—he reeked of cop. So he worked job-to-job, always roving, never partnered up. Which was okay with him. He wasn't going anywhere. No promotions in his future. And they couldn't fire him. So he was just doing time.

I knew all about that.

I also knew one place I could get what I wanted . . . if Nadine's friend was really all she said she was.

"He was a man," Morales said, surprising me out of my thoughts.

"Who?" I asked him.

"Wesley," Morales said, touching the brim of his hat as a goodbye. Or maybe a salute.

Driving away, I shoved in a cassette and let the blues flow over my thoughts. What's a "man" to Morales, anyway? Someone who walked his own way, I guessed, same way Morales himself did. What was he saying, then? That this Homo Erectus guy . . . wasn't?

It was like trying to knit a sweater from cigarette smoke. I gave it up.

The whisper-stream isn't all lies. I'd never heard of this "Gatekeeper" the Prof had talked about, but I knew who might. Queen Thana, the voodoo priestess who had told me the truth about myself. My destiny. And, maybe because I understood she already knew—I guess I never really will know why—I told her the truth about myself, too. What happened to me when I was a little kid. First time I ever said it out loud. She told me I was a hunter. That was true—I'd been looking for a missing baby when I'd come to her, following a twisty-scary trail. She told me two more things: I had to be what I am—I could change my ways, but I couldn't change myself. And not to come back.

After that, it all happened. I went into a house of beasts looking for a captured kid. At least, that's what I told myself. But I went in shooting. Killing, really. The only gunfight was at the end. And if they hadn't had guns down in that basement—where a kid was trussed up for the sacrifice, the videocams ready to turn blood into money—it would have been just killing then, too. In the exchange, they all died. Even the kid.

I'd gone into that house hunting my childhood. Not the ones who did those things to me. They were gone. I couldn't dig them up and kill them again. But their descendants. Their heirs. Their . . . tribe. When it was done, it almost did me too. No rationalization worked. I know who killed that kid. I know it was me. I know I didn't mean to. I know they were going to kill him anyway.

None of it helped.

For a long time, I wouldn't touch a gun. I prayed for Wesley's ice to come into my soul. He was my brother. We had suckled at the same poisonous breast. Only he could save me from going down into the Zero, it was pulling at me so hard.

Things happened since then. A lot of years. And the last time I held a gun in my hand, it was to protect my family. I never got to pull the trigger. Michelle was closer, and she got off first. And roared away on the back of Crystal Beth's motorcycle as a team of feds drove a convoy of explosives toward the Hudson River.

That was 26 Federal Plaza, the giant downtown government building that houses IRS, FBI, INS—everything the New Nazis hated.

That's what Morales had been talking about. But it was just talk. Nobody really cared, not with hundreds of Hitler-worshippers in prison . . . and the plot to make Oklahoma City look like a pipe bomb defused.

I was rambling. Not out loud—that would have scared me. But in my head, still. And I didn't like the sound.

Queen Thana wasn't the only witch I knew. And now I had to see if Nadine's friend was going to bring me the offering I'd need for the other one.

"Can you stop by sometime?" Lorraine's voice, on the phone at Mama's, as casual as if she wanted me to pick up a bunch of forwarded mail that had piled up for me at her house.

"Sure," is all I told her.

I hung up. Walked through the back of Mama's kitchen into the alley, climbed in the Plymouth, and headed over to the place I still thought of as Crystal Beth's safehouse.

I didn't recognize the woman who answered the door downstairs, but she must have been expecting me because she forked over a folded piece of paper and slammed the door in my face.

Under a streetlight, I opened the paper. Just an address. I got back in the Plymouth.

I guess I was expecting a dyke bar, but it turned out to be a little diner—one of those aluminum-sided things—standing right off the Red Hook waterfront like a leftover from the Fifties. Inside, I could see they'd ripped out all the old fixtures and set up a bunch of wooden tables so it looked like a regular restaurant.

The crowd was dressed too good for the neighborhood, but I knew it was only a short drive from Brooklyn Heights and other trendy sections, so I wasn't that surprised—New Yorkers are real adventurous when it comes to eating.

A woman behind the counter saw I was alone and waved her hand in the direction of some empty tables. I took the smallest one I could find—round, with a butcher-block top. I opened the menu and looked around.

I couldn't tell what the game was. The diner was in a borderland, but the clientele was all from one side of the line. Yuppies are major consumers, but most places won't let narcotics in the door. Mama has the same rule, and I never asked why. Could be morals, could be the untrustworthy nature of the traffickers. Or how easily homicide comes into play when you fuck with poppies or powder. It doesn't matter. Truth is, every thief knows, it's not for nothing they call it "dope."

Maybe it was a restaurant for real. A waitress came over, asked if I wanted anything to drink. I asked her for some lemonade by touching it on the menu with my finger. She nodded and moved off.

Then I spotted the big guy in a corner, drawing something. I'd seen him before, in another joint. The one where I'd first met Crystal Beth. He looked over at me, like he was bored from working, giving his eyes a rest. His head moved about a quarter of an inch. I sensed someone just behind my left shoulder, but I didn't look up.

"In the back," a voice said.

I got up, saw the voice belonged to a stocky woman with an expressionless face.

"I'll follow you," I told her.

She shook her head. No.

I walked down a narrow corridor, past the restrooms, to a door marked STORAGE.

"That one," the woman said.

It opened when I turned the knob. I stepped into an empty room. It was absolutely bare, except for a pocket door. I stood there, knowing there was a lens watching from somewhere, my hands open at my sides.

The flat door slid into the wall. I stepped through.

Lorraine was standing there. "Thanks, Trixie," she said to the stocky woman. "You got here quick," she said to me.

"Quick as I could," I answered her.

Then I saw why she had called. Xyla. Sitting by herself in a corner of the room in one of those orthopedic computer chairs they have for people who spend hours in front of the screen. And the screen was huge—looked like a TV instead of a monitor. The entire wall was nothing but cyber-machinery: lights blinking, hard drives whirring, modem connections buzzing and howling . . . searching for openings.

I walked over behind Xyla's chair. The screen in front of her was filled with numbers and letters and symbols, all strung together, like they'd turned an autistic kid loose at the keyboard.

"I got him," Xyla said, not turning around.

"You sure?" I asked her.

"Pretty sure. I got . . . let me check . . ." She hit the keys so fast her fingers were a blur. ". . . four hundred and eighty-eight responses. But most of them were just to the addy—they couldn't even open the message I sent, just wanted to talk, you know. He's got his own home page now, so I figure maybe one of his fans—"

"What's a home page?"

"A website. Like some companies have. You know: www, whatever, dot com? It's a domain. A webmaster runs it, and it's only devoted to one topic. We have . . ." She glanced over her shoulder at Lorraine.

"He knows," Lorraine said. "Crystal Beth told me she told him about ours."

Xyla nodded. "Okay. Anyway, this one isn't actually *his,* okay? I mean, he didn't set it up or anything. And it's not a true domain, just a personal home page. Like a fan page, I guess you'd call it. They're all over the Net. Some cyber-guy thinks a horror writer is hot stuff, so he starts a fan page for him. They usually post a few pictures, maybe some news about upcoming books or appearances. Like that. But the big feature is the message board."

I gave her a puzzled look, but quickly figured out she was just drawing a breath before she went on: "You can leave messages, okay? Sometimes the star . . . or the writer, or the singer, or whoever the cyber-guy set the home page up for . . . actually answers, but that's like a big thing . . . real rare. Usually it's just fans of whoever the home page is for—talking to themselves, you know? Like who should play what character in the movie, like that."

"And this guy has one of these home pages?" I asked her.

"Yeah. In fact, there's about a half-dozen of them. One's even in Japanese."

"And people write to these message boards with stuff for him?"

"Sure. Mostly it's like 'Right on!,' you know? I mean, they're *fans,* right?"

"Of a serial killer?"

"Oh, please," Xyla said. "First of all, that's nothing new. Charles Manson has a website. *Plenty* of people get turned on by serial killers. Go to the movies, read a book—serial killers are hot stuff. But this one, it's . . . different. I figured, at first, it was mostly gay guys writing, just being . . . encouraging, you know? But once he started blasting those child molesters, it's like *everyone's* on his side. You can see it everywhere. They call him HE. For his initials, I guess it meant, once. But now it's like 'he,' understand? Like 'He said so,' see?"

I did see. I'd sure seen

HE RULES!

graffiti'ed all over town. Thought it was another of those religious-nut organizations pasting their crap up the way they always do.

"Anyway, so, I got a bunch of hit-backs, like I said," Xyla went on. "But only three even opened up the encryption, and two of those were *obviously* from geeks."

"How'd you know that?"

" 'Cause it worked just like you said," she replied. "That velociraptor bit. The other two, they started in with *Jurassic Park.* The movie, right? And they wanted me to send them a gif, and—"

"A what?"

"A picture. Digitized photograph. Just wanted to see if I was a boy or a girl, my best guess. So lame . . . like anyone couldn't send someone else's picture. Anyway, I knew it couldn't be them. But this one . . . it's him, I bet. Take a look for yourself."

She hit some keys again. The screen blinked, went all blue, then flicked back into white. Xyla pointed at the lettering:

>>Send proof. One (1) word. No more.<<

"Jesus Christ!" I said. "That *has* to be him. You're right. Can you get an address from what he sent?"

"Not a chance." Xyla laughed. "The guy's *way* ahead of me. It's not just his addy that got nuked, it's the whole ISP."

"Huh?"

"It doesn't matter," she said, an undercurrent of impatience in her voice at having to explain such simple stuff to the older generation. "Look. No, I can't trace it. Nobody could. He built it himself, from scratch. And he's probably got more . . . that he's only going to use one time and do the same thing. It probably only existed for a few seconds. It's gone forever. Very, very slick," she said, admiringly.

"But if you can't find him . . . if his address is gone . . . ?"

"I can't find *him,*" she said. "That's true. And I could *never* find him if I couldn't at least get into the server. I can't believe he actually *built* one just to send one lousy message. He's not just smart, I'll tell you something else about him—he's rich. Whatever he's got, it cost more than all this," she said, sweeping her arm to indicate the bank of machinery in the room, "times a hundred."

"So what do we—?"

"Well, I don't have his address, but he has mine. At least, he did. I nuked it myself, soon as I heard from him, like I told you I would. I figure, we keep playing, right? Send out another message, just like I did before. He must have known what was going to happen. That's why he said 'one word only,' see? I'll put it out there again. He *does* lurk. He'll see it. And, if it works, he'll reply to whatever new addy I send it from, then nuke himself off again, see?"

"Yeah," I told her.

"So," Xyla asked, her fingers poised, "what's the word?"

I told her, playing the only card in my deck, watching the name of the ice-man pop up on the giant screen:

wesley

I tried the radio on the drive over to my place. No music that didn't belong in elevators. No surprise. The all-news station was all-crime. No surprise there either. I tried talk radio. Mistake. Some "expert" was saying depression is America's number-one mental illness. Chump. You want to know about America's number-one mental illness, consult a proctologist.

Pansy was glad to see me anyway.

The next morning was so bright and crisp it made the badlands look pretty through my window. Until you looked close. Like those magazine photos of Tibet. The ones that don't show the Chinese troops.

I thought maybe I'd start looking for the witch I needed, playing it that Nadine's friend would come through. Then I realized . . . I didn't know anything about the witch but her name. The name they gave her, and the name she took for herself. I knew her daughter's name . . . but that kid would be a teenager by now. She could have moved. Disappeared, even. The only one I could have asked was the guy who got me involved with her in the first place. Julio. The one she watched die, gleeful witchfire crackling in her eyes. I still had her phone number, but it had been so long. . . .

I thought it through. Nothing. Then I worked with the singing bowl Max had given me. I never wondered why he had such a thing himself. Max can't hear, but I know he can feel vibrations—better than anyone else I know. So, when he held it in his hands, maybe . . .

Pansy liked the sound too. I was getting pretty good at it. When I came back around, I made the decision. If she was still there, okay. If not, I'd try and trace her through her daughter. But I wasn't going to open that coffin unless I had something to ask for.

So I went back to waiting.

Part of the waiting was sex I had with a girl named Lois. I wasn't looking for her—she just turned up in a place I was and we went back to her apartment. If the action had been in a movie, the critics would have called the whole scene gratuitous.

"Just like old times," she said, when we were finished.

That was the truth. She'd greeted me with "Hello, stranger," and that's the way I left.

I stayed down in the whisper-stream, sifting and sorting, looking for anything that could get me what I needed. That "message-board" thing Xyla told me about was nothing new. It works that way down here too. At the intersection of a few wires, I picked a rumble from a finger—someone who sets up jobs but never does them himself. Some fingers are amateurs—cable-repair guys, utility company workers, deliverymen—anyone who gets access to a house and has a chance to look around, check the security, see if there's a dog, anything worth stealing, like that. But this particular guy was a pro, and he only fingered big jobs. An armored car, this one was supposed to be. And the finger didn't just have the route, he had an inside man. A driver who wanted a piece of whatever haul he got "robbed" of—willing to take a few good knocks to make it look real too, and guaranteed to hold his end of the take for no less than five years before spending a penny. Sounded like gold. Unless you listened close. The way I saw it, the finger had finally gotten popped himself. And instead of diming out people who'd worked opportunities he'd pointed out in the past, the cops were using him to catch the crew who'd been doing cowboy jobs on armored cars all over the East Coast the past year or so. The cowboys didn't seem all that organized—they'd just cut off the armored car with their own jalopy, jump out wearing ski masks and body armor, rake a full-auto burst across the windshield to get the driver's attention, then hold up a grenade . . . high, so the driver could see what would happen if he didn't open up. Sometimes they scored—one take was near a million—sometimes they struck out. In fact, the one driver they killed was piloting an empty truck, on his way back from a dropoff. So the FBI probably figured the hijackers for some of the White Night crowd, refinancing their coffers after so many of them had been captured last year.

I thought the feds were wasting their time. The guys they were looking for weren't even pros themselves, so they wouldn't be tuned in. No working pro would care if a pack of Nazi asshole amateurs went down, but the finger was marked lousy now. No matter how it played out, he was done.

I didn't know if Lincoln was bugging Davidson for "progress-report" crap, but it wouldn't matter. We already had his money, and Davidson wouldn't even bother telling me about things like that.

The more I thought about it, the more I figured this Homo Erectus guy was already well away. It had only been a couple of weeks—not enough to make the fag-bashers brave again, sure—but he hadn't done his bit for a while, so he could be anywhere.

Maybe I was right about that. Maybe it was the other stuff that brought him back. Maybe he never left.

The other stuff was copycat. It started small: A child molester just released from prison had his address published in the paper—seems he decided the only suitable housing he could find was about a hundred yards from a kids' school. Some people paid him a visit one night. And lit a fire. It was an amateur arson, but good enough to total the house. And if the freak hadn't moved fast, he'd have been barbecued.

I knew it wasn't the killer's work. So did the cops, I was sure. But the papers didn't. And they started playing it up again.

Smart fucking move. A while back, the papers decided to do a series on the Bloods. Not the real-thing, L.A. gangsta Bloods, this was about the East Coast version—a few guys who got together in the joint, awarded themselves OG status and started talking the talk. Probably began in response to the Latin Kings and the Netas—two Hispanic gangs who formed themselves Inside for protection, the same way it always starts. But the balance had shifted. Rikers Island was more Hispanic than black now. If the Latino gangs had joined forces, they could have ruled. Naturally, that didn't happen. When I was Upstate, it was usually black against white, with the Latins trying to stay out of the crossfire. Now it was the whites' turn to play that role. The papers did what they usually do: interview some "spokesman" and print it all like it was gospel.

Next thing was a wave of random slashings all over the city. Usually box-cutter jobs, usually to the face. Word was that you had to cut someone to be a Blood, and all these dumb-fuck kids wanted to be in . . . so they went out slicing. And when the cops responded to the media with their usual sweep-arrest thing, they scooped a lot of nasty little weasels, but no real Bloods.

The Bloods found out the wannabes were even imitating the triangular cigarette burns that proved you were in. And so they started issuing more press releases, working the pay phones in the jailhouses to call the newspapers collect, disclaiming any responsibility for the slashings, warning the wannabes they'd be "dealt with" as soon as they came Inside. And as long as they were on the line with the press, they couldn't pass up the opportunity to dump on their Hispanic counterparts.

So the Latin Kings demanded equal time. And the newspapers were eager to comply. Each reporter dutifully printed the usual rant about how the gangs were community-improvement and racial-pride organizations. Sure, they could *be* violent, if they were forced to, but their purpose wasn't crime, it was . . . uh, you know, political.

Sure. The papers, especially the columnists, provided a perfect forum for the Bloods and the Kings to death-diss each other publicly. All the leaders ended up in total lockdown, but the slashing continued Inside. And the publicity only got more kids wanna-being.

The Mayor pledged to wipe out the new scourge, convinced that winning the last election against the lamest candidate the Democrats had come up with in half a century made him a national model for city management. Yeah. Like the ATMs in New York City strip bars are proof of our "economic revival."

Sure enough, the cops started finding Crips too. No, not the Compton Crips. This crew was mostly crack dealers flying colors.

Perfect. Now you had Hispanic kids approaching black kids, asking, "You a Blood?" and slashing away no matter what the answer. You had some kids afraid to wear red or blue, while others proudly flew the colors without the credentials, risking attack from both sides.

So, when the freak's house got burned down, it wasn't a big surprise that whoever wrote to the papers bragging about doing it signed off with "HE Rules!" Not pretending to *be* him, just *with* him.

Then the gates opened again.

The first four seemed unrelated at first. A stockbroker in his twenties, a middle-aged manager of the service desk at a car dealership, an unemployed guy who lived alone but wasn't on welfare, and a woman who had once run a day-care center on the West Coast.

They all had two things in common. Each had been shot in the head at close range, in their own home. The papers weren't saying, but the implication was that it was the same weapon too.

The other common denominator was computers—they'd all been involved in freakish cyber-stuff.

The stockbroker and the unemployed guy were after boys, haunting the chat rooms. The manager liked little girls. They didn't find any evidence that he did any more than collect pictures of them. He was trading the pictures too. But if the cops learned the identity of any of the kids in the photos, they weren't saying.

The woman was looking for "models." Said she ran an agency, and promised girls big bucks for a few hours' work. All she wanted was teens or younger. "Hairless" was her favorite description for the merchandise. One exchange the cops pulled off her computer's hard drive was between her and a twelve-year-old who'd already been "posing" for a year. The girl had a little sister, and was negotiating a price for her, seeing her own market value dropping with age, moving up to agent status.

This time, as soon as he spoke up, the papers didn't wait to print what he had to say.

> Impostors beware! I do not seek converts. I am a hunter, not an evangelist. Those last four were all targeted for their crimes against gays, lesbians, and bisexuals. A warning here: I am well aware that two of the targets met their victims through so-called "homosexual" chat rooms. This perversion will not be tolerated. Anyone who links homosexuality to pedophilia will be dealt with. *Anyone.* The other two were dispatched because their conduct fuels the fires of discrimination and violence against us. Finally, no crimes are to be committed in my name. None. Should my name be linked, in any way, to an incident of

violence, the perpetrators will be viewed as antithetical to my mission. For all I know, the pedophile whose house was burned was targeted because of a misperception that he was "homosexual." I have gone to great lengths to disabuse the world of the notion that molestation of children is "homosexual" even if committed by perpetrators of the same gender as the victim. That myth is homophobic. Homophobia breeds gay-bashing. And gay-bashing now brings death. The equation is simple. The rules have been explained. Unless a public disavowal of self-identification as "homosexual" by major pedophile organizations is forthcoming within the next two weeks, escalation will occur.

So he was here. In the city. Had to be. No way to do all those close-up hits without having someplace local to disappear into.

I spent a lot of time thinking. Almost like being back Inside. Only I wasn't thinking about getting out, I was focused on getting in. Into him.

He wasn't a chess player, not that kind of killer. No, he played outside the lines. *Made* the rules. So I went outside the lines myself. Off the chessboard. Considered what nobody seemed to be thinking about: All we had was the letters. And the murders. Did it have to be a man? Or even *one* man? There was nothing to show one man *couldn't* have done everything he'd pulled off . . . no simultaneous murders in different parts of town, nothing like that. The letters were all in the same voice. No question about that. As distinctive as a fingerprint—egotistically individualized beyond the ability of any group-composition effort, no matter how shared their rhetoric. And too concise to be group work anyway. But if he did have partners, he'd know how to keep that off the screen.

And why respond to that "velociraptor" bait at all if he didn't want to . . . what? He already had the biggest forum anyone could hope for. All the newspapers published his letters the minute they came in, usually on the front page. I knew they were translated into other languages too. Fan pages on the Internet. He wasn't threatening anyone if they *didn't* publish, like that Unabomber maniac. He didn't have a fucking "manifesto" he wanted in print. And he sure as hell wasn't looking for a book-and-movie deal.

I couldn't make it work. But I had to work *from* someplace, so I settled on three assumptions: he was working solo; he was based here; he was willing to talk to me if I was the real thing—not a cop, from the other side of the line.

And if Wesley's name didn't prove that to him, I was out of luck.

A few days passed. And when the pedophile organizations didn't produce the public statements he wanted, didn't admit they were not "gay," but just child molesters, he went even farther off the board.

"KIDDIE SEX TOUR" PLANE EXPLODES OVER PACIFIC!

Some version of that headline blazed across the front page of every paper in the world. For once, the TV networks were ahead in the race—this time they had footage, and video beats print every time. But the footage wasn't much . . . mostly of the futile rescue efforts.

There had been no irregular communication from the plane just before it vanished from the radar screens. No warning, no hint. No nothing.

But though nobody expected a bombing, the anchorman made it clear that his network had known about the flights for a while. I tuned in somewhere in the middle of his somber-voiced speech:

> At the time of the crash, our In-Depth Investigative Team had already been working on the shocking story of "kiddie-sex tourism" in Southeast Asia. The changing economic climate in that region has paralleled a change in child prostitution practices. Thailand was originally considered the worst offender, but Thai brothels are now largely staffed with women and children brought across the border from Myanmar, while Goa, Sri Lanka, and especially the Philippines are all significant purveyors. The ID Team has learned that the charter service, which

> had advertised under the name "Budding Blossoms," has been in operation for several years. We now go to Mary Jo Sanstrom, on board a SEATO vessel which is part of the search-and-rescue operation. Mary Jo . . .

A woman wearing a khaki jumpsuit and a camouflage cap standing against a backdrop of endless sea . . .

> John, there are no apparent survivors of the devastating explosion. The activity you see behind me has been under way for several hours, but we are told the search is now concentrated on recovering the black box, although helicopters are continuing to work close to the ocean surface, hoping against hope. The passengers had all apparently purchased "package deals," the specifics of which are not known at this time. However, UN-agency sources state bluntly that the tours were exclusively for pedophiles who wanted sexual access to child prostitutes in an environment free of danger from prosecution.

They cut away to a tall, lanky man with a beard and glasses, standing in the middle of a small office with haphazard piles of books everywhere. He looked like a professor. Talked like one too:

> Sure, the government says that child prostitution is illegal, and claims that offenders are always prosecuted to the full extent of the law. But virtually every international agency concerned with the protection of children from sexual exploitation has debunked those claims. Indeed, there is plenty of printed material explicitly advertising "safe" sex with children in . . .

The camera quickly played over the glossy covers of some brochures. Just glimpses—a little girl licking a lollypop; a little boy running on the beach, naked, his back to the camera—the lens furtive and guilty, knowing it was lingering too long as the professor kept right on talking:

> . . . those countries. Some of these so-called "tour" companies offer "guidebooks," while others offer "on-site services" which means . . .

The camera snuck another look at images on a computer monitor, this time blurring out the details.

Then back to the anchor:

> But not everyone is convinced that operations such as "Budding Blossoms" actually deliver what they promise. . . .

As his words trailed off, they segued to an outdoor taped interview, with some disheveled-looking little guy who claimed to be the "coordinator" for various groups "exposing" the kiddie-sex tours as a scam. He babbled about how anyone going to the Philippines looking for sex with a child was going to end up in jail. Claimed all the "exposés" about kiddie-sex tourism were actually encouraging freaks to go there. Whoever was editing the tape cut him off in the middle of a stumbling rant about his "authenticated" website and replaced him with a young Asian woman with harsh eyes who called him a fraud:

> If it's such a scam, how come that charter service has been running so long and so successfully? The reason that flight was full was because so many previous flights had gone so "well" for those degenerates. They live by word-of-mouth. Why don't you pull the passenger manifest? I'll bet you find it shows the name of plenty of repeat customers.

Then back to the anchorman, live:

> Although law-enforcement sources have not released the manifest to which Ms. Hong referred, the ID Team has obtained a copy, and airline sources confirm that many of the passengers on Flight 0677 were, indeed, repeat customers. And we *have* learned that a number of those on board had criminal records involving sexual abuse of children. However, the essential mystery now is what caused the plane to spontaneously explode. Stay tuned to this station for updates as they occur. . . .

Turned out they didn't need the black box. Or even an investigation. He did all that for them. His message was front-page everywhere.

> Warnings were issued. And duly ignored. Consequences were promised. And duly delivered. I now utilize this forum for three distinct reasons, each of potential value to apparently disparate but occasionally interlocking constituencies of interest.
>
> (1) Flight 0677 was deliberately destroyed. It was neither accident nor negligence. I most sincerely recommend neither conspiracy theorists nor lawyer feeding-frenzies be tolerated by the media or the public.
>
> (2) There were no "innocents" killed. Collaborators are subject to the same punishment as principal actors. You are now on notice as to the rules of engagement. For those of you who fail to comprehend such argot, I will simplify: If you aid, abet, facilitate, or even transport others to the scene where children are sexually exploited, you are a target. The same rules, including the collaborative crime of harboring the enemy, apply, of course, to gay-bashing.
>
> (3) The mass execution was made possible only by the volitional act of a thief. One on board Flight 0677. The methodology was as follows: An obviously expensive, alligator-bound world atlas measuring approximately 5 × 9 × 3″ and containing elaborate, full-color maps on silk-shot paper with numerous pull-outs, a compartment for holding personal papers, and other indicia of extreme cost (including, but not limited to, 18-karat gold corner clips and ribbon markers) was "left" in the Men's Room at LAX. The specific Men's Room was located just outside the gate area to Flight 0677. The person who stole the book was specifically and actually monitored. Had a passenger *not* booked on that flight taken the book, he would have been intercepted. Needless to say, the person who did take the book did *not* turn it in to the authorities, but simply pocketed his prize. That prize contained, in addition to the above-described contents, a sufficient amount of plastic explosive to

> blow out a considerable portion of the airplane, guaranteeing its inability to remain aloft. The timing mechanism was set so that, even allowing for deviation caused by weather or intruding flight patterns from other aircraft, the explosion would occur over water, limiting the damage to those on board. I commend to your attention this simple method of destroying aircraft. Any half-baked terrorist could have duplicated my feat, not targeting any particular flight but claiming responsibility as soon as the explosion occurred. As such "packages" will pass through existing scanners without incident, any dedicated, competent individual willing to play the odds with the requisite patience *will* succeed. The only method of defense against such eventualities is for those who "find" property to turn it over to the proper authorities. I believe it is safe to state that such activity is highly likely to increase in the immediate future. Consider this (still another) public service.
>
> This time, he only signed his initials.

But that still didn't mean he had a partner. There had been more than enough space between the last murders here and the flight out of L.A. for him to have made the trip with ease.

It did tell me one thing. Whatever he looked like, it wouldn't be remarkable. He was a blender, a natural camouflage man. He wasn't obese, he wasn't flashy, he wasn't . . . Sure, he wasn't anything but white either.

Yeah, *that* narrowed it down. The guy I just described, he could be me.

I was at Mama's when she called.

"I have it," she said. And hung up.

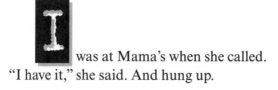

It was almost three in the morning when she'd called, so I was outside her apartment house in fifteen minutes. I didn't like the doorman eyeballing me more than once, but I didn't see a way around it either. If he thought it was unusual for someone to be calling at that hour, he didn't show it . . . just rang up and got the okay for me to enter the elevator.

She must have been right at the peephole—the door opened even as I raised my knuckles to rap. The rose lighting was back on. Otherwise, the place was shrouded. "Go sit down," she told me, standing aside.

I gave up trying to solve the mystery of her three chairs and just took the middle one, letting her play any way she wanted.

She looked ghostly, floating across the room toward me. Barefoot, in a gauzy white robe that wrapped her body—a frame, not a cover. She took the nearest open chair, reached over, and pulled mine around so we were facing each other.

"I believe you," she said.

"Which means . . . ?"

"I believe you wouldn't . . . do what you said. I believe you . . . Oh, never mind. Look, here it is, okay? She . . . asked around. Like you said. I don't know about this 'theory' of yours, but you're right about one thing—they have the men who did that drive-by."

"Have them?"

"*Found* them, I should have said. They're dead. And one of the people killed in the crowd—you were right about that too. The police think it was murder. I mean, deliberate murder. The rest was only for . . . what do you call it? Camouflage? I don't know. But the cops say it was business. Professional business. They think they know who gave the order. That's what you want, right?"

"That's what I want."

"Well, I have it," she said.

"But you want to play with it first? Or you want me to place a fucking bid? What?"

"Why are you so . . . hostile?" she asked softly. "I've been nice to you. It was fun . . . flirting, right? I know you liked it."

"We've already been there," I told her.

"You *really* hate them, don't you?" she said, leaning so close I could feel her breath.

"Who?"

"Child molesters."

"Who doesn't?" I said, sloughing it off, staying clear of whatever was lightning-bolting around the rose-lit room.

"You should spend more time where I do," she said, an ugly undertone to her soft voice. "And you *said* to ask. You said it was okay. You *told* me to do it."

"What are you talking about?"

"My . . . friend. The cops. All that. It was easy, she said. They all . . . a lot of them anyway . . . they know you. Or about you, at least. I even know about those murders—the ones in the South Bronx."

"Jesus Christ, *that's* the kind of sorry two-bit rumor your pal came up with? That story's a fucking fossil."

"I know what you think," she said, sliding the gauzy robe off her shoulders. "You think I'm trying to get you to . . . admit something, right?"

"That's why you keep taking your clothes off? So I'll see you're not wearing a wire?" I laughed at her.

I could see her face flush. Or maybe it was just the reflected light.

"I'm just more . . . comfortable this way," she told me. "I don't like clothes. I don't like people to wear clothes. It's another thing to hide behind."

"Yeah, sure. You spend half your life in a gym, you've got a beef with *clothes*? You're more confident without your clothes, that's all. Because you're an overmatch against most everyone else that way."

"I'll bet I'd be with you."

"No contest," I acknowledged.

"You don't want to play at all, do you?"

"No."

"Why not?"

"I'm not a player."

"What does that mean? You don't have sex unless you're in love?"

"No. It means I smoke cigarettes but I don't light them with sticks of dynamite."

"You don't trust me?"

"I'd have to upgrade a cubic ton to *dis*trust you," I told her, keeping my voice level. "You got me over here because you said you had what I wanted. Instead of giving it to me, you start asking me about some murders I'm supposed to have committed. I tell you I don't want to fuck you," I said, dropping my voice, letting a harder tone bleed through, "you tell me I'm a liar. I told you before: Behavior is the truth. What's the game? I say: 'Sure, you've got a body that would get a rise in a morgue,' and you say, 'Well, *you're* not getting any of it'? Would that make you happy? Is that your game? Okay, I'll pay that much, if that's what it takes. You're a gorgeous woman."

"But . . . ?"

"But you can't get juice from marble," I told her.

"What does that mean?"

"How many different ways you want me to say it? You've got a stake in this. Not the same one Lincoln and those other guys have. Yeah, I know, you told me: You 'love' this guy. And you just want to protect him, right? Sure, fine. I'll buy it, that's what you want. And I played right along, didn't I? You think I'd turn him over to the cops for a pass on one of my own cases, then don't help. But you already *did* that, right? Checked me out. Found out some stuff. Enough to convince you that, whatever else I am, I'm not a rat. So here I am. And what do I get? Another strip show. More of your stupid teasing. And some questions about . . . bullshit crap that couldn't be your business."

"How do you know?"

"What?"

"How do you know it isn't my business? All right, I shouldn't have said what I said. It was stupid. I'll tell you what she . . . my friend . . . told me. She said there was a . . . cult or something. Or maybe just a ring of perverts. They were making torture films. Of little kids getting raped. The cops were looking for them, all over. There'd been a murder . . . a baby's murder. It all got confused. But this is what they know for sure: They were all in a house. In the South Bronx, like I said. Some people went into that house and killed them. Every one of them. And they, the cops, they all say it was you. Your work. My friend asked, if they thought you did all that, how come you'd never even been arrested for it? You know what they said? They said they didn't have any proof but it was the kind of thing Burke would do. They said you're a homicidal maniac when it comes to . . . them."

I heard Wesley's machine voice in my head. "Every time one of those diddlers gets done, your name comes up on the radar screen.

Killing people, it's a business. You start making it personal, you're dead meat yourself."

I went with it and used it. Like I always do when Wesley talks to me. "Look, it's no secret that I hate those freaks," I told her. "But the rest of it, that's just lazy-ass cop-speak for 'We can't find who really did it, so we'll just chalk it up to Burke.' How many people was I supposed to have killed, anyway? Couple a hundred?"

"No," she said, her voice soft and serious. "But a lot. A lot more than were in that house, too."

"And you believe that?"

She reached over and put her hand on the inside of my thigh. It didn't feel sexual . . . more like she was checking for a pulse. "Yes," she said. "I believe it. And this Wesley . . . he helped you, too."

"Wesley's dead," I told her. Seemed like that's all I'd *been* telling people for a while. "Didn't your cop pal tell you that?"

"Yes. She told me about it."

"All about it?"

"I . . . think so. Why?"

"You're ready to do something for me, to trust me, because you believe I killed a bunch of baby-rapers, right? That's your story. *Today's* story, anyway. If you know how Wesley died, you know he didn't go out alone."

"I know what he did. That . . . explosion. At the school."

"And who died in that?" I put it to her. "Kids, right? Lots and lots and lots of kids. You hate baby-rapers, you want to help me because I do too. You think I did a bunch of killings. You think Wesley was my partner. If that was true, then my 'partner' killed more kids in a few minutes than any of those freaks could do in ten lifetimes."

Her eyes did that flicker-thing again. Not blinking—a light going on and off. It was over in a second. She took a deep breath. Not showing off this time—like she needed strength.

"Maybe he had his reasons," she said.

"To kill kids?"

"Yes."

"You pay your shrink by the hour or do you get a volume discount?"

"I don't have a shrink," Nadine said. "I don't need one. I know what I need. And you have it."

"I already said—"

"Stop! I'm not playing either. Just listen. The man the cops think ordered that murder—of the gay guy in the park—is someone named Gutterball Felestrone. And the name of the man who was killed is Lonnie Cork. 'Corky' is what they called him." She took a deep, shuddering breath. Let it out. Looked directly into my eyes. "And the man Felestrone hired was your friend. Wesley."

I waited, not wanting to cut her off if she had anything more. But she was done. She looked exhausted, as if saying those few words had wasted her.

"Okay," I told her, starting to stand up.

She jumped to her feet and shoved me with both hands against my chest. I fell backward into the middle chair, Nadine on top of me. "Don't even think about it," she said into my ear. "You promised! You said if I got that information for you I could be in on it."

My hand went to her back, fingers searching for the spot on her spine that would stop her cold if she ended up acting as crazy as she was talking.

"You *will* be in on it," I said calmly. "What you just got was a piece of the puzzle. Maybe, I can't even be sure about that. And it's a *big* puzzle, girl. You think you were gonna just throw some clothes on and come with me? Right now?"

She grabbed the sides of the chair with both hands and pulled, hard, jamming her body into mine so deep I had to turn my head to breathe. "You think what you want," she said into my ear. "You do what you want, too. But when you meet him, I have to be there. That's our deal. Nothing else. Nothing less. Understand?"

"How could I guarantee—?"

"He *is* going to meet you," she hissed at me. "I know it. I'm trusting you. What I told you . . . it might make it happen. And I'm going to be there. So that nothing happens to him, understand?"

"Yeah, sure. I got it. He's the one man in the world you want to fuck, so—"

She punched me in the face so fast and hard that I didn't have a chance to get my hand up. But I stabbed a two-finger kite deep into her heavily muscled rib cage before she could do it again. She gasped and slid off me.

"You dirty fucking *pig*!" she snarled at me from the floor. "I would *never* . . ."

My mouth tasted bloody. Some of it probably sprayed on her

when I bent down to tell her: "Don't ever do that again. What did you think, you insane bitch? We were gonna handcuff ourselves together until this is over?"

"You better not—"

"Don't threaten me," I said. "Far as I'm concerned, you're with them. You were there when the deal was made. If I *do* get this guy to meet me, you can be there. And then I'm gone. Whatever you do after that, it's on you. I'll be all square then. Earned the money, right?"

She didn't answer.

"Right?" I asked her again, shoving my face within inches of hers.

She didn't flinch. Locked eyes with me for a long few seconds. "All right," she finally said.

The whole crazy scene hadn't taken long. There was enough of the night left for me to reach out for a woman who loved the dark.

It had been, what? Six, seven years. But this was her time. If the number was still good . . .

I found a pay phone and pushed the buttons, remembering you needed an area code to reach Queens from Manhattan now. It rang only twice before it was picked up.

"Hhhmmm?" is what it sounded like. It was enough.

"It's me," I said.

"I knew you would come."

"I—"

"I know," she said in her witchy voice. "Now, yes?"

"Yes."

"Come," she whispered.

I was driving through a time warp. Nothing had changed. The same car, the same streets. And, when the Plymouth's headlights picked it out, the same house. I drove around to the back, the way I always had. The garage door was closed. The house was dark. I got out, walked to the back door.

It opened while I was still on my way. She was wearing a red slip dress the exact same shade as her flaming hair. Even the spike heels and the lipstick matched. As if she'd had years to shop for this minute.

"Hello, Jina," I said.

She stepped in to me, her face in my neck, hands locked around me. "Say my name," she whispered. "My real name. You didn't come for Jina. She's not for you."

"Strega," I said.

She cooed, licked the side of my face like a cat. A silk-tongued cat, but one with fangs and claws. Then she turned and grabbed my hand, leading me through the house to that ice sculpture of a living room I'd spent so much time in. Terror time. The chair was still there, too. She pulled my jacket off my shoulders. I sat down. She went off somewhere. I closed my eyes.

"Here," she said. On her knees next to the chair, holding my cigarettes and matches.

I lit the smoke, blew a jet out my nose.

"You look the same," I told her.

"I will always look the same to you," she said. "You know that. But that's not what you came for. I know you. Tell me what you want."

"It's a long story. How much of it do you—?"

She climbed into my lap, snuggled against me. "Remember what we did, right in this chair?" she asked softly.

"Yes. How could I—?"

"Forget? I don't know. You're a man. I don't know what men forget. I know what *I* don't forget. You saved my Mia. You found Scotty's picture. And you made that . . . filth dead. While I watched. I sleep with you inside me. Not inside my heart. You don't want my heart. Not the part of it that's left. That's only for Mia."

Mia was her daughter. That's how I'd met Strega. She was being threatened. By some freak who'd been watching her jog in the nearby park, saying he was going to do something to her child if she didn't . . . do what he wanted. Julio remembered me from the joint, and he called, gave me the job. He didn't want it done by the Family, so he needed a mercenary. One he could trust, is what he said. Made sense.

There wasn't much to the job. Max and I found the freak. We hurt him. He didn't like pain. We promised him much more if he ever came near the woman again. He never did.

But then it whirlpooled. Her daughter had a pal, a little kid named Scotty. And somebody in a clown suit had taken a Polaroid of Scotty being raped. Scotty thought they had captured his soul, and his therapist couldn't convince him otherwise. Strega hired me to get that picture back. And she helped too. Witch's help. We had sex in this chair. She didn't want to use anything but her mouth. And I had to tell her she was a good girl every time she was done. I should have known then, but I was too focused on staying alive. The maggot who had taken Scotty's picture was half of a husband-and-wife team. And they'd hired muscle—a White Night gang I knew from Inside. I had to walk that tightrope. Then I had to sit in a room with a human so foul that killing him would have given me an orgasm. And listen while he spooled out evil, showing me how pedophiles computer-networked their traffic in trophies . . . pictures of raped babies. It ended in murder and arson. Later, two more fires: one in Strega's hands as she burned the Polaroid I'd found in front of Scotty; one in her eyes as she told me the truth about her Uncle Julio.

It was years later when that score got squared. The vicious old gangster had used me once and gotten away with it, but he went to the well once too often. He started it with Wesley, then he couldn't make it stop. So he tried to middle me, figuring the ice-man would kill the messenger and forget the message. But it was Julio who went down—his neck broken on a bench near La Guardia, Strega watching from the car as it happened.

I don't know how she did some of the things she did. But I knew her word was platinum, her heart was steel, and her touch terrifying.

So I told her the truth.

"I still don't understand," she said when I was finished. "You already have the money, yes?"

"Yes."

"So . . . Ah, it's the woman. This woman. Your woman. The one who got killed?"

"I . . . think so."

"You're a very religious man, aren't you, Burke? It's always in you. This isn't for love. Did you love her?"

"I . . . guess I did."

"But you can't bring her back, no matter what you—"

"Did you ever hear anything about . . . a Gatekeeper?"

"Oh God, not *that* thing. Yes, you crazy, dangerous man, I've 'heard.' Do you believe it?"

"No. I just—"

"It's only for the evil," she said softly. "Or those who *did* evil. It's from the same root. The revenge root. Are you saying you loved an evil woman? Is that why you came to me?"

"No. She wasn't evil. The opposite."

"So even if there is a Gatekeeper, what good would it do you?"

"None, I guess. I just . . . heard about it. And I thought I'd ask you."

"Want me to kiss you?" she asked, hand drifting into my lap.

"No."

"I know you don't. But someone made that mistake, didn't they? With a lot less evidence than this, huh?" she whispered, flicking her long thumbnail just under the head of my cock. The response was a match in gasoline, but she just kept holding me, gently, waiting for an answer.

"Yes. That happened."

"Some woman thought you wanted her, but you didn't?"

"Yes."

"And she's involved too?"

"I . . . think so."

"But she doesn't know you?"

"No."

"Know how *I* know? That she doesn't know you?"

"No."

She grabbed my cock around the shaft, squeezed hard, made one of her little sounds deep in her throat. "I asked you what you wanted. That never works on you. It hurts you to say you want something. Anything. So you never say. But if *I* asked *you* . . . if I said, 'Could I?' you would have said something different, huh?"

I didn't answer. It was like it always was with her. She frightened me past fear.

"Some men like to be asked. Begged, even. If I got down on my knees and begged, would you like that?"

"No."

"Why wouldn't you? It would be a very pretty sight, wouldn't it?"

"Sarcasm isn't pretty," I told her.

"Ummmm," she moaned. "I don't beg, and you don't take orders. It's so hard, huh?" She squeezed my cock again, chuckling, enjoying her magic tricks. Like always.

"You want to know why I came?" I asked her.

"You want me to stop playing with you?"

"No. It feels . . . nice. I just want . . . something else. Like I said."

"You can have it," she promised, breath soft against my face. "Whatever it is. You know that."

"The way this started—the drive-by—I learned some things about that. It was a hit. Somebody was deliberately taken out, the rest of it was just cover. The guy who ordered the hit was Gutterball Felestrone. The dead man was Lonnie Cork . . . 'Corky,' they called him."

"So? Gutterball's with the Donatelli crew. And they're part of the—"

"Yeah, I know all that. Listen for a minute, okay? The way I heard it, when Gutterball made the . . . arrangements, it was on the phone. And the guy he thought he was talking to—the hit man—it was Wesley."

"Wesley's—"

"Right. But he's the key to all this."

"How could he be, my poor baby? All Wesley is, is a ghost. A rumor. People talk about him in the street like he was a god, but he was a killer, that's all."

"That's not all he was," I told her. "I know. I know . . . him. We came up together."

She nibbled at the carotid artery in my neck, waiting.

"Look," I said, "here's what I need to know: Is it true? All *I* got is a handful of rumor. I don't even know if the stuff about Gutterball is the real thing. Maybe it's just cop-talk bullshit."

"Ah. *That's* what you came for, isn't it?"

"Yes."

"But you could find out some other—"

"I don't think so," I said. "Or I would have."

"Are you afraid?" she asked me.

"I'm always afraid," I told her.

"I know. I didn't mean . . . that. I mean . . . this. *Of* this. *You* don't think Wesley's alive, right?"

"Right."

"Because, you know, it's true, some say he's not gone. That he never died. That he's still . . . working. Some even think he's the one doing all this . . . killing now."

"But not you."

"No. If Wesley was still here, I'd know it."

"Will you do it?"

"I already said I would. But you have to trade."

"Trade what? First you say you'll—"

"I swore I would always protect you," she hissed, "and I will. But you have to let me do it my way. My way, the way I know. I'll get what you want—it won't be hard. I have all the wires. But I need something . . . need you to do something."

"What?"

"I need you in me. I need to taste you. So sweet. It banishes the . . . I'm not going to tell you. I want to taste you again."

"All right."

"Yes. And I want her too. I want to see her."

"Who?"

"This woman who doesn't know you."

"Why would you—"

"Ssshhh," she said, holding her fingers against my lips. "You don't ask now. Two things. For what you want. Will you do them? Do them both?"

"Yes," I told her.

"Do one now," she said, her mouth dropping onto me.

Pansy and I watched first light come, sitting together. I wondered if I'd ever watch it come with a woman next to me. I knew Strega would do whatever she promised. She was a woman without boundaries, but she hated liars. In her mind, "they" were all liars. I knew who "they" were. . . . It was a secret she'd shared with me, and I never with her, but we were the same. She knew I lied. Knew it was part of what I did. But I didn't lie to her, and I guess that kept the wolfpack of her witchery at bay.

I remembered one of the first things the Prof taught me Inside. "Nothing be strong if it don't play long, Schoolboy. Insistent, persistent, and *con*sistent, that's the train you got to ride."

I didn't know why I was doing this anymore.

"You go there, now, okay?"

"Where, Mama?"

"Girl who eat here call. Her place. Now, okay?"

"I'm rolling," I told her.

Broad daylight, but I moved the Plymouth through the badlands without attracting even a glance. Just another rustbucket on its way to one of the dozens of bootleg, no-license repair joints in that part of Bordertown—no big thing.

Mama had to mean the same place I'd found Xyla the last time. But I thought they wouldn't open until it was time for the supper crowd.

Sure enough, when I pulled into the parking lot, it was deserted.

I got out, unsure of myself. But before I could make a move, Trixie came out a side door I didn't know was there, and made a waving motion at me. I walked over to where she was standing, as evenly balanced as if she was tuned to the earth's rotation. The way Max stood.

Xyla was at her computer chair, but the screen was blank in front of her.

"It's the screen-saver," she said over her shoulder by way of explanation. "He came back. There's a file. But I haven't opened it. Wait a minute, and you'll see what I mean."

She tapped some keys. The screen came to life. "It was all encrypted, but this is as far as I went," she said. On the screen, I saw:

> Your ID accepted. Dialogue will now commence. A file is attached. *Warning!* If any attempt is made to copy this file, to print it, or to enter it in any way, it will vanish. Further, be advised that it will appear in chroma-blue, rendering it impossible to photograph. Further, understand that, once opened, it will remain on screen only long enough to be read at an appropriate speed. It will then vanish. When it disappears, you will be required to furnish certain information in order to see the next transmission. I estimate approximately twelve (12) transmissions before you have viewed the total. The transmissions were originally not intended for publication until my death. However, I am now prepared for that death, metaphorically speaking. And I expect you to aid therein. All will become clear as you read. I am certain whoever sent the original contact messages on your behalf will tell you that there is no technological means to determine if other individuals view the screen along with you. This same individual will tell you that my own expertise in this area far exceeds their own. View the following *alone*. It is for your eyes only. When the screen clears, you may summon your confederate(s), as some cyber-communication will be required. When ready, open the attached file.

"You want me to open it?" Xyla asked.

"If I understand him right, something's going to show up then? Something I can read?"

"Yeah. But not copy. Or even take a picture of. You have to scroll down, like this," she showed me, tapping an arrow key, "to read it. Better do it pretty quick—I don't know what 'appropriate' reading speed means to someone like him, but I can guarantee, if you try and scroll backward, you're gonna lose it all, understand?"

"Yeah."

"Okay. When you're ready, just hit this key," she said, pointing. Then she got up and left the room, leaving me alone.

I took a deep breath. Lit a cigarette, grateful for the empty ashtray someone had placed right next to Xyla's machine table. Then I hit the key. The screen danced for a good long minute, then it turned white. Words popped up—in some shade of blue I'd never seen before.

Any moderately discerning individual could deconstruct the failures of Leopold and Loeb simply through perusal of the tabloids of that era. Yellow journalism notwithstanding, there *was* no "Leopold and Loeb." There was a "Leopold," and there was a "Loeb." The media created the illusion of "oneness." Ironically, that illusion originated in a delusion of the participants. A shared delusion. Folie à deux, the psychiatrists call it.

[Of course, these are the self-same psychiatrists who call child molestation "pedophilia." That same flock of politically driven sheep who change their own bible—the Diagnostic and Statistical Manual of Mental Disorders . . . or, as they term it so worshipfully, the "DSM"—as the dictates of grantsmanship command. At one time, they characterized homosexuality as a "mental disorder," subject to the profession's varied and sundry "treatments," all of which were doomed to fail. Today, homosexuality is viewed as a "life-style," an equally stupid misunderstanding of reality. In truth, homosexuality is genetic. Its manifestations may be more or less syntonic with the individual so marked, but that is internal. Only the behavior is external.]

Christ, I thought to myself. *That's what it's been about all along, huh?* But I kept scrolling, reading fast, knowing I'd have to remember it later.

Forgive the digression. A mind such as mine multi-tasks constantly—insights simply fly off the diamond-faceted surface of my intellect. And because insights

have value only in proportion to their dissemination . . . this journal.

A brief word about the journal itself. My art demands egolessness. Hubris has ruined many aspirants to greatness. And as I aspire even higher—to nothing less than uniqueness—egotism is not permitted to intrude upon my work. No "Please catch me before I kill again!" notes to the police; no bombastic letters to newspapers; no "unconscious" clues left at the scene of my crimes.

What was this lunatic talking about? He's a goddamned specialist *at writing letters to the newspapers. . . .* I hit the scroll key before I got lost in that thought.

To the world, I am a criminal. A professional. And in my specialty, anonymity and success are inextricably intertwined.

But I am, above all else, an artist. Where is the ego in art? That has long concerned me. Should the true artist be satisfied with his art? Or must he share it with others, subject it to their critical appraisal, and await trepidatiously their biased and agenda'ed response?

The answer continues to elude me. So I compromise. This journal is a meticulous record of my art. As matters now stand, it will be released, automatically, upon my death. Should I change my thinking on the subject, it could be released sooner. For now, it shall remain covert.

Am I replicating the mistake of so many others who have walked this road before me unsuccessfully? Am I creating evidence to be used against me in some future trial, as though I were a demented mail-bomber or religious fanatic? No. Rest assured, access to this journal will occur only upon my express consent. The encryption codes are known only to me, locked in my perfect memory, never put to paper. Any attempt to access this computer will crash the hard drive. Any "recovery" software will yield only gibberish. And a random program designed to reveal the password

would require a mainframe running at capacity for approximately 7.44 years to locate its target.

Of course, all of that is secondary to the vial of sulfuric acid inside this very computer, its trigger set to discharge the contents should any unauthorized intrusion be attempted.

Further, I vary from the garden-variety psychopath in one fundamental way. No matter how insane the act, no matter how horrific the consequences, the actor will always find those who approve—even worship—his conduct. Incarcerated serial killers receive fan mail and marriage proposals. Murderers of those who work in abortion clinics are admired by those who claim to be "pro-life" (ignoring, of course, the unintended irony which so often accompanies the activities of the terminally stupid: i.e., some of the victims are *pregnant* women who would have given birth until "aborted" by the heroic killers). The homicidal arsonist of black churches is a "freedom fighter" to his fellow race-haters. The list is endless.

But I am not of that undistinguished (and indistinguishable) ilk. I am no herd animal—I stand alone. Should I be captured, I would be alone as well. What I do is done by no other. And I do not cloak my art in the pretensions of politicians or the alibi of insanity.

I have no politics. And I am the sanest, most rational person any of you will ever encounter.

But to return to my theme: Leopold and Loeb were not "one." Therefore, each divisible half could betray the other. And so they did.

Although they thought of (and referred to) themselves as Nietzschean "supermen," they were, in fact, a pair of pathetic little sociopaths, cringing together in the wet darkness of their fears. The kidnapping they engineered was beyond incompetence: Their cover story was tissue paper; they actually *rented* the vehicle in which the victim was transported; the ransom note was typed on a machine stolen from their fraternity house. . . . The list is

endless. One of the blunderers even left his eyeglasses at the scene of the disposal.

And once apprehended, they tripped over each other in their eagerness to shift the blame.

Money, and perhaps Darrow's brilliant dispositional arguments, saved them from the rope. But it was their sexuality that caused their eventual doom. Although it quickly became known that their relationship was homosexual—indeed, rather pedestrian master-slave homosexual—what was ignored was the fact that the kidnapping itself was a sex crime. No, I do not refer to the mutilation of the little boy's genitals (although that might have alerted even the most incompetent forensic psychologist), but to the fact that the very mutuality of the act was sexual in and of itself . . . much as many gang rapes of females are, in reality, homosexual orgies engaged in by those in deep denial. For additional criminological reference, see the literature regarding so-called "fag-bashing." Some are content to be in denial, others attempt to destroy that which they are unable to successfully deny.

One of the secrets of my continuing success is my refusal to deny anything.

What the fuck? was all my mind could react with. *He says he never denies anything, but he's some supercreature way above sex? How could this be the same guy blowing up half the damn city in a war against fag-bashers?* Or would the rest of this lunatic's little journal take me to that answer . . . ?

Denied their grotesque mutuality, Leopold and Loeb were physically separated in prison. Loeb the "master" quickly learned that he had no such power over anyone but Leopold. His lesson was a fatal one—he was stabbed to death in the prison shower room. Leopold reconfigured his sexuality into suppression, and lived to be paroled some three decades later.

But while failure to properly execute a kidnapping is

near-universal, the reasons for failure run across a lengthy continuum. Hickman failed because he was an incompetent, a defective of low intellect and excessive self-esteem. Krist failed despite his intelligence because his plans were insufficiently flexible. And he did not work alone. Speaking of which: Hauptmann, of course, was a pawn.

Although most failures occur at the point where the kidnapper must recover the ransom money, a listing of every failure would exhaust human language. A successful kidnapping is high art.

I have made that art my own. Redefined it. I am a perfectionist. Alone and unfailing.

I was still trying to connect what he was saying with what was happening now when the screen went blank. Then it bloomed in bright red, with black lettering clear against it.

>>Summon your operator now. A question will follow. It must be answered in order to see my next journal entry.<<

"Xyla!" I called out.

She bounced into the room, shooed me out of the chair, and took over. "Ready?" she asked me.

"I don't know," I told her truthfully.

We both watched the screen. In another few seconds, his message came, this time in a regular font, black letters on a white screen:

>>Prove link, you ↔ Wesley. Three (3) names. No more. Send immediately.<<

"What words?" Xyla asked me urgently, her fingers poised.

I told her. Watched the screen carry the message.

Candy. Train. Julio.

Driving back, I wanted the safety of my cave. My head hurt from it all. It started reasonably . . . for a lunatic. That whole gay thing. But he was saying he was a kidnapper. The best in the business. What business? There hadn't been a successful kidnapping in years. Nothing remotely resembling the perfection he was bragging about. When had he first written this? Why was he sending it to me? And what did Wesley have to do with a . . . "metaphorical" death?

Was he saying all those homicides meant something other than what they were? Was *any* of his journal true? I . . . couldn't get it. So I stuffed as much as I could deep into my memory, packing a suitcase for a long journey.

I was in Mama's that night. The Prof had left word he'd roll by, and I waited to . . . I don't know what I wanted. Maybe just to be with the only father I'd ever had, just for a little while. Before I did something I knew was going to end ugly.

My father came in with his son. They sat down. The old man looked at me . . . and, for the first time, I realized he *was* an old man. I mean, he *had* to be, right? But it never came to me so hard as right that moment.

He didn't ask me anything, just had his soup and waited. When he was done, I told him.

"Okay, let me get this straight. Motherfucker sends you his 'journal'? A diary, like those teenage girls keep? Only this one, it's about him being the all-time ace of snatch artists?"

"Not the whole thing, Prof. It was . . . a piece, like."

"There's more, then? He gets his pleasing from teasing?"

"I don't think so. It could be techno—maybe he could only maintain security with so much data at a time. But it feels like . . . You remember those serials you told me about, the ones they had at the movies when you were a kid?"

"Oh yeah. Those were some *boss* cliffhangers, son. Kept you coming back for more, that's the way they scored."

"Right. That's what this feels like."

"He gets you hooked, so you don't book?"

"Sure. But why would he care? The only thing he wants from me has something to do with Wesley—that name really opened his door. And, remember what I told you, he said he was ready to die. And I was going to help him."

"But not die-die, right? Meta-something die. That don't mean the real deal."

"No. I don't know what . . . The way it started, I thought he was going to go into a rant about being gay, you know? But he dropped that in a flash, switched to the kidnapping thing."

"Then here's what's true, *that* ain't new."

"Because . . . ?"

"Because the motherfucker may be crazy—hell, he sure *is* crazy—but no way he's stupid, right? If he's king of the kidnappers, you won't know it from the papers. Like I said, that ain't the play, no way, not today. The drug boys do snatches, but it's to get back their powder or make somebody go along with the program, not a ransom deal."

"So you think this is an old journal?"

"What the man said, right? Got it stashed in some computer in case he's caught or something. . . ."

"No. In fact, he said, if anyone tried to get at it, the whole thing would get nuked."

"But it was getting him off," the Prof said, flatly. "*Had* to be. Keep fucking records of your own heists—what kind of righteous thief does that?"

"You got me. He says he's a pro. He came across like there's no way he's got partners."

"He figured out a way to do snatches without partners, man's good," the Prof conceded. "But he still sounds like the kind of fool I came up with . . . you know, a motherfucker so dumb, you tell him somebody with a gun's coming for him, he runs around looking for a knife."

"Those they still have," Clarence said gravely.

"Always *gonna* have," the Prof assured him. "Like they wasn't *born* stupid enough, they got to practice."

"Prof," I asked him quietly, the same volume we used to speak on the yard, so many years ago. But straight ahead, not out of the side of my mouth. "Can you tell me anything?"

"Got two things to tell you, Schoolboy. Only one you gonna listen to."

"You sure?"

"Here's the first one: Walk away. Fast."

The little man looked at me until my eyes dropped. "Thought so," he said. "Here's the other. Motherfucker's tied to Wesley some way. And the way I see, only one way that could be."

"Which is?"

"He's afraid of him," the Prof said.

"Wesley's dead," I said. My theme song now, I guessed it was.

"And people still not afraid of him?" the Prof challenged. "You know what they say. You know where they say it. Wesley may be dead, but he ain't in the ground. Some be saying Wesley went down to the Crossroads, see if he could meet the Devil. Not like Robert Johnson did. Not to make no trade. To *meet* the man, to get it on. And the way it's told, the Devil, he never showed. Remember, nobody did no autopsy. Every once in a while, the wire starts humming: Wesley's coming. You hear it too, what do you do?"

"Get out of the way," I told him, all truth.

"I don't think this crazy motherfucker's got even *that* much sense," the Prof said solemnly.

We were still sitting there when Mama told me I had a phone call. It was just after midnight.

"What?" I said into the receiver.

"I have what you want." Strega's voice. "You bring me what I want now."

"I don't know if she's—"

But the witch-woman was gone.

“Where are we going?”

“Never mind. You said you wanted in. This is how it has to go.”

“Right now?”

“Yes.”

“Oh, all right. I’ll meet you—”

“No. Stay there. I have to make sure you’re . . . okay before we go.”

“What does that—?”

I hung up on her.

She was wearing jeans and a white T-shirt, a thin red leather jacket held over one shoulder.

“Hold it,” I told her. “I want you to bring something with you.”

“What?”

“You know that mask you told me about?”

“Yes . . .”

“That.”

“Why?”

“Go get it,” I told her.

She stared at me for a long second, then went somewhere into the darkness. When she came back, she had it in her hand. Black leather, just like she described, right down to the zipper for the mouth.

“How do you get this over a full head of hair?” I asked her.

“She doesn’t . . . Oh: it laces up the back, see?”

I turned it over, saw what she meant. “Okay,” I said, “let’s go.”

There’s lots of ways to cross the river into Queens, but I had to make my move before I took any of them. I pulled under the FDR underpass, turned off the ignition. Handed her the mask.

“Put it on,” I told her.

“Me?”

"You. Where I'm taking you, I don't want you to remember the route."

"You could use a—"

"I don't trust blindfolds. And I'm not gonna tranq you; it would take too long to bring you around."

"Isn't there any other way?"

"Sure," I told her. "Get out."

I walked her around to the back of the Plymouth, opened the trunk, showed her how much room there was back there, even with the padded fuel cell cutting into the space. Showed her the blankets I had for Pansy, the air holes for breathing.

"No," is all she said.

"Then we're down to two choices," I bluffed, knowing I had to have her with me. Knowing Strega. "You can wear the mask, or I can take you back to where I got you."

"I never had it on," she said. "I always wondered what it felt like. Some doms I know, they try their gear on themselves. Like a paddle, you know? See how hard it's really going to sting? But I never . . ."

"Yes or no?"

"All *right,*" she said, walking away from me.

Inside the car, she pulled the mask over her head. I laced it up, not tight. She found the zipper herself, pulled it across. "It's hard to breathe like this," is all she said.

"I won't smoke," I promised her.

I wasn't worried about some cop spotting the mask. All the glass in the Plymouth is tinted, and I could just tell Nadine to yank it off if I spotted any company. She didn't say another word for a while. I was just turning off the BQE when she spoke again.

"You like this?"

"Like what?" I asked her.

"Me. Keeping me . . . restrained."

"You're not restrained," I told her. "This isn't some bondage trip. I don't want you to see where you're going. Big deal."

"You said you don't trust blindfolds. Why?"

"Because they don't always work."

"How do you know?"

"Because I've had them on me, bitch. All right?"

"Playing a—?"

"You're not going to make me lose my temper," I promised her. "Playing? No, not playing. I was a child. And people were . . . It doesn't matter. You're not with me. There's nothing you need to know about me. We made a deal. I'm keeping my end. But the person I'm taking you to, maybe they don't want you to be able to find them on your own. Is that so fucking shocking to you?"

"I'm sorry."

"No, you're not. You don't have a truly sorry bone in that body you're so proud of. But it doesn't matter. You being sorry wouldn't help me, even if it was true. You don't even know what you'd be being sorry for. You're just making it up. Filling in the blanks. Look, you don't want to do this, just tell me. I'll turn around, you can take the mask off. Then I'll drive you back to your place."

"I *said* I was sorry."

"Oh. Yeah, I get it now. You're sorry that you might have been a little too cute, even for you. There's something *you* want. It's marked all over you. I don't know what it is, and—"

"I *told* you I—"

"Yeah, I forgot. You love this guy. And you want to help him. And you don't trust Lincoln and his crew and you sure as hell don't trust me. Got it. It's all playing with you, huh? All games? No matter what happens, you go back to your leashes and your collars and your chains and your other toys. Me, I'm *in* it, understand? So how about you just shut up, okay?"

I could feel her vibrate next to me, but she didn't say another word for the rest of the trip.

I wasn't surprised to see the garage door open. Two far-apart cars inside the murky space. I backed the Plymouth in carefully, but there was no risk—plenty of room on both sides. I got out and hit the switch—the door came down. The place went pitch-black then, but I'd been ready for it. I opened the passenger door and helped

Nadine get out. Then the door opened, the one that leads right into the first floor of the house.

Strega was standing there, waiting. She was wearing a long-sleeved white silk something that was cut off around her diaphragm and a tiny black spandex skirt. Her fiery hair was lustrous and loose. Her stockings had some kind of sparkle-dust woven into them, picking up glints of light over her ankle-strapped black spikes.

"Bring her over here," she said, her voice witchy and low.

I did that. Strega turned and walked. I followed her until we got into the living room. A couple of the baby spots were on, but it was shadowy elsewhere. If the spots had been rose-colored, it would have looked a lot like Nadine's joint.

At a nod from Strega, I unlaced the mask. Nadine yanked it off before I was finished, the heavy muscles standing out on her bare arms. She shook her head hard, resettling her hair without touching it. I stepped to the side as she and Strega faced each other.

"So this is the girl who's helping you, huh?" Strega said to me.

"This is the girl I told you about," I said, not asking for her judgment, just telling her I'd delivered the goods, kept my promises.

"What's your name?" Strega asked her.

"Nadine."

"I'm Jina. And he's mine," she said, pointing at me like I was an unlicensed dog she was claiming from the pound.

"You're welcome to him," Nadine said. "I'm only here because—"

"Oh!" Strega said suddenly. "I see. You're not into men at all, huh?"

"I'm a lesbian," Nadine said proudly, folding her arms under her breasts.

Strega walked around Nadine like the bigger woman was a statue, not saying anything for a long minute. "Sit down," she finally said, pointing at a chair.

Nadine sat back, crossed her legs, waiting. Strega perched herself on the ottoman that matched the chair, imitated the other woman's gesture.

"Yours?" Strega asked her, holding the leather mask.

"Yes," Nadine replied, eyes and voice steady.

"Oh, you like to *spank,* huh? What do you think?" she said, getting up. "You like to spank *me*?"

"I don't know you," Nadine said, like she was answering questions at a job interview.

"Ahhh . . . and I thought I had such a tempting ass too," Strega said, bending forward and making a kissing sound at Nadine. "Get up," she said suddenly.

Nadine did it, standing still and calm, taller than Strega.

"Take a better look, maybe you'll change your mind," Strega told her, turning her back on Nadine and walking away. Nadine followed her into the darkness.

They were gone long enough for me to smoke through a pair of cigarettes. Not chain-smoke either—plenty of time in between. I went somewhere else then, closing my eyes.

"You asleep, baby?"

Strega's voice. I opened my eyes. She was alone.

"No," I told her. "Where's—?"

"Oh, she's nice and safe. But she has to stay there. It's not her business what you want to know, right?"

"Right."

"I have to whisper," she said, turning her back and dropping into my lap.

I didn't say anything, waiting. When she finally settled herself, her voice was calm, like she was giving me the recipe for something.

"Gutterball ordered it, all right. You know how he got his name? He was a bowler, a pro bowler, when he was younger. Like calling some fat guy Tiny, I guess. Anyway, Corky was angling, and Gutterball wanted him off the count. Corky wasn't made, so Gutterball didn't need the okay, but he—Corky, I mean—he was with some Irish guys. Some *bad* Irish guys, you understand what I'm saying? So it had to look good."

She slipped her hand inside my pants. Said, "Oh, not interested, huh?" then chuckled at her own pun before she went on: "You know what was the real slick part? Corky, he thought *he* was gonna do someone. I mean, that's why he was there. At that gay rally. What they told him was, the mark's gonna come strolling by. *Behind* him, like, understand? So Corky, he *knows* there's gonna be a car there. The way I got it, they made a few passes, let Corky see them and everything. How it was *supposed* to go, Corky stands at the very back of the crowd, close to the sidewalk, get it? Then, when the mark comes down the sidewalk, the guys in the car, they tap the horn three times, real quick. Corky turns around, blasts him, and just keeps running into the car and off they go. The cover fire was supposed to protect Corky. A real slick plan."

"You saying Gutterball wanted them *all* gone?"

"I don't know. They weren't his honchos or anything, but they were in his crew. The way I heard it, Wesley told him he was gonna get Corky, but . . ."

"Wesley?"

"Wesley," she said softly. "Gutterball talked to him himself. Made the whole deal on the phone. You know how Wesley works."

"Yeah. But how could Gutterball be sure it was—?"

"That's what he said himself. You know what Wesley told him? New deal. Nothing up front. COD. How could Gutterball lose behind that?"

"But how would Wesley know Gutterball wanted—?"

"I don't know. *Gutterball* didn't know. He thought he was being set up. So he met with him and—"

"He met with Wesley?"

"That's what he said. Oh, he didn't *see* him—just a man, in the shadows. But whoever it was, he knew Gutterball's business, knew what Corky was up to . . . everything."

"Jesus."

"Wesley—"

"It wasn't Wesley."

"O*kay,* baby. Sssshh. Who*ever* it was, all right? He said he was back in town, and he knew some people wouldn't believe him. That's why he was changing the deal. He didn't ask for it all up front, like you'd expect . . . especially since that whole war started back then, when they wouldn't pay him, remember? He said he'd prove who he was."

"It stinks," I said. "How'd Gutterball know he wasn't talking to the law, for chrissakes?"

"He said he could tell. I don't know what else to say. You've been around Wesley. No cop could ever . . . Wesley has his own . . . I don't know what you'd call it. But it wasn't a cop. And there damn sure *was* a killing."

"More than one."

"I know. Gutterball, he paid *fast,* I promise you. It's Wesley's style, right down to the end. No witnesses, right?"

"Yeah. But anyone could've—"

"Sure, honey. Whatever you say."

"The other ones who died . . . the ones in the crowd. It was all for . . . nothing."

"That's Wesley too, baby boy."

"He'd—"

"—do it just like that, and you know it. Wesley'd burn a building down to get one of the tenants. He did it before. And he couldn't have known your girlfriend would be . . ."

"Gutterball, you think he'd talk to me?"

"Not in life. He's not gonna talk, period. Even if they drop him for this, he's never saying a word. You can always juice a jury or scam the parole board. But Wesley . . . Gutterball wouldn't be safe, no matter where they put him. Anyway, it doesn't look like that's gonna happen. Gutterball, he's golden now. Word is, Wesley's working for him. You know what that means."

"Sure. It means they're a pack of retards."

"Whatever you say. But they're a *scared* pack of retards, that's the truth."

"It wasn't Wesley," I told her.

"Burke, I wasn't there, okay?"

"I know. Thank you."

"You know how to thank me."

"Strega, not now. I . . ."

"Sssshhh," she hissed.

"Where is she?" I asked her later.

"You ready to go? Is that what you're saying?"

"Yes."

"When are you coming back?"

"I don't know."

"No, you don't. But I'll know. And I'll be here. I never forget. Give me something."

"What?"

"Something of yours. That," she said, pointing to my wristwatch, "I'll take that."

I didn't say anything as she unsnapped the bracelet and pulled it off my wrist.

"Hmmm," she said, rubbing her thumb over the crystal. "Come on, I'll give her back to you. And you don't need the mask. I don't care if she knows where I live. She'll never come back. Unless I tell her to."

Strega led me to a back bedroom. It was dark. I saw Nadine, sitting on a straight chair in a corner, facing out. Her legs were pressed primly together, hands in her lap.

"Come on," I told her. "We're going."

She got up and came with me.

"I want to talk to you," she said as I turned onto Metropolitan Avenue, heading straight down to the Williamsburg Bridge, no traffic at that hour, a clean run.

"Talk," I told her.

"You know what she did?"

"Who?"

"Strega. She told me her real name. With me. Back in that room."

"I don't have a clue. Nothing she did would surprise me."

"She told me to sit down. In that chair. I did it. Then she slapped my face. Not . . . playing, like we do. But to . . . get my attention. So I'd listen. I could tell. She has a voice like a snake. It scared me. But only a little. She said if I did anything to hurt you she'd make me dead. Slow dead. Rotting from the inside. She said she was a witch. And she told me something about myself to prove it."

"Which was . . . ?"

"I don't have to tell you," she said, in a little girl's adamant voice. "She said I didn't have to tell you. But she knew. Nobody knows, but she knew. She said I could have my secret. Everybody has secrets. But not from her. She said you were in her. Inside her. Not like sex . . . I don't know what she meant, but I know she meant it."

"So she guessed something about your past and you—"

"She wasn't guessing. And it doesn't matter. I wasn't going to hurt you anyway. But I have to see him. Even if it . . . Whatever happens, I have to see him. You promised. You said if I—"

"I'm keeping my promises," I told her. "To everyone. But I can't *make* things happen. All I can do is *try* to make them happen, understand?"

"Yes. I know. I'm sorry if I—"

"It doesn't matter now," I told her.

I pulled up outside her apartment building. "Where's your mask?" I asked her, looking in the back seat.

"It's hers now," Nadine said. "She told me to give it to her. Are you going to call me when—"

"Yes," I lied.

I had the Plymouth in motion the second she slammed the door.

I thumbed the cellular into life, tapped out Mama's number. I don't use speed-dial—cloning cell-phone numbers is a big-time felony, and if this one fell into the wrong hands, I wouldn't want anything that could connect back to me. I never even touch the damn thing without gloves on.

"Gardens," Mama answered.

"Anything?"

"Yes. Girl call. Say, more come in, okay?"

"Got it," I told her, and aimed the Plymouth in the right direction.

"He sent another," Xyla said, excitement clear in her voice. "Same as last time. You want to look at it, right?"

"Yeah."

"Okay. You remember how to do it?" she asked, getting up from her chair.

"I do. Thanks."

I lit a cigarette and pulled the curtains aside. There he was:

This is my ninth experience. Of the prior eight, I collected the ransom in five. I consider this to be a laudatory record of success. Perhaps I could have increased the collection percentage, but at the cost of increasing risk. My way is unalterable, however—unless and until each and every step is flawlessly executed, in sequence, with the proper response from the target, I simply retire from the field.

The first step, obviously, is research. How many kidnappings have failed when it develops that the parents simply lack the appropriate resources? To demand a half-million-dollar ransom from a man whose net worth is in five figures is the act of a fool. A doomed fool.

As I write this, I realize the value of the writing. It clarifies my own thoughts. And helps me to express them to you . . . the eventual reader. Thus, in reviewing the last paragraph, I came to realize that I have omitted a vital step. One that comes before research. Indeed, before anything. It is, doubtless, one of the many aspects of my modus operandi that distinguishes me from other operators. What is this critical distinction, you might ask? The answer is: A trial run. Not with the intended victim, but with the entire process.

Thus I began my kidnapping career by deconstructing the totality into segments, then practicing the various aspects independently so as to avoid even the possibility of detection. So, for example, I might research Family "A" as to finances, but conduct surveillance of Family "B" as

to terrain and so on. In point of fact—verified by the records, which are appended hereto—I captured four separate children successfully before I ever sought ransom of any kind. Each technique was perfected before moving on to the next.

I scrolled down fast, looking for the records he was talking about, but all I got was:

Forgive the rambling. I realize it is a conceit to assume that the (future) reader will be as fascinated with my thought processes as I myself am, but not all conceits are axiomatically invalid. Again, it is a matter of risk versus gain. If you are interested, then I must include everything or you will be cheated. If you are not, what has been lost?

Research is only a small portion of my success. Another operative factor is clinical purity. That is, no secondary motive. Too many kidnappers are, in fact, perverts or degenerates. Sadists, child molesters, rapists . . . those of that odious breed. The ransom demand is mere protective coloration over their actual intent—the true force which drives them.

I have no such demons within me. I take only children because: (a) they are more gullible; (b) they are less capable of physical resistance; (c) they are more likely to be ransomed, if only because the dictates of society so require.

The children are never returned. No matter how careful the kidnapper, some risk is always inherent in returning a victim. And while children are, in fact, weaker and easier to gull than adults, their powers of observation are extraordinary, their memories excellent, and their post-traumatic revelations have convicted more than one perpetrator.

I never kill with force. Not one child yet has refused the food I offered. Death follows, painlessly. The bodies are never found. No, not out of some sadistic desire to deny the parents the "closure" so beloved of the self-

aggrandizing, but from the knowledge that forensics is a weapon I must deflect to the fullest extent possible.

Often, the children must be kept alive for some protracted period of negotiations, that complex dance in which the parents attempt to avoid the inevitable and the police interfere regardless of my instructions. In fact, at this point in my career, I *expect* police intervention. A routine, predictable annoyance.

Which is undoubtedly what led me to my most recent decision . . . to kidnap the child of an organized-crime kingpin. Viewed logically, it squares fully with my own precepts. The target: (a) has the necessary cash resources; (b) believes his child to be exempt from attack because of some archaic "code" allegedly governing conduct between gangsters; and (c) will not notify the authorities.

If this works as anticipated, I may sub-specialize in this area for the foreseeable future.

As soon as the screen started to change color, I knew what was coming. I hardly got her name out of my mouth before Xyla came bounding into the room, dropping into the chair I had just vacated with the springy grace of a gymnast. His message came in seconds:

>>Your prior proof acknowledged. Further transmissions from me on pure exchange basis. Next installment available only upon revelation of Wesley work not known to law enforcement. Maximum length = 5 words. Send *now*.<<

I stepped behind Xyla, put my hand on her shoulder. "Five words maximum? I'll go the son of a bitch a couple better," I told her. "Type this":

blowgun dart

"Any idea why he only wants such short messages?" I asked as soon as her fingers left the keyboard.

"It could have something to do with his security software, but it's too much for me to figure out," she replied. "You'd think it would be the other way, right? I mean, he'd want to keep *his* transmissions as short as possible, limit his exposure. Are they longer?"

"Much longer," I told her.

"It *couldn't* be something as simple as an attached file," she mused. "Maybe . . . I don't know. You want me to poke around, see if I can—"

"No!" I interrupted her sharply. "Don't look for him at all. Stay away. Just get word to me anytime he makes contact again, okay?"

"Okay. Sure, if that's what you want. Lorraine said—"

"Sure. Thanks, Xyla. I really appreciate this."

"You don't look so good," she said.

"Little girl, I never look good."

"Stop that! I mean, you look . . . I dunno, drained or something. Was it his message?"

"Oh yeah," I told her.

I thought I had it then. Organized crime—no, preying on organized crime—that was going to be his specialty . . . if whatever thing he was doing at the time he wrote his journal worked out. Which it obviously must have, if he was still out there somewhere.

I wondered if any of it was true. Any of anything.

"You heard me," I told the voice on the phone. "Every kidnapping which resulted in the kid not being returned. *Ransom* kidnappings, money successfully changes hands, kid never found, nobody ever arrested. Got it?"

"Sure. But you're probably asking the wrong man."

"How so?"

"I can get all the *reported* cases that meet your search criteria."

"Meaning?"

"Look, I'm a journalist," Hauser's gruff voice came back over the phone, "not a cop. I can work Nexis easy enough, but that's a media database; it won't get you anything that *didn't* make the papers, see?"

"Sure. I got that other part covered."

"And what's in it for me?"

"I just told you," I said, hanging up on him. Hauser was only going through his reporter's dance. He's an info-trader, so under any other circumstances, I'd have to promise him access to something—a story, an exclusive . . . whatever. But I've known Hauser for a long time. Being a father is the most sacred thing in his life. Telling him I was looking for a child-snatcher was enough, and we both knew it.

"Let me write this down," Nadine said. She turned her back on me and left her living room, to return in a minute with a grid pad like architects use and one of those gel-handled pens that're supposed to conform to your fingers as you hold then. She looked at me expectantly.

"Kidnappings," I told her. "*Successful* kidnappings. From organized-crime bigshots. Not *reported* to the cops, but known to them anyway, okay? And the kid is never returned."

"Murdered?"

"What word didn't you understand?"

"I'm sorry," she said, meekly.

"Look, this is no risk to your friend. Just computer access. She can always say she's ambitious—looking to step up, work a cold-case file on her own time, score a promotion—if they ever tie anything to her."

"It doesn't matter. She'll do—"

"Yeah, I heard that speech," I told her. "Got it memorized."

"Do you hate me?" she asked suddenly.

"Hate you? For being a pain in the ass? Don't be stupid."

"I wasn't. I mean, I know I—"

"*Hate.* You got any idea what that word really means, you spoiled bitch? The way you people talk . . . Someone's mad at you so you say, 'Oh, he's going to *kill* me,' right? We don't speak the same language."

"'You people.' What does *that* mean?"

"It means, not *my* people," I told her.

I was with my people when I told them the next piece the killer had sent me.

"He kills kids?" the Prof asked, jolted.

"Yeah. He says so, anyway. Not for fun. Like . . . cleaning up after himself. Or maybe just some techno-glitch, to a guy like him."

"You know guys like him, mahn?" Clarence asked.

"Sure. So do you. People aren't human to them. They're just objects. Pieces on a chessboard. The only thing that holds guys like that in check is fear. They think they can get away with something—anything—they do it."

"Sure, mahn. There are plenty like that. But this—"

"He's just . . . better at it," I said. "That's all."

"Nah, bro, there's more we know," the Prof said.

"What's that?"

"He wouldn't be so loud if he wasn't so proud," the little man said.

"I don't know," Strega whispered. She was in my arms, me carrying her. She wanted that, sometimes. I never knew why, but I always did it, walking her through that spooky house like she was a child I was trying to cuddle-coax back to sleep.

"But you could find out," I said. It wasn't a question.

"I can find out anything from . . . them. They have no secrets from me."

"Nadine said she had no secrets from you either."

"Ah, that one. She lied to you, Burke."

"About what?"

"She told you some fairy story, right? She didn't start out gay. . . ."

"Yeah, she said something like that."

"You know how guys—the ones who don't get it—say lesbians hate men?"

"Sure."

"She's not lying about that," Strega said against my neck. "She hates men."

"That wouldn't make her a—"

"I don't know if she likes women either. She likes sex. And women are the only ones she's going to have it with."

"Yeah, I know. I heard all about—"

"She's not a dom either," Strega said softly. "Not in her heart. The role's playing *her,* understand? She's just building walls. Like the way she builds her body."

"What?"

"It's safer where she is. Like I'm safe now," she whispered against me.

I rubbed my thumb in small circles at the base of the witch's neck, quieting her while I thought about what she said. Walls. Prison. In there, everyone has to have a role. Predator or prey. No Switzerland option. You don't *have* to fuck some kid to mark your territory, but some went that way. "Shit on my dick, or blood on my knife," is what the wolves greet you with when you're a young fish, a first-timer. That's what drives so many of them into gangs Inside. That's a role too. By the time I went in, I already knew the truth I later heard the Prof tell to so many new kids: "If they try, they got to die." I had a shank in my waistband when I hit the yard for the first time. Being raised by the State in those prison-prep schools teaches you all that. But why would this woman need to . . . ?

"I get it," I lied to Strega. "It's not men she hates, just sex with—"

"She'd have sex with you. She wants to, you know. Bad."

"I *don't* know. She's a game-player. I don't know her game. It doesn't matter."

"Because you don't want her?"

"Because I'm not playing."

"But you want to play with me, don't you?" she asked, witchy.

I knew who it was even as the phone was ringing at Mama's. And I was on my way in a couple of minutes more.

We had it down to a routine by now. I hardly had the match to my cigarette before he showed again:

I have the child now, here with me. Her name is Angelique, but her school records indicate she prefers "Angel." She is 10+ years, in apparently excellent health.

The abduction was simplicity itself. The child is the first to be picked up each morning by the bus from the private school she attends. Her nanny accompanies her to the end of the drive, where the bus stops each morning, but my observations indicated that the nanny (a young woman who may have been selected for other than her child-care abilities, but I acknowledge that to be mere speculation on my part, albeit consistent with the pattern displayed by the girl's father in other dealings) was always bored and inattentive, often to the point where she did not even respond when the child spoke to her.

The private school is quite discreet. Their bus is virtually unmarked—a smallish vehicle, dark green in color, with the school's name gilded subtly in Olde English script across the door panel.

The regular driver had answered the knock at his door earlier that morning. He saw . . . well, me: Dressed in a standard-issue government suit, carrying a well-traveled briefcase. He let me in without complaint, albeit with an air of victimized resignation. Had the school thoroughly vetted its employees, they would have known their driver had a prior conviction for child molestation. Actually, he had been allowed to plead guilty to a lesser, statutorily euphemized offense, but the facts were there for anyone with the will to search them out. The driver had long since completed his parole (and it was in another state entirely), but he had grown acculturated to answering the questions of white males who had a certain look about them.

That look comes easily to me: My features are both unremarkable and mobile.

The driver lived alone, in a small cottage owned by the school. Occupancy of the cottage and personal off-duty use of the bus apparently were intended to compensate for the inadequacy of his salary . . . barely past minimum wage.

The driver's death would be discovered rather quickly. It was not, as you might imagine, a gratuitous homicide on my part. Functionally, it accomplished two things: (a) immobilization, guaranteeing that he would not give the alarm before my work was completed, and (b) demonstrable evidence that the kidnapper would, in fact, kill. The latter tends to add emphasis to negotiations.

I was well prepared with a cover story had the nanny questioned me, but none was necessary. The child ran toward the bus even as I approached, and the nanny turned her back and started toward the house before I had even opened the doors.

The child said, "Where's Harry?" and I told her Harry was sick—I was the relief driver. I knew from my research that such an emergency-substitution system was in place, but I could not know if it had ever been utilized during the period of time the child had been attending the school. Still, she made no protest, and took her seat calmly.

Less than a quarter-mile from her house, I pulled over to the side of the road into a spot shielded by overgrowth. Within ninety seconds, the child was rendered unconscious—chloroform on a sterile handkerchief—and carried from the bus into the car I had waiting.

There was some degree of exposure during the fifteen-minute drive to the house I had prepared, but it was minimal. The child was sleeping in the trunk, I could easily explain my presence should there be any inquiry, and I expected to be invisible, with my captive totally secured, before any of the other children's parents called to complain about the bus being late.

When the child awoke, it was near noon. Many children are frightened when they find themselves captured, but this one was quite stoic. I showed her the basement where she would remain, including the TV set (complete with video-game connectors), the private bathroom, the small refrigerator, and the convertible sofa. She nodded

gravely as I explained she had been kidnapped; that it was like a game adults play . . . a game for money.

She appeared to understand (and to readily accept) the concept of extortion.

I told her that she was free to move around or do anything that she wished while I was present, but that when I had to leave—occasionally in order to complete the financial arrangements—I would have to restrain her. I showed her how the restraints worked, how comfortable they actually were, and how she could use the remote to work the television, and that she could easily reach the bathroom and refrigerator should she require either—I never expected to be gone for more than a very short time anyway.

I asked her if there was anything I could get her to make her stay easier. She wanted books. I had anticipated this—her school records indicated she was a scholarly child. But, of course, any individual shopping for children's books in the next few days would have aroused suspicion. Especially a stranger. I was prepared: With over one hundred separate titles, all age-appropriate and of great variety. The child seemed absolutely delighted with the selection. I told her she could take all the books with her when I released her, expecting even greater happiness. However, she said she would not be allowed to have so many books.

When I asked her why that should be—after all, her life seemed filled with various—and, frankly, conspicuous—possessions, she just replied, "That's what they say."

"Who is 'they'?" I asked her.

"Them."

I did not press the point, preferring to establish as harmonious a relationship as possible.

The screen flickered, indicating he was done. I called Xyla in, and waited for the rest. It didn't take long.

>>Mortay? Wesley's work? Yes or No?<<

Was this maniac into myth-busting now? Mortay had been the reigning champ of the anything-goes death matches some degenerates were holding in a giant basement, but he couldn't handle the whisper-stream saying Max could beat him. He put it all on the line. Threatened to kill Max's baby to force a match. Right after he said that to me, one of his men was shot from a nearby rooftop. The real target was Mortay, but he'd moved faster than any human I'd ever seen, and the sniper picked off what was left. The sniper wasn't Wesley . . . but that's what everyone thought.

Mortay finally got dead. Although the cops couldn't be certain-sure about it, the whisper-stream knew. After I'd shot him a bunch of times in that deserted construction-site excavation, I'd kicked a grenade into his mouth, folded his hands over his face, and pulled the pin.

In a way, that's what started all this. I didn't know until much later that Mortay was already on Wesley's list. The freak was too out of control for the mob guys who paid him to make snuff videos—taking hookers right off the street for actresses—so they gave the work to Wesley. But before the ice-man could get it done, our crew had handled it ourselves. It cost Belle her life, and me my love.

If I'd known the maggot was on Wesley's list, I would have just stepped aside and waited for the inevitable. But after the way it went down, the whisper-stream gave me the hit-man tag. A street brand that I could never shed, not in some places.

And then the stupid *cafone*s who'd contracted with Wesley said they wouldn't pay off, because he hadn't done the job; I had.

That's when Wesley started killing them all.

Was this guy asking me who was on the roof that night Mortay almost got smoked? Or was he trying to find out what kind of a man I was? Didn't matter. No way I was going to have Xyla type El Cañonero's name into her machine. He had been the only other pro sniper working the city then, but he wasn't with me. He was a soldier for some Puerto Rican Independentistas, doing a job for me that night in exchange for something I would do for them. And I wasn't going to say I did Mortay myself, either. So I played his question straight.

no

is what Xyla sent him.

When you're interrogating a suspect, you can sometimes get him to tell you the truth by letting him think you already know it. Did the killer really understand the "blowgun dart" message I'd sent him? Or was he playing me, waiting patiently?

And was he asking me about Mortay because he already knew the truth, testing to see how reliable my answer might be to something he *didn't* know, down the line?

No way for me to even guess. But I knew this much: It was still Wesley, to him, *all* Wesley, somehow.

"Nothing," Hauser told me two days later.

"What do you mean, 'nothing'?"

"I mean nothing. Zero. Zip. *Nada.* Not one case meets your search criteria. There were cases where a child disappeared . . . but no ransom demands. There were cases where there was ransom demanded and paid, and the child was later found . . . dead. But nothing along the lines you told me to look for."

"Fuck!"

"You're still on this, right?" Hauser asked.

"Yeah."

"So I'm still in it if there's something I can—"

"You have my word," I told him, and hung up.

His next message just picked up from where the last one left off. I was as locked to it as if the previous one had still been on the screen, seamless.

Children vary as widely as adults. Perhaps more so, as they are still in the process of formation, and their possibilities and potential have not yet adapted to the

dictates of socioeconomic survival. This child, however, was different in a way I had not observed previously. Some children go almost mute with the trauma of separation, some are garrulous. But, always, they are intensely self-absorbed—understandable, I acknowledge, in the circumstances under which I come into contact with them—wondering "What is going to happen to me?" to the exclusion of all else. This child, however, expressed such an apparently genuine interest in the mechanics of my art that I found myself in discussions which had an eerie "peer" quality about them.

[Of course, had she been older and more sophisticated, she would have concluded that discussing the specifics of my methodology with a person who could later describe same to the authorities would be counterindicated. Indeed, the fact that I remained unmasked throughout should have been sufficient to provide a clue as to each child's fate. None seemed to notice. Or, perhaps, they were determined not to notice—I am not a psychologist.]

But this child seemed utterly fascinated with the mechanics of kidnapping. And hers was not the gory fascination of a child, but the mature fascination of an interested adult. This was no difficult deduction on my part. Indeed, her first question was:

"Aren't you worried they could trace the ransom note?"

I was temporarily taken aback by her question, but, rather than ensuring my silence, it seemed to almost compel me to disclosure. An egotistical desire to share my art, perhaps? I do not believe so. After all, that is the purpose of this journal.

Still, I showed her how I used only electronic ransom notes. I tape complete television series—sit-coms are the best because they are more likely to possess the requisite longevity—in order to acquire a word bank. "All in the Family," "Leave It to Beaver," "The Brady Bunch" had sufficient running time to provide all I needed. Next, I use a digitizing apparatus to separate the individual words. The final edit assembles the note. The child had a little bit of difficulty following me—I realize that my vocabulary is occasionally excessive and that I tend toward the pedantic—but when I explained that my technique was the same as clipping words from newspapers and pasting them to paper, she grasped the principle perfectly. When I demonstrated—by forming the message "Angelique is a pretty girl" from "The Brady Bunch" (actually, the best source of girl's names, for some reason unknown to me—I have never actually watched an episode) word bank—she clapped her hands.

After she had something to eat—I let her choose from a variety of foodstuffs I had assembled . . . it reduces the feeling of powerlessness in the captive—I showed her that the messages were on micro-cassettes. All I had to do was dial the target's home number and, when the phone was answered, play the tape. Good luck to the FBI and its so-called "voiceprints."

"My father has a . . . thing on his phone," the child piped up. "They'll know where you called from."

Was she mocking me? It didn't seem so—her little face was serious. Almost . . . concerned.

So I took out some more of my equipment and explained how a blue-box system worked. A telephone recognizes a hyper-specific series of electronic beeps. When I dial out using the box, it goes into an 800 loop—the best ones to use are those which have chronically heavy traffic . . . any of the conventional credit-card services will do—and re-emerges locally, so whatever rudimentary device of her father's the child was referring to would only recognize the 800 number (which is based in a faraway state) if it recognized anything at all.

"Are you going to call from here, then?" the child asked.

I patiently explained that, while I could, indeed, call from the location in perfect safety, there was no phone installed. Sophisticated technology is a two-edged sword, and taking chances is for amateurs.

"So you have to go out?" she asked.

"Yes."

"Shouldn't you take me with you?"

"Why would I do that?"

"So I couldn't . . . escape."

I assured the child I was more than satisfied with the restraint system I had established, speaking to her as if she was a colleague in the enterprise rather than its victim . . . which seemed to best match her own affect. Obviously, I realized that she was attempting to beguile me into giving her an opportunity to attract attention once we were outside, but I was not angered. In fact, I had a sincere respect for her wit. And for her will to survive.

Yet I did not tell her the entire truth. Once I have successfully completed the capture phase of my operation, it is vital to remain in the hideout until target-contact is established. The message had long since been recorded, and the central computer in my residence . . . [I must digress here: I work from home, in my perfectly legitimate occupation of independent computer consultant. My small, modest house is rather isolated from the neighbors by the landscaping and they all know my habit is to remain inside for literally weeks at a time, working on some complex computer problem. I earn a moderately respectable income yearly, and dutifully report it all. None of my neighbors have ever been inside my house, nor I in theirs. But even were they to inspect the premises, they would find nothing untoward. That is, unless they discovered the opening to the tunnel, which leads from my basement all the way through to a heavy stand of trees on a three-acre plot which all the neighbors fear will someday be sold to a developer. After all, it is owned by a corporation with precisely that stated purpose. Their petty suburbanite fears are groundless. I, in fact, own the land. Inside the house is my principal computer.]

Let me resume: The principal computer is never disengaged. I can access it via telephone from anywhere in the world. A certain code will trigger its auto-dial feature and, after the appropriate loops, it will reach the

target. As soon as the phone is picked up and voice recognition—any human voice—occurs, the previously recorded message will be played.

So I will not actually leave the premises, just the basement. I use a portable phone to reach the computer. Even should the call be inadvertently intercepted—it is, after all, a radio transmission—it would not reveal anything but a series of connection-beeps. I make only one call per phone, and then discard it. After I reduce it to untraceable rubble, of course.

There was no need to tell the child this. I have learned that children are especially sensitive to commitments . . . even those made by their captors. The promise to return, for example. One might imagine the children would be happy if I never returned. After all, they are incapable of seeing deeply into the future—very much instant-gratification creatures, indeed. So with a plentiful supply of food—including, of course, the sort of so-called "junk food" many children are not allowed by their parents—and toys and games, they would not worry about being rescued. Yes, they might easily become bored—that is always a concern. But you would surmise that the return of their captor would hardly be greeted with pleasure. Yet, surprisingly, that has not been my experience. Without exception, each child was absolutely overjoyed when I returned. It took me considerable time to synthesize this data. My conclusion was as stated: The keeping of promises is critically important to children.

Therefore, I told the child I was going out to make the first call, but would return within two hours. I then simply went upstairs, dialed up my home-base computer, and waited patiently for the time to pass.

He finished the way I'd gotten used to by then—if I wanted to see the next installment, I had to pay up front. His question was a simple one this time:

>>Marco Interdonato. Wesley?<<

Marco Interdonato. Sure, I remembered that one. A spring-bomb in a public storage locker at La Guardia. Another of the killer's tests? Trickier than before, maybe? That one *was* Wesley's work. It was in the goodbye letter he'd left with me, the one where he took the weight for killing Mortay. And Train. And some other things I'd done. Maybe it convinced the cops. Maybe it didn't. But it wasn't something they ever leaked to the papers, so . . . It was like the blowgun-dart thing again. How the fuck could he *know* such things?

If I said Wesley's name now, would I be ratting him out . . . or confirming he was dead? I figured the killer could have put it all together without any inside knowledge. Morales always said Wesley left his fingerprints all over every job, and he wasn't talking forensics. That left only one way to play it:

yes

Xyla typed it in.

"Is there anything I could do to make you hot?" Nadine asked me. Her outfit didn't go with the question—she was wearing a gray jersey workout suit, and her hair was dank with sweat, like she'd been pushing herself hard just before I'd come to her place.

"You mean *you* you?"

"That's right. *Me* me."

"And by 'hot,' you mean aroused?"

"Yes!" she snapped, impatient now.

"What difference would it make?" I asked her.

"I want to have sex with you."

"Huh? From the minute I met you, all you've been telling me is how bad I want you, right? What a liar I am when I say I don't. So . . . what is this, another stupid game? I fuck you, that proves I'm a liar? Look, all men are liars. I'm no exception. You already have all the answers, why don't you just write 'Burke' on a vibrator and be done with it?"

"Why are you *like* this?" she demanded, stepping close to me. She smelled like a sweaty-sweet girl. No estrogen pheromones, just . . . girl-smell.

"Me? I'm not 'like' anything. I'm me."

"And *you* . . . you *don't* want to fuck me?"

"You know what? Sure. Who wouldn't? You got all the stuff. But you don't smell like pussy to me," I said, hoping that going crude would end this game . . . whatever it was.

"Oh yes?" she asked, standing right against me. "What do I smell like?"

"Like a trap," I told her.

She turned her back on me and walked a few feet away. Then she whirled around and stood looking at me for a few long seconds. And disappeared.

When she came back, she was wearing a pair of loose wide-leg white cotton shorts and a pink T-shirt, barefoot, smelling of soap. She took the chair next to mine. Asked: "What did you mean?"

"About . . . ?"

"Me smelling like a trap. What does that mean?"

"You got the information I wanted? The stuff you *said* you had to get me over here."

"I have it," she promised. "And you can have it. If you'll just answer my question. Honestly. One time. Will you do that?"

I looked at her cobalt eyes until I was sure she was connected, deciding what to tell her . . . deciding it would be the truth. I wasn't sure I needed anything more from her anyway. But I also sensed that she'd smell a lie this time. And that if she did, and it turned out that I *did* need her again, there'd be nobody home when I rang the bell.

"I think you're crazy," I told her, my voice low and carefully controlled. "I mean . . . clinically insane. Don't ask me why. Don't ask me what the diagnosis is. But you're . . . nuts. There's something about you so . . . off, I don't know what else to call it."

"You mean, like some *Fatal Attraction* thing?"

"No. I mean something like you having AIDS and wanting to spread it around before your time is up."

"*What? You're* the one who's crazy. I never even heard—"

"—of what? Spare me. There's been dozens of guys charged with murder for doing exactly that, and you know it. Or you're out of touch."

"Yes," she almost snarled, "dozens of *men.* But you can't name one woman who—"

"Sure I can. You're talking percentages, that's all. Like saying *most* child molesters are men. Or that most serial killers are. But not *all,* right? It's bound to happen. A woman with your body . . . you could probably kill a few hundred while you still looked good. And who knows how many they'd spread it to. If—"

"*Stop!* I do not have AIDS. Come on," she said, standing up. "I know a clinic, a private one on East Eleventh. We'll go together. You and me. Right now. Tell them we're going to be married, and we want to exchange results, okay? You get mine, I get yours. You don't have to give your name, just a code number. Fair enough?"

"Sit down," I told her. "It was an example, that's all. I didn't say I smelled AIDS on you. I just said it was some kind of major-league craziness . . . and I gave you an example of that, okay?"

"I don't have AIDS."

"All right. Fine. You don't have AIDS. Whatever you say. It doesn't matter to me."

"You wouldn't care if I—"

"I don't care if you live or die," I told her. "I work real hard at that—not caring about people who don't care about me. You say you don't have AIDS, I believe you. But you *are* crazy. And you *are* dangerous. And there's nothing you could do, no outfit you could put on, no girlfriend you could invite over . . . nothing that could make me take a chance against that."

"Is that what *she* told you?"

"Who?

"Strega? Strega the witch. Is that what she said? That I was crazy?"

"She didn't say anything about you," I lied. "Believe me, jealousy isn't her game."

"Then why would you—?"

"I don't have time to spell it out for you. Only reason you want to know is so you can camouflage it better, right?"

"Of *course* not! Camouflage what? That I'm 'crazy'? Don't be an idiot. I just want to know why *you* think so."

"Not today. Just get me the—"

"But you *will* tell me, right?"

"If you—"

"Not today. I don't care. But you'll tell me. Someday."

"Sure."

"I don't have any paper," she said.

"What? So this was all a—"

"I don't have any paper because there isn't any. Just listen to me for a minute, please? My . . . friend looked. Just like you asked. There is *nothing* in there."

"Not a single—"

"Not one single organized-crime figure whose child was kidnapped and not returned. Not one, period. But my . . . friend says maybe there's a reason for that."

"And that would be . . . ?"

"NYPD only has local records. Kidnapping, it's a federal offense. And there's Mafia in other cities. She said what you need is an FBI contact. They'd have a record of *every* kidnapping and—"

"And you just happen to have a friend who works there?"

"No," she said, almost sadly. "I don't. But I thought the information would be . . . helpful. I mean, at least it's something. A new place to look . . ."

I left her sitting there. She looked like a sad little girl. In a translucent mushroom cloud of menace.

"Why would you want this information?" Wolfe asked, not playing the game the way she always did. Away from me now. Maybe forever.

"What difference does that make?" I asked her. "You're in the business. You sell stuff. I want to buy some of it."

"You sell stuff too. And now you're *in* stuff, aren't you?" she asked, her gray eyes empty of even a hint of warmth.

"Not what you think," I told her. "On the square."

"What you're into? Or what you're telling me?"

"What I'm telling you."

"Is Wesley gone?" she asked me bluntly, cobra-killer eyes unblinking.

"He's dead," I said. Wondering if she'd take that for an answer.

"Kidnappings. Ransom paid. Child never returned. No arrests, no clearances, no nothing. And the targets are all Family members?"

"Yes."

"Going back . . . how far?"

Damn. Wolfe was the first one to think that way. Like a hunter. "Uh, twenty years," I said, pulling it at random.

"That's a big search."

"A big price, you mean. It's computers, right? How long could it take?"

"Everything wasn't databased back then," she said. "They only started keeping certain records recently."

"But kidnappings . . . that's been *federale* territory since Hoover was wearing a dress."

"Sure. But, still . . . they have to code it in by hand from those days. It may not be all done yet. And if you want—"

"I don't care what it costs," I told her.

She stood there facing me, hands at her sides, clenched, not giving ground. "If I find out you're in business with Wesley, I'll take you down myself," she said. Then she walked away.

"This one'll take a while to come up," Xyla told me, her eyes deliberately averted from the screen. "I can tell by the pre-coding when the message came in."

"How'd you learn all this stuff?" I asked her, more to kill time than anything else.

"I had to pretty much teach myself," she said. "It's mostly men—boys, really—who understand it. And you can't get them to teach you much."

"Why not?" I asked. "I don't mean to be offensive, but you're a pretty girl. I'd think those kids would be falling all over themselves to—"

"The opposite." Xyla laughed. "Cyber-boys are always flexing their little muscles, you understand? Like, if I go to the beach . . . I walk by, guys show off, understand?"

"Sure."

"Well, it's the same thing in Cyberville. Only the muscles they have, they're not real. I mean, I can't bench-press four hundred pounds. But I *can* do anything on a computer they can do—it doesn't take strength, just knowledge. If they give me theirs, they can't . . . pose, you know?"

"Yeah," I said. "And you figured that out yourself?"

"You want to know the truth?" she asked. "A man taught me. Not computers—what I just told you. And as soon as I snapped to it, I realized I'd have to learn the cyber-stuff myself. So I did."

I saw the screen change. "That's—"

"It's coming up?" she interrupted.

"Yeah."

"See you later," she said, walking out of the room.

The killer continued his serial. The same way. I watched it come up, then started to scroll. . . .

I had been careful to act on a Monday. Not only are reaction times typically slower on Monday mornings, it is a major "sick day" for civil servants, and late starts are also common. In addition, USA Today does not have a weekend edition, and I wanted to give the targets maximum opportunity to post their answer as directed without having to wait. A Tuesday response was impossible, and even Wednesday was unlikely. A drive to the airport would be necessary. Anyone buying USA Today from a regular newsstand might attract attention in a small town, and anyone buying on two consecutive days certainly would. Such risks must be minimized.

Obviously, this is a part of the operation where a confederate would be invaluable. But even had I not ruled this out on practical grounds, I confess that my artistic sensibilities would be offended by the appearance of

collaboration with others. I refer, of course, to *internal* appearance—externally, the appearance of having confederates involved in kidnappings is, indeed, one of the critical elements of success.

The nearest airport was approximately 77 minutes, depending on road conditions. [I was not willing to make the trip during the early-morning hours, at least not until there was considerable commuter traffic. The additional investment of time was worth the cover traffic would provide.] A minimum of three hours' absence was thus required, so Wednesday was out of the question.

Fortunately, the child was quite capable of self-entertainment. The two-day wait passed uneventfully, and I did not have to resort to the tranquilizers some of the other children had required. At the age of ten—and a highly precocious ten she was, although her school records had not so indicated—boredom plays a significant role in counter-tranquillity. I asked the child if she wanted to play with any of the dolls I had purchased, realizing, from experience, that some children would eagerly accept a new doll while others only wanted their own—something I could not assure, depending on the circumstances of the original capture. The child refused, but made no reference to any doll of her own. Perhaps she was already outgrowing such things. . . .

Common thugs have "equipment" for their crimes. I have a repertoire. This includes a working knowledge of the developmental milestones in children and their unique linguistic capacities. One must be careful, for example, never to use "tag" questions when conducting interviews. One does *not* ask a child: "It's really nice that it has stopped raining, isn't it?" This common lawyer's trick requires that the responder confirm the proposition in order to answer the question: i.e., to agree that it *had*, in fact, been raining, even if the child was not aware that it had been and could observe only the fact that it is *now* not doing so. I have also learned that an engaged child is a less anxious child, and so I delicately questioned my captive to ascertain her tolerance for engagement. As it developed, she was profoundly uninterested in what I had been assured were "age-appropriate" games.

However, I did have a variety of higher-level board games on hand, ranging in difficulty. Her favorite proved to be something called Risk, a strategy-based game not intended for children her age. . . . I had added it almost as an afterthought. I explained that Risk was not really designed for only two players, and she quickly grasped the concept of playing two roles simultaneously. I was prepared to let her win a moderate number of games, balancing a child's natural competitiveness against the need to maintain intellectual challenge for her, but it proved unnecessary: There is sufficient luck in any game which involves rolling dice so that she managed to win legitimately a number of times. I noted with interest that she did not insist on keeping score, nor did she "celebrate" her victories.

"What's a game that has the right design?" she asked suddenly.

"I don't understand."

"Well, you said Risk isn't really for two players. There must be games that *are*, right?"

"Certainly. There are card games—casino, gin rummy, and others of that sort."

"Do you have cards?"

"Uh, no, I don't."

"Can you get some? When you go out?"

"I can," I told her, remembering that every airport in the world sells such items.

"What else?"

"What else?"

"I mean, besides cards. What other games?"

"Oh. Well, there's checkers. And chess."

"Do you have them?"

"No, I'm afraid I don't."

"Can you—?"

"Yes, Angelique," I said. "I can try to find a set while I'm out."

"No, I didn't mean that. Couldn't you . . . make one?"

"Make a . . . oh yes, I see. Actually, I have no such skills. But *you* do. So if I provided the schematic—"

"What's a schematic?"

"It's like a plan. A picture of how something works."

"You draw pictures?" she asked, an unreadable look on her face.

"No, child. Not pictures, plans. There's a great difference."

"What's the difference?"

Realizing I should have anticipated just such a question and incorporated the answer in my prior explanation, I mentally resolved to concentrate with greater task-oriented precision. "A plan is something that can be drawn with instruments, say a ruler, or a protractor, or a T-square. A diagram. Art is freehand. Very individual. No two pieces of art are ever exactly the same."

"Can't people copy art?"

"Certainly they can try. But a true connoisseur could always distinguish between an imitation and the genuine article."

"What's a connoisseur?"

"A person who is especially knowledgeable about a certain subject. It could be food, or antiques, or even wild animals, for that matter."

"But it has to be a thing?" the child asked.

"A . . . thing?"

"Yes. Those are all things, right? Not something you do."

"Well, certainly, one could be a connoisseur of . . . oh, I don't know . . . say, ballet. Or football. Those are not objects, they are performances. Do you understand?"

"But could you do them yourself and still be one?"

"I am not certain I—"

"Could you, like, be an artist and still be a . . . connoisseur of art?"

"Ah. Yes, to be sure. In fact, there are those who say one cannot be a great writer unless one is also a connoisseur of writing . . . as an art form, do you see?"

"Sure! That's me. I love to draw, and I love to look at . . . paintings and stuff. So I guess I'm a connoisseur, aren't I?"

"Well, that would depend on the criteria you employ."

"I don't—"

"I mean," I corrected myself, "whether you had good taste. In other words, if you liked only very fine art, you could be a connoisseur."

"I like everything."

"Well, then, you—"

"But I don't like everything the same. I mean, I like some stuff a lot better. So could I be a—?"

"Yes, child. That's correct. You certainly could be. Shall I show you the . . . drawing of the game?"

"Yes, please."

Using the edge of a hardcover book, I quickly roughed in a diagram of a checkerboard—sixty-four identical squares. Then I used a half-dollar to make a pair of circles. "See, Angelique? There will be thirty-two pieces, half of them one color and half of them another. And we put them on a board that will look like this. Do you think you could make one?"

"Sure I could. But I'd need some construction paper. Do you know what that is?"

"Not only do I know," I told her, a trace of pride perhaps in my voice, "I have some right here." [In fact, I always keep a plentiful supply for my captives, having found that making the sort of mess children create with brightly colored paper occupies some of them for long periods of time.]

When I gave her the paper and a pair of scissors (with rounded tips) she set to work. When we took a break for the midday meal, she was so absorbed I had to summon her twice.

The checkerboard was finished by mid-afternoon. I pretended not to notice the child's progress, concentrating on the portable computer's screen. [Yes, obviously, the computer will contain incriminating evidence. But should I be apprehended in the company of a captive, it would be coals to Newcastle.]

"It's ready!" she called out, and I got up to see her project.

My astonishment was impossible to conceal . . . which was fortuitous, as it seemed to delight the child. The board was composed of what appeared to be several dozen layers, a multi-colored laminate (the top of which was a dazzling white) on which she had drawn the squares to perfection. My amazement, however, was reserved for the pieces themselves. Although each was a disk of the same size, and although the thirty-two of them were equally divided between a sort of Day-Glo orange and a misty blue (I had not disclosed to the child that the traditional colors are red and black), each piece was individually decorated with a tiny drawing . . . everything from butterflies to bears to houses and cars. The work was as complex and delicate as scrimshaw and, to my not-untrained eye, displayed no less skill.

"This is absolutely remarkable," I told the child.

"Do you like it?"

"Very much. It's . . . magnificent."

"It's for you, all right? To keep. Like a present?"

"I will treasure it," I told her solemnly, realizing even as I spoke that it too would be evidence and I could not keep it, but . . .

"Can we play now?" she asked.

"After dinner," I promised.

The screen switched colors. I knew what was coming, so I called out Xyla's name.

>>Queensboro Bridge: (1) You present? (2) Caliber?<<

I said some words to Xyla and she made them appear on the screen:

(1) yes (2) .223 Remington

She hit the keys, and my message disappeared. Somewhere in cyber-space, I had just told a killer I was with Wesley when he'd done one of his hits. And proved it.

You know how it is—you talk different things over with different people. I had no one to talk this over with. No point guessing what the next installment would be, or how it would end. I couldn't make a move until he was finished with his story. If it was a story.

Nadine called me at Mama's. Asked: "Do you have anything yet?"

"No," I told her, and hung up, not even sure if I was lying.

When I called Strega to ask her the same question, she just hissed at me, asked what I *really* wanted. So I hung up on her too.

I know a brilliant guy when it comes to unhinged minds. Doc runs a little private clinic now, but I'd met him in the joint—he'd interned as a prison shrink. I could have asked him, I guess. But there just didn't seem any point. He always said I knew more about freaks than he did.

You could only ask the Mole techno-questions. And Michelle only emotional ones.

Mama knew money. Max knew combat.

The Prof knew it all. But he didn't know this.

I had the lines out. But I couldn't do anything until I got a bite.

I spent a lot of time with Pansy. Wondering how much time she had left. They say Neos are a long-lived breed. But Pansy had already gone past where they said. She looked okay—fatter, slower, maybe, but okay. I took her to a vet I know in Brooklyn. He's not a guy I like—he works pit-bull fights for cash—but when it comes to medical stuff for someone you love, you look the other way. He said she was in good shape: heart, lungs, all that. Nothing wrong with her. "She's just old," the vet said.

"Me fucking too," I told him as I forked over the money.

I was in the Plymouth, on my way back from wasting a couple of hours with a punk who said he wanted to buy three crates of guns. But he didn't show me the cash and I sure wasn't showing him any guns first. Reason the conversation took so long, neither of us knew if the other was ATF. He didn't feel that way to me. Just some disturbo who wanted to talk politics and had been thrown out of too many bars, so he set himself up as a buyer and got an audience that way. Pitiful stupid loser. When the ATF *did* drop him, he'd shriek "Entrapment!" all the way to Leavenworth.

The cell phone throbbed next to my heart. I unholstered it, said: "What?"

"Incoming." Xyla's voice.

I punched the throttle.

There was no expectation of immediate response on my part. Indeed, the voice message transmitted had provided different directions entirely:

> **We have your daughter. She has not been harmed in any way. This is not personal. We are professionals. Do not notify the authorities. This can be resolved very easily if you cooperate. Place an ad in the Personals column of USA Today which states: "Lost at O'Hare Airport: Saudi Arabian passport number 125689774. Repeat: 125689774. Reward for return. No questions asked." When we see the ad, we will contact you by this same method. Any attempt to**

trace calls will be detected by our equipment and the subject will be terminated without further contact. You may, however, record any incoming calls so that you need not rely on your note-taking ability.

I have found that allowing the target to tape calls provides them with a measure of reassurance. Even the most cooperative of victims can be subject to attacks of nervousness, and I would not want such a mental state in those whose *precise* cooperation would be required throughout the process.

USA Today was selected because of its status as a "national" newspaper, available from a wide variety of totally anonymous outlets. The ad itself has the ring of authenticity: While I cannot be certain without hacking into the passenger manifests of various airlines—something of which I am certainly capable—logic compels the conclusion that some Saudi nationals have passed through America's busiest airport within the two weeks or so preceding the placement of the ad. Further, because it is a common practice of contraband-traffickers to place apparently innocent ads which contain a series of numbers, those in law enforcement who scrutinize such placements on a regular basis would assume the ad I requested to be in that category, never connecting it to my actual intent.

Finally, of course, no physical contact is required for me to read the ad . . . or to read subsequent entries in that same forum.

My next task was to monitor local radio, alert to any news of the kidnapping. There was no such reference. Although I had little fear of being discovered accidentally, the thought of roaming search parties of self-righteous locals, any of whom would trade their paltry futures for a few minutes' exposure on television, was not comforting to me. By then, the bus would have been discovered. But even had I been careless enough—and I assure you, I was not—to leave some indication of my brief presence, any

bus occupied on a daily basis by a dozen or so schoolchildren would prove beyond the forensic capabilities of any local operation. In my work, I rely to some extent upon the jealousy and territoriality of local jurisdictions, and do not expect FBI involvement for a minimum of seventy-two hours. And the FBI, following its own procedures for excluding known prints, would be required to take exemplars from all of the children who habitually ride that bus. Amazing though it will sound to the uninitiated, my experience indicates that at least one of the families of the children who were not kidnapped will balk at this intrusion into their "civil rights," thus delaying the process even further.

None of that is of any consequence.

Then he was done.

I had my mouth open to call Xyla when she walked in. Almost like she knew how long it was going to take me.

"Question coming?" she asked.

"Always has, so far," I replied.

It took less than a minute.

>>Last address?<<

Whose address did this maniac want? Mine? Wesley's? Wesley never had an address. The last time I'd seen him face to face, it was in an abandoned building he was using as a staging area . . . before his last strike. Was he trying to tie me to . . . No, what was the point? All this . . . information. Fuck it. I spoke to Xyla and she made it appear on the screen.

Meserole Street

My answer to his last question had been a pair of guesses. Even if I was right and he was asking about Wesley, the ice-man's last hideout wasn't actually on Meserole Street, it was just off the corner.

But I couldn't give you the number of the building if my life depended on it. That neighborhood probably didn't even have a goddamned zip code.

He was getting cute now. No reason for it.

None I understood, anyway.

"Not a single one," Wolfe said.

That was all she said. I felt . . . surrounded. We were in the no-man's-land under the Williamsburg Bridge. Someone I didn't recognize was standing off to one side, holding a revolver. It was pointed at the ground, but I was close enough to see his left hand on his right wrist. And that the piece was cocked. Mick was somewhere behind me. Max had always figured him for a karateka of some kind, but we'd never known for sure. Pepper was in the front seat of her car, watching, the motor running.

Me, I was alone.

Wolfe was looking at me, a glowing red neon *I Don't Trust You!* sign in her gray eyes. Cold gray now.

"Can you—?"

"On what you gave me, no."

"Then I—"

"Just give me the money," Wolfe said.

I guessed I'd sent the killer what he wanted. When I opened the next message, he was right back . . . continuing from where he'd left off.

When I returned—allegedly from making a telephone call from some remote location—the child was munching calmly on some cookies, a glass of juice at her elbow, her face half buried in one of the books I had procured in anticipation of her stay. If the restraints bothered her in any way, it was not apparent.

"Did you call them?" she asked, looking up as casually as if I had been a legitimate member of her household who had gone out to perform some mundane task.

"I did," I told her. "But there will be no response from them for a minimum of forty-eight hours. This whole process will take a certain amount of time."

"How much time?" That was a reasonable question, especially from a child's perspective. Usually, I am careful to keep the estimate quite short (bearing in mind, of course, that even the modified form of sensory deprivation attendant to keeping a captive away from all sources of natural light is sufficient to completely blur the concept of "days"), but I sensed that this child was simply asking for information, and not emotionally invested in the response.

"It could be as long as two or three weeks," I said.

"Is it ever longer?" she asked.

I watched her eyes, aware that innocence is often a mask. Had she deduced my true calling from my prior conversation? Or was she somehow baiting me into revelation? Could she simply be curious? I decided to make no assumptions. . . .

"Why do you ask that? Do you think I have done this sort of thing before?"

"Oh, you must have," she said, her little face perfectly serious. "You know everything about it. Nobody's very good at something the first time they try it, are they?"

"Well," I explained, "there is a difference between talent and skill."

"I don't understand," she said.

"Let us assume you have a natural talent for . . . oh, I don't know, say painting, all right? Now, you would be quite good at it as soon as you picked up a brush. That is, you would have a natural . . . aptitude for it. But the more you practiced, the better you would become."

"I have a natural talent," the child piped up.

"And what is that?" I asked her.

"I can draw."

"Can you?" I asked, simply to engage the child. Her work on the checkerboard pieces rendered her declaration quite superfluous.

"Yes, I can. I don't mean trace, or color either. Not like a baby. I can draw."

"What do you draw?" I asked her, drawing her (pun intended) further away from the potentially frightening aspects of her situation.

"I can draw anything," she said with the smug confidence of the very young.

This disturbed me. I pride myself on being fully equipped, studying the child I capture well in advance to be prepared for any eventuality. For example, I once took a child who was diabetic. It was greatly reassuring to inform the parents on my very first call that I was aware of the problem and our "nurse" was on hand with all appropriate medications. Improvisation is not my forte, and leaving the hideout to obtain materials was out of the question. Still, I asked the child: "What do you need to draw?"

She looked at me questioningly, but said nothing. Clearly, she required a further explanation.

"What . . . materials?" I asked. "Paper, pencils . . . what sort of implements do you require?"

"Oh!" she said brightly. "I have everything. Right in my backpack."

A momentary flash of paranoia—that is, paranoia in the classic psychiatric sense, not the functional hypervigilance which is the trademark of a successful practitioner of my profession—overcame me for an instant, but then I told her she was free to get what she needed.

"I can't reach it," she said.

And I saw she was speaking the truth. Her restraints permitted significant freedom of movement, but I had placed the backpack in a far corner of the basement, and it was, in fact, beyond her grasp. I walked over and picked it up. Professional experience commanded that I search it thoroughly . . . but the finely honed instincts—which are, obviously, not "instincts" at all, being not bio-genetic but actually the synthesis of sufficient experiences so that they surface as quickly as if encoded—developed over those same years caused me to hand it to the child without examination.

She took it from me as though she expected nothing less. Some captives are querulous and demanding. Others are abject and fearful. Some are floridly terrified, others virtually mute. This one fit no such definition. She was . . . at peace. Not with the resignation that comes over an individual when all hope is gone, but with the sense that the future, while immutable, was acceptable.

"Is everything there, Angelique?" I asked.

"My name isn't Angelique," she replied, not looking inside the backpack.

"Angel, then," I offered.

"My name is Zoë," she said in a voice that brooked no disagreement.

I avoided the usual adult trap of condescension and merely said, "My apologies, Zoë. Now . . . is everything there?"

"You didn't open it," she replied.

"I . . . don't understand."

"You didn't open it," she repeated. "From the time I got on the bus, I was the only one who had it. It's always been with me."

"And so . . . ?"

"So if you didn't open it, whatever was there is still there, see?"

"Yes. That was a very good deduction. You'd make a good detective," I told her, mentally chastising myself for overlooking the obvious—if I were interested in protecting a child from kidnapping, I would certainly have affixed a tracking device in some way, and a backpack would be quite suitable. I would not make such a mistake again.

"I would?" she asked, checking my face carefully.

"You certainly would," I assured her, my voice brisk and professional. "A good detective works only with the facts. Anything that is not a fact should be ignored."

"There'll be detectives, won't there? Looking for me, I mean."

"Certainly. They have probably already begun."

"But they won't find me, will they?"

"No, child, they won't."

"Because you're smarter than them, right?"

"I am. . . . It is not strictly a matter of intelligence," I explained. "It is more a matter of careful planning and skillful execution. There is no accounting for random chance, but—"

"So they *could* find me?" she interrupted.

"It is possible. Nothing is one hundred percent certain in these matters. There is always *some* chance."

"Oh," is all she said.

"Don't you want to draw?" I asked her.

"I always want to draw."

"Then why not . . . ?"

"I don't want you to be mad," she said, her voice tentative.

"Why would I be angry?" I asked her, hoping to teach by example the difference between insanity and annoyance—people are so imprecise in their verbiage, but only children seem capable of learning.

"Because I want to draw you," she said, her eyes wide and alert.

A conundrum was thus produced. The child's intelligence was manifest, a phenomenon not to be ignored. Therefore, despite my desire to make her stay with me as pleasant and stress-free as possible under the circumstances, surely she realized that a sketch of her own kidnapper would be of great value to the authorities. On the other hand, she certainly had ample opportunity to use her eyes, if not her skill at drawing, and my features were, presumably, memorized. If I refused her request, it might supplement the illusion that she was, eventually, to be returned. Conversely, it would perhaps distress her. On balance, I elected to compromise.

"You may certainly draw me, if you wish," I told her. "But under the circumstances I'm sure you will understand you'll have to leave the . . . artwork here when you leave."

"It was for you anyway," she said. "I never keep what I draw."

I pondered this internally. Children are generally guileless, but that is a rule to which there are many exceptions . . . some characterological, but most situational. Children are extraordinarily self-absorbed—a characteristic often retained into adulthood. But that sort of analysis did not figure in my assessment—globalization is not a valid problem-solving tool. Why would the child never keep her own handiwork? Under other circumstances, I would have simply asked the apparently invited question. But the child's mien was that of someone who did not expect to be questioned, so I merely said:

"Very well. How would you like me to . . . pose?"

"You don't have to do anything," she assured me. "I can just draw while we . . . talk or something, okay?"

"All right."

She opened her backpack and removed a thick drawing tablet and several pencils.

"I have pastel sticks too," she said, noticing my observations. "But I don't draw people with them. Not until I'm done with the pencils."

"Very sensible," I told her. "Pencils are more precise, aren't they?"

"They're sharper," she replied, as though amplifying her agreement.

She busied herself at the tablet. I watched her work, dark hair spilling over her face, almost obscuring it from view. I glanced at the tablet and noticed that a good many pages had been removed. Apparently it was true that the child did not keep her work once it was completed. I . . .

"How long does it usually take?" Her voice intruded into my thoughts, startling me. Even without glancing at my watch, I realized some considerable time had passed.

"How long does what take, Zoë?"

She smiled, perhaps at my use of the name she had selected. "For them to . . . I mean, don't you have to talk to them? So you can . . ."

"Oh. I understand what you mean now. There is no set rule. Sometimes it takes several weeks for the entire arrangements to be worked out."

"What's the shortest time it ever took?"

"Nine days," I answered without thinking. Immediately, I began to berate myself internally for my foolishness. The answer I gave the child was an honest one, but it would not be as reassuring as I had hoped.

"But this will probably take longer, won't it?"

"Yes. Absolutely," I told her, grateful that she was not going to fixate on a nine-day period and become anxious if it were exceeded.

"You're hard to draw," she said.

"Why is that?"

"Your face keeps . . . shifting. I don't know, I'm not sure. You have to draw the skull."

"The skull?"

"The skull beneath the skin. You have to draw that first. That's the part that stays the same."

"I'm not sure I follow you exactly," I told her. "May I have a look?"

"No!" she replied, the first hint of sharpness in her voice since I had captured her. "I don't like anyone to see my drawing until I'm done. Sometimes I don't get it right, and I have to keep doing it. So I don't like anyone to see it until it's true. Please?"

"Certainly," I assured her. "Every artist must work in his or her own way."

She smiled gratefully and went back to work.

On her first night, I asked the child her normal bedtime, but she was vague in response. Offered a choice of evening meals, however, she became animated. When I told her that, yes, she could mix several of the meals I had planned, incorporating components as she wished, she clapped her hands in delight. After great deliberation, she chose spaghetti, spinach, and
liver.

"Do you think that's gross?" she asked.

"As a matter of fact, I think it is quite creative," I told her. "I believe I'll have the same."

The child helped with the cooking. She ate her meal with relish, but watched me anxiously until I assured her that, indeed, her mixed selection was delicious.

"And very good for you too," she added.

Realizing that, for whatever reason, she was not going to be precise about her normal bedtime, I told her that she could, while she was staying with me, go to bed anytime she wished. After all, there would be no school for her in the morning.

"Are you going to do it?" she asked.

"Do what?"

"Teach me. I have a friend. Jeanne Ellen. She's home-schooled. Do you know what that is?"

"Certainly. Some states permit—"

"Are you going to do it?" she interrupted.

"Do . . . what?"

"Home-school me," she replied, as though I were a bit slow.

"Well, I . . ."

"I have most all of my books with me," she said, a pleading undertone to her voice. "And you have *lots* of books here too, the ones you got for me, I mean."

I began to protest that I was not familiar with her coursework, but quickly self-edited. After all, how complex could a fifth-grade curriculum be, especially given the abysmal state of American education generally?

"All right," I agreed. "But you had better get ready for bed, just in case you fall asleep."

"I don't have any pajamas."

"My apologies. I showed you the books, but not the clothes. Over there in the chest of drawers. Take a look. It's all new, of course. I had to guess at your sizes, but I believe I was quite accurate."

The child immediately ran over to where I had indicated and began pawing through the clothing. It was all of good quality, but not up to her usual standard, I assumed.

"Can I keep all this?" she asked, surprising me. After all, if she was not permitted an excess of books, why . . . ? Still, I did not pursue the issue.

"Of course," I said. "But now go put on your pajamas, all right? You can use the bathroom."

She trotted off without a word, emerging in about fifteen minutes. I had no anxiety about the time lapse—escape from the bathroom was impossible and it was devoid of potential weaponry.

"I brushed my teeth," she announced when she emerged, wrapped in the pink terry-cloth bathrobe I had purchased in anticipation of a little girl's natural modesty in the presence of a stranger.

I made up the bed for her, and sat down to read. I left the television on. In the past, that had always succeeded in eventually lulling the children to sleep. But this one proved remarkably resistant. It was almost midnight when I looked up to find her wide awake.

"Are you having trouble getting to sleep?" I asked her.

"No. I'm just not sleepy."

"All right."

"But I *should* sleep, right?"

"Well, of course. At some point, everyone—"

"Could you read me a story?" she asked. "That would make me sleepy, I know it."

"I—"

"There's lots of books," she reminded me. "And I haven't read hardly any of them."

"Do your parents usually read to you before you—"

"No," she said, her voice flat. "Please?"

I found a book about a mother polar bear and her cub and their various adventures as they crossed the Arctic ice cap in search of food. True to her word, she was fast asleep before I got a dozen pages into it.

She appeared to sleep peacefully.

I felt Xyla in the room, but she wasn't standing where she could see the screen.

"This was a lot longer one, huh?" she asked.

"Yeah. I don't know what it means. . . ."

"I thought he was limiting transmission time to prevent us from fingering him, but he has to know there's no way to do that with these little cookies—they're files with programs—he keeps mixing in there. Not going over an open line."

"But when you send him the answer to all his questions . . . ?"

"I don't think he's there, waiting for it. I think the program he's using just files it someplace else. He could open it whenever he wanted. I think maybe—"

I held up my hand to silence her, watching his question pop up:

>>Age first contact?<<

I wasn't going to guess what he meant anymore. I played it the way it looked: how old was I when I first met Wesley? Truth is, I wasn't sure. But I gave Xyla a number for him anyway.

12

I could never bring Wesley's face into my mind. Never see it clearly. He didn't look like anything. He was a generic . . . never got a second glance from anyone. Most of his targets never saw him at all. This is where I'm supposed to say "except for his eyes," right? People who write those serial-killer porno books never met the real thing. Anyway, Wesley was no serial killer. He was an assassin. And his eyes didn't show you anything. Nothing about him did.

I can hear his voice, though. Clear as if he was right next to me. It was a machine's voice, lifeless, no inflection. Just a communication device. I remember every word from the last time we talked:

"Something about a kid?" the ice-man had asked me, wondering how I had stumbled across his business.

"Yeah."

"That soft spot—it's like a bull's eye on your back."

"Nothing I can do," I said. Lying to Wesley was . . . wasted.

"It's not your problem, right?" he asked me, trying to understand. "Not your kid."

"I didn't want it like this," I told him. "I wanted to be . . . something else."

"What?"

I dragged on my smoke, knowing I'd finally have to say it. I looked deep into the monster's empty eyes. "I wanted to be you," I said.

"No, you don't. I'm not afraid. Of anything. It's not worth it."

Even as he said that to me, so many years ago, I knew it was true. But when we were coming up, Wesley was the icon. He was never afraid, even when we were kids. I don't mean he was ready to go to Fist City with another guy over some insult. But he *would* take your life if you put your hands on him. Not right then and there—Wesley was no slugger. But someday. Guaranteed. It was all over the street, even then. You fucked with Wesley, you were dead. Money in the bank. Earning compound interest.

After he got out of prison that last time, I guess he figured he might as well make a living at what he was.

Wesley had a different mother than me. But his birth certificate had the same blank spots mine did.

He saved my life once, when we were kids. A stupid thing. Me and another guy in the gang, lying on the rat-slime next to the subway tracks, our heads on the rail. Train coming. First one to jump back loses. I was ready to die right then. Die for a rep I'd never be around to enjoy. To have a name to replace the one I'd never been given. Wesley was the one who pulled me back, just in time. The other guy had already jumped, but I hadn't seen it . . . not with my eyes closed.

Later, when Wesley went to work, I never went near him. Once in a while, he'd reach out for me. Whatever he wanted, I would do it. Not because I was afraid of him. Wesley didn't work like that. No robberies, no extortions, no scams. Wesley killed people. That was his work.

When he got tired of his work, he finished it. By doing as much of it as he could in one monstrous move.

The whisper-stream still throbs with it. Wondering if the ice-man had another way out. I knew he didn't. Knew he wanted to go. I read the note he'd left behind—mailed to me just before he walked his last walk.

But as long as the whisper-stream flowed, Wesley would never die.

"You ever watch two girls have sex?" Nadine asked me, a sheaf of paper in her two clasped hands, still trafficking in a product I didn't want.

"Yes."

"Ever do it with them?"

"Why?"

"I thought maybe if I put on a little show for you first—me and my . . . friend—you might change your mind. Ever see a real pony girl? I'm a *good* rider."

I let out a long breath to show her my patience was low. "I already told you once—there's nothing you could do. Now either give me that stuff or not."

But all the paper she'd tempted me over to her house with was crap. Her cop pal had looked a bit deeper, that's all. And came up empty.

The guy who opened the door was big, six-six minimum, and built to match. He had a mild face, rimless glasses, short-cropped hair. I remembered him from the place I'd met Crystal Beth, always sitting off in a corner, drawing. And he'd been at this joint too, the first time I'd come. What was his name . . . ? Oh yeah:

"Where's everybody else, Rusty?" I asked him.

"Uh, there was a little thing. Earlier. They'll be back soon."

"Okay. I'll just—"

"He's here," Xyla announced, standing in the doorway to the computer room.

"Uh, see you later," the big guy said.

As soon as we got into her room, Xyla opened him up.

To my surprise, the child did not rush through the evening meal in her eagerness to play the new game. Indeed, she politely inquired if she could, again, select the menu and, given permission, spent the better part of an hour examining the various options before making a decision. Which was: Pasta in a cream sauce of her own creation speckled with chunks of albacore.

"It would be better with bread," she assured me.

"Bread doesn't keep well," I replied. "And since we are going to be—"

"Well, couldn't you pick some up? When you go out the next time, I mean?"

"I will . . . try," I finally agreed, understanding intuitively that the child was not referring to typical manufactured bread—she expected me to visit an actual bakery. That was out of the question. Still, if I remembered correctly—and, in fact, I have never failed to remember correctly—there was a bakery of some sort right within the airport.

We ate in relative silence, for which I was grateful. The child's manners were superb—she invariably asked if I would pass a condiment rather than reaching for it herself. But her visage appeared troubled.

"Is something wrong, Zoë?" I asked.

"Do you like it?"

"It?"

"The *food*. Do you like the food?"

"It's delicious."

"Well, you didn't *say* anything."

"That was bad manners on my part," I said, truthfully enough. "I was enjoying it so that I forgot myself."

"Oh, that's all right," she said, smiling. "I just . . . When people don't say anything, I never know . . . I mean, I always think . . ."

"I promise to tell you what I'm thinking, Zoë. How would that be?"

"Oh I would *love* that. You're not . . . teasing, are you? You'll really tell me?"

"I certainly will. But only when you ask, fair enough?"

"Okay! And I won't ask all the time, I swear."

"Whenever you like, child."

Throughout the rest of the meal, we talked around pockets of silence, but never once did she ask what I was thinking.

"Can I do it myself?" she asked as we started to clean up after dinner.

"I thought it would be easier if we both did it."

"No. I mean, yes, maybe it would. But it doesn't have to be easier, does it? I mean, I would like to do it myself. It would be fun."

"Very well, Zoë. And thank you."

"You're welcome." She smiled.

Not having access to a newspaper, I flicked on the television set to watch PBS as the child busied herself in the kitchen portion of the basement.

I must have been resting my eyes, half-listening to the television, when the child tapped me on the shoulder. Startled, I turned to her, waiting for her to speak.

"What's that?" she asked, pointing at the screen.

It only took a second to ascertain. "Some footage of tribal warfare," I told her.

"Why are they killing everyone?"

How to explain xenophobia and its natural byproduct, genocide, to a child? "They hate each other," I tried for simplicity, knowing what was coming next.

"Why?"

I was not disappointed, but no closer to an explanation. It was clear that the child was not trying to be annoying, that she was deeply puzzled by what appeared, on its surface, to be patent insanity. Yet, in thinking through to a response accessible by a child of Zoë's age, I could not escape the internal logic. After all, tribalism is per se insanity. Still, I made another attempt:

"Do you know about Indians, Zoë? Have you ever studied about them in school?"

"Not really. But I know . . . something about them, I guess."

"All right. You know Indians are aligned into tribes, yes?"

"Yes. Like Apaches and Navahos and—"

"That's right. Now, even today, there are tribes too. In the Balkans, in Africa, in the Middle East. And some of them hate each other. They have for many, many years. Sometimes, when that kind of hatred builds up long enough, one tribe attempts to exterminate the other."

"Exterminate? Like with—"

"Yes, like with termites in a house. But the difference is . . . it would be . . . as if the goal was to exterminate every single termite from the face of the earth. So no more termites would exist anywhere."

"But . . . people . . . ?"

"To a virulent tribalist, people of other tribes are the same as termites. Mere vermin, to be disposed of by any means at hand."

"They all want to kill each other?"

"Yes."

"In . . . these different places?"

"In other places too, Zoë. Kurds and Iraqis. Turks and Armenians. Serbs and Croats. Hausa and Ibo. The list is endless."

"But not in America, right?"

"Child, what you must understand is that those thoughts are everywhere. In America too, certainly. Do you know anything about Adolf Hitler?"

"Yes. He was an evil man. He wanted to kill all the Jews."

"That is correct. And there are people in America who still follow Hitler."

"They want to kill all the Jews too?"

"Yes. And there are others who want to kill all the blacks. And blacks who want to kill all the whites. And—"

"Why?"

"The reasons are too complex to explain simply, Zoë. Some are mentally ill. Some are inadequates who can only feel superior by denigrating others. Some are profiteers, who make money from hatred. Some actually believe in a sort of manifest destiny—that God has designated them to rule the earth."

"Will America be like that someday?"

"It is not impossible," I told her. "With the technology for mass destruction so readily available that any moron can kill thousands all by himself, race war in America is not out of the question."

"So where is it safe?"

"There's no *place* that is safe, Zoë. Only people are safe."

"I'm safe now, right?"

"Yes, you are perfectly safe here."

"Do they kill children too?"

"Exterminators do not discriminate on the basis of age," I explained.

She started to cry then. I was . . . confused by that reaction, especially as I had assured her of her own safety. Her immediate safety, in point of fact, and children have a more truncated view than adults—the "future" to them usually is not very much beyond the present. I had no wish for the child to be in distress, and vaguely understood that I could have responded to her inquiries in a way different from that which I had elected. Still, beyond the usual platitudes so beloved of adults, I was bereft of any actual comfort potential, and I sensed that Zoë would be impervious to hollow clichés. However, by the time I had reasoned all this through in what I acknowledge to be a laborious fashion, the child quieted down, utilizing some self-soothing inner mechanism I could not immediately detect.

"Aren't we going to play checkers?" she asked me, rubbing her eyes as though to banish traces of her just-departed tears.

It induced no consternation that the child grasped the principle of checkers almost immediately. By that time, I had grown accustomed to her quickness. We played only three games—"practice games," she termed them—with me showing her the consequences of each move as she proposed it, before she announced she was ready to play "for real."

This proved problematic. Unlike Risk, checkers is a finite activity, with all probabilities susceptible to near-instantaneous calculation. Therefore, it was impossible for the child to defeat me. And having proposed the activity myself, it would be unseemly for me to dominate the contest. Fearing she might detect a deliberate miscue, I provided full disclosure: "You understand, Zoë, this game really isn't for children."

"Why not?" was the reply, as expected.

"Well, because it takes years to actually win a single game. Years of practice. And most children don't have the patience for that."

"I'm very patient," she assured me.

"I am certain that you are. But, still, won't you get bored playing if you never win?"

"It's still playing," the child said. "It's just not winning."

That comment seemed far too sagacious for a child of her age, but I allowed it to pass and we began to play "for real."

Zoë lost every game for almost three hours without a word of complaint.

"Sleepy," she finally said, her head lolling.

I did not think it proper to undress the child, so I simply opened the bed and placed her there, covering her against a possible chill.

##

"Would it work if we put something inside first?" the child asked me early the next morning.

"I'm not certain what you're asking," I told her. Which was certainly the truth.

"Inside the biscuits."

"I don't . . ." I began, but then, upon actually looking at what I had been doing, I understood the question. The "biscuits" to which the child had been referring were not fresh from a bakery. Rather, they came in a tube designed to be stored in a refrigerator. One simply pops open the tube by pulling a strip down the side of the container. Inside, there are eight white disks of dough which, if placed in the oven for the requisite time, emerge as biscuits. I eat such products frequently. So frequently, in fact, that I go into auto-pilot mode as I cook for myself, never paying attention to the process.

"You want to put something inside the biscuits *before* they are baked?" I asked her.

"Yes, please."

"Why would you want to do that, Zoë?"

"Just to make it different. Maybe . . . even better. Just to . . . I don't know . . . see what happens. Do you think it would work?"

"I must say I don't know. The biscuits are a specific design. If they are separated to insert something, that might alter the result. And whatever was inserted would be subjected to the same degree of heat for the same duration."

"But can't we *see*?"

"If you like."

"Goody!" the child exclaimed, clapping her hands. She immediately began to forage through the entire supply of foodstuffs, holding up various options much as an artist might examine a dab of color before applying it to canvas. She finally settled on an entire palette: Celery, onion, radish, parsley, and other herbs.

"Are you going to put all that in the biscuits?" I asked her.

"No, silly. Each biscuit gets a different one."

"Very intelligent," I complimented her. "That increases significantly the prospects of success for at least a portion of the experiment."

"And they might *all* be good too."

The child was still during the baking process, but stole occasional glances at the oven. When the timer sounded, she reached it before I did. She turned the oven off, opened the door, and took out the metal tray with the biscuits, being careful to wrap her hand in a towel first. I never use a pot holder for such tasks and the child had apparently observed my propensity for utilizing whatever was at hand.

"They *look* real good," she said, holding out the tray.

I was constrained to agree. The appearance of the finished product did not vary visually from what I had grown accustomed to over the years.

"Which one do you want?" she asked.

"Do you remember which is which?"

"Yes," she said proudly. "Just tell me which one you want, and I'll pick it out."

"Oh, the . . . parsley."

"Here!" she said, reaching unerringly for the correct biscuit. She watched as I took a tentative bite. It tasted as it usually did but, perhaps, there was just a hint of parsley . . . ?

"It's quite good," I told her.

"See?"

"Yes, I do. Now perhaps you would like to sample one yourself?"

"I'm going to try the onion," she declared.

We then reversed roles, me watching her with some interest. "Ummm! It's really, really good!" she sang out.

The radish biscuits—she had, for some reason, made two of those—were, we both agreed, the least successful of the batch. "Now you have your own recipe, Zoë," I told her.

"My own?"

"Certainly. You are the originator, so it is certainly your own."

"You mean it's a secret?"

"Not necessarily. I only mean you hold the key. If you share your recipe with anyone else, they could certainly pass it along. But if you keep it to yourself, only you will know."

"You know too."

"I promise I shall never tell another living soul."

"Swear?"

"Yes, child. I swear."

"What should I call it?"

"Well, what about 'Zoë's Secret Recipe'?"

"No, I don't like that. It's not really a secret, it's more like a . . . they *look* the same, right? As the regular ones?"

"Yes, they do."

"So it would be a surprise? If you ate one and you didn't know?"

"Absolutely."

"Zoë's Surprise," the child said. "That's what I'm going to call it."

"Perfect," I assured her.

True to her word, although the child insisted on playing checkers throughout the day, she never once complained about not winning. In between, she busied herself with drawing. Although she watched television programs when I did, she displayed no independent interest in the medium. Nor was she at all drawn to the video games, the first of my captives who resisted such temptation. She continued to be somewhat ceremonious about meals, but as it mollified her to be allowed to alter either content or presentation, I silently acquiesced to the point where it became the norm.

I observed her closely for signs of dissociation, especially as she displayed no anxiety whatever concerning the progress of reunification with her family. Some children segue into an altered state to cope with unbearable trauma and, despite my best efforts, children have reacted in such a manner occasionally. However, Zoë was fully oriented—albeit often preoccupied—at all times. And although her curiosity was, in general, boundless, it was all outwardly focused.

"I'm going to be gone when you get up tomorrow morning," I told her. "I have to go out and check the newspapers, and pick up some of the things you wanted. But I have to leave quite early to do that, do you understand?"

"Yes. But can't I—?"

"Zoë," I said patiently, "it would be impossible to take you along. I already explained—"

"Not that. I just wanted to . . . Oh, never mind."

"Wanted to . . . what, child?"

"Never *mind*!" she blurted out, stamping her foot. The first display of willfulness I had observed. I made a decision not to press her, and she soon returned to what I had come to understand was her normal affect.

In order to encourage her to go to sleep earlier than usual—I myself could not rest until she had achieved that state—I read her another story.

As soon as she was asleep, I disabled the computer, proofed the surroundings, and tested the restraints. Everything was in order.

I awoke at 4:00 a.m.—my wristwatch has a silent alarm which causes it to throb against my pulse. After showering and shaving, I selected an anonymous business suit and a well-used carry-on bag. But when I re-entered the main room to have a cup of tea before I left, Zoë was up and bustling about.

"Why are you up so early, child?" I asked her.

"Well, I had to make breakfast, didn't I?"

"It's too early for you to eat. Why don't you go back to—?"

"Not me, you. You have to eat something before you go out. It's important to always have something in your stomach."

"Very well," I told her, not wishing to cause her any distress when she would be alone for so long.

She made an omelet with several different ingredients. I didn't watch her closely, preferring to be surprised. It was excellent, despite the pale color and altered texture.

"What did you put in this, Zoë?"

"Cream cheese and red peppers."

"Well, you've done it again. This is quite astounding."

"You won't forget, will you?"

"Forget what?"

"What you're going to get. When you're out?"

"A deck of playing cards," I told her. "And some fresh bread, if I can find it."

"You *did* remember."

"It wasn't a very complex task," I told her. "Why would you expect me to . . ."

"People forget stuff," she said, dismissively.

"My memory is flawless," I responded.

"I wasn't . . . Never mind."

Not wishing to evoke another tantrum, I did not pursue the matter. After testing the security of the restraints, I said goodbye to Zoë and left the hideout from the first floor.

The drive was uneventful, as I had hoped. The radio had nothing about the kidnapping, despite my enduring its repetitive blather for the entire trip. I was fortunate enough to locate a spot in the short-term parking lot, the advantage being the coin-operated meters as opposed to a human being who filled the same role in the larger lot. The rates were near-extortionate, but a full hour was permitted, so there was no risk of an identifying ticket from one of the uniformed drones eagerly circling awaiting just such an opportunity.

The young woman at the airport concession counter rang up my innocuous purchases: People magazine, a lurid-covered paperback book, a deck of playing cards, and, of course, USA Today. I made certain that, upon inquiry, she would not recall a man matching my "description" as having purchased only the newspaper. She pulled a receipt from the cash register and handed it to me along with my change, never making eye contact. I placed them in my carry-on bag, a round-trip ticket to a nearby city in my inside breast pocket against the unlikely chance of being asked to produce a reason for my presence.

The airport did, indeed, feature a bakery. I purchased three loaves of French bread, then made my way out of the terminal toward where a group of people had gathered to smoke. I had a pack of cigarettes in my pocket, opened with several missing, in preparation. It was not at all uncommon for ticketed passengers to wait outside until the last moment in order to ingest as much nicotine as possible in the fresh air (the contradiction apparently lost upon them) to fortify them for the coming deprivation. However, once certain I was not being shadowed, I simply proceeded across the various walkways until I reached my car. I left the airport as undetected as I had entered.

As an act of self-discipline, I did not examine the newspaper until I re-entered the basement. The child looked up when I entered, her artwork spread in front of her, classical music of some kind playing on the radio.

"Hi!" she said brightly.

"Hello, Zoë."

"Did you get—?"

"Of course," I assured her, pulling out the deck of cards and the French bread.

"No, I meant . . . did you get the paper?"

"Yes."

"And did they—?"

"I don't know yet," I told her. "Let's see."

Apparently, the child took that statement as an invitation (although it was not so intended, I could not fault her for taking the words literally) and perched herself on the arm of the chair I was occupying as I searched for the appropriate section.

The response was there. Precisely as instructed. I pointed it out to Zoë.

"Does that mean they'll buy me back?" she asked.

"It would appear so," I replied. "But it may be a ploy of some kind."

"What's a ploy?"

"A ruse. A . . . trick."

"Oh. How will you know?"

"There are stages to these operations. As we progress, the truth will emerge."

"But you are going to ask them for money, right?"

"Certainly. That is the whole purpose."

"Do you have a lot of money?"

"I . . . don't know, child. I suppose that would depend on what 'a lot' means to you."

"Do you have a million dollars?"

"Yes," I told her truthfully. "I have considerably more than that, in fact."

"Oh."

She was silent after that, getting up and going back to her drawing. After some time passed, I realized that I had been puzzling over her reaction to my last statement. A logic gap was apparent, but the sequence eluded me.

"Zoë," I asked, "weren't you surprised?"

"At what?"

"When I told you I had so much money."

"No."

"Well, then, weren't you surprised that I would do something like this for money when I already had so much?"

"No. My father has a lot of money too. Millions and millions. And he always wants more."

"Ah. But, you understand, child, I don't do this for the money. Do you know why I do it?"

"Because you're a connoisseur, right?"

I was stunned. There was not a trace of sarcasm in the child's statement. Yet how could she . . . ? I quickly recovered, and asked her: "Why do you say that, Zoë?"

"Well, because of what you said. Before. Remember? You said you could be a connoisseur of . . . something, right? And also *do* it too. Like my drawing."

"I remember."

"Well, what you do, it's like . . . acting, right? And other people do it, but they don't all do it the same."

"How do you mean, other people do it?"

"Kidnapping. It happens all the time. On TV, you see it. My father talks about it sometimes."

"About you being kidnapped?"

"No, about other kids. What he saw on TV."

"I see. And you think I do this because it's my . . . art? Like what you do?"

"Sure."

"But your drawing, it's designed for . . . display, isn't it? You want other people to see what you did?"

"Sometimes."

"All right, sometimes. But nobody will ever see what I do."

"Yes they *will*. They just won't know it was you. Like a painting on a wall."

"But artists sign their paintings."

"I don't sign mine."

"Ever?"

"Never. I never sign mine. They tried to make me. In school. But I wouldn't do it."

"Still, they would know it was you."

"What do you mean?"

"If they displayed different drawings that the whole class did, wouldn't everybody know which one was yours?"

"Yes. But only in the class. If you put my drawings up in another place, nobody would know it was me."

"But they could still admire them, couldn't they?"

"Yes."

"Then—"

"That's like you," she interrupted. "You don't sign your . . . stuff either. Or you'd go to jail. You can't sign it. But people see it. And you know it was you."

That evening, I began to teach her how to play chess.

I knew what was coming next. Looked around. Xyla wasn't there. I called her name and she came running just in time for the next question to come up:

>>Where Candy?<<

I couldn't figure out if he was testing or really asking, but it didn't matter, the answer was the same.

dead

Luther Allison's "Cherry Red Wine" was searing out of the Plymouth's speakers as I drove back. About an unfaithful woman who drank so much wine that the earth around her grave turned the same color. I wondered what color the dirt would be around wherever they'd put Candy. Whatever color human hearts are, I guess. Ripped-out human hearts, sold to the highest bidder.

I'd given the maniac her name earlier on. And two more: Train and Julio. It'd be easy enough for him to find out who Train was. Who he'd been, anyway: the leader of a baby-breeder cult. There was a contract out on him, and Wesley was holding the paper. But Candy came into it. Hard Candy. She went back with me and Wesley. All the way back. I hadn't seen her in years, didn't recognize her when I met her again—all that plastic surgery. But when she took off her contacts to show me those yellow eyes, when she told me things that nobody but she could have known, I believed her. Candy was in business for herself by then. I can't think of a name to call her, but she sold sex. Packaged it, any way you wanted. Train had her daughter, and she wanted the kid back. I . . . got into it.

All of this happened around the same time. And it was more connected than I'd ever nightmared. Train and Candy were partners. Her daughter was a toy. And Candy thought I'd be her tool.

It didn't work out like that. First, Wesley warned me off Train. Later, we ended up trading targets. I took Train. Julio too. Wesley did mine, then claimed them all in his suicide note.

But not Candy. When we were all kids, when all of us were doing wrong, all building sins, Wesley was magnetic north on her compass. He never knew. I don't think it would have made any difference to him. Wesley was too lethal to mate; never had a real partner. And Candy . . . she worshipped the ice in Wesley just as I did. But it penetrated her. Took her.

Citizens would say there was no difference between them, but they'd be missing it. Wesley was walking homicide, but he never did it for fun. It was fun for Candy, all of it. Even selling her own daughter to freaks, and chumping me into getting the kid back after she'd been paid for the merchandise.

I've got enough regret in me for the things I've done in my life to fill a chasm. But Candy . . . *killing* Candy . . . that wasn't one of them.

Wesley died never knowing what happened to her. But now my secret was shared. With a . . .

"He's *crazy,* baby," Michelle said. "You can't make sense out of crazy. You'll just make yourself crazy trying."

"He's not crazy."

"Burke! Listen to yourself. That stuff you told me. The 'messages' he's sending you. He kidnaps kids and kills them. That's his 'art.' He's foaming at the mouth, sweetie. If the people running around making a hero out of him knew . . ."

"Michelle, there hasn't been one murder since he started . . ."

"Started . . . what?"

"These messages. To me. It's like . . . those murders were all some kind of . . . You know how you have to prove?"

She knew what I meant by the word. Had to do it herself too many times on the street not to. "Sure," she said.

"Credentials," I said, finally finding the word I was looking for—the word that kept echoing through all of this. "He's the real thing. I just can't see what he wants."

"Wesley," she said softly.

"Wesley's—"

"—dead. Sure. But that's what all his little crazy 'tolls' are about, right?"

"Tolls?"

"The price, honey. Like stud poker. You have to pay to see his next card. Every time, isn't that true?"

"Yeah."

"Well, then, that's the link," she said, like she was telling me it was Monday, so certain.

"No, it isn't," I said, all of a sudden getting it. "I am."

"Xyla around?" I asked Trixie.

"She was. But she had to . . . do something. Said she'd be back in a couple of minutes. You don't mind waiting, right?"

"Not at all." I don't know why, but there was no sense of urgency in me. I knew the killer's next message was somewhere in that computer, just waiting for Xyla to open it up. But I wasn't in any hurry to see it.

"Crystal Beth was my sister," Trixie said, snapping me out of wherever I'd gone to.

I just looked at her, waiting.

"This . . . guy. The one Xyla got you to. You think he killed them?"

"Who?"

"Whoever killed Crystal Beth. He kills fag-bashers, right?"

"Yeah. There's no guarantee he'll ever get the right ones. He hits at random."

"So why do you want him?" she asked, stepping closer to me. A shadow changed behind her. Rusty. The big guy who was always drawing. He didn't say a word, just bowed slightly. I returned it. And finally got it—I'd have to say the right thing to this woman if I wanted Xyla to open another message.

"Some people . . . some gay people . . . they hired me to reach out to him. See if he needed any help. Getting away, I mean."

"And you were willing to do that?"

"I'm trying to find whoever killed Crystal Beth," I told her. "And maybe he's the path."

"Yeah. Okay. I mean, I'm no serial-killer groupie but . . . I mean, it's not like he's killing kids or anything. Everyone knows how *you'd* feel about that."

Her face was a study in repose, brown eyes alive but calm. And right then I knew. Xyla was slicker than the killer thought. And, somehow, she'd read his damn messages too.

I didn't say anything.

Xyla swept into the room. Trixie and Rusty backed away.

"Ready to have your look?" Xyla asked, so upbeat and innocent.

"Sure," I told her.

The following morning, it was time for the next phase of the operation. Again telling Zoë that I would be making a call from outside, I simply went upstairs and activated the staged sequence in the computer with the "contact-target" command. Within minutes, a call would be placed to the subject's home. Whether picked up by an answering machine or a person, I was reasonably confident that it would be recorded. The digitized paste-up was ready to send, one of a menu of choices available to me telephonically via button-sequence selection. As the target had indicated compliance via the newspaper ad, I was able to proceed to the next step without the annoying game-playing that sometimes results when the target's response is placed other than as precisely directed.

When the phone was answered at the target's home, the following message would come across the line:

> Thank you for your cooperation. If you wish proof of the child's health and safety, please so indicate by affixing a piece of *red* material to the flagpole in front of your residence. This may be an object of clothing, a scrap of cloth . . . anything at all, so long as it is unmistakably red. As soon as we observe this, we will prepare and transmit the appropriate proof.

There is an element of bluff—and, thus, of chance—in all operations. Requiring the target to attach a piece of red material to the flagpole in front of their house is a classic example. Certainly, I was aware of the flagpole. Now was the time to balance the value of instilling the belief that they were under constant observation against the risk of revealing the somewhat mechanized nature of my contact systems. Restated: I would necessarily assume that they would, indeed, attach the red material, and act as if that were a fact. If I was correct in my assumption, it would exacerbate their sense of being under observation . . . and increase my safety by decreasing their willingness to participate in any law-enforcement exercise designed to ensnare me. However, if they refused (or were unable) to attach the material and I sent the promised proof anyway, it would surely disclose that they were *not* under active surveillance, threatening the credibility of my entire presentation to date.

Although not given to introspection, I do understand that my exercises contain an element not purely intellectual. That is, the intellectual portion is *reduction* of risk. But were I able to eliminate *all* risk, my art would be truly completed and any repetition thereof utterly banal and meaningless. Were I ever to achieve perfection, I would cease at the apex.

Downstairs again, I found the child wearing some sort of coveralls, busily engaged in cleaning the kitchen area.

"Did you call them?" she asked by way of greeting.

"I did."

"Did they say anything?"

"I would have no way of knowing, child. It was a one-way conversation. Remember? I explained how it worked."

"Oh. I didn't know you did that for all the . . . phone calls. Just maybe for the first one."

"No. In fact, I will never actually speak to . . . the people."

"What people?"

"Whoever your parents designate to act for them. Sometimes, the parents have . . . difficulty in dealing with the emotional stress of the situation, and they have others act for them."

"Like the police?"

"That is the most likely."

"My father won't do that," the child said. Not smugly, but with clear assurance.

I did not pursue the matter. Although the child seemed far too clever to be deceived about her father's actual occupation—he is listed as the owner of a waste-removal firm in the business directory—there was no point in providing her with the information known to me.

"Do you want to help me make a film, Zoë?" I asked instead.

"Like a movie?"

"Somewhat. Actually, it's a videotape. You see that equipment over there? In the corner?"

"Yes. I saw it before. We have that too."

"In your house?"

"Yes."

"For surveillance?"

"I don't know. What's . . . surveillance?"

"Like the cameras they have in banks. To watch people who come on the premises."

"Oh. I don't know if we have those. My father has a camera. In the basement, just like this."

"Like this basement?"

"No. Never mind."

As this was a time when maximum participation was required, I again bowed to the child's "Never mind" trademark. "What we have to do is make a short tape, Zoë. So everyone can see you are alive and well. Do you want to help?"

"Sure!"

"All right. But we're going to have to play a trick on . . . the people who see the tape. Are you willing to help with that too?"

"What kind of trick?"

"Well, the only way to get the tape to them is to mail it. That takes two or three days. But it will take almost a whole day for me to go away and mail it. If I mailed it from around here, they would know we are close by."

"And we don't want that?"

"No. Certainly not. The further away they believe us to be, the better. And if the date is . . . advanced . . . they will believe it was mailed immediately after it was made, do you understand?"

"You mean, like, pretend it's already tomorrow?"

"Precisely. Can you do that?"

"That's easy. What else do I have to do?"

"Just say hello. Tell them you're fine, and nobody has harmed you. That you want to come home, and to please do whatever 'they' say."

" 'They'?"

"Yes, Zoë. It is much safer for me if the . . . if your parents and whoever is helping them believe there is more than one person involved in . . . this."

"Okay. I get it."

"There's nothing to be nervous about, child. We can try it as many times as you like until we get it just right."

"I'll get it right the first time," she said confidently.

As it developed, her confidence was neither misplaced nor overstated. At the first take, the child looked directly into the camera and said:

"Hi! It's me, Angelique. I'm fine. Everybody is being very nice to me here. It's Saturday morning and I just watched my show. You have to do everything they say, okay? Bye!"

"That was excellent!" I complimented her. "Now we must prepare the package."

"How do we do that?"

"Well, the most important thing is to leave no forensic traces."

"What's 'forensic'?"

"Something that could be used as evidence. Say, a fingerprint, or a drop of perspiration . . . That's why I always work under absolutely sterile conditions," I told her, holding up my surgical-glove-covered hands for emphasis. "But an equally important part of presentation is misdirection. Do you know what that is, Zoë?"

"Like magic tricks?"

Again, I was brought up short by the child's fund of knowledge. Or was I making unwarranted assumptions? "What do you mean?" I asked her, in order to determine.

"Well, like with the rabbit in the hat, right? They make you look at something else, so you don't see what they're doing."

"Yes. That is called 'legerdemain.'"

"Leger . . ."

". . . demain. It means, sleight of hand."

"Oh. Anyway, how can you do that with this . . . stuff?"

"Do you see this little mark?" I asked her, holding the cardboard sheath for the videocassette at an angle for her inspection.

"It's a little . . . I can't see. . . . Oh! It's a little piece of paper with a . . . number on it."

"That's correct. Actually, it's a tiny portion of a price code which was affixed at the point of origin—where the cassette was originally purchased. That was in Chicago. I also have this," I said, showing her a postage-meter tape which displayed the next day's date, "Chicago IL," and a perfectly legitimate meter number. "I am going to fly to Chicago with the tape we just made and mail it from there."

"How did you get it?"

"I was in Chicago some time ago. On business. After some period of reconnaissance, I discovered a twenty-four-hour public photocopying establishment which was very poorly staffed in the early-morning hours. I merely came in with a very large job and, when the clerk was distracted with its complexities, changed the date on the postage meter in the store, made several tapes, and then changed the date back."

"But how did you know what date you would need?"

"Actually, child, I did not know. Not at that time. But I was reasonably certain of the time period. And, if events proved to be such that the none of the tapes would work, they would be easy enough to discard."

"Oh. Then you're going to Chicago?"

"Yes. This evening, in fact."

"I'm going to be alone at night?"

"Yes, you are. You won't be frightened, will you?"

"No. I won't be afraid. I just . . ."

"What, child?"

"I just don't like to be alone in the dark. Could I leave a light on?"

"You may leave them all on if you wish, Zoë. But I have another idea, if you like."

"What?"

"Well, there is some flexibility in my schedule. I could leave rather late this evening . . . after you're asleep. And I could return while it is still daylight tomorrow. How would that be?"

"Great!" she exclaimed.

We had another astoundingly complex dinner, played several games of checkers—all of which the child lost—watched the news briefly, and then I read her a story until she fell asleep.

##

The late-night flight to Chicago was, as expected, quite full of passengers, mostly businessmen returning to their homes for the weekend. I landed at O'Hare just after 2:00 a.m., took a cab into the Loop driven by an individual whose command of English seemed limited to that particular destination, dropped the package into a mailbox on Michigan Avenue, and returned to O'Hare. By ten o'clock on Saturday morning, I was back in the hideout, eating a complicated breakfast.

"How long will it take?" Zoë asked.

"For this particular phase, or the entire operation?"

"For . . . for them to get the film I made."

"The United States Postal Service has the capacity to deliver within two days, but we should figure three days on average. However, we must also assume the Chicago mailbox won't even be emptied until Monday, and receipt at . . . the other end won't be until Thursday."

"Couldn't they, like, trace it?"

"The envelope? I don't believe so, child. I don't know, and frankly doubt, that the mailers supplied by the post office itself are identifiable by location, but, just to be sure, I have a supply from various cities on hand, and I was careful to use one from Chicago. The label was typed on a machine I constructed from several ancient typewriters, and that concoction itself was destroyed as soon as I was finished. The package was sealed with a type of packing tape available commercially through a dozen different mail-order houses. And any 'tracing,' as you put it, would only add to the mystery, not solve it. There is absolutely nothing which would give a key to our current whereabouts."

"It's going to take *much* longer than nine days, isn't it?"

"Considerably more," I replied.

"Can we start school, then?"

"School?"

"*Home* school. Remember? I told you my friend—"

"—Jeanne Ellen."

"Yes! You *do* remember. You were just teasing."

"I would not . . . ah, well, perhaps."

"So? Can we start?"

"There is no school on weekends," I informed her.

"But you *study* on weekends, don't you? Didn't you do that? When you were in school?"

"I was . . ." I stopped, wondering why the next words simply would not come. Momentarily puzzled, I quickly changed the subject: "That was a long time ago," I said. "What's important is the way people do things today."

"Well, I want to study. I always study. Not just my homework either. All right?"

"Very well. Do you want to get your schoolbooks?"

"Okay!" She almost flew across the basement in her eagerness, and proudly presented me with a stack of well-worn texts. I took them from her and began to leaf through them in the hopes of recognizing an appropriate starting point. It was impossible to ignore the fact that virtually every page was covered with Zoë's drawings. Although she had been careful not to obscure the actual words, the margins were completely decorated, and even the white space between paragraphs was not spared. Her mathematics book was creative to the point of genius—the child had connected various equations with drawings that seemed, in some symbolic way, to link the numbers with the art. The depth was breathtaking.

"Are you okay?" I felt the child's small hand tugging at my sleeve.

"Of course, child," I replied. "I was merely absorbed in the book, looking for—"

"But you were doing it for an *hour*!" she said, her voice not so much complaining as . . . nervous? Frightened? I could not determine.

"Ah, well, that is likely to occur when a person gazes at works of art. One becomes lost in the work."

"You were looking at my drawings?"

"Yes, I was. They are quite . . . remarkable. But aren't your teachers . . . annoyed at your defacement of the books?"

"They used to be. But now they know I won't turn them in at the end of the year. My father has to buy them. From the school, I mean. So they don't get mad anymore."

"Are you bored, Zoë?"

"No! I'm having a good time. Really."

"I didn't mean here, child. I meant in school. Do you draw during class because the material is so boring?"

"I don't know. I always do it, I guess."

"And then you learn the material at home? By yourself?"

"I . . . guess. I always do my homework, so nobody ever gets mad."

"But what about your grades? Your . . . report card, I suppose it would be called."

"I always get all A's," she said, without the expected vein of pride in her voice, just stating a fact.

"Is that right? Your parents must be very pleased with your performance."

"My . . ." The child looked stricken, unable to complete her thought. She stood frozen, an unconnected look on her face. It was . . . familiar, in a way I myself could not articulate.

"Your grades, Zoë," I said gently. "Weren't they pleased with your grades?"

She did not respond. I had observed both catatonia and elective mutism in captured children previously, but this was neither of those states. Acting on some perhaps primal instinct, I wrapped her in a blanket and carried her over to

the couch. She responded only by curling up in a tight fetal ball.

It was almost forty-five minutes before she stirred. If she was surprised at finding herself under the blanket, she gave no sign. "Are we going to study?" she asked.

"It seems you have already mastered the material in your own books," I told her. "Perhaps you would be interested in learning something about computers . . . ?"

"Sure!" she said enthusiastically, throwing off the covers and coming over to where I was working on the portable machine.

Two hours later, she was sufficiently familiar with the basics of programming to create a small module of her own. Once she did that successfully, I opened a modified version of a drawing program and showed her how she could use the electronic stylus to create freehand drawings on the screen.

She was still working on acquiring the feel of the stylus when I told her it was time for supper.

Oh, I knew him then. But I couldn't figure out if he was testing me or telling me. I called for Xyla, playing out the lie that she couldn't retrieve what had just disappeared from the screen.

"Want me to—?"

"Just a minute," I told her. "There'll be one of his questions next. Let me ask you something, what does this stuff mean?" I pulled a pad of paper off the desk and wrote down the symbols he'd been using.

"Oh," she said smiling. "The ** marks around a word is the same thing as italics. Most computer programs won't let you underline unless you're connecting with someone using the same ISP. Some people use ###### for chapter breaks, like if they're sending you something in segments. And the >> and <<, those are quote marks, but you only use them when you're quoting something that's already on the screen from another person, see? I don't know why he uses them the way he does. You understand?"

"I . . . guess."

"Oh, you'll get used to it," she promised brightly. "I wonder when he's going to—"

His message interrupted her.

>>You ever conduit?<<

I was with him by then. I couldn't see why, but I could see where.

yes

It was supposed to be a job. A job of lies. All liars. Every one of them. And I fit right in. I work for money, but I live for revenge. If I'd had a target, if I'd known who took Crystal Beth, I never would have gotten into this whole thing.

First I thought, this killer, maybe he had a list somehow. You want a list of all the neo-Nazis, you ask ZOG. But if you want a list of all the fag-bashers, who is there to ask? Maybe this guy? And, sure, I'd get him out of here in exchange for that list—Crystal Beth's killers would have to be on it somewhere.

But once we connected, I could see it. He had no list, this Homo Erectus maniac. He had a fetish. Like any serial killer. That's why they're so hard to catch. Random hitters, triggered by something too common to protect—blondes, hookers, gay hitchhikers, red shoes, priests—symbols, not individuals.

Whatever he was, he'd started out snatching kids. Hard to tell if killing the kids was anything other than what he said it was—that he was an artist, and killing the kids was no more than keeping his paint-brushes clean. But all the record searches came up empty.

Was he some kind of insane fiction-writer, playing out his fantasy to thousands of people at once, me thinking I was the only one? Or just too much of a narcissist to keep his light under a bushel?

Why Wesley?

If I could get that, I could get him.

But it was hard to care, and I couldn't figure out why I did. Whoever put Crystal Beth in the ground, that's where *they* were too, thanks to the hit man—if what Strega said was true.

And I believed it was. Strega did things no man could understand, but she wouldn't lie.

Responsibility isn't a legal thing. If the hit man, the one Gutterball thought was Wesley, if he did the other two from the drive-by car when they got to the garage, then the only one in the crowd *he* took out himself was the guy on the spot, Corky. Crystal Beth, she was an accident. One of those "casualties of war." Casual. No malice. Just . . . in the way. And the guys who had laid down the cover fire that claimed her were already taken care of.

The drive-by, that's what had triggered this maniac. At least, that's what I thought at first. But he didn't come across as gay in his transmissions. He didn't come across as sexual at all.

Like Nadine . . . With all her flash and fire, she didn't have any hormones I could smell. Said she was gay, and maybe she was. And making people do what you want, that's sexual, in its own way. But she had a piece missing. Like there was no "Nadine" at all, just some collection of parts.

No point me looking anymore. I had to wait for the end of his story. And the punch line.

"You kind of done admiring this guy, huh?" I asked Xyla, probing gently.

"What do you mean?"

"Well, you used to talk about what a cyber-genius he is, all like that. Last few times, you haven't said a word."

"He hasn't shown me anything new," she replied, a little too glibly, her face slightly flushed.

I wondered what Trixie and Rusty and the rest of her crew thought. Because I was sure that whatever Xyla knew, they did too. I gave her the nod, and she opened his latest:

> **It is very important to me that my captives do not suffer. Infliction of pain would be an affront to my art. Physical pain, that is. I am not without comprehension**

that my art causes emotional pain, but I am deeply concerned that its practice never replicate sadism—a repulsive "disorder" which, upon observation, I refuse to characterize as such. That is, I consider sadism, especially sexual sadism, to be a conscious decision on the part of its wielder. Clearly, there is a market for such hideousness—witness the enormous pornography industry which has attempted to fill the vacuum created by demand. And my personal investigations have proven that the market is by no means limited to *staged* depictions of the most graphic, even terminal, torture. Even assuming, as I do, that many if not most of the proffers are from government agents—parenthetically, I do not consider such activity to be "entrapment," as the essence of same is to induce conduct to which the "victim" is not otherwise disposed—there exists a significant demand for such product. A mental disorder, then? I think not. I suspect, if one were to seek venture capital for a magazine catering to schizophrenics, one would find the prospects bleak indeed.

Ah, so many "masters" out there, convinced of their superiority, never realizing that their obsession makes them as susceptible to manipulation as the "slaves" they "collar." But such games are, in fact, just that. Games. To be played as children play: Immaturely, focusing on immediate, tactile gratification.

But when the jolt fades, when they require reality, when their sadism can only be satisfied not with the *appearance* of unwillingness but its actuality, then pain becomes the goal. Such humans are beneath contempt. They fancy themselves "superior," but they are pitifully dependent creatures, fools who believe they *are* the power, but who come alive only when the power is supplied by others—proving them to be as self-determining as an electrical appliance.

I know power. I was born to it, I believe. And I use it to create. My art.

The next days passed without incident. Indeed, my recollection of them is . . . flawed, perhaps. I do recall promising the child some additional art supplies. Or was it condiments? I realized that to ask her again would be to damage the fragile connection between us, so I merely resolved to obtain a sufficient quantity of anything she might potentially have requested when I left the hideout.

Friday's telephone message to the target was simplicity itself:

> If the proof you requested is sufficiently satisfactory to you and you wish to proceed with negotiations, please so indicate by replacing *red* as previously instructed with *yellow*. It is not, repeat *not* necessary that the material be similar, only the location.

That evening, Zoë became agitated, claiming that I had not been listening to her. No explanation would satisfy the child. In truth, I was at a loss for such explanation myself, vainly attempting to fill in the apparent gaps in our conversation in confabulatory fashion. I remembered a phrase from one of the TV shows Zoë and I had watched together, some trendy serial about "relationships" she said she had not been allowed to watch at home but had heard about from her friends at school. I told her, "My mind must have been somewhere else."

The child came over to the chair where I had been slumped—itself somewhat remarkable, as I pride myself on my correct posture—and said, "I know." Then she shyly kissed my cheek. It may surprise you to learn that this was not such an unusual event during the term of my career. Children, once their survival instincts have been activated, often attempt to curry favor with captors. However, there was none of that quality about this child's conduct. While puzzling, it posed no danger to the operation, so I resolved to consider it post-completion, a time always more conducive to contemplation.

Saturday morning brought with it the next phase. Again, assumption-upon-assumption: (1) the target had, in fact, placed the red material on the flagpole; (2) the target had, in fact, received the video of the child; (3) the target had, in fact, decided to open negotiations and had so signified by replacing the requisite marker as directed.

The latter assumption is not, as the amateur might assume, auto-warranted. On several occasions, I have encountered parents who simply refused to negotiate—whether in blind obedience to police instructions or because the child's return was not desired, I have no way of ascertaining to any degree of scientific certainty. While it would be possible to theorize that some negotiation offers would be rejected on the ground that the child him/herself was a participant rather than a victim—a not-uncommon occurrence among teenagers of the ultra-wealthy class—I avoid this by capturing only children too immature to concoct such a scheme. And, on one occasion, my research failed. It was impossible to convince the child's father—a notorious drug-lord of foreign ethnicity—that I was not the representative of a rival gang but an independent entrepreneur. As a result, no money changed hands. I consider such an attempt imperfect, but a learning experience. Nevertheless, I had assumed no risk of discovery, as the target insisted on his view of reality, attacking the rival gang with great ferocity. While Zoë's father was himself a member of organized crime—indeed, if my information was accurate, the head of a continuing criminal enterprise—I was unconcerned about him misperceiving the facts. Kidnapping children of enemy gang leaders seems a cultural phenomenon—common among some groups, unheard of in others. As always with such groups, morality is not an issue (despite the wishful thinking of some screenwriters). Only tactics are of importance. There is a Darwinistic quality to establishment and maintenance of ongoing criminal-group activity, and media exposure is, eventually, antithetical to survival. So those "sources" so highly prized by newspaper reporters are rarely in possession of *working* knowledge. That is, they may know names, dates, places, and events. But they do not understand the interstitial tissue which binds the enterprise. Thus, their information may destroy a gang, but cannot be used to replicate one.

I have developed a pre-recorded menu which allows me to "converse" with targets without actually speaking. The target is presented with a series of questions and directions. The response determines which menu item I then select. The R&D component was rather lengthy, but I now have the system perfected, reducing not only risk of identification but the length of all conversations.

Therefore, with both assumptions and equipment in place, I dialed the target's home.

"Hello?" A man's voice, crisp with tension, but without that crackling underpinning of anxiety characteristic of most in his position.

I tapped a button on my console and the pre-recorded voice said: "You have the proof. Do you now understand that we have your child? Answer 'yes' or 'no' *only*, please."

"Yes."

"Do you understand that your child is unharmed, and will remain unharmed if we conclude our business successfully?"

"Yes."

"Are you prepared to pay for your child's safe return?"

"Yes."

"Have you notified the authorities?"

"No."

"The price is seven hundred thousand dollars, U.S. currency. Confirm you understand: Seven hundred thousand dollars."

"I under—I mean . . . yes."

"By what date will you be prepared to pay?"

"Uh . . . give me, three, four days, okay?"

"The date you have selected is suitable. Now listen carefully. Do you have a method of electronic banking?"

“Yes.”

(It was well he answered as he did, as I knew the truth.)

“Can you place the money in an account subject to your *immediate* transfer authorization?”

“Yes.”

“During what hours can such transfers be effectuated?”

“Uh, what . . . twenty-four hours. I mean, anytime at all.”

(So the target was experienced in such matters. My guess was that he probably utilized one of those easily penetrated Cayman Islands bank accounts.)

“Friday. Nine-fifty-seven a.m. Have you marked that time?”

“Yes.”

“*Prior* to that time, you will dial up the account in which the money is placed. At nine-fifty-seven precisely, I will call. You are to recite the account number I read to you then and *immediately* authorize the transfer. Do you understand?”

“Yes.”

“We will know within approximately thirty-five seconds if you have complied. If you have done so, the child will be released within the hour, and returned to you by close of business the same day. Do you understand?”

“Yes.”

I terminated the conversation.

It was always hard to tell when his transmissions ended. Every single time, I scrolled down until I hit a blank wall. I did it that time too. When the screen started to change colors, I was ready. I thought about trying to answer him myself—I had been watching Xyla each time and I thought I could do it—but there wasn’t any point if she’d already seen his stuff. And I couldn’t shake the thought that she had. His next toll didn’t ask for a fact from the past. I had to look at it a couple of times to make sure what he *was* asking:

>>Wesley. Me. Difference? One word<<

Time to see if I could find a button to push. "Send him this," I told Xyla, and watched.

professional

come up on her screen.

If I had it figured right, my response would be a stake in his heart. But even if it was, I knew it wouldn't kill him. Vampires I understood. What else is a child molester but a blood-bandit who breeds others of his tribe from his own venom? But this guy was way past that.

And I wondered if he'd keep playing by his own rules.

Back at my place, I sat down with Pansy to watch some TV. She used to love pro wrestling years ago, but now she hates it. I don't understand why, but she's real clear about it. Her favorite is this Japanese soap opera, *Abarenbo Shogun.* Maybe soap opera isn't right, but I don't know what else to call the damn thing. It takes place in eighteenth-century Edo, where the Shogun has a secret identity as the resident bodyguard for the boss of the firefighter brigade, and it's all about him bringing truth and justice to his subjects. He does it with his sword, and the body count is even higher than the old *Untouchables* used to be. Every time, it ends with the Shogun revealing his true identity to the perps and ordering them to commit seppuku. They, quite reasonably, refuse and decide to fight it out. Fat fucking chance. The Shogun also has a pair of ninjas working for him, a young guy and a dazzlingly beautiful girl who looks like a geisha most of the time and only lets her hair down when she's slashing and stabbing. The bad guys always retreat behind their hirelings, and the Shogun has to hack his way through to them. He faces off by cocking his sword to display the royal crest—the same flashy way movies show a guy jacking a round into the chamber—and starts his walk, complete with special theme music. The outcome is not in doubt. At the end, he orders his ninjas to finish off the main culprits. Pansy knows her TV.

Anyway, when I finally got cable here, I learned that there's an all-news TV show too, just like the radio. I clicked it on. Another dead baby. Beaten to death. ACS wasn't giving out any explanations, although it admitted the family was "known" to them. ACS: that's "Administration for Children's Services." When I was a kid, they called it BCW. They've changed the name half a dozen times since then, usually after a bunch of babies die.

Even when they die, it doesn't amount to much. I remember the last big media-play murder. Kid doesn't show up for school for a whole year. Nobody even checks. Finally, they come around looking. Little girl's not there. Turns out the mother's boyfriend strangled her to death while the mother held the kid's hands so she couldn't struggle. Then they wrapped the body in plastic and duct tape and trucked it through the snow in a laundry cart to a Dumpster near a vacant lot. The DA offers the mother probation for her testimony, and she gets on the stand and tells it like it happened. The jury's so full of hate for the DA letting her walk away, they convict the guy only of manslaughter, not murder, trying to divide the blame by sending a message. Same way the jury did with Lisa Steinberg's killer—his girlfriend got a free pass from the DA too. Wolfe had that kind of case once. Only she took them *both* down, not going for the sure-thing conviction of the man by free-passing the woman.

I remembered the "social worker" I had when I was a kid. One of them, anyway. A young girl . . . although I guess she looked pretty old to me then. All I remember about her was her mouth. Her lying mouth. I never looked at her eyes.

Fuck it. I got up, worked Pansy through a few of her routines, just to keep her sharp. She loves that. I don't get the way people train dogs. There's really nothing to it. You wait long enough, the dog will do anything you want. When you see it, you reward it. Sometimes you have to create the situation so it happens, but that's not so hard. There's no reason to hit a dog. Every time I think about people doing that, I . . . think about how people starve racing greyhounds, run them until they're used up, then round them up and shoot them. And how scumbags feed their pit bulls gunpowder. The fucking morons think it makes the dogs tough. All it does is eat the linings of their stomachs, so they get ulcers and they're always in pain. Makes them vicious, not tough.

I met a lot of guys who fit that exact description over the years. And vicious hurts the same as tough when you're on the receiving end. I took a lot of beatings until Wesley pulled my coat. We were just kids, but he knew the truth. "They're easier when they're sleeping," he whispered to me one night in the dorm.

When I walked into Nadine's apartment, she told me to have a seat—she had to get something. I took the middle chair. There was a tape playing on the screen. Pony girl, just like she'd bragged about. A chubby blonde on her hands and knees, wearing some kind of mask with little leather ears sticking up, a bridle bit in her teeth, a harness fitted around her upper body. Nadine was riding her, using a crop on the blonde girl's rump, directing her around a room I didn't recognize—not the one I was sitting in.

It ended like you'd expect. Nadine waited for the tape to go blank before she came back in.

"She loves it," Nadine said.

I didn't say anything.

"She calls me up and begs for it," Nadine kept on. "She usually comes before she even starts eating me."

"That the cop?" I asked her.

"Yep."

"Okay. I already got *that* message. So what's your point?"

"A *true* submissive will do whatever you tell her. She'd come right over and suck your cock if I snapped my fingers. And she doesn't like men . . . not at all."

"I still don't get your point."

"I just want you to keep your promise."

"What promise? The only thing I ever told you was—"

"—that I'd get to meet him. Be there with you when you did."

"*If* that happens."

"It'll happen," she said confidently. "It was meant to happen."

"Better stick to your toys and games," I told her. "I don't see a crystal ball around here."

"Never mind," she said. "I know it. So it doesn't matter *what* you believe. That won't change anything."

"Yeah, fine. So . . . why the videotape?"

"You know why," she said. "And you'll be back."

Where I went back to was where I'd find Xyla. And there he was, waiting:

"It is all a matter of timing," I told Zoë later that day. "Any transfer, electronic or paper, can be traced. However, I have set it up so that, within minutes after the money reaches the receptor account, it will be transferred from there to twenty-one *other* accounts in various parts of the world. As soon as the transfer is effectuated, the receptor account will automatically close. A trace will dead-end at the bank. By the time the authorities discover how the money was distributed, it will have been emptied from each of the new accounts into a funnel account, and *that* account too will be closed . . . with the money withdrawn."

"That sounds hard."

"Not really," I said, annoyed at myself for the ascertainable trace of pride in my voice. "The Swiss are quite cooperative in such ventures. They have a long history of separating money from morality."

"What does that mean?"

"It simply means that they will not question—indeed, they will deliberately avert their eyes from—the *source* of cash so long as they are paid a goodly sum for their 'handling' of it."

"Oh."

"Are you certain you understand, child?"

"Sure. Maybe they're not bad themselves, but they don't care if *you're* bad, right?"

"Yes, that is a worthy approximation."

"Doesn't that make *them* bad, too?"

"One could certainly argue that, Zoë."

"Do they?"

"Do they what?"

"*Argue* about it?"

"Oh. Yes, certainly. In fact, such arguments seem to provide an endless source of entertainment for some individuals. But nothing changes as a result."

"People always do it, right?"

"Do what, Zoë?"

"Bad things. I mean, it's not new. People always did bad things, didn't they?"

"Yes. And good things. That is human nature, to be both bad and good. Or to have that potential within us, anyway."

"So it's a choice?"

"I don't follow—"

"You can be good if you want, right? I mean, nobody *has* to be bad . . ."

"It's not that simple, child. But, generally speaking, I believe you are correct."

Oh, he was on the money there, the crazy bastard. The first time I really understood it, I was in prison. Reading. I killed a lot of time doing that. I remember something about a "choice of evils." And it made me think. About the other guys in there. How some didn't have much choice. The thieves, mostly. If you wanted to live like a human being, if you were culled out of the herd when you were little so you couldn't earn honestly, what was left? But the ugly ones—the rapists, the child molesters, the torture freaks—they weren't bad guys the way thieves were, they were stone evil. And it was their choice. That's what they picked. They didn't do it for money, they did it for fun. That's what evil is, when you strip away the crap. It's choice. This guy wasn't sick. The way he was telling it, the rules didn't apply to him, that's all. He was above it. Above everything. He was killing kids for art. And that was his choice. I snapped out of it and started scrolling again, fast now, to make up for the lost time.

“Okay. Can we play chess now?” the child asked.

I agreed. And, as I anticipated, she learned the rudiments of the game with alacrity.

There was a languid, drifting quality about the next several days. My memory of them is . . . imprecise. Zoë continued to prepare her impossibly elaborate meals. I read . . . I believe I read . . . some technical manuals. We played chess together and I began to introduce her to plane geometry. She worked on her drawings.

Tuesday night she woke me up, saying she was afraid. She would not elaborate further. I allowed her to sleep in my bed, sitting next to her in a chair. It appeared to comfort her, and she eventually fell asleep. I suppose I did too. When I awoke, it was Wednesday morning.

Wednesday night, I explained the remainder of the operation to the child. She listened, fascinated as always. Suddenly she looked up at me.

“I know who you are,” she announced.

“What is it you know, child?” I asked her. “My name?”

“No. It doesn’t matter. I have a name I call you, but I won’t tell you what it is. But I know who you are.”

“And who is that, Zoë?”

“You’re my hero,” she said solemnly. “You came to rescue me. Just like in the story I read. I was a princess. Sort of. And you came to rescue me.”

“I do not—”

“That’s your art,” the child said eagerly. “You’re always saying, we have our art. You and me. Zoë me. I draw. And you rescue little kids.”

Try as I might, she refused to discuss the subject further. I saw no reason to interfere with her childish coping mechanisms. I detest cruelty.

Thursday night, Zoë said: “I’m going to tell you a secret.”

“What secret is that, child?”

“I know your secret,” she said.

Friday morning ran like a Swiss watch—pun intended. I returned to the hideout.

"It's time to say goodbye, Zoë," I told her.

"I know," she said, eyes shining as though a special treat were in store.

"Zoë, I have a . . . new art now. One I must practice and learn very well before I can reach the heights of my old art. You are the last of that, do you understand?"

"Yes."

"Zoë, you cannot come with me, child. Do you understand?"

"No!" she said sharply. "I *can* come with you. I'll help you. Kill her. Kill Angelique. Kill her now!"

Angelique drank the potion I prepared for her. I held Zoë while Angelique departed.

As with all art, practice is essential. Someday, I shall achieve the same perfection with my new art as I had with what I have now discarded.

I will return to this area soon.

To practice.

What the *hell*? What was he telling me . . . that this was the last transmission? There was only one way to read it—I'd seen it coming a while back. But if he changed and started on. . . No, it was just . . . insane.

"Xyla!"

She was there before the last syllable of her name left my mouth. Dropped into the computer chair, waiting.

>>explain last answer<<

First time he didn't put a word limit on my response. So I *had* stung him. "Type this," I told Xyla. Then I watched it come up on the screen.

any freak can kill random targets.
a professional hits only the target
he is assigned to. *any* target.

When Xyla tapped one last key, the message vanished.

"He's gone now, right?" I asked her.

"He's gone *every* time," she said, shrugging her shoulders. "He can come back anytime he wants, but only if I ask him to. . . ."

"What do you mean?"

"The way it works, I change *my* address each time too. Then, later, I send out a message with the new one."

"But . . . he knows you've got plenty of time to set up. So you could be waiting to trap him every time he sends a message, right?"

"Sure. He knows. Doesn't matter. The only time his own modem is actually open is that last little thing at the end—when I send to him. He receives it, and the whole thing comes down. Fingering it would be a waste of time."

"But if you *don't* send him a new address . . . ?"

"Hmmm," she said. "I see what you mean. He couldn't reach me. Unless he could . . ."

". . . do what I wanted *you* to do," I finished for her. "Right?"

"Right. You think he can?"

"I think he will," I told her.

"How could you possibly—?"

"Because I know who he is now," I said.

"You want *what?*" Wolfe laughed. "A list of every Family man hit during the past . . . what did you say, ten years? . . . Sure. I can get that for you. Only the printout wouldn't fit in the trunk of your car."

I was standing in the same box I'd been in the last time I'd met with her. Only this time, besides the pistol, the man I didn't recognize had something else—a honey-colored pit bull on a snap lead. I'd seen that pit before—she scared me more than the gun.

Yeah, I was standing in the same place, all right. And Wolfe was showing me where I stood with her.

"There's that many?" I asked her.

"It would be 'that many' even if you were talking just the metro area," she said sarcastically. "New York, New Jersey, Connecticut—give me a break. And *national,* come on!"

"I just thought . . ."

"You know what?" she said, shifting her posture to a more aggressive one, dropping her voice just a fraction. "I think you're in something way over your head. You think there's a pattern somewhere, that's obvious. But the database is so huge, you couldn't find it without some serious computer. . . . Oh! You found yourself some new friends, huh?"

"I don't know what you're talking about."

"And I don't know what you're doing. But I really only came here to tell you this. We're done, you and me. You want to know about dead mobsters, ask your pal—he put more of them in the ground than anyone else."

She turned and walked away. Her crew stayed in place until I did the same.

The sheets on Strega's bed were silk. The same color as her hair. Her body slid between gleam and shadow, mottled by the candle's untrustworthy light.

"Tell me the rest," she whispered at me. "Quick, before I get hungry again."

"Dead guys. Assassinations, not accidents. And they have to have been on the street when it happened, not in the joint. Murders, okay? Unsolved murders."

"Wesley did—"

"For*get* Wesley," I said, harsher than I'd meant to. "Listen. I know the list would be too long. You—"

"I'm still working on what you asked me before. You can't get something like that in—"

"I know. Forget that too. Come here."

She crawled over to me. Looked down. I shook my head. She dropped hers until her ear was against my mouth.

"This won't be in any computer," I told her, speaking soft. "I could do that myself. It has to be a whisper. Dead guys. Mob guys. And they had to have been fucking their own little girls before they—"

"Aaahhh," she moaned, her fingernails raking my chest. I could feel the blood. She licked it off her talons, kneeling straight up now, witchfire loose and wild in her eyes.

"Not Julio," I told her softly. "That one's done, remember? All done."

She started to cry then. I pulled her down to me, held her against my chest, rubbed her back.

A long time passed.

"I can find out," she finally said, the steel back in her voice. "But you have to tell me why."

"You said you'd do anything for—"

"I *will* do anything for you," she hissed. "I already have. You're in me. Forever. I would never let anyone hurt you. But if he's doing . . . that—killing them—I don't want to do anything that would—"

"He's stopped," I said, sure it was the truth. "And he's moved on."

"How do you—"

I pulled her close to me. And, for the first time in all the years I'd known her, I told her some of my secrets.

I spoke to the ice-man the way I always do. In my mind. If I told people that Wesley answered, they'd institutionalize me. But regular people don't get it. We have our own language, the Children of the Secret. It's garbled gibberish to anyone else. But that wasn't my link to Wesley. He was my true brother. We had gene-merged in the crucible of the State system for abused and abandoned kids. Even the grave couldn't silence him when I reached out.

And when I saw the next message from the killer, I knew Wesley was right.

>>select target<<

is all he sent.

I sat there, smoking a cigarette all the way through, waiting. It got too much for Xyla. "Aren't you going to answer him?" she finally asked.

"He doesn't expect an answer," I told her. "If I put one in right now, he'd get suspicious."

"I don't get it," she said.

"I think I do," I told her. "Just send this":

`come back. 72 hours.`

She typed it in.

"This means I have to leave my same addy up there, you understand that, right?"

"I think I understand it better than you think," I told her. "Go ahead and nuke your address, girl. My best guess—he's already found you."

"You mean . . . ?"

"Yeah. I'll be back. Three days from right now."

How much did the killer really know? Everyone thought Wesley was a machine, but they had it wrong. Wesley was just . . . focused. Right down to a laser dot. He studied his prey, but he didn't know anything outside of that. Didn't matter to him. This guy—this super-killer, how much could he know about Wesley's jobs? How they worked? The last part of his journal—at least, the last part he'd shown me—said he was going to hunt them too. But . . . "them"? I had to play it like it was a category he hunted, not a group. It was the only thing that made any sense. And if I was right, there'd only be one match.

"He's gone," I said.

"You're . . . sure?"

"Absolutely," I told Lincoln, scratching behind Pansy's ear. "He's well away. No chance of getting caught. He's a million miles from here."

"What's he . . . like?" one of the men in the back of the room asked me.

"That wasn't the deal," I said. "You wanted him safe. You got him safe."

"He's right." Nadine's voice cut into the room. She was seated at the same table, but she'd replaced the lank-haired skinny woman with the same chubby blonde pony girl I'd seen in her little home video. "There hasn't been a killing for weeks. The cops are just blowing smoke."

"It *changed* things, though," another woman said from across the room. "It's . . . different now."

"Sure," an older man said, "you can walk down Christopher Street without the back of your neck tingling every time you see a crowd of straights now. There hasn't been a fag-bashing for a good while. They're scared. *He* did that. But what makes you think it's going to last?"

"He showed us the way," Nadine spoke up. Like she was talking about Jesus. Walking to Mecca. Following the Tao.

"What does *that* mean?" one of the younger guys asked, the sneer just below the surface.

"They didn't stop because they saw the light," Nadine said, an orator's organ-stop in her voice, speaking to the whole room. "They stopped because they were afraid. They're *still* afraid. They're afraid of *him.* And now he's gone. But he doesn't have to go. . . ."

"What are you talking about?" Lincoln demanded.

"Nobody knows who he is, right?" Nadine shot back. "All they have is two things: letters to the newspapers . . . and dead bodies. It'll be quiet for a while. Maybe a long while, I don't know. But when they . . . when they start going after us again, well . . . who says *we* can't write letters to the newspapers?"

"Sure, but they only *printed* the letters because they were authentic," Lincoln said.

Nadine got to her feet. Eye-swept the room a couple of times to make sure everyone there was riveted to her. She took a deep breath.

"We could make ours authentic too," she said. Softly. But everyone in the place heard her.

"This is Tracy," Nadine told me in the alley outside the room where they'd met, a nod of her head indicating the chubby blonde.

"Pleased to meet you," was all I could think to say.

"Turn around," Nadine ordered her.

The blonde did it.

Nadine stepped over to the blonde, pushed her until the other girl's face was right against the wall. Then she reached around the blonde girl's waist, and did something with her fingers. The blonde girl made some sound, too low for me to understand. Nadine yanked down the blonde girl's jeans and her underpants in one two-handed pull.

"Stay!" she said.

Pansy stayed too. Watching. She didn't know what was going on, but the hair on the back of her neck was up.

It was dark in the alley.

"Light one of your cigarettes," she said to me, just this side of a command.

I did it, wondering why even as the match flared. She snatched it out of my mouth. Looked at the glowing tip. Smiled ugly. "Want some of that?" she said, pointed at the chubby blonde.

"No," I told her.

"Then go away," she said, dropping her voice. "I'm going to play with her. Right out here. In public. When I'm done, she'll carry my brand. Think about that. And remember your promise. I cleared it with the rest of them. You got your money. But you better not be—"

"I'm still working," I said.

Then I snapped my fingers for Pansy to heel and walked out of the alley.

Why did that crazy girl think she could pull me in with sex games? I couldn't figure it out. Couldn't understand the cigarette thing either. That wasn't me. Ever. It always made me . . . I could never get it, never get the part where people yearned for what other people had done to me. But I guess I did get it after all. The freaks, they set things in motion. Sometimes they make more of themselves. Sometimes they create their own hunters. I guess they don't . . . know. Or care. I never asked one. Except when I was a kid. I remember crying, "Why?" And I remember him laughing.

I never knew what to do with all that hate until Wesley told me. A long time ago. "Fire works." The ice-boy never played, not even back then. Not even with words.

"Rocco LaMarca," Strega whispered to me late the next night.

"You're sure?"

"He ran a big crew. Mostly in Westchester. The carting industry. But he lived in Connecticut. New Canaan. Very classy. Not even a whisper about him. Called himself Ronald March."

"And he was—?"

"The cops thought it was a mob hit. An ice pick in the eye. You know what that means—he saw something he shouldn't have. And they cut his tongue out too. Saying he *said* something about what he saw."

"But how do you know he's—?"

"It wasn't a sanctioned hit. The Family doesn't know who did it. But they knew about his daughter. He made . . . films of her."

"For money? Like—?"

"No. Just to . . . show off. His . . . power. I mean, he *said* it was business. Showed the films to a few of the boys who were in that end. You remember Sally Lou?"

Strega, telling me she knew everything. Sally Lou ran the mob's kiddie-sex business before Times Square felt the Disney steamroller. I love it. Disney cleans up Times Square, but they hire a convicted child molester to direct one of their movies. People protested, but the studio ranted on about giving people another chance. Sure, once it came down to money, all of a sudden, Disney's got more faith in "rehabilitation" than an NCAA recruiter.

Sally Lou had gone down around the same time Mortay did, all part of that same horror show that cost me my love and launched Wesley on his last rampage.

A lot of thoughts. But all I said to Strega was: "Yeah."

"Well, Sally Lou was one of the ones who saw it. But LaMarca never turned it over. So Sally Lou, he asked around; like, what was the guy up to, right? And that's when the word came back. He had a daughter. So they put it together. The filthy slime. He was—"

"I know," I said, stroking her hair. "What happened to her? To the daughter?"

"Nobody knows," Strega said.

Meaning she didn't. But she knew everything else. And her answer to my next question was the last tile dropping into the mosaic. I could read it then, even through the haze of blood.

"It was almost fifteen years ago," Wolfe said quietly. "September twenty-seventh, nineteen eighty-four."

"I got him now," I told her.

"You're really working this?" she asked, disbelief the strongest element in her voice.

"I'm not a good liar," I lied. "There's nothing more for you to do. You got paid. We're square. You think what you want about me. Make your judgments. Maybe someday I'll tell you about it."

"Why 'maybe'?"

"I think you know," I told her. "I think you've always known. You don't want . . . me. I got that. I'm doing this for me. The way I do everything, right? For me, that's what you think. But you had me wrong, and one day you'll know that. Even if I don't tell you myself."

"Burke . . . wait!"

I just kept walking.

"Write it down on a piece of paper," Xyla told me. "I can't tell how to spell it from what you're saying. And what if you're—"

Her mouth popped open as her computer screen shifted.

>>name?<<

was all it said. And

gutterball felestrone. 50-50

is all she typed back.

"He *did* find me," Xyla said. "Christ, he's good. I could never have found *him.*"

"I did," I told her. "Get ready. He's going to come back. And pretty soon, I think."

I guess he wanted to make sure I wouldn't miss it. Gutterball's last meal had been in his favorite restaurant, a mob joint deep in what of Little Italy still survived the all-borders Chinatown encroachment. Nobody walked in there and blasted him, but someone had gotten into the kitchen. Gutterball was dead before the EMS ambulance managed to bull its way through the clogged streets. Gutterball always had the same thing: spaghetti and sausage with oregano-laced sauce—gravy, he called it. The newspapers had all that. The autopsy report was made public. The sauce had a little extra spice in it, that night. "Enough ricin to kill a regiment," the pathologist was quoted as saying. "After the first swallow, he never had a chance."

"Would it be a true death?" I asked the woman. Her office was jumbled and serene at the same time. She had no desk, just a couple of easy chairs and a couch. No computer screen, not even a file cabinet.

"It . . . could. Do you know if there were any others?"

"No."

"Do you know—?"

"I told you everything," I said. "Everything I know. Doc said you're the best there is. At . . . this stuff."

She flashed a smile. "This 'stuff,' as you call it, is . . . variable. That is, it depends on so many things. From what you told me, all I can say is that it *could* be. But only if the subject felt completely, totally safe."

"Safe? I don't get it. I mean—"

"It would be a true death only if the dead person never came back—that *is* what you're asking, isn't it? And I'm giving you the best answer I can. As long as the . . . environment was safe, really truly safe . . . if the . . . original conditions never resurfaced, then, yes, it could be a 'true death,' as you put it."

"How do you know he'll—?"

"I don't," I told Lorraine. "But I have to be ready in case he does."

"And you're sure he's the one who—?"

"Yeah."

"I'll get a cot put in here," she said. "The bathroom's right through that door over there. You want food, just walk into the kitchen, I'll take care of it."

"Thanks."

"I would like to go with you," Rusty said quietly. I hadn't even noticed him before he spoke.

"It can't work like that," I replied, bowing slightly to show my respect for what he was offering.

"What kind of dog is that?" Xyla asked me.

"She's a Neapolitan mastiff," I told her. "Aren't you, sweetheart?"

Pansy ignored me, watching Xyla. I saw a look pass between them. And I recognized it. "You love dogs, don't you?" I asked Xyla.

"Oh, I *do*. I have a—"

"Yeah. Whatever. Listen, do *not* feed her, understand?"

"I wasn't gonna—"

"Yeah, you were," I told her. "It won't matter. She wouldn't take food from a stranger anyway."

"I guess I'm busted," she said, face reddening. It was a pretty sight in that machine-cold room, like a flower blooming at the base of a prison wall.

"I'll call you when it's time," I told her, lying back on the cot and closing my eyes.

I wasn't surprised when Xyla's computer screen started blinking at 3:44 a.m. Sure. Let him think the machine was sitting in my house—that's what the test was all about.

>>50-50<<

his message said. I told Xyla what to do, and she hit her keyboard:

yours $125K

Xyla was about to get up, but I put my hand on her shoulder, telling her he wasn't done.

>>why target?<<

"He's using ICQ," Xyla said excitedly. "He's there. I mean . . . somewhere. But he's on the line."

"He won't stay long. Just type what I tell you."

Cork unauthorized

His response popped up almost immediately.

>>next?<<

4 names. major money. but they want to deal direct

"What does that—?" Xyla asked.

"Ssshhh," I told her. "He wants that too. You'll see."

>>understand. but no face-to-face<<

they don't want that either. afraid

>>then?<<

want proof

>>*names* = proof<<

no. want proof he's alive

>>*you* tell them<<

polygraph

>>understand. you know who i am?<<

think so

>>not *look* same<<

so?

>>how pass polygraph then?<<

only question: did i talk to him in person?

>>understand. you *do* know who i am.<<

yes

>>no more talk. next message, instructions for meet<<

got it

The screen flickered, glowed red, then yellow. Then Xyla's computer just shut itself off.

"Fuck!" she snarled, flicking switches like a madwoman.

I watched her in silence. It was almost a half-hour before she pushed herself away from the computer, rolling her chair back across the room, sweat-drenched.

"He crashed it," she said. "Thunderbolt. I've heard about them, but I didn't know if they were real."

"What's a thunderbolt?"

"A giant spike. Electrical. It's transmitted over the modem during ICQ. When the sender signs off, it's activated."

"You lost all your data?"

She gave me one of those "What are you, stupid?" looks young girls probably memorize in the cradle. "Of course not. That's in a separate unit. I don't leave anything connected. All he spiked out was my software. But there was a *ton* of that. It's gonna take me a couple of weeks to . . ."

"I'm sorry," I told her. Even as I realized that his attack on Xyla's setup was another message: whatever meeting he was going to set up wasn't going to be soon.

I learned a lot of trades in prison. Not the ones the rehab-geeks talk about. The ones we all learn, some better than others. Trades have tricks. One of them I did learn was how to use time you're stuck with. And that's what I did while I was waiting for the finale.

"I know the whole thing now," I told my family.

They were all there this time: Michelle and the Mole, Terry sitting between them. The Prof and Clarence. Max and Immaculata. Even little Flower was around someplace, probably playing with the cooks in the back. Mama hawk-eyed the kitchen area, getting up every couple of minutes to check on her granddaughter.

Nobody said anything, waiting for me to fill in the blanks. I did it. Slow, taking my time, testing every link before I added it to the chain.

When I was done, the Prof was the first to speak. "If it's written in blue, it must be true," the little man said. "He found the Gatekeeper."

"Prof!" Michelle snapped at him. "Stop it! This is insane enough without a bunch of superstitious—"

I reached over and took Michelle's hand, squeezing it gently. "Prof," I asked, "you said the only way to work it is to give them a soul for every one the . . . dead guy took, right?"

"One for one, son," he agreed.

"That plane . . . the sex-tour one. I figure that probably evened the score."

"It is impossible to transmit matter in that way," the Mole said, earning a loving glance of approval from Michelle.

"Nobody knows some—" Clarence started, defending his father.

"Both true," Mama said.

We all looked toward her, but she nodded at Immaculata, the first time I'd seen her defer. Mac gulped at the honor, knowing it had to be her profession Mama was deferring to, not her wisdom—Mama believed nobody under seventy knew anything of value from their own life experience. "Psychologically," she began, "a belief can become a fact to the believer."

"But this ain't no nut," the Prof stepped up.

"He wouldn't have to be . . . crazy," Mac told him. "Just a . . . believer. He might be rational in all other senses of the word. But if you 'reason' from a false premise, any conclusion, no matter how logically it follows, will be wrong, do you see what I'm saying?"

"Both true," Mama said again, not disrespecting Immaculata's answer, but making it clear it wasn't enough.

"All right," Immaculata said. "Look at it this way. Some believe this . . . Wesley never actually died, yes? But there was no . . . support for that proposition. This recent rash of murders, they represent a sort of 'proof,' seemingly to underscore the presence of . . . Ah, look: Those who think Wesley never actually died or those who think he could return from the dead . . . merge. Into a belief system. If it is 'Wesley' doing these murders in the minds of the believers, he *has* come back, understand?"

Mama nodded gravely, a gesture of complete support. Immaculata bowed her gratitude for the recognition.

"It doesn't matter!" Michelle said sharply. "He's not a threat to us. There's no reason to get . . . involved with him. It's over. Let him do whatever he—"

Max bowed slightly. Put his two fists together, then made a snapping motion. Volunteering to do the job if I could get him close enough.

I bowed my thanks, knowing it was impossible. "Both true, Mama?" I asked her.

She pointed at the Prof, then at the Mole.

We waited, but she was done.

"Me first," the Prof said, stepping up to the challenge. "If this guy found the Gatekeeper, he'd have to bring a whole *bunch* behind what Wesley did, right?"

Nobody moved. It hadn't been a real question.

"And he *did* that, right?" the Prof continued. "Ain't no question but the motherfucker's *qualified.*"

"If that would work," the Mole said, his mild voice throbbing with the one electrical current that always hit his circuits, "the Nazis could . . ."

"To bring Hitler back, they would have to kill six million people," Clarence said. "If they could do that, why would they need . . . ?"

His voice trailed off into the silence as we all let it penetrate. But it took the Prof to say it out loud: "You all just heard the word. You got it, Schoolboy?" he asked me.

"Anyone who could kill six million people wouldn't have to bring Hitler back," I said slowly. "He'd *be* Hitler."

Immaculata looked up. "Yes. And this killer, he wants to be . . ."

"Wesley," I finished for her.

"Why?" the Mole asked. "Wesley was . . ."

"No," I told them all. "Wesley *is.* Check the whisper-stream. He'll never die. They never found a body. You say his name, people start to shake. It's not some ghost they're afraid of."

"You think if he kills enough he will have the same . . . respect Wesley has, mahn?" Clarence asked. "That is insane. It is not the count of the bodies that—"

"My son just got it done," the Prof said. "No way you take Wesley's name just by playing his game."

I saw where he was going, and cut him off. "Everything he did, it's like an improved version of Wesley," I said. "Every hit tied to Wesley, this guy copied. He works just like Wesley did. Wesley wasn't just a sniper. Neither is this guy: he uses bombs, poisons, high-tech. That's why he wanted that damn . . . 'assignment.' When I challenged him. Told him that any freak can be a random hitter. Wesley took contracts. He was a missile. All he needed was a name. This guy, he took a name from me and did the job because *he* wants a name. He wants Wesley's."

"Never happen," the Prof said. "Nobody could take Wesley's place. Wesley'll never die. And the only way to never die is *to* die, right? No matter what this guy does, no matter how many fucked-up letters he writes to the newspapers, you know what they're gonna say: it's Wesley's work. He can't change that."

"He's a shape-shifter," I told them. "But that's not the whole thing. I understand what Mama meant now. You too, Mac. All of you. It *is* all true. If this guy starts doing Wesley's work—taking contracts, making people dead on order—then he *is* Wesley, see? When people whisper Wesley's name, they're talking about *him.* And he'll know that, wherever he is."

"But you said his . . . journal was all about kidnapping children and—" Immaculata said, dropping her voice, eye-sweeping the place to make sure her little girl wouldn't hear what lurked past her circle of love.

"At *first,*" I told her. "But I get the impression that it's old. He did it a long time ago. He's an . . . artist. And he finally decided that the highest art was homicide. As a kidnapper, he was the best there was. No contest. He didn't need his name in the paper, he *knew.* He probably thought he was the greatest killer too. I think *that's* what he said his new art was going to be. Not killing child molesters, killing mobsters. Or . . . maybe both. I don't know. But I figure, he started doing it. And kept it up, same way he did the kidnappings. For the 'art,' right? But when he snapped to it . . . when he figured out that there was someone ahead of him . . . that he was in a contest he couldn't win . . . that's when he figured out he had to *be* Wesley. That's his art now."

"Motherfucker's *way* past crazy," the Prof said.

"Sure," I said. "So what? He can't be Wesley except through *me,* understand? Gutterball *thought* he was dealing with Wesley when he sent out that hit. That's why I sent this guy right back at Gutterball. There's nobody left to—what's that word you always use, Mac?—*validate* him. Except me. Gutterball was an idiot. That's not news. But me . . . If I go into the street and say I saw Wesley, who's gonna deny it? Everyone knows how we . . . were."

"And with all those baby-rapers getting hit, it just *reeks* of you, honey," Michelle said, nodding her head in agreement.

"He said it right at the beginning. Of that freakish 'journal' he sent me. 'Folie à deux,' remember? I told him I could get him mob contracts, but I'd have to say I *saw* Wesley, get it? He made me send him all this stuff, prove I was the real thing. That I was with Wesley. All the way back to the beginning. I don't know where he got some of his info, but it was on the money, all of it. So now, the way he figures it, if I see *him,* I *did* see Wesley. He *is* Wesley now—the way he figures, he's proved that. Taken over. So he's going to meet me, I'm sure of it."

"But, honey, what's the point?" Michelle asked me. "He can't do anything to you—not if he wants you to . . . do what he said. If you don't do it, he's on his own. Why meet with him?"

Max grabbed Michelle's hand to get her attention. With his other hand, he reached over and tapped my heart. Pointed to himself, then to Immaculata. Finally, he made the sign of a man shooting a pistol.

"Oh God," Michelle gasped. "You mean—?"

"It was him," I told her. Told them all. "If he's the one Gutterball talked to on the phone, then he's the one who did the hit in Central Park. Did it the same way Wesley would have. A couple of flunkies to lay down cover fire, make a diversion, then a surgical strike. And wipe out the witnesses. Gutterball must have known it was gonna cost him those two other guys. Maybe he wanted them gone anyway—got three for the price of one."

Immaculata cleared her throat, threading delicately, the way she always does. "But, Burke, if that's true . . . this . . . killer, he wasn't the one who shot Crystal Beth."

"He made it happen," I said flatly. "He knows a thousand ways to kill. If he'd used any other one, she'd be here today. Right here. With me."

Something must have happened to me after I said that. When I came around, I was in a chair in the basement, my family all around me. I didn't ask how I got there—Max could carry me as easy as a wino could lug a bottle wrapped in a paper bag.

I opened my eyes. Looked at the only people I loved on the whole planet. "I don't know if you can make up for things," I told them, calming down. "He killed a lot of little kids. Then he stopped. And killed a lot of scum. I don't know if they were child molesters or mob guys or both . . . at first. Then it was fag-bashers. Then pedophiles. Maybe whoever's keeping count thinks his scales are balanced. But not me. Michelle was right. What do I care if he was planning to kill every last freak on the planet? Because now he's . . . stopped. He's going to be Wesley now. A contract hitter. And you know what? It doesn't matter anyway. He killed Crystal Beth. Got her killed, same difference. He wants to be Wesley so bad—I'm going to send him someplace where he can talk to him face to face."

"You ain't alone, home," the Prof reminded me.

"You want Terry to hear this?" I asked Michelle.

"It's not up to her," Terry said, his still-changing voice on man-sound now. "I know how I got my mother," he said, reaching over to touch her. "And my father," he said, bowing his head toward the Mole. "I know what you . . . did, Burke. Then, I mean. I'm in this too. Whatever you want to do, I want to do it too. If someone took my . . ."

He didn't finish. Didn't have to.

"There's no way," the Prof said. "He's not gonna walk into a room. Motherfucker don't take no risks. No way you're gonna get a piece past whatever he's got set up either."

"Mole?" I asked.

"If he has the correct equipment, he could pick up any weapon, in any form, just from its composition. Even plastic explosive. Thermal-image scanners could. . . . I have . . . devices. Very small. But they would not be . . . invisible if he were properly equipped."

Max leaned over, tapped each of my hands, spread his into a question. Could I kill him with my hands if I got close enough?

"I don't know," I told him honestly. Max has been training me for years and years, but I never got that good at any of the techniques. I can hit pretty hard, and I can take a shot and keep coming. And if I got my hands on any vital spot—and focused hard on why I was there—maybe. But it could never be a sure thing.

"It will not work," the Mole announced.

"Mole, I think I can—"

The Mole held up his hand for silence. "He will not *let* you get close enough. Remember?"

Sure. I knew what he meant. Like Wesley. This killer would keep a safety zone around himself. Wesley usually did it with an Uzi. I don't know what this guy would use, but the Mole was right—he'd use something.

"We could put a tracking device on you," the Mole said. "But you would have to discard it before you stepped into his zone."

"Fair enough," I told him.

"*Not* enough," the Prof said. "This team needs a scheme."

They all argued for a while. I just sat there, slumped in the chair. When they ran out of gas, I told them how I wanted to do it.

"I'm not rebuilt yet," Xyla said. "How could I—?"

"I need a message sent to him. I don't care if you send it on this machine. Send it the same way you sent the first one. He'll get it. I don't need an answer. When he bangs back in . . . when you have this all back up . . . he'll either go for it or he won't."

"I can do that," she said. "Trixie has a little halfass Mac I could—"

"Sure," I stopped her.

She grabbed a pen. I waved her away, wrote it down myself, and handed it to her.

not coming alone. bringing woman. she *direct* connect. she *only* one who can validate in certain areas. can *not* make it happen without her. not negotiable. you pick time, place, conditions . . . anything you want. but if can't bring woman, no go.

"Jesus," Xyla said. "He might not answer at all now."

"That's his choice," I told her. "Just like this whole thing's been since he started."

"This is the only way," I told her.

"You're . . . serious?" Nadine asked.

"Dead serious. I'm keeping my promise. But this is the way I'm going to keep it. I don't trust you. There's only one way I can—"

"How do I know you'll—?"

"You don't," I told her. "You don't know anything. Take it or leave it," I said.

"No!" I whispered to Strega. "No handcuffs. No chains. You have to keep her—"

"She'll *like* them," the witch hissed at me, glancing over at Nadine standing in the farthest corner of the white living room, her back to us. "If she tastes it herself, she'll know how it feels when she—"

"No."

"Burke, if I have to keep her for—"

"If you can't do it, say so. But you *can't* chain her, understand? No restraints."

"How else could I watch her twenty-four-seven?"

"You know how," I told her.

I didn't feel guilty about leaving Nadine there. Poison wouldn't have a chance against Strega—she drank it for nourishment.

I needed the time to get everything ready. And I needed Nadine with me when I went to meet the killer. Needed her to come when she was called, no hesitation. Once he opened the window, I knew it was going to be just a narrow crack. And if I moved wrong, a guillotine.

I kept thinking about my hands. I'd boxed in prison. I wasn't really any good at it. The Prof got me started. He'd always wanted to train a fighter. Knew how to do it too. But it was a long time before I understood what I was really being trained for. When I first started, I'd be fine until I got hit with a good shot. Then I'd go off. Take three to give one. All I—finally—learned from boxing was self-control. Staying inside myself even in battle. I did learn that much. Max tried to teach me too. And I learned some of his stuff. But I never worked at it. Never . . . got it, I guess. I don't know.

I don't like fighting, maybe that's the problem. I can't see hitting someone to hurt them. And if someone's going to hurt me, I can't see hitting them at all. Wesley told me he once killed a guy in the joint when he was just a kid. The guy was part of a crew, and they'd told Wesley he had a choice: give up some head to one of them, or get gang-banged by them all. Wesley picked the easier one. That made sense to them, but they didn't know what "easier" meant to Wesley. He got on his knees, but then he rammed the guy in the stomach and got his hands on his throat. And held the guy's head in place while some anonymous guard at the other end of the tier threw the switch that racks the bars on all the cells. The guy's skull crumbled like it was papier-mâché.

The reason Wesley did it that way was because there'd been a shakedown, and the hacks had taken the shank he had stashed in his cell. Didn't matter—he always got it done.

So I thought about dying. But even if I could get enough explosives past whatever security he'd have set up, I couldn't be *sure.*

My hands, then. All I had. But not for his throat. To push a button.

I hit the post with a perfect two-knuckle strike, driving *through* it, not at it . . . the way I'd been taught. I hardly felt my hand. My mind was right.

"That's mine," Strega said. "Don't touch it."

I turned and saw her in the corner of the shadowy basement. "Where's—?"

"In the bathtub," Strega said. "With no towels. And if she steps out of it wet, she'll fry like an omelet."

"Jesus," I said, looking down at my hand.

"I said don't *touch* it," Strega ordered, coming toward me. She was naked, her hair tied back with a black ribbon. She grabbed my hand. It was bloody around the knuckles. "Mine!" she said, like a two-year-old just learning the word. She licked the blood off. Then she squeezed my hand, hard. Some new drops blossomed. She pulled my knuckles into her mouth, sucked until she came, spasming, me with one arm around her to keep her from falling.

The bathroom door on the second floor was standing open. Strega stepped in. I looked over her shoulder. Nadine was in the tub, lying back, her eyes closed. Strega pulled a pair of plugs from their sockets, disconnecting the red-coiled heaters which were standing sentry on the soaked tile floor. Then she tossed a heavy black mat down, dropped to her knees, and started gently rubbing Nadine with a bar of soap, crooning to her.

Nadine's eyes never opened. I couldn't tell if she even knew I was there.

After a minute, I wasn't.

I spent a lot of time waiting, some of it at the joint where Xyla had her war room in the back. I watched Rusty draw, wondering how he could do that and scan the room at the same time. Listened to the table-talk around me. Drifted. Knowing the answer was somewhere in me. Knowing I couldn't force it out.

I went back Inside. When we were all doing time together. Maybe not together. I mean, Wesley was in there with us, but he wasn't *with* us. Wesley wasn't with anyone. But we were close enough so that we wired anything back to him that he'd need.

That's when we found out this guy was looking to take Wesley off the count. Tower. I don't know if that was his name or his handle. Didn't matter—his true ID was tattooed on his forearm, the swastika dripping blood. That was years ago, before they announced their kills with the spiderweb on the elbow. He wanted a shank, and he wanted it from Oz. That's because Oz made the best shanks in the whole joint. Only problem is, he wanted it for five cartons of smokes, and the going rate was ten. Oz was a very pale guy. Not prison-complexion pale, his natural color. Even his hair was almost white. He was some kind of Scandinavian, about as Aryan as you could get, but Tower didn't see him that way. Tower wasn't bargaining—although that's what it would sound like to you if you only heard the audio and didn't get the implied threat in the way he loomed over Oz. That's when the Prof stepped in:

"Where you been, chump?" the little man asked Tower. "You know nothing's on sale in the jail. You want a shank, you tap your bank. Far as I'm concerned, ten crates for one of my man's pieces—hell, that price is *nice,* Jack."

Tower looked down at the Prof, making up his mind. Big mistake. I was in position by then. And I'd already paid *my* ten cartons. "Tomorrow, motherfucker," Tower said to Oz, saving face. "Bring the best you got." Then he stalked away.

Oz was there the next day, but Tower never showed. That stirred the whisper-stream, but it wasn't until later that I learned the truth.

"Damnedest thing I ever heard of," Doc mused in his office. He liked an audience. And I liked to listen. "They find him dead in his cell. Looked like he went in his sleep. Not a mark on him. But the tox was bad—I mean, *deadly* bad."

"So he OD'ed?" I asked.

"Not on curare!" Doc snorted. "But once they saw *that,* then they *really* did the job. They found it in his ear."

"What?"

"A little dart. Beautiful piece of work, fluted and everything, like you'd make in a lab."

"Somebody threw—?"

"No way, Burke. It was *deep.* Cruz said he recognized it. You know what he said it was? A fucking *blowgun* dart! Can you believe that? Last time I checked, we didn't have any rain-forest pygmies here."

"So how come the Man didn't shake down the whole place?" I asked him. That's what happened every time there was a stabbing and the weapon wasn't recovered at the scene.

"What would be the point?" Doc responded. "It was weeks old by the time they found it. Whoever did it certainly got rid of it by then. Or took it apart, turned it back into whatever he made it from. Who knows?"

"Who cares?"

"You got a point," Doc agreed. "No way this'll kick off a race thing—Tower locked in H Block."

I just nodded. H Block was all white. Not all AB, true, but all white, for sure. Everyone in there didn't have the same politics, but they had the same color.

Same color as Wesley.

And when I'd sent "blowgun dart" to this super-killer, he'd just nodded from his cyber-hideout. He knew. So I had to play it like he knew it all.

I was going to get close to him soon. But there'd be bars. Some kind of bars. My hands wouldn't do it.

A muscular guy with deep-glazed eyes staggered past us. He bumped into Rusty, knocking the big man's drawing tablet onto the floor. Rusty didn't say anything, just bent to pick it up.

"You got a fuckin' problem?" the guy asked, speech slurred but fists clenched.

"There's no problem," I told him.

"I wasn't talking to you, motherfucker," he said to me, eyes only on Rusty.

Before he finished, Trixie was standing next to him, off to the side. "What's he been drinking?" she asked the waitress.

"V and V," the girl said.

"You're out of here," Trixie told the muscular guy.

"Fuck you, butch."

"Step off!" she warned him.

"I'll fucking step—"

Rusty shoved the heavy wood table he was sitting at right into the guy's knees, driving it so hard you could hear bone snap. The drunk dropped.

"Goddamn it, Rusty!" Trixie yelled at him. She reached down, hooked the guy's belt, and dragged him off somewhere. The waitress went with her.

"What's a 'V and V'?" I asked Rusty.

"Vodka and Vicodin," he told me. "Lots of fools taking that now. Really gets you wrecked."

Freddy Fender's "Wasted Days and Wasted Nights" mocked me from the Plymouth's speakers as I headed back to my place.

When I got upstairs, I saw Pansy had Max's singing bowl on the floor. She was just nosing it around with her snout, not biting it or anything. But she must have worked hard to get it down from the shelf where I'd put it.

"You like the sound, girl? Is that what you're trying to do?" I asked her.

Pansy just looked at me.

I sat on the floor next to her, worked the wooden whisk until the bowl began to sing.

And then I went into it.

When I came back, I had the weapon. A bomb. A bomb built in hell. I knew it was there. I knew I could bring it with me. But I didn't know if I could detonate it.

And then there was nothing left.

I wasn't worried about walking out of there alive. Without me, the killer couldn't be.

"She knows what we're doing," Strega whispered at me from her silky bed.

"So what?"

"It's part of her . . . discipline. She has to know."

"All right," I said softly, knowing I was near the edge, dancing with a witch.

"Now she has to have more."

"What?"

"She has to watch. I'm going to bring her in here. And make her watch us."

"No."

"Yes. You know how I hold her? How I keep her here?"

"No."

"I love her," Strega said. "And she loves me. I let her . . . here," she whispered, guiding my hand to between her legs, a moist soft trap.

"Because you—?"

"Because *she,*" the witch said. "Understand? We're the same . . . some ways. The same. She wouldn't let a man . . . either. But me . . ."

"I already know she's gay."

"She's not," Strega said, dropping her face, nipping at my cock. "Me either."

"Look, I don't care what you—"

"She has to watch," Strega hissed at me, nipping harder. "And, if you want, we could all . . ."

"No."

"I wouldn't let her hurt you, my darling. I'll be right here."

"I don't want her near me—not like that."

"Oh, yes you do, baby. My baby. But you're afraid. You never have to be afraid when I'm here. When I'm alive. Even when I'm not, I'll always be with you."

"Strega," I asked her, sitting up, tugging at her hair to pull her face away from my cock, "did you ever meet the Gatekeeper?"

"She has to watch," the witch said. Like the Gatekeeper herself; always a price.

"Just . . . watch, right?"

"If that's all you—"

"Just *watch,*" I told her, surrendering. Hating a piece of myself but staying within the circle surrounding my life. Everything costs. Everybody pays . . . and I'd paid so much to learn even *that.*

"Hmmmm . . ."

"And then you'll tell me?" I asked, telling myself it would be over soon. And then I'd know. Not why Strega did things, but what she knew. What I needed.

"Yessss . . ." she whispered.

Strega disappeared. I lay there, my back against some propped-up pillows, smoking and waiting. Knowing it wasn't about giving in to Strega, or doing what she wanted. No, whatever it was, she was doing it for me. But she was a witch, and she couldn't work without her charms.

Nadine walked in. Nude. I couldn't see her face in the shadowy light Strega seemed to bring with her as she followed the bigger girl into the room. Strega stood next to Nadine, her right hand somewhere behind the other woman.

I watched them watch me.

Strega crawled onto the bed between my legs. Then she stopped, well short of reaching me. "No closer, understand?" she said.

I couldn't figure out what she was talking about. Strega was a witch, not a tease. And I was . . . limp, anyway. Frightened. Strega always frightens me. This was worse. There was lightning in the room. No thunder, just the soundless pressure of electricity ready to crackle into life. Or take it.

Strega got up, went back to where she had been standing. Then Nadine crawled onto the bed. I was frozen. If she . . .

Nadine stopped, right where Strega had. And stayed there, arching her back as Strega knelt on the floor behind her and took her. Nadine's eyes gleamed, but they weren't seeing me. She made a throaty sound. Strega hissed into her. I couldn't *not* look at them.

Nadine let go, exploding inside. Even her overdeveloped arms wouldn't hold her as her shoulders dropped and her face hit the bed, only inches from me. Strega slithered across Nadine's back until her mouth was on me.

"It works now, doesn't it, baby?"

I didn't want it to, but it did.

Nadine never moved, staying face-down on the red silk sheets. Strega gulped hard—but she didn't swallow the way she always did. She yanked hard on Nadine's hair and when the bigger girl's face came up, Strega kissed her. Deep and long.

"You're in her now too," Strega said when she was done. "I washed your blood. It's mine. I can give it to whoever I please."

I couldn't move. My spine was frozen. But I'd paid the tolls.

Trixie approached my table, telling me it was time without saying a word. I got up and followed her to the back room.

"Incoming," Xyla said, over her shoulder.

I watched the screen.

>>Meet. Now.<<

where?

>>ground rules: (1) no "friends"; (2) no weapons<<

understand

>>pay phone. corner 23rd and 1st. go there now. one hour. no more. await call. follow instructions.<<

bringing woman, remember?

I had Xyla type, stalling for time as I thumbed my cellular into life.

"Hmmmm," Strega answered.

"Get ready to ride," I told her. "Right now. Corner of Twenty-third and First."

"We're ready."

"Now!" I told her, hitting the "End" switch just as his response popped up on the screen.

>>yes. *you* remember. same rules for her.<<

ok

>>leave *now* one hour, no more.<<

The huge digital clock above Xyla's computer read 02:12. Sure, no traffic at that hour. I'd be able to get where he said on time, no matter where in the city I was. He couldn't know the woman wasn't with me already. I told Xyla to type:

leaving now

"He's gone," she said, fingers tapping impotently.

In another minute, so was I.

I knew he had the technology to monitor cellular traffic, but he couldn't hear me speak face to face. "Pay phone. Twenty-third and First," I told Clarence as I opened the door to the Plymouth.

"With you, mahn," the islander said, strolling over to his own car. They'd all be there, most of them before me.

I couldn't afford to be stopped, so I kept well within the limits all the way over. Still, I was there with a good twenty-five minutes to spare. I opened the transmission tunnel and pulled out the ice-cold untraceable pistol. Not for him—in case somebody was using the pay phone.

But it was deserted. I put the gun back.

A flame-colored Porsche Boxster roared up across the street from the pay phone. Strega, flying her flag.

I walked over to her, not feeling his eyes, but believing in them. No way he wouldn't have the whole terrain covered. I couldn't see any of my crew, and hoped he couldn't either. I bent down just as her window lowered.

"He's going to call me on that phone," I told her, nodding in its direction without turning my head.

"Kiss me," she commanded.

Her tongue was fire in my mouth.

"Give me your hands."

She licked the backs of them across the knuckles.

"Mine is stronger," she said. "I'll send her over in a minute."

"Then go," I told her.

"I'll never go," she witch-promised me. "And if you do, I'll bring you back."

Nadine walked across the street to where I was standing at the pay phone. The Porsche roared away.

"He's going to call and—"

"I know," she said. She was dressed in a pair of cut-off jeans and a pink T-shirt, plain white sneakers and sweatsocks on her feet. If she felt the chill in the night air, she didn't show it.

I lit a cigarette.

"She did that," Nadine said to me.

"What?"

"Burned me. With a cigarette."

"She doesn't smoke. . . ."

"On purpose. So I would understand."

"Understand what?"

"What *I* did. To . . . my friend. She said if I hurt you she would find me in hell. I had to wear her brand when I met . . . him."

"And you just—?"

"You don't understand," Nadine said quietly. "But she does."

"I—"

The phone rang.

"The woman with you—is she the one?" the voice asked.

"Yes," I replied, knowing I could be talking to a tape recording, not wasting an atom of concentration on the voice.

"Turn around."

I did it. Waited. Nadine didn't move, so I was looking over her shoulder.

"You are under observation. Full thermal. Discard all weapons, recording devices, and transmitters now."

"Don't have any," I told him.

"See building directly ahead of you to the right? Gray stone. Twenty-nine stories?"

"Yes."

"Security box to right of door. Access code is: thirteen thirty-three thirty-nine zero three. Repeat."

"Thirteen. Thirty-three. Thirty-nine. Zero. Three."

"Enter building. Summon elevator. Last car on your left. Enter. Follow instructions."

I heard a disengagement *click!*

"Let's go," I told Nadine.

The building had twin front doors of thick glass, each with a long vertical brass handle. I punched in the numbers. Pulled on the handles. Nothing. The muscles between my shoulders tightened. I took a deep breath through my nose and pushed. The doors opened inward. We walked across a medium-sized lobby with an unattended doorman's desk. The last elevator to my left was standing open. We stepped inside. As the door closed, I saw a typed note taped to the control panel.

PRESS → 21-11-19-4

I did that. The car started to rise. A digital indicator showed each floor as we passed. When it reached 29, it kept on going. *Like my old place,* I thought. *Crawl space . . . off the charts.*

The elevator door opened into an archway. I knew what it was right away. Security gauntlet. The most sophisticated detector made, as sensitive as an MRI. I'd seen one like it before. On the private penthouse floor of a terrified billionaire with enough cash to indulge his paranoia.

I didn't waste time worrying about the zipper in my jacket or my belt buckle or . . . anything. He'd trust his machines. I just said, "Come on" to Nadine and started to walk through it.

The place was operating-room cold. I felt Nadine behind me, her hand fluttering against my shoulder. At the exit end of the archway was a small table, standing just off to the right. The only thing on it was a box about the size of an eight-by-ten photograph. I looked down at it. Greenish glow. I placed my right hand flat, making sure my fingerprints would register. I looked around. A tiny red light was standing above a door a few feet away. Even in the murky light, I could tell that the door was built hard and heavy. I could feel Nadine's breath against my neck. It was ragged but not frightened. More like . . . excited.

The red light blinked off. I walked to the door. Couldn't see a knob. I pushed gently. It opened, swinging free. I stepped inside, Nadine so close now she almost shoved past me.

The floor was carpeted. I could feel it, but I couldn't see it. A single strand of blue neon tubing ran all around the walls. That was the only light. I could make out two metal chairs, a coffee table between them, standing lengthwise so the chairs were close together. On the table, a long narrow tray full of sand, like one of those miniature Buddhist gardens.

I took the chair to the right, furthest from the door, showing him I knew I couldn't get out if he didn't want me to. Nadine sat down next to me. The blue neon amped up just enough for me to see what was in front of us. A wall of thick plastic, like they use in liquor stores, only this one had no money slot. Lexan, probably. I could make out a shape behind it. Seated. Impossible to tell if it was a man or a woman.

"The instructions I taped to the inside of the elevator car—did you bring them with you?" a voice asked. A man's voice, coming from speakers somewhere on my side of the glass. No way to tell if it was his own or an electronically altered version.

"No. I left them there," I said.

"Good. If your . . . friends overheard the coordinates to enter the building and try the elevator, I presume they will push the same sequence. It has been reprogrammed."

"They won't—"

"If they do that," the voice continued, as if I hadn't spoken, "the doors will seal. And unless they came equipped with gas masks, they are already dead. The stairway is secured against anything other than low-yield explosive, and I have it on both visual and audio right in front of me. That option is closed as well."

"I played this square," I told him. "I'm alone. And unarmed. You must have your own way out of here."

"Of course."

"So. You want to do business or I wouldn't be here, right?"

"Yes. Questions first."

"Mine or yours?"

"Mine. Why is the woman with you?"

"Not now," I told him.

"You have no options," the voice said.

"Yeah, I do. If I gave a damn about dying, I wouldn't have looked for you in the first place."

"I would have found you."

"I know that now, but I didn't when I started. I know what you want. You can't get it snuffing me. I'm sure you got gas jets in the ceiling. Probably got electricity in these chairs too. I got the message, pal. I'm surrounded. It's no new experience for me. Your questions have nothing to do with her. She's here because she wants to be. Ask her whatever you want . . . when you and me are done."

"You are in no position to bargain."

"No? You think you know me. You don't. You think you know Wesley. You don't know him either, for all your fucked-up 'research.' Otherwise I wouldn't be here. What's your problem? We can't leave. And we can't hurt you. Do what you want—I don't give a good goddamn."

The voice was quiet after that. Nadine twitched in her chair. I probably shouldn't have said anything about electricity. I breathed through my nose, shallow.

Time passed.

"I thought you would have wanted one of your cigarettes by now," the voice said, like he had all the time in the world. "By the way, purely as a matter of interest, what brand did Wesley smoke?"

"Dukes," I told him. "Same as me."

"Dukes? I am not familiar with—"

"New York has a humongous tax on smokes," I said. "Lots of states do. Contraband creates opportunity. There's major traffic in bringing them up from North Carolina. Tobacco country. 'Dukes,' get it? You buy them from a wholesale jobber down there, truck them up here, sell them for fifty percent retail, and everybody scores. Doesn't matter what the brand name is—Dukes is what they call smuggled smokes. Me, I smoke whatever's on the truck that month, understand?"

"Certainly. Nothing in your profile indicates a connoisseur's taste, even in something so mundane."

His voice wasn't anything like Wesley's. The voice coming through the speakers was machine-altered. Wesley *was* a machine.

I waited.

"I am in no particular hurry," the voice said, picking up on my thoughts. "Even if your . . . friends have this building under surveillance . . . even if you have notified the authorities . . . I am able to leave undetected."

"And then blow the building?"

"Perhaps," he acknowledged, like it was no big thing. "I may choose to do so, but only if—"

"I understand," I told him. I could feel shock waves of surprise from behind the glass partition, but he didn't say anything.

Neither did I. Nadine had stopped twitching. A heavy, thick smell came off her. Not fear, something I couldn't put a name to.

I concentrated on my breathing.

Time passed.

"Why did you search for me originally?" he finally asked.

"A group of gay people wanted to protect you. They were afraid you'd be captured. They wanted me to find you, get you out of the country to someplace safe."

"Ah. You understand that—"

"You can leave whenever you want?" I cut in deliberately, trying to shift his balance, even if only a little bit. "And that this was never about fag-bashing?"

"Correct. On both counts."

"You had a long rest," I told him.

"A . . . rest? No. Not a rest. I went . . . quiescent. Once I had mastered my art, there was no . . . challenge."

"You were always above us, huh?"

"I *am* above you, Mr. Burke. In all ways."

"Yeah," I said, thinking of his velociraptor icon. And the killing claw. "So far above you couldn't get your ear to the ground, much less down into the whisper-stream. But it wasn't until you did that you learned the truth."

"Your . . . idiolect is unfamiliar to me."

"You were the greatest kidnapper ever," I said quietly. "Perfect."

"I was," he acknowledged, accepting his due.

"You mastered that art," I told him, shifting my gears, trying to jam his. "And you switched to another. I never did get that last piece."

"Piece?"

"Of your journal. That was your last kidnapping, right?"

"Yes."

"Then you switched to homicide?"

"Assassination," he corrected me. "Yes."

"Your journal was ambiguous," I said. "What was the new art? Killing mobsters? Killing incest fathers? Killing child molesters? What?"

"Ah. Because the first target fit all those criteria?"

"Yeah."

"The target was pedophiles," he said. "From the very beginning."

"But you . . . practiced on . . . what?"

"Anyone," he said. Dry ice.

"Sure. And when you were ready, that's when you switched from your private journal to the letters to the newspapers. And it almost worked."

"Almost? Please, Mr. Burke, don't be ludicrous. I am universally acknowledged as the—"

"Not in the whisper-stream," I chopped him off. "You got a higher body count . . . maybe . . . than Wesley, but so what? Every single one of his hits was bought and paid for. Someone *else* picked the target. Down here, there's talk of a guy called the Trustee. Supposed to be managing a fortune some old gay guy left . . . for killing fag-bashers. And word is, this Trustee got to Wesley. And all this work, it's his, not yours."

"Where is this mythical 'down here' of yours?"—the machine not altering the sneer in his voice.

"You like 'grapevine' better? It doesn't matter. Back alleys, prison tiers, waterfront bars. Crimeville, understand? Not for citizens. That's where Wesley lives. You say his name there, people tremble. He starts his walk, somebody's gonna die. Everybody knows."

"Wesley is dead," he said, repeating my line now.

"To who?" I challenged him. "He went out the way he wanted. But maybe he went someplace else. Some say he never really left. That he had some tunnel under the school, or that it was a remote-control robot's voice the cops heard or . . . whatever. You know how people talk. *You've* got a way out of here. Who's to say Wesley didn't?"

"Yes. But the circumstances are—"

"And others, they say he came back."

"From the dead?" The voice dripped sarcasm.

"Yeah. You never heard about 'Reaching Back' either, huh? You're so far above us, you can't see down through the clouds. Wesley's alive. He can't die. And I know that's what you want."

"What *I* want?"

"Why else all this? I'm no threat to you. You don't bite on that Internet bait, you're well away. Vanished. Like you did before.

"But you figured the only true test of art is immortality. Like a statue or a painting or a book that people still look at hundreds of years after it's done, right? *Your* art . . . it dies with you. I don't know how old you are, but you *are* going to die. And all your little 'journals' will end up as some cheap paperback book. There's only one way for you to get where you want to go. And that's why I'm here, isn't it? You need me to set up some more hits. As Wesley's 'agent,' right? That makes him alive. And that makes you him."

There was such silence I could hear heartbeats. A slow, steady thump. I was so calm I was almost comatose. Once you're over the line, the tension stops. Maybe it was Nadine's heart I heard. I never looked her way.

"Yes," he finally said.

I waited. It wasn't time yet. He wasn't . . . exposed enough for my one strike.

"How would it work?" he finally asked me.

"There's people I could talk to. See in person. They know me and Wesley were . . . They know I can reach him. I was—"

"You were the original suspect when my most recent . . . artistry started," he cut in. "Why was that?"

It wasn't time to fire yet, but I cocked the hammer. "One of the people that was killed in the drive-by. She was my woman."

"Ah. And the police thought you were seeking revenge."

"Yes."

"That *is* your reputation. Is it true?"

"Yes."

"And when did you decipher the coding?"

"Later on," I said. "You needed a way to justify killing a whole lot of people quickly. So the body counts would put you up there with Wesley. But you didn't want the police making connections—you wanted to spell it out for us. And you wanted some way to say Wesley was alive too. I don't know how you found out that Gutterball wanted—"

"He was not . . . discreet about it. I happened to access an individual he had attempted to . . . retain for that purpose."

"And then all it took was a phone call? And some meeting in the shadows?"

"Yes. He . . . quite readily accepted that he was speaking to . . ."

"Wesley."

"Yes."

"So you resurrected Wesley and kicked off the killings at the same time. It was . . . brilliant. No way the cops ever make *that* connection. Only problem is, it trapped you too."

"What does *that* mean? I am hardly the one trapped here."

"Listen to what you just said." I spoke quietly, willing him closer. "You couldn't have imitated Wesley's voice. You never heard it. Nobody's ever *really* heard it. So how come Gutterball went for the whole thing unless he *already* believed Wesley was alive? It's like I told you, pal. Wesley *can't* die. Not down here, he can't."

"Ah," he said smoothly. "So, in fact, I do not require your 'services' at all, do I, Mr. Burke? Let me ask you another question . . . purely for my own edification: Do you hold me responsible for the death of your . . . girlfriend? You do understand that I only executed the target. The rest was . . ."

"I understand," I lied. "No way you could have known who else would be there."

"Your statement does not square with other information I have unearthed about you, Mr. Burke."

"If you were really convinced of that, why have me here?"

"Ah. Well, in simple terms—and please believe me, I do not intend to be insulting—your personal animosity, to the extent it exists at all, is of no concern to me. You are . . . powerless, shall we say. My . . . research sources are, as you so adroitly pointed out earlier, dissimilar to yours. And I concede that your . . . reputation is, to some extent, inaccurate. When I began my final . . . quest, long before I ever made contact, it quickly became apparent that you were linked to Wesley. However, it also became apparent that there was a commingling at some juncture, so that various homicides were misattributed between you."

"What does it matter?" I asked him.

"Matter? Nothing. I was simply explaining that I have no direct method of ascertaining whether your rather legendary commitment to vengeance is valid. Regardless, I am both invulnerable as to you and needful of your . . . services, for which I am prepared to pay. Or, at least, until you so adroitly pointed out your own uselessness, I *was* prepared to pay. I do assume your reputation as a man-for-hire is factual . . . ?"

"Yeah. It is. But I'm no hit man. Wesley—"

"*Wesley* was a rank amateur," he said, his tone sounding more human now, even through the mechanical barrier. "How he achieved such . . . immortal status is beyond my comprehension. I assume it was the rather theatrical way he elected to exit which retroactively amplified his rather pedestrian accomplishments as an assassin."

"Amateur?" I taunted him. "Amateurs do things for fun. Like you do. Amateurs call it fucking 'art.' Like you do. Wesley, he got paid. And he never missed. You gave Wesley a name, you got a body," I said, echoing the Prof. "The only body they never got was his."

"Have you ever read any of Conan Doyle's works, Mr. Burke? Sherlock Holmes, surely you are familiar with that fictional detective? Holmes was a *self-described* amateur. And, simultaneously, the king of his profession. Performing feats for compensation is not a higher art."

"Maybe where you live," I told him.

"Where I live . . . doesn't matter. *That* I live is all that is of importance. Vital importance. I am Wesley now. His immortality is mine. I no longer require your services. Any works of art erected after Wesley's demise which are attributed to him are, in fact, mine. When this 'whisper-stream' of yours speaks, as it will forever, every time it says his name, it will be *me* of which it speaks. Do you understand?"

"Sure. You're gonna blow this building. *After* you get out. So everyone'll say: That's Wesley—he knows how to blow things up and still walk away. You're an identity-thief."

"My work was superior to his in every aspect!" he said, sharply. "His identity *is* mine, now. I have not 'stolen' it, I have ascended to it. And then *transcended* it. And you have, unwittingly, already identified my work . . . my recent work . . . as his. That is not theft, it is proper attribution. Anything less would be plagiarism."

"How can you be sure I did that?" I asked him.

"Oh, I have no doubts," he said. "Mr. Felestrone is proof enough of that."

"How can you be sure?" I repeated.

"Pure art will out. Time is its only test. Axiomatically, I cannot personally verify such things. It is an act of faith."

"And you did it all for art?"

"For *my* art. I do not fit any of those pitiful law-enforcement 'profiles.' I do not live to kill. In fact, I killed to live . . . although I do not believe you are capable of comprehending such a concept other than in the most elemental terms. No 'motivation' drives my work. The motivation is the work itself."

"Bullshit," I told him calmly.

"Surely you are not fool enough to believe you can anger me into accessibility, Mr. Burke? Am I supposed to rise to your transparent bait and physically attack you in some way? Your attempt is ludicrous. Do you know what an osmotic membrane is?"

"Yeah. A one-way barrier. You can cross over to the other side, but you can't step back."

"Ah. You surprise me. I would not have thought—"

"I did a lot of reading in prison," I told him.

"Which apparently included a good deal of pop psychology," he said dryly. "Nevertheless, this barrier—the one which separates us now—is, in fact, osmotic. You could enter the area I now occupy, *if* I so elected. See . . . this!" he said.

A yellow light suddenly blinked on to my right. It looked like it was floating in air.

"What you see is a projected beam. It will open the barrier between us."

"A door in the Lexan?"

"If you will. I prefer my own analogy—it is more . . . applicable to the instant situation, especially given the wires embedded in the glass. Do you wish to come closer, then, Mr. Burke?"

"No," I told him. "I'm fine right here." I lit a cigarette, leaned back in my chair, blew smoke at the invisible ceiling.

"Then you wish to retract your absurd statements concerning my alleged 'motivations' for my art?"

"Sure," I told him. "I'll do that. I figure there's a better way."

"What are you—?"

"I know you," I told him. I didn't know if he could feel that truth—maybe it would just wash against the glass, never touch him. But it was all I had. I couldn't see his eyes. A freak's eyes always get soft and wet—sex-wet—when he talks about his fun. Wesley's eyes were as dry as his bloodless heart—killing was work to him. "And I know you don't want me going out and being your 'agent,'" I sneered softly at him. "Once was enough. Now you want this all to vanish. Everything. You figured it out a long time ago. Immortality requires death. And that part you said I'd never understand . . . killing to live? I know who you killed to live."

"Do you actually believe I—?"

"Why don't *you* tell him?" I said, turning to Nadine. "It's time now. You wanted this so bad. Now you're here. Tell him."

"I . . ." she started to speak, then stopped.

Velociraptor. A combination of crocodile and bird. Both survived. He claimed that for his own. Time to find out if he'd split or stayed mixed. It was all I had. I sucked the smoke deep into my lungs again, knowing it had to be perfect or I was done. "Go ahead. Tell him. Tell him the truth . . . Zoë."

She gasped so hard her whole body shuddered in the chair. She got to her feet, shakily. Stood with her hands behind her back, one knee slightly bent. A little girl.

"You are my father," she said into the darkness. "You gave me life. I waited for you. Inside. But I knew you would come for me someday."

"You're—" His voice cracked, clear even through the microphone.

"You never killed her at all," I told him, flat, no more debating. "Not *all* of her. That last journal entry was as cute as it gets. You figured out Angelique was a multiple. And you knew why she was. But that wasn't what did it. It was when she recognized *you* that everything . . . changed. Changed forever. You killed the alter. Killed Angelique. And left this other one behind. I don't know how you did that, but . . ."

I let my voice trail off. Then I spoke right at Nadine's back: "Where did you wake up?"

"I . . . don't know," she said, her voice still a child's. "It was in . . . California, somewhere. The police found me. I was . . . they said I was . . . amnesic. They put me in a hospital. I never . . . They looked, but they never found . . . I was . . . adopted. Not really adopted . . . a foster home. They named me. Nadine. I was very . . . intelligent. But I couldn't remember. I was . . . somewhere else. Inside. Waiting. I'm an architect. I knew I loved . . . design. And I hated men. I was never with a man. Ever. I . . . waited. And when my father started to . . . avenge . . . I felt the pull. I always . . . knew, I think. But not . . . I'm still not . . . I'm Zoë. Now. I am."

The speaker spit out, "You could not . . ." but his voice trailed off.

"You know the truth," I told him, calm and quiet and centered as deeply as I ever had been in my life. "You only killed Angelique. That's when your art was done. When you found out the real reason why you did it. She taught you. She's not lying. You are her father. But she was the one who gave *you* life."

"My life is art. And my art is death."

"Yes. And you're done now. You're Wesley. You can't die. So you can't stay either."

"I know," he said. A human voice now. He must have switched off the distorter in the microphone.

"Take Zoë with you," Nadine begged him. "I wanted to go with you then. I can help you now. I can be with you. I don't want to be here."

She was crying then. I didn't move, even when the cigarette started to burn the tips of my fingers.

"Come here, child," he finally said.

Nadine walked forward. Touched the yellow button. And stepped into the darkness.

I heard a faint click as the Lexan door closed again.

I sat there, frozen, watching the barrier.

A white-orange fireball exploded in front of my eyes. The room rocked.

I got off the floor, surprised I was still there. I knew what was coming next. Wesley was going out again. The same way. I wondered how much time I had even as I ran toward the waiting elevator.

"Reprogrammed," the maniac had said. I didn't touch any of the buttons in the elevator. I climbed onto the railing and shoved the flat of my hand against the ceiling. The security panel yielded. I climbed out of the car and looked across. Empty black space. Sure—only that one car went to the secret top floor. But the blackness ahead of me wasn't the Zero. There *had* to be other cars. I slipped the gloves onto my hands, wished for a flashlight. The stairway was sealed at the bottom. This way was my only shot. And a timer somewhere was ticking away my life. How much was left before he turned into Wesley for real?

I jumped, reaching out for the cable I couldn't see. I hit it with my chest, grabbed on as hard as I could. Got a grip but it was too greasy—I lost it and started to free-fall. I . . . crashed onto the roof of the car below. Felt the wind go out of me. Didn't fight it, waiting even as my mind screamed the opposite command. I got a breath. Clawed around frantically until I found the panel's handle. Yanked it up and dropped inside. Stabbed the button for the ground floor, willing the damn thing to drop like a stone.

It opened into the lobby. I sprinted toward the thick glass doors and pulled with all my strength. Locked! Sure, the son of a bitch wouldn't do anything without a backup plan. Alive, I could tell the truth. I pounded on the door. Useless. I looked around frantically, knowing it was coming and . . .

The night lit up. The quad beams of my Plymouth, aimed right at the door. I semaphored wildly. The Plymouth backed up, tires squealing, spun into a J-turn, and shot toward me, rear end first like they do in Demolition Derbies. I backpedaled toward the elevator as the Plymouth roared right up the steps and crashed into the doors, splitting them wide open. I ran for the passenger door, wrenched it open, and dove inside as the big car lurched forward, bouncing down the steps, fishtailing as it hit the street, then shot toward the FDR.

I looked over at the driver and caught Wolfe's Satan-slayer smile. "Controlled collision," she said. "The Mole wanted to work the lock, but the Prof said it was probably rigged. So we waited. When we saw you, it was time."

"I . . ."

"I know you do," Wolfe said, as the night behind us turned into flame.

It was probably getting light outside somewhere, but none of it penetrated into Mama's.

"All she did was love him," Wolfe said. "And he must have hated all the freaks, just like she did. Why didn't he just go on and—"

"It was his choice," I told her. "She knew his secret. She loved him for it, but he had no love left in him. He wanted to go, but he wasn't going to leave anyone who would make excuses for him. You know how they talk about a choice of evils? He had all the choices. And evil was the one he chose."

"I don't think that's true," Wolfe said. "I think he loved her. The only way he could."

"He was just . . . what, then?"

"I don't have a name for it."

"Doesn't matter. He's gone now."

"You're not," she said, leaning toward me, her hand on mine, gray eyes soft with something I'd never seen before. "And it's your time now. Your time to choose."

A Note About the Author

Andrew Vachss has been a federal investigator in sexually transmitted diseases, a social caseworker, and a labor organizer, and has directed a maximum-security prison for youthful offenders. Now a lawyer in private practice, he represents children and youths exclusively. He is the author of eleven novels, a collection of short stories, three graphic series, and *Another Chance to Get It Right: A Children's Book for Adults.* His work has appeared in *Parade, Antaeus, Esquire,* the *New York Times,* and numerous other forums.

Further information about Andrew Vachss and his work is available on his website, "The Zero," at www.vachss.com, and at www.Choiceofevil.com.

A Note on the Type

The text of this book was set in a typeface called Times New Roman, designed by Stanley Morison for *The Times* (London), and introduced by that newspaper in 1932.

Among typographers and designers of the twentieth century, Stanley Morison was a strong formative influence, as typographical adviser to the Monotype Corporation of London, as a director of two distinguished English publishing houses, and as a writer of sensibility, erudition, and keen practical sense.

In 1930 Morison wrote: "Type design moves at the pace of the most conservative reader. The good type-designer therefore realizes that, for a new fount to be successful, it has to be so good that only very few recognize its novelty. If readers do not notice the consummate reticence and rare discipline of a new type, it is probably a good letter." It is now generally recognized that in the creation of Times Roman, Morison successfully met the qualifications of his theoretical doctrine.

Composed by Stratford Publishing Services,
Brattleboro, Vermont
Printed and bound by R. R. Donnelley & Sons,
Bloomsburg, Pennsylvania
Design and hand-lettering by Virginia Tan